Simon Cal

Robert Keable

Alpha Editions

This edition published in 2023

ISBN : 9789357931328

Design and Setting By
Alpha Editions
www.alphaedis.com
Email - info@alphaedis.com

Contents

THE AUTHOR TO THE READER

The glamour of no other evil thing is stronger than the glamour of war. It would seem as if the cup of the world's sorrow as a result of war had been filled to the brim again and again, but still a new generation has always been found to forget. A new generation has always been found to talk of the heroisms that the divine in us can manifest in the mouth of hell and to forget that so great a miracle does not justify our creation of the circumstance.

Yet if ever war came near to its final condemnation it was in 1914-1918. Our comrades died bravely, and we had been willing to die, to put an end to it once and for all. Indeed war-weary men heard the noise of conflict die away on November 11, 1918, thinking that that end had been attained. It is not yet three years ago; a little time, but long enough for betrayal.

Long enough, too, for the making of many books about it all, wherein has been recorded such heroisms as might make God proud and such horror as might make the Devil weep. Yet has the truth been told, after all? Has the world realized that in a modern war a nation but moves in uniform to perform its ordinary tasks in a new intoxicating atmosphere? Now and again a small percentage of the whole is flung into the pit, and, for them, where one in ten was heavy slaughter, now one in ten is reasonable escape. The rest, for the greater part of the time, live an unnatural life, death near enough to make them reckless and far enough to make them gay. Commonly men and women more or less restrain themselves because of to-morrow; but what if there be no to-morrow? What if the dice are heavily weighted against it? And what of their already jeoparded restraint when the crisis has thrown the conventions to the winds and there is little to lighten the end of the day?

Thus to lift the veil on life behind the lines in time of war is a thankless task. The stay-at-homes will not believe, and particularly they whose smug respectability and conventional religion has been put to no such fiery trial. Moreover they will do more than disbelieve; they will say that the story is not fit to be told. Nor is it. But then it should never have been lived. That very respectability, that very conventionality, that very contented backboneless religion made it possible—all but made it necessary. For it was those things which allowed the world to drift into the war, and what the war was nine days out of ten ought to be thrust under the eyes of those who will not believe. It is a small thing that men die in battle, for a man has but one life to live and it is good to give it for one's friends; but it is such an evil that it has no like, this drifting of a world into a hell to which men's souls are driven like red maple leaves before the autumn wind.

The old-fashioned pious books made hell stink of brimstone and painted the Devil hideous. But Satan is not such a fool. Champagne and Martinis do not taste like Gregory powder, nor was St. Anthony tempted by shrivelled hags. Paganism can be gay, and passion look like love. Moreover, still more truly, Christ could see the potentiality of virtue in Mary Magdalene and of strength in Simon called Peter. The conventional religious world does not.

A curious feature, too, of that strange life was its lack of consecutiveness. It was like the pages of *La Vie Parisienne*. The friend of to-day was gone for ever to-morrow. A man arrived, weary and dirty and craving for excitement, in some unknown town; in half an hour he had stepped into the gay glitter of wine and women's smiles; in half a dozen he had been whirled away. The days lingered and yet flew; the pages were twirled ever more dazzlingly; only at the end men saw in a blinding flash whither they had been led.

These things, then, are set out in this book. This is its atmosphere. They are truly set out. They are not white-washed; still less are they pictured as men might have seen them in more sober moments, as the Puritan world would see them now. Nor does the book set forth the author's judgment, for that is not his idea of a novel. It sets out what Peter and Julie saw and did, and what it appeared to them to be while they did it. Very probably, then, the average reader had better read no further than this....

But at any rate let him not read further than is written. The last page has been left blank. It has been left blank for a reason, because the curtain falls not on the conclusion of the lives of those who have stepped upon the boards, but at a psychological moment in their story. The Lord has turned to look upon Peter, and Julie has seen that He has looked. It is enough; they were happy who, going down into the Valley of the Shadow of Death, saw a vision of God's love even there. For the Christ of Calvary moved to His Cross again but a few short years ago; and it is enough in one book to tell how Simon failed to follow, but how Jesus turned to look on Peter.

R.K.

PART I

Ah! is Thy love indeed
A weed, albeit an amaranthine weed,
Suffering no flowers except its own to mount?
Ah! must—
Designer infinite!—
Ah! must Thou char the wood ere Thou canst limn with it?

FRANCIS THOMPSON.

CHAPTER I

London lay as if washed with water-colour that Sunday morning, light blue sky and pale dancing sunlight wooing the begrimed stones of Westminster like a young girl with an old lover. The empty streets, clean-swept, were bathed in the light, and appeared to be transformed from the streets of week-day life. Yet the half of Londoners lay late abed, perhaps because six mornings a week of reality made them care little for one of magic.

Peter, nevertheless, saw little of this beauty. He walked swiftly as always, and he looked about him, but he noticed none of these things. True, a fluttering sheet of newspaper headlines impaled on the railings of St. Margaret's held him for a second, but that was because its message was the one that rang continually in his head, and had nothing at all to do with the beauty of things that he passed by.

He was a perfectly dressed young man, in a frock coat and silk hat of the London clergyman, and he was on his way to preach at St. John's at the morning service. Walking always helped him to prepare his sermons, and this sermon would ordinarily have struck him as one well worth preparing. The pulpit of St. John's marked a rung up in the ladder for him. That great fashionable church of mid-Victorian faith and manners held a congregation on Sunday mornings for which the Rector catered with care. It said a good deal for Peter that he had been invited to preach. He ought to have had his determined scheme plain before him, and a few sentences, carefully polished, at hand for the beginning and the end. He could trust himself in the middle, and was perfectly conscious of that. He frankly liked preaching, liked it not merely as an actor loves to sway his audience, but liked it because he always knew what to say, and was really keen that people should see his argument. And yet this morning, when he should have been prepared for the best he could do, he was not prepared at all.

Strictly, that is not quite true, for he had a text, and the text absolutely focused his thought. But it was too big for him. Like some at least in England that day, he was conscious of staring down a lane of tragedy that appalled him. Fragments and sentences came and went in his head. He groped for words, mentally, as he walked. Over and over again he repeated his text. It amazed him by its simplicity; it horrified him by its depth.

Hilda was waiting at the pillar-box as she had said she would be, and little as she could guess it, she irritated him. He did not want her just then. He could hardly tell why, except that, somehow, she ran counter to his thoughts altogether that morning. She seemed, even in her excellent brown costume that fitted her fine figure so well, out of place, and out of place for the first time.

They were not openly engaged, these two, but there was an understanding between them, and an understanding that her family was slowly recognising. Mr. Lessing, at first, would never have accepted an engagement, for he had other ideas for his daughter of the big house in Park Lane. The rich city merchant, church-warden at St. John's, important in his party, and a person of distinction when at his club, would have been seriously annoyed that his daughter should consider a marriage with a curate whose gifts had not yet made him an income. But he recognised that the young man might go far. "Young Graham?" he would say, "Yes, a clever young fellow, with quite remarkable gifts, sir. Bishop thinks a lot of him, I believe. Preaches extraordinarily well. The Rector said he would ask him to St. John's one morning...."

Peter Graham's parish ran down to the river, and included slums in which some of the ladies of St. John's (whose congregation had seen to it that in their immediate neighbourhood there were no such things) were interested. So the two had met. She had found him admirable and likeable; he found her highly respectable and seemingly unapproachable. From which cold elements much more may come than one might suppose.

At any rate, now, Mrs. Lessing said nothing when Hilda went to post a letter in London on Sunday morning before breakfast. She would have mildly remonstrated if the girl had gone to meet the young man. The which was England once, and may, despite the Kaiser, be England yet once more.

"I was nearly going," she declared. "You're a bit late."

"I know," he replied; "I couldn't help it. The early service took longer than usual. But I'm glad to see you before breakfast. Tell me, what does your father think of it all?"

The girl gave a little shrug of the shoulders, "Oh, he says war is impossible. The credit system makes it impossible. But if he really thinks so, I don't see why he should say it so often and so violently. Oh, Peter, what do you think?"

The young man unconsciously quickened his pace. "I think it is certain," he said. "We must come in. I should say, more likely, the credit system makes it impossible for us to keep out. I mean, half Europe can't go to war and we sit still. Not in these days. And if it comes—Good Lord, Hilda, do you know what it means? I can't see the end, only it looks to me like being a fearful smash.... Oh, we shall pull through, but nobody seems to see that our ordinary life will come down like a pack of cards. And what will the poor do? And can't you see the masses of poor souls that will be thrown into the vortex like, like...." He broke off. "I can't find words," he said, gesticulating nervously. "It's colossal."

"Peter, you're going to preach about it: I can see you are. But do take care what you say. I should hate father to be upset. He's so—oh, I don't know!—*British*, I think. He hates to be thrown out, you know, and he won't think all that possible."

She glanced up (the least little bit that she had to) anxiously. Graham smiled. "I know Mr. Lessing," he said. "But, Hilda, he's *got* to be moved. Why, he may be in khaki yet!"

"Oh, Peter, don't be silly. Why, father's fifty, and not exactly in training," she laughed. Then, seriously: "But for goodness' sake don't say such things—for my sake, anyway."

Peter regarded her gravely, and held open the gate. "I'll remember," he said, "but more unlikely things may happen than that."

They went up the path together, and Hilda slipped a key into the door. As it opened, a thought seemed to strike her for the first time. "What will *you* do?" she demanded suddenly.

Mrs. Lessing was just going into the dining-room, and Peter had no need to reply. "Good-morning, Mr. Graham," she said, coming forward graciously. "I wondered if Hilda would meet you: she wanted to post a letter. Come in. You must be hungry after your walk."

A manservant held the door open, and they all went in. That magic sun shone on the silver of the breakfast-table, and lit up the otherwise heavy room. Mrs. Lessing swung the cover of a silver dish and the eggs slipped in to boil. She touched a button on the table and sat down, just as Mr. Lessing came rather ponderously forward with a folded newspaper in his hand.

"Morning, Graham," he said. "Morning, Hilda. Been out, eh? Well, well, lovely morning out; makes one feel ten years younger. But what do you think of all this, Graham?" waving the paper as he spoke.

Peter just caught the portentous headline—

"GERMANY DECLARES WAR ON RUSSIA,"

as he pulled up to the table, but he did not need to see it. There was really no news: only that. "It is certain, I think, sir," he said.

"Oh, certain, certain," said Lessing, seating himself. "The telegrams say they are over the frontier of Luxembourg and massing against France. Grey can't stop 'em now, but the world won't stand it—can't stand it. There can't be a long war. Probably it's all a big bluff again; they know in Berlin that business can't stand a war, or at any rate a long war. And we needn't come in. In the City, yesterday, they said the Government could do more by standing out. We're not pledged. Anderson told me Asquith said so distinctly. And, thank God, the Fleet's ready! It's madness, madness, and we must keep our heads. That's what I say, anyway."

Graham cracked an egg mechanically. His sermon was coming back to him. He saw a congregation of Lessings, and more clearly than ever the other things. "What about Belgium?" he queried. "Surely our honour is engaged there?"

Mr. Lessing pulled up his napkin, visibly perturbed. "Yes, but what can we do?" he demanded. "What is the good of flinging a handful of troops overseas, even if we can? It's incredible—English troops in Flanders in this century. In my opinion—in my opinion, I say—we should do better to hold ourselves in readiness. Germany would never really dare antagonise us. They know what it involves. Why, there's hundreds of millions of pounds at stake. Grey has only to be firm, and things must come right. Must—absolutely must."

"Annie said, this morning, that she heard everyone in the streets last night say we must fight, father," put in Hilda.

"Pooh!" exclaimed the city personage, touched now on the raw. "What do the fools know about it? I suppose the *Daily Mail* will scream, but, thank God, this country has not quite gone to the dogs yet. The people, indeed! The mass of the country is solid for sense and business, and trusts the Government. Of course, the Tory press will make the whole question a party lever if it can, but it can't. What! Are we going to be pushed into war by a mob and a few journalists? Why, Labour even will be dead against it. Come, Graham, you ought to know something about that. More in your line than mine—don't you think so?"

"You really ought not to let the maids talk so," said Mrs. Lessing gently.

Peter glanced at her with a curiously hopeless feeling, and looked slowly round the room until his eyes rested on Mr. Lessing's portrait over the mantelshelf, presented by the congregation of St. John's on some occasion two years before. From the portrait he turned to the gentleman, but it was not necessary for him to speak. Mr. Lessing was saying something to the man—probably ordering the car. He glanced across at Hilda, who had made some reply to her mother and was toying with a spoon. He thought he had never seen her look more handsome and…. He could not find the word: thought of "solid," and then smiled at the thought. It did not fit in with the sunlight on her hair.

"Well, well," said Mr. Lessing; "we ought to make a move. It won't do for either of us to be late, Mr. Preacher."

The congregation of St. John's assembled on a Sunday morning as befitted its importance and dignity. Families arrived, or arrived by two or three representatives, and proceeded with due solemnity to their private pews. No one, of course, exchanged greetings on the way up the church, but every lady became aware, not only of the other ladies present, but of what each wore. A sidesman, with an air of portentous gravity, as one who, in opening doors, performed an office more on behalf of the Deity than the worshippers, was usually at hand to usher the party in. Once there, there was some stir of orderly bustle: kneelers were distributed according to requirements, books sorted out after the solemn unlocking of the little box that contained them, sticks and hats safely stowed away. These duties performed, paterfamilias cast one penetrating glance round the church, and leaned gracefully forward with a kind of circular motion. Having suitably addressed Almighty God (it is to be supposed), he would lean back, adjust his trousers, possibly place an elbow on the pew-door, and contemplate with a fixed and determined gaze the distant altar.

Peter, of course, wound in to solemn music with the procession of choir boys and men, and, accorded the honour of a beadle with a silver mace, since he was to preach, was finally installed in a suitably cushioned seat within the altar-rails. He knelt to pray, but it was an effort to formulate anything. He was intensely conscious that morning that a meaning hitherto unfelt and unguessed lay behind his world, and even behind all this pomp and ceremony that he knew so well. Rising, of course, when the senior curate began to intone the opening sentence in a manner which one felt was worthy even of St. John's, he allowed himself to study his surroundings as never before.

The church had, indeed, an air of great beauty in the morning sunlight. The Renaissance galleries and woodwork, mellowed by time, were dusted by that soft warm glow, and the somewhat sparse congregation, in its magnificently isolated groups, was humanised by it too. The stone of the chancel, flecked with colour, had a quiet dignity, and even the altar, ecclesiastically ludicrous, had a grace of its own. There was to be a celebration after Matins. The historic gold plate was therefore arranged on the retable with something of the effect of show pieces at Mappin and Webb's. Peter noticed three flagons, and between them two patens of great size. A smaller pair for use stood on the credence-table. The gold chalice and paten, veiled, stood on the altar-table itself, and above them, behind, rose the cross and two vases of hot-house lilies. Suggesting one of the great shields of beaten gold that King Solomon had made for the Temple of Jerusalem, an alms-dish stood on edge, and leant against the retable to the right of the veiled chalice. Peter found himself marvelling at its size, but was recalled to his position when it became necessary to kneel for the Confession.

The service followed its accustomed course, and throughout the whole of it Peter was conscious of his chaotic sermon. He glanced at his notes occasionally, and then put them resolutely away, well aware that they would be all but useless to him. Either he would, at the last, be able to formulate the thoughts that raced through his head, or else he could do no more than occupy the pulpit for the conventional twenty minutes with a conventional sermon. At times he half thought he would follow this easier course, but then the great letters of the newspaper poster seemed to frame themselves before him, and he knew he could not. And so, at last, there was the bowing beadle with the silver mace, and he must set out on the little dignified procession to the great Jacobean pulpit with its velvet cushion at the top.

Hilda's mind was a curious study during that sermon. At first, as her lover's rather close-cropped, dark-haired head appeared in sight, she had studied him with an odd mixture of pride and apprehension. She held her hymn-book, but she did not need it, and she watched surreptitiously while he opened the Bible, arranged some papers, and, in accordance with custom, knelt to pray. She began to think half-thoughts of the days that might be, when perhaps she would be the wife of the Rector of some St. John's, and later, possibly, of a Bishop. Peter had it in him to go far, she knew. She half glanced round with a self-conscious feeling that people might be guessing at her thoughts, and then back, wondering suddenly if she really knew the man, or only the minister. And then there came the rustle of shutting books and of people composing themselves to listen, the few coughs, the vague suggestion of hassocks and cushions being made comfortable. And then, in a moment, almost with the giving out of the text, the sudden stillness and that tense sensation which told that the young orator had gripped his congregation.

Thereafter she hardly heard him, as it were, and she certainly lost the feeling of ownership that had been hers before. As he leaned over the pulpit, and the words rang out almost harshly from their intensity, she began to see, as the rest of the congregation began to see, the images that the preacher conjured up before her. A sense of coming disaster riveted her—the feeling that she was already watching the end of an age.

"Jesus had compassion on the multitude"—that had been the short and simple text. Simple words, the preacher had said, but how when one realised Who had had compassion, and on what? Almighty God Himself, with His incarnate Mind set on the working out of immense and agelong plans, had, as it were, paused for a moment to have compassion on hungry women and crying babies and folk whose petty confused affairs could have seemed of no consequence to anyone in the drama of the world. And then, with a few terse sentences, the preacher swung from that instance to the world drama of to-day. Did they realise, he asked, that peaceful bright Sunday morning, that millions of simple men were at that moment being hurled at each other to maim and kill? At the bidding of powers that even they could hardly visualise, at the behest of world politics that not one in a thousand would understand and scarcely any justify, houses were being broken up, women were weeping, and children playing in the sun before cottage doors were even now being left fatherless. It was incredible, colossal, unimaginable, but as one tried to picture it, Hell had opened her mouth and Death gone forth to slay. It was terrible enough that battlefields of stupendous size should soon be littered with the dying and the dead, but the aftermath of such a war as this would be still more terrible. No one could say how near it would come to them all. No one could tell what revolution in morals and social order such a war as this might not bring. That day God Himself looked down on the multitude as sheep having no shepherd, abandoned to be butchered by the wolves, and His heart beat with a divine compassion for the infinite sorrows of the world.

There was little more to it. An exhortation to go home to fear and pray and set the house in order against the Day of Wrath, and that was all. "My brethren," said the young man—and the intensity of his thought lent a certain unusual solemnity to the conventional title—"no one can tell how the events of this week may affect us. Our feet may even now be going down into the Valley of the Shadow of temptation, of conflict, of death, and even now there may be preparing for us a chalice such as we shall fear to drink. Let us pray that in that hour the compassion of Jesus may be real to us, and we ourselves find a sure place in that sorrowful Heart."

And he was gone from the pulpit without another word. It would have been almost ridiculous if one had noted that the surprised beadle had had no "And now to God the Father ..." in which to reach the pulpit, and had been forced to meet his victim hurrying halfway up the chancel; but perhaps no one but that dignitary, whom the fall of thrones would not shake, had noticed it. The congregation paid the preacher the great compliment of sitting on in absolute silence for a minute or two. For a moment it still stared reality in the face. And then Mr. Lessing shifted in his pew and coughed, and the Rector rose, pompously as usual, to announce the hymn, and Hilda became conscious of unaccustomed tears in her eyes.

The senior curate solemnly uncovered and removed the chalice. Taking bread and wine, he deposited the sacred vessels at the north end of the altar, returned to the centre, unfolded the corporal, received the alms, and as solemnly set the great gold dish on the corporal itself, after the unmeaning custom of the church. And then came the long prayer and the solemn procession to the vestry, while a dozen or two stayed with the senior curate for the Communion.

Graham found himself in the little inner vestry, with its green-cloth table and massive inkstand and registers, and began to unvest mechanically. He got his coat out of the beautiful carved wardrobe, and was folding up his hood and surplice, when the Rector laid a patronising hand on his shoulder. "A good sermon, Graham," he said—"a good sermon, if a little emotional. It was a pity you forgot the doxology. But it is a great occasion, I fear a greater occasion than we know, and you rose to it very well. Last night I had half a mind to 'phone you not to come, and to preach myself, but I am glad now I did not. I am sure we are very grateful. Eh, Sir Robert?"

Sir Robert Doyle, the other warden, was making neat piles of sovereigns on the green cloth, while Mr. Lessing counted the silver as to the manner born. He was a pillar of the church, too, was Sir Robert, but a soldier and a straight speaker. He turned genially to the young man.

"From the shoulder, Rector," he said. "Perhaps it will make a few of us sit up a little. Coming down to church I met Arnold of the War Office, and he said war was certain. Of course it is. Germany has been playing up for it for years, and we fools have been blind and mad. But it'll come now. Thank God, I can still do a bit, and maybe we shall meet out there yet—eh, Mr. Graham?"

Somehow or another that aspect of the question had not struck Peter forcibly till now. He had been so occupied with visualising the march of world events that he had hardly thought of himself as one of the multitude. But now the question struck home. What would he do? He was at a loss for the moment.

The Rector saved him, however. "Well, well, of course, Sir Robert, apart from the chaplains, the place of the clergy will be almost certainly at home. Hospital visiting, and so on, will take a lot of time. I believe the Chaplain-General's Department is fully staffed, but doubtless, if there is any demand, the clergy will respond. It is, of course, against Canon Law for them to fight, though doubtless our young friend would like to do his share in that if he could. You were in the O.T.C. at Oxford, weren't you, Graham?"

"Yes," said Graham shortly.

"The French priests are mobilising with the nation," said Sir Robert.

"Ah, yes, naturally," replied the Rector; "that is one result of the recent anti-clerical legislation. Thank God, this country has been spared that, and in any case we shall never have conscription. Probably the Army will have to be enlarged—half a million will be required at least, I should think. That will mean more chaplains, but I should suppose the Bishops will select— oh, yes, surely their lordships will select. It would be a pity for you to go, Graham; it's rough work with the Tommies, and your gifts are wanted at home. The Vicar of St. Thomas's speaks very highly of your gifts as an organiser, and doubtless some sphere will be opened up for you. Well, well, these are stirring times. Good-morning, Mr. Graham."

He held out his hand to the young man. Mr. Lessing, carefully smoothing his silk hat, looked up. "Come in to luncheon with us, will you, Graham?" he said.

Peter assented, and shook hands all round. Sir Robert and he moved out together, and the baronet caught his eye in the porch. "This'll jog him up a bit, I'm thinking," he said to himself. "There's stuff in that chap, but he's got to feel his legs."

Outside the summer sun was now powerful, and the streets were dusty and more busy. The crowd had thinned at the church door, but Hilda and Mrs. Lessing were waiting for the car.

"Don't let's drive," said Hilda as they came up; "I'd much sooner walk home to-day."

Her father smiled paternally. "Bit cramped after church, eh?" he said. "Well, what do you say, dear?" he asked his wife.

"I think I shall drive," Mrs. Lessing replied; "but if Mr. Graham is coming to luncheon, perhaps he will walk round with Hilda. Will you, Mr. Graham?"

"With pleasure," said Peter. "I agree with Miss Lessing, and the walk will be jolly. We'll go through the park. It's less than half an hour, isn't it?"

It was arranged at that, and the elders drove off. Peter raised his hat to Sir Robert, who turned up the street, and together he and Hilda crossed over the wide thoroughfare and started down for the park.

There was silence for a little, and it was Peter who broke it.

"Just before breakfast," he said, "you asked me what I should do, and I had no chance to reply. Well, they were talking of it in the vestry just now, and I've made up my mind. I shall write to-night to the Bishop and ask for a chaplaincy."

They walked on a hundred yards or so in silence again. Then Hilda broke it. "Peter," she began, and stopped. He glanced at her quickly, and saw in a minute that the one word had spoken truly to him.

"Oh, Hilda," he said, "do you really care all that? You can't possibly! Oh, if we were not here, and I could tell you all I feel! But, dear, I love you; I know now that I have loved you for months, and it is just because I love you that I must go."

"Peter," began Hilda again, and again stopped. Then she took a grip of herself, and spoke out bravely. "Oh, Peter," she said, "you've guessed right. I never meant you to—at least, not yet, but it is terrible to think of you going out there. I suppose I ought to be glad and proud, and in a way I am, but you don't seem the right person for it. It's wasting you. And I don't know what I shall do without you. You've become the centre of my life. I count on seeing you, and on working with you. If you go, you, you may ... Oh, I can't say it! I ought not to say all this. But..." She broke off abruptly.

Graham glanced round him. They were in the park now, and no one in particular was about in the quiet of the sidewalk. He put his hand out, and drew her gently to a seat. Then, leaning forward and poking at the ground with his stick, he began. "Hilda, darling," he said, "it's awful to have to speak to you just now and just like this, but I must. First, about ourselves. I love you with all my heart, only that's so little to say; I love you so much that you fill my life. And I have planned my life with you. I hardly knew it, but I had. I thought I should just go on and get a living and marry you—perhaps, if you would (I can hardly speak of it now I know you would)—and—and—oh, I don't know—make a name in the Church, I suppose. Well, and I hope we shall one day, but now this has come along. I really feel all I said this morning, awfully. I shall go out—I must. The men must be helped; one can't sit still and imagine them dying, wounded, tempted, and without a priest. It's a supreme chance. We shall be fighting for honour and truth, and the Church must be there to bear her witness and speak her message. There will be no end to do. And it is a chance of a lifetime to get into touch with the men, and understand them. You do see that, don't you? And, besides—forgive me, but I must put it so—if *He* had compassion on the multitude, ought we not to have too? *He* showed it by death; ought we to fear even that too?"

The girl stole out a hand, and his gripped it hard. Then she remembered the conventions and pulled it away, and sat a little more upright. She was extraordinarily conscious of herself, and she felt as if she had two selves that day. One was Hilda Lessing, a girl she knew quite well, a well-trained person who understood life, and the business of society and of getting married, quite correctly; and the other was somebody she did not know at all, that could not reason, and who felt naked and ashamed. It was inexplicable, but it was so. That second self was listening to heroics and even talking them, and surely heroics were a little out of date.

She looked across a wide green space, and saw, through the distant trees, the procession of the church parade. She felt as if she ought to be there, and half unconsciously glanced at her dress. A couple of terriers ran scurrying across the grass, and a seat-ticket man came round the corner. Behind them a taxi hooted, and some sparrows broke out into a noisy chatter in a bush. And here was Peter talking of death, and the Cross—and out of church, too.

She gave a little shudder, and glanced at a wrist-watch. "Peter," she said, "we must go. Dear, for my sake, do think it over. Wait a little, and see what happens. I quite understand your point of view, but you must think of others—even your Vicar, my parents, and of me. And Peter, shall we say anything about our—our love? What do you think?"

Peter Graham looked at her steadily, and as she spoke he, too, felt the contrast between his thoughts and ordinary life. The London curate was himself again. He got up. "Well, darling," he said, "just as you like, but perhaps not—at any rate until I know what I have to do. I'll think that over. Only, we shan't change, shall we, whatever happens? You *do* love me, don't you? And I do love you."

Hilda met his gaze frankly and blushed a little. She held out a hand to be helped up. "My dear boy," she said.

After luncheon Peter smoked a cigar in the study with Mr. Lessing before departure. Every detail of that hour impressed itself upon him as had the events of the day, for his mind was strung up to see the inner meaning of things clearly.

They began with the usual ritual of the selection of chairs and cigars, and Mr. Lessing had a glass of port with his coffee, because, as he explained, his nerves were all on edge. Comfortably stretched out in an armchair, blowing smoke thoughtfully towards the empty grate, his fat face and body did not seem capable of nerves, still less to be suffering from them, but then one can never tell from appearances. At any rate he chose his words with care, and Graham, opposite but sitting rather upright, could not but sense his meaning.

"Well, well, well," he said, "to think we should come to this! A European war in this century, and we in it! Not that I'll believe it till I hear it officially. While there's life there's hope, eh, Graham?"

Peter nodded, for he did not know what to say.

"The question is," went on the other, "that if we are carried into war, what is the best policy? Some fools will lose their heads, of course, and chuck everything to run into it. But I've no use for fools, Graham."

"No, sir," said Peter.

"No use for fools," repeated Mr. Lessing. "I shall carry on with business as usual, and I hope other people will carry on with theirs. There are plenty of men who can fight, and who ought to, without disorganising everything. Hilda would see that too—she's such a sensible girl. Look at that Boer affair, and all that foolery about the C.I.V. Why, I met a South African at the club the other day who said we'd have done ten times as well without 'em. You must have trained men these days, and, after all, it's the men behind the armies that win the war. Men like you and I, Graham, each doing his ordinary job without excitement. That's the type that's made old England. You ought to preach about it, Graham. Come to think, it fits in with what you said this morning, and a good sermon too, young man. Every man's got to put his house in order and carry on. You meant that, didn't you?"

"Something like that," said Peter; "but as far as the clergy are concerned, I still think the Bishops ought to pick their men."

"Yes, yes, of course," said Mr. Lessing, stretching himself a bit. "But I don't think the clergy could be much use over there. As the Canon said, there will be plenty to do at home. In any case it would be no use rushing the Bishops. Let them see what's needed, and then let them choose their men, eh? A man like London's sure to be in the know. Good thing he's your Bishop, Graham: you can leave it to him easily?"

"I should think so, sir," said Peter forlornly.

"Oh, well, glad to hear you say it, I'm sure, Graham, and so will Mrs. Lessing be, and Hilda. We're old-fashioned folk, you know.... Well, well, and I suppose I oughtn't to keep you. I'll come with you to the door, my boy."

He walked ahead of the young man into the hall, and handed him his hat himself. On the steps they shook hands to the fire of small sentences. "Drop in some evening, won't you? Don't know if I really congratulated you on the sermon; you spoke extraordinarily well, Graham. You've a great gift. After all, this war will give you a bit of a chance, eh? We must hear you again in St. John's.... Good-afternoon."

"Good-afternoon, Mr. Lessing," said Graham, "and thank you for all you've said."

In the street he walked slowly, and he thought of all Mr. Lessing had not said as well as all he had. After all, he had spoken sound sense, and there was Hilda. He couldn't lose Hilda, and if the old man turned out obstinate—well, it would be all but impossible to get her. Probably things were not as bad as he had imagined. Very likely it would all be over by Christmas. If so, it was not much use throwing everything up. Perhaps he could word the letter to the Bishop a little differently. He turned over phrases all the way home, and got them fairly pat. But it was a busy evening, and he did not write that night.

Monday always began as a full day, what with staff meeting and so on, and its being Bank Holiday did not make much difference to them. But in the afternoon he was free to read carefully the Sunday papers, and was appalled with the swiftness of the approach of the universal cataclysm. After Evensong and supper, then, he got out paper and pen and wrote, though it took much longer than he thought it would. In the end he begged the Bishop to remember him if it was really necessary to find more chaplains, and expressed his readiness to serve the Church and the country when he was wanted. When it was written, he sat long over the closed envelope and smoked a couple of pipes. He wondered if men were killing each other, even now, just over the water. He pictured a battle scene, drawing from imagination and what he remembered of field-days at Aldershot. He shuddered a little as he conceived himself crawling through heather to reach a man in the front line who had been hit, while the enemies' guns on the crest opposite were firing as he had seen them fire in play. He tried to imagine what it would be like to be hit.

Then he got up and stretched himself. He looked round curiously at the bookcase, the Oxford group or two, the hockey cap that hung on the edge of one. He turned to the mantelpiece and glanced over the photos. Probably Bob Scarlett would be out at once; he was in some Irish regiment or other. Old Howson was in India; he wouldn't hear or see much. Jimmy—what would Jimmy do, now? He picked up the photograph and looked at it—the clean-shaven, thoughtful, good-looking face of the best fellow in the world, who had got his fellowship almost at once after his brilliant degree, and was just now, he reflected, on holiday in the South of France. Jimmy, the idealist, what would Jimmy do? He reached for a hat and made for the door. He would post his letter that night under the stars.

Once outside, he walked on farther down Westminster way. At the Bridge he leaned for a while and watched the sullen, tireless river, and then turned to walk up past the House. It was a clear, still night, and the street was fairly empty. Big Ben boomed eleven, and as he crossed in front of the gates to reach St. Margaret's he wondered what was doing in there. He had the vaguest notion where people like the Prime Minister and Sir Edward Grey would be that night. He thought possibly with the King, or in Downing Street. And then he heard his name being called, and turned to see Sir Robert Doyle coming towards him.

The other's face arrested him. "Is there any news, Sir Robert?" he asked.

Sir Robert glanced up in his turn at the great shining dial above them. "Our ultimatum has gone or is just going to Germany, and in twenty-four hours we shall be at war," he said tersely. "I'm just going home; I've been promised a job."

CHAPTER II

At 7.10 on a foggy February morning Victoria Station looked a place of mystery within which a mighty work was going forward. Electric lights still shone in the gloom, and whereas innumerable units of life ran this way and that like ants disturbed, an equal number stood about apparently indifferent and unperturbed. Tommies who had found a place against a wall or seat deposited rifle and pack close by, lit a pipe, and let the world go by, content that when the officers' leave train had gone someone, or some Providence, would round them up as well. But, for the rest, porters, male and female, rushed up with baggage; trunks were pushed through the crowd with the usual objurgations; subalterns, mostly loud and merry, greeted each other or the officials, or, more subdued, moved purposefully through the crowd with their women-folk, intent on finding a quieter place farther up the platforms.

There was no mistaking the leave platform or the time of the train, for a great notice drew one's attention to it. Once there, the Army took a man in hand. Peter was entirely new to the process, but he speedily discovered that his fear of not knowing what to do or where to go, which had induced him (among other reasons) to say good-bye at home and come alone to the station, was unfounded. Red-caps passed him on respectfully but purposefully to officials, who looked at this paper and that, and finally sent him up to an officer who sat at a little table with papers before him to write down the name, rank, unit, and destination of each individual destined that very morning to leave for the Army in France.

Peter at last, then, was free to walk up the platform, and seek the rest of his luggage that had come on from the hotel with the porter. He was free, that is, if one disregarded the kit hung about his person, or which, despite King's Regulations, he carried in his hands. But free or not, he could not find his luggage. At 7.30 it struck him that at least he had better find his seat. He therefore entered a corridor and began pilgrimage. It was seemingly hopeless. The seats were filled with coats or sticks or papers; every type of officer was engaged in bestowing himself and his goods; and the general atmosphere struck him as being precisely that which one experiences as a fresher when one first enters hall for dinner at the 'Varsity. The comparison was very close. First-year men—that is to say, junior officers returning from their first leave—were the most encumbered, self-possessed, and asserting; those of the second year, so to say, usually got a corner-seat and looked out of window; while here and there a senior officer, or a subaltern with a senior's face, selected a place, arranged his few possessions, and got out a paper, not in the Oxford manner, as if he owned the place, but in the Cambridge, as if he didn't care a damn who did.

Peter made a horrible hash of it. He tried to find a seat with all his goods in his hands, not realising that they might have been deposited anywhere in the train, and found when it had started, since, owing to a particular dispensation of the high gods, everything that passed the barrier for France got there. He made a dive for one place and sat in it, never noting a thin stick in the corner, and he cleared out with enormous apologies when a perfectly groomed Major with an exceedingly pleasant manner mentioned that it was his seat, and carefully put the stick elsewhere as soon as Peter had gone. Finally, at the end of a carriage, he descried a small door half open, and inside what looked like an empty seat. He pulled it open, and discovered a small, select compartment with a centre table and three men about it, all making themselves very comfortable.

"I beg your pardon," said Peter, "but is there a place vacant for one?"

The three eyed him stonily, and he knew instinctively that he was again a fresher calling on the second year. One, a Captain, raised his head to look at him better. He was a man of light hair and blue, alert eyes, wearing a cap that, while not looking dissipated, somehow conveyed the impression that its owner knew all about things—a cap, too, that carried the Springbok device. The lean face, with its humorous mouth, regarded Peter and took him all in: his vast expanse of collar, the wide black edging to his shoulder-straps, his brand-new badges, his black buttons and stars. Then he lied remorselessly:

"Sorry, padre; we're full up."

Peter backed out and forgot to close the door, for at that moment a shrill whistle was excruciatingly blown. He found himself in the very cab of the Pullman with the glass door before him, through which could be seen a sudden bustle. Subalterns hastened forward from the more or less secluded spots that they had found, with a vision of skirts and hats behind them; an inspector passed aggressively along; and—thanks to those high gods—Peter observed the hurrying hotel porter at that moment. In sixty seconds the door had been jerked open; a gladstone, a suit-case, and a kit-bag shot at him; largesse had changed hands; the door had shut again; the train had groaned and started; and Peter was off to France.

It was with mixed feelings that he groped for his luggage. He was conscious of wanting a seat and a breakfast; he was also conscious of wanting to look at the station he was leaving, which he dimly felt he might never see again; and he was, above all, conscious that he looked a fool and would like not to. In such a turmoil he lugged at the gladstone and got it into a corner, and then turned to the window in the cleared space with a determination. In turning he caught the Captain's face stuck round the little door. It was withdrawn at once, but came out again, and he heard for the second time the unfamiliar title:

"Say, padre; come in here. There's room after all."

Peter felt cheered. He staggered to the door, and found the others busy making room. A subaltern of the A.S.C. gripped his small attaché case and swung it up on to the rack. The South African pulled a British warm off the vacant seat and reached out for the suit-case. And the third man, with the rank of a Major and the badge of a bursting bomb, struck a match and paused as he lit a cigarette to jerk out:

"Damned full train! We ought to have missed it, Donovan."

"It's a good stunt that, if too many blighters don't try it on," observed the subaltern, reaching for Peter's warm. "But they did my last leave, and I got the devil of a choking off from the brass-hat in charge. It's the Staff train, and they only take Prime Ministers, journalists, and trade-union officials in addition. How's that, padre?"

"Thanks," said Peter, subsiding. "It's jolly good of you to take me in. I thought I'd got to stand from here to Folkestone."

H.P. Jenks, Second-Lieutenant A.S.C., regarded him seriously. "It couldn't be done, padre," he said, "not at this hour of the morning. I left Ealing about midnight more or less, got sandwiched in the Metro with a Brigadier-General and his blooming wife and daughters, and had to wait God knows how long for the R.T.O. If I couldn't get a seat and a break after that, I'd be a casualty, sure thing."

"It's your own fault for going home last night," observed the Major judiciously. (Peter noticed that he was little older than Jenks on inspection.) "Gad, Donovan, you should have been with us at the Adelphi! It was some do, I can tell you. And afterwards..."

"Shut up, Major!" cut in Jenks. "Remember the padre."

"Oh, he's broad-minded I know, aren't you, padre? By the way, did you ever meet old Drennan who was up near Poperinghe with the Canadians? He was a sport, I can tell you. Mind you, a real good chap at his job, but a white man. Pluck! By jove! I don't think that chap had nerves. I saw him one day when they were dropping heavy stuff on the station, and he was getting some casualties out of a Red Cross train. A shell burst just down the embankment, and his two orderlies ducked for it under the carriage, but old Drennan never turned a hair. 'Better have a fag,' he said to the Scottie he was helping. 'It's no use letting Fritz put one off one's smoke.'"

Peter said he had not met him, but could not think of anything else to say at the moment, except that he was just going out for the first time.

"You don't say?" said Donovan dryly.

"Wish I was!" ejaculated Jenks.

"Good chap," replied the Major. "Pity more of your sort don't come over. When I was up at Loos, September last year, we didn't see a padre in three months. Then they put on a little chap—forget his name—who used to bike over when we were in rest billets. But he wasn't much use."

"I was in hospital seven weeks and never saw one," said Jenks.

"Good heavens!" said Graham. "But I've been trying to get out for all these years, and I was always told that every billet was taken and that there were hundreds on the waiting list. Last December the Chaplain-General himself showed me a list of over two hundred names."

"Don't know where they get to, then, do you, Bevan?" asked Jenks.

"No," said the Major, "unless they keep 'em at the base."

"Plenty down at Rouen, anyway," said Donovan. "A sporting little blighter I met at the Brasserie Opera told me he hadn't anything to do, anyway."

"I shall be a padre in the next war," said Jenks, stretching out his legs. "A parade on Sunday, and you're finished for the week. No orderly dog, no night work, and plenty of time for your meals. Padres can always get leave too, and they always come and go by Paris."

Donovan laughed, and glanced sideways at Peter. "Stow it, Jenks," he said. "Where you for, padre?" he asked.

"I've got to report at Rouen," said Peter. "I was wondering if you were there."

"No such luck now," returned the other. "But it's a jolly place. Jenko's there. Get him to take you out to Duclair. You can get roast duck at a pub there that melts in your mouth. And what's that little hotel near the statue of Joan of Arc, Jenks, where they still have decent wine?"

Peter was not to learn yet awhile, for at that moment the little door opened and a waiter looked in. "Breakfast, gentlemen?" he asked.

"Oh, no," said Jenks. "Waiter, I always bring some rations with me; I'll just take a cup of coffee."

The man grinned. "Right-o, sir," he said. "Porridge, gentlemen?"

He disappeared, leaving the door open and, Donovan opening a newspaper, Graham stared out of window to wait. From the far corners came scraps of conversation, from which he gathered that Jenks and the Major were going over the doings of the night before. He caught a word or two, and stared the harder out of window.

Outside the English country was rushing by. Little villas, with back-gardens running down to the rail, would give way for a mile or two to fields, and then start afresh. The fog was thin there, and England looked extraordinarily homely and pleasant. It was the known; he was conscious of rushing at fifty miles an hour into the unknown. He turned over the scrappy conversation of the last few minutes, and found it savoured of the unknown. It was curious the difference uniform made. He felt that these men were treating him more like one of themselves than men in a railway-carriage had ever treated him before; that somehow even his badges made him welcome; and yet that, nevertheless, it was not he, Peter Graham, that they welcomed, or at least not his type. He wondered if padres in France were different from priests in England. He turned over the unknown Drennan in his mind. Was it because he was a good priest that the men liked him, or because they had discovered the man in the parson?

The waiter brought in the breakfast—porridge, fish, toast, and the rest— and they fell to, a running fire of comments going on all the time. Donovan had had Japanese marmalade somewhere, and thought it better than this. The Major wouldn't touch the beastly margarine, but Jenks thought it quite as good as butter if taken with marmalade, and put it on nearly as thickly as his toast. Peter expanded in the air of camaraderie, and when he leaned back with a cigarette, tunic unbuttoned and cap tossed up on the rack, he felt as if he had been in the Army for years. He reflected how curious that was. The last two or three years or so of Boy Scouts and hospitals and extra prayer-meetings, attended by the people who attended everything else, seemed to have faded away. There was hardly a gap between that first war evening which he remembered so clearly and this. It was a common experience enough, and probably due to the fact that, whereas everything else had made little impression, he had lived for this moment and been extraordinarily impressed by that Sunday. But he realised, also, that it was due as much to his present companions. They had, seemingly, accepted him as he had never been accepted before. They asked practically no questions. So far as he could see, he made no difference to them. He felt as if he were at last part of a great brotherhood, in which, chiefly, one worried about nothing more important than Japanese marmalade and margarine.

"We're almost there, boys," said Bevan, peering out of window.

"Curse!" ejaculated Jenks. "I hate getting my traps together in a train, and I loathe the mob on the boat."

"I don't see why you should," said Donovan. "I'm blest if I bother about anything. The R.T.O. and the red-caps do everything, and you needn't even worry about getting a Pullman ticket this way over. Hope it's not rough, though." He let a window down and leaned out. "Looks all right," he added.

Peter got up with the rest and began to hang things about him. His staringly new Sam Browne irritated him, but he forgot it as the train swung round the curve to the landing-stage.

"Get a porter and a truck, Donovan," said the Major, who was farthest from the door.

They got out nonchalantly, and Peter lit a cigarette, while the others threw remarks at the man as to luggage. Then they all trooped off together in a crowd that consisted of every variety of rank and regiment and section of the British Empire, plus some Waacs and nurses.

The Pride of Folkestone lay alongside, and when they got there she seemed already full. The four of them got jammed at the gangway and shoved on board, handing in and receiving papers from the official at the head as they passed him. Donovan was in front, and as he stepped on deck he swung his kit-bag back to Peter, crying:

"Lay hold of that, padre, and edge across the deck. Get up ahead of the funnel that side. I'll get chairs. Jenko, you rotter, get belts, and drop eyeing the girl!"

"Jolly nice bit of fluff," said Jenks meditatively, staring fixedly across the deck.

"Where?" queried the Major, fumbling for his eyeglass.

"Get on there, please, gentlemen," called a ship's official.

"Damn it! mind my leg!"

"Cheerio, old son, here we are again!"

"I say, Tommy, did you get to the Alhambra last night, after all? What? Well, I couldn't see you, anyhow."

To which accompaniment, Peter pushed his way across the deck. "Sorry, padre," said a V.A.D. who blocked the way, bending herself back to let him pass, and smiling. "Catch hold," called out Donovan, swinging a couple of chairs at him. "No, sir, it's not my chair"—to a Colonel who was grabbing at one already set out against the rail.

- 24 -

The Colonel collected it and disappeared, Jenks appearing a moment later, red-faced, through the crush. "You blamed fool," he whispered, "it's that girl's. I saw her put one here and edged up on it, only some fool got in my way. Still (hopefully), perhaps she'll come back."

Between them they got four chairs into a line and sat down, all, that is, save Jenks, who stood up, in a bland and genial way, as if to survey the crowd impartially. How impartially soon appeared. "Damn!" he exploded. "She's met some other females, weird and woolly things, and she's sitting down there. No, by Jove! she's looking this way."

He made a half-start forward, and the Major kicked his shins. "Blast!" he exploded; "why did you do that, you fool?"

"Don't be an infant, Jenko, sit down. You can't start a flirtation across the blooming deck. Here, padre, can't you keep him in order?"

Peter half raised himself from his chair at this, and glanced the way the other was looking. Through the crush he saw, clearly enough for a minute, a girl of medium height in a nurse's uniform, sideways on to him. The next second she half-turned, obviously smiling some remark to her neighbour, and he caught sight of clear brown eyes and a little fringe of dark hair on the forehead of an almost childish face. The eyes met his. And then a sailor blundered across his field of vision.

"Topping, isn't she?" demanded Jenks, who had apparently been pulled down into his chair in the interval.

"Oh, I don't know," said Graham, and added deliberately: "Rather ordinary, I thought."

Jenks stared at him. "Good Lord, padre," he said, "where are your eyes?"

Peter heard a little chuckle behind, and glanced round to see Donovan staring at him with amusement written all across his face. "You'll do, padre," he said, taking a pipe from his pocket and beginning to fill it. Peter smiled and leant back. Probably for the first time in five years he forgot for a moment what sort of a collar it was around his neck.

Sitting there, he began to enjoy himself. The sea glittered in the sun and the Lees stretched out opposite him across the shining gulf. Sea-birds dipped and screamed. On his left, Major Bevan was talking to a flying man, and Peter glanced up with him to see an aeroplane that came humming high up above the trees on the cliff and flew out to sea.

"Damned fine type!" said the boy, whose tunic, for all his youth, sported wings. "Fritz can't touch it yet. Of course, he'll copy it soon enough, or go one better, but just at present I think it's the best out. Wish we'd got some in our circus. We've nothing but ..." and he trailed off into technicalities.

Peter found himself studying Donovan, who lay back beyond Jenks turning the pages of an illustrated magazine and smoking. The eyes interested him; they looked extraordinarily clear, but as if their owner kept hidden behind them a vast number of secrets as old as the universe. The face was lined—good-looking, he thought, but the face of a man who was no novice in the school of life. Peter felt he liked the Captain instinctively. He carried breeding stamped on him, far more than, say, the Major with the eyeglass. Peter wondered if they would meet again.

The siren sounded, and a bustle began as people put on their life-belts. "All life-belts on, please," said a young officer continually, who, with a brassard on his arm, was going up and down among the chairs. "Who's that?" asked Peter, struggling with his belt.

"Some poor bloke who has been roped in for crossin' duty," said Jenks. "Mind my chair, padre; Bevan and I are going below for a wet. Coming, skipper?"

"Not yet," said Donovan; "the bar's too full at first for me. Padre and I'll come later."

The others stepped off across the crowded deck, and Donovan pitched his magazine into Bevan's chair to retain it.

"You're from South Africa?" queried Peter.

"Yes," replied the other. "I was in German West, and came over after on my own. Joined up with the brigade here."

"What part of Africa?" asked Peter.

"Basutoland, padre. Not a bad place in a way—decent climate, topping scenery, but rather a stodgy crowd in the camps. One or two decent people, but the majority mid-Victorian, without a blessed notion except the price of mealies, who quarrel about nothing half the time, and talk tuppenny-ha'penny scandal the rest. Good Lord! I wish we had some of the perishers out here. But they know which side of the bread the butter is. Bad time for trade, they say, and every other trader has bought a car since the war. Of course, there's something to be said for the other side, but what gets my goat is their pettiness. I'm for British East Africa after the war. There's a chap written a novel about Basutoland called 'The Land of To-morrow,' but I'd call it 'The Land of the Day before Yesterday.' I suppose some of them came over with an assortment of ideas one time, but they've struck no new ones since. I don't advise you to settle in a South African dorp if you can help it, padre."

"Don't suppose I shall," said Peter. "I've just got engaged, and my girl's people wouldn't let her out of England."

"Engaged, are you? Thank your stars you aren't married. It's safer not to be out here."

"Why?"

Donovan looked at him curiously. "Oh, you'll find out fast enough, padre," he said. "Wonder what you'll make of it. Rum place just now, France, I can tell you. There's the sweepings of half the world over there, and everything's turned upside down. Fellows are out for a spree, of course, and you can't be hard on a chap down from the line if he goes on the bust a bit. It's human nature, and you must allow for it; don't you think so?"

"Human nature can be controlled," said Peter primly.

"Can it?" retorted the other. "Even the cloth doesn't find it too easy, apparently."

"What do you mean?" demanded Peter, and then added: "Don't mind telling me; I really want to know."

Donovan knocked out his pipe, and evaded. "You've got to be broad-minded, padre," he said.

"Well, I am," said Peter. "But ..."

"Come and have a drink then," interrupted the other. "Jenko and the Major are coming back."

"Damned poor whisky!" said the latter, catching the rail as the boat heaved a bit, "begging your pardon, padre. Better try brandy. If the war lasts much longer there'll be no whisky worth drinking this side. I'm off it till we get to the club at Boulogne."

Peter and Donovan went off together. It was a new experience for Peter, but he wouldn't have owned it. They groped their way down the saloon stairs, and through a crowd to the little bar. "What's yours?" demanded Donovan.

"Oh, I'll take the Major's advice," said Peter. "Brandy-and-soda for me."

"Soda finished, sir," said the bar steward.

"All right: two brandies-and-water, steward," said Donovan, and swung a revolving seat near round for Graham. As he took it, Peter noticed the man opposite. His badge was a Maltese Cross, but he wore a flannel collar and tie. Their eyes met, but the other stared a bit stonily. For the second time,

Peter wished he hadn't a clerical collar. The next he was taking the glass from the South African. "Cheerio," said Donovan.

"Here's to you," said Peter, and leaned back with an assumption of ease.

He had a strange sense of unreality. No fool and no Puritan, he had naturally, however, been little in such an atmosphere since ordination. He would have had a drink in Park Lane with the utmost ease, and he would have argued, over it, that the clergy were not nearly so out of touch with men as the papers said. But down here, in the steamer's saloon, surrounded by officers, in an atmosphere of indifference to him and his office, he felt differently. He was aware, dimly, that for the past five years situations in which he had been had been dominated by him, and that he, as a clergyman, had been continually the centre of concern. Talk, conduct, and company had been rearranged when he came in, and it had happened so often that he had ceased to be aware of it. But now he was a mere unit, of no particular importance whatever. No one dreamed of modifying himself particularly because a clergyman was present. Peter clung to the belief that it was not altogether so, but he was sufficiently conscious of it. And he was conscious of liking it, of wanting to sink back in it as a man sinks back in an easy-chair. He felt he ought not to do so, and he made a kind of mental effort to pull himself together.

Up on the deck the world was very fair. The French coast was now clearly visible, and even the houses of the town, huddled together as it seemed, but dominated by a church on the hill. Behind them, a sister ship containing Tommies ploughed steadily along, serene and graceful in the sunlight, and above an airship of silvery aluminum, bearing the tricoloured circle of the Allies, kept pace with the swift ship without an effort. Four destroyers were visible, their low, dark shapes ploughing regularly along at stated intervals, and someone said a fifth was out of sight behind. People were already beginning to take off their life-belts, and the sailors were clearing a place for the gangway. Peter found that Donovan had known what he was about, for his party would be close to the gangway without moving. He began to wonder uneasily what would be done on landing, and to hope that Donovan would be going his way. No one had said a word about it. He looked round for Jenks' nurse, but couldn't see her.

It was jolly entering the port. The French houses and fishing-boats looked foreign, although one could hardly say why. On the quay was a big notice: "All officers to report at once to the M.L.O." Farther on was a board bearing the letters "R.T.O." ... But Peter hardly liked to ask.

In fact, everything went like clockwork. He presently found himself in a queue, behind Donovan, of officers who were passing a small window like a ticket office. Arriving, he handed in papers, and was given them back with a brief "All right." Beyond, Donovan had secured a broken-down-looking one-horse cab. "You'll be coming to the club, padre?" he asked. "Chuck in your stuff. This chap'll take it down and Bevan with it. Let's walk. It isn't far."

Jenks elected to go with his friend the Major, and Donovan and Peter set off over the cobbles. They joined up with another small group, and for the first time Peter had to give his name as he was introduced. He forgot the others, as soon as he heard them, and they forgot his. A big Dublin Fusilier officer with a tiny moustache, that seemed ludicrous in his great face, exchanged a few sentences with him. They left the quay and crossed a wide space where a bridge debouched towards the railway-station. Donovan, who was walking ahead, passed on, but the Fusilier suggested to Peter that they might as well see the R.T.O. at once about trains. Entering the station gates, the now familiar initials appearing on a row of offices before them to the left, Peter's companion demanded the train to Albert.

"Two-thirty a.m., change at Amiens, sir," said a clerk in uniform within, and the Fusilier passed on.

"What time is the Rouen train?" asked Peter in his turn, and was told 9.30 p.m.

"You're in luck, padre," said the other. "It's bally rotten getting in at two-thirty, and probably the beastly thing won't go till five. Still, it might be worse. You can get on board at midnight, and with luck get to sleep. If I were you, I'd be down here early for yours—crowded always, it is. Of course, you'll dine at the club?"

Peter supposed he would.

The club entrance was full up with officers, and more and more kept pouring in. Donovan was just leaving the counter on the right with some tickets in his hand as they pushed in. "See you later," he called out. "I've got to sleep here, and I want to leave my traps."

Peter wondered where, but was too much occupied in keeping well behind the Fusilier to think much. At a kind of counter a girl in a W.A.A.C. uniform was serving out tickets of one sort and another, and presently the two of them were before her. For a few francs one got tickets for lunch, dinner, bed, a bath, and whatever else one wanted, but Peter had no French money. The Fusilier bought him the first two, however, and together they forced their way out into the great lounge. "Half an hour before lunch," said his new companion, and then, catching sight of someone: "Hullo, Jack, you back? Never saw you on the boat. Did you ..." His voice trailed off as he crossed the room.

Peter looked around a little disconsolately. Then he made his way to a huge lounge-chair and threw himself into it.

All about him was a subdued chatter. A big fire burned in the stove, and round it was a wide semicircle of chairs. Against the wall were more, and a small table or two stood about. Nearly every chair had its occupant—all sorts and conditions of officers, mostly in undress, and he noticed some fast asleep, with muddied boots. There was a look on their faces, even in sleep, and Peter guessed that some at least were down from the line on their way to a brief leave. More and more came in continuously. Stewards with drinks passed quickly in and out about them. The Fusilier and his friend were just ordering something. Peter opened his case and took out a cigarette, tapping it carefully before lighting it. He began to feel at home and lazy and comfortable, as if he had been there before.

An orderly entered with envelopes in his hand. "Lieutenant Frazer?" he called, and looked round inquiringly. There was no reply, and he turned to the next. "Captain Saunders?" Still no reply. "Lieutenant Morcombe?" Still no reply. "Lieutenant Morcombe," he called again. Nobody took any interest, and he turned on his heel, pushed the swing-door open, and departed.

Then Donovan came in, closely followed by Bevan. Peter got up and made towards them. "Hullo!" said Bevan. "Have an appetiser, padre. Lunch will be on in twenty minutes. What's yours, skipper?"

The three of them moved on to Peter's chair, and Bevan dragged up another. Peter subsided, and Donovan sat on the edge. Peter pulled out his cigarette-case again, and offered it. Bevan, after one or two ineffectual attempts, got an orderly at last.

"Well, here's fun," he said.

"Cheerio," said Peter. He remembered Donovan had said that in the saloon.

CHAPTER III

Jenks being attached to the A.S.C. engaged in feeding daily more than 100,000 men in the Rouen area, Peter and he travelled together. By the latter's advice they reached the railway-station soon after 8.30, but even so the train seemed full. There were no lights in the siding, and none whatever on the train, so that it was only by matches that one could tell if a compartment was full or empty, except in the case of those from which candle-light and much noise proclaimed the former indisputably. At last, however, somewhere up near the engine, they found a second-class carriage, apparently unoccupied, with a big ticket marked "Reserved" upon it. Jenks struck a match and regarded this critically. "Well, padre," he said, "as it doesn't say for whom it is reserved, I guess it may as well be reserved for us. So here goes." He swung up and tugged at the door, which for some time refused to give. Then it opened suddenly, and Second-Lieutenant Jenks, A.S.C., subsided gracefully and luridly on the ground outside. Peter struck another match and peered in. It was then observed that the compartment was not empty, but that a dark-haired, lanky youth, stretched completely along one seat, was regarding them solemnly.

"This carriage is reserved," he said.

"Yes," said Jenks cheerfully, "for us, sir. May I ask what you are doing in it?"

The awakened one sighed. "It's worked before, and if you chaps come in and shut the door quickly, perhaps it will work again. Three's not too bad, but I've seen six in these perishing cars. Come in quickly, for the Lord's sake!"

Peter looked round him curiously. Two of the four windows were broken, and the glory had departed from the upholstery. There was no light, and it would appear that a heavier body than that designed for it had travelled upon the rack. Jenks was swearing away to himself and trying to light a candle-end. Peter laughed.

"Got any cards?" asked the original owner.

"Yes," said Jenks. "Got any grub?"

"Bath-olivers and chocolate and half a water-bottle of whisky," replied the original owner. "And we shall need them."

"Good enough," said Jenks. "And the padre here has plenty of sandwiches, for he ordered a double lot."

"Do you play auction, padre?" queried what turned out, in the candle-light, to be a Canadian.

Peter assented; he was moderately good, he knew.

This fairly roused the Canadian. He swung his legs off the seat, and groped for the door. "Hang on to this dug-out, you men," he said, "and I'll get a fourth. I kidded some fellows of ours with that notice just now, but I know them, and I can get a decent chap to come in."

He was gone a few minutes only; then voices sounded outside. "Been looking for you, old dear," said their friend. "Only two sportsmen here and a nice little show all to ourselves. Tumble in, and we'll get cheerful. Not that seat, old dear. But wait a jiffy; let's sort things out first."

* * * * *

They snorted out of the dreary tunnel into Rouen in the first daylight of the next morning. Peter looked eagerly at the great winding river and the glory of the cathedral as it towered up above the mists that hung over the houses. There was a fresh taste of spring in the air, and the smoke curled clear and blue from the slow-moving barges on the water. The bare trees on the island showed every twig and thin branch, as if they had been pencilled against the leaden-coloured flood beneath. A tug puffed fussily upstream, red and yellow markings on its grimy black.

Jenks was asleep in the corner, but he woke as they clattered across the bridge. "Heigh-ho!" he sighed, stretching. "Back to the old graft again."

Yet once more Peter began to collect his belongings. It seemed ages since he had got into the train at Victoria, and he felt particularly grubby and unshaven.

"What's the next move?" he asked.

Jenks eyed him. "Going to take a taxi?" he queried.

"Where to?" said Peter.

"Well, if you ask me, padre," he replied, "I don't see what's against a decent clean-up and breakfast at the club. It doesn't much matter when I report, and the club's handy for your show. I know the A.C.G.'s office, because it's in the same house as the Base Cashier, and the club's just at the bottom of the street. But it's the deuce of a way from the station. If we can get a taxi, I vote we take it."

"Right-o," agreed Peter. "You lead on."

They tumbled out on the platform, and produced the necessary papers at the exit labelled "British Officers Only." A red-capped military policeman wrote down particulars on a paper, and in a few minutes they were out among the crowd of peasantry in the booking-hall. Jenks pushed through, and had secured a cab by the time Peter arrived. "There isn't a taxi to be got, padre," he said, "but this'll do."

They rolled off down an avenue of wintry trees, passed a wooden building which Peter was informed was the English military church, and out on to the stone-paved quay. To Peter the drive was an intense delight. A French blue-coated regiment swung past them. "Going up the line," said Jenks. A crowd of black troops marched by in the opposite direction. "Good Lord!" said Jenks, "so the S.A. native labour has come." The river was full of craft, but his mentor explained that the true docks stretched mile on mile downstream. By a wide bridge lay a camouflaged steamer. "Hospital ship," said Jenks. Up a narrow street could be seen the buttresses of the cathedral; and if Peter craned his head to glance up, his companion was more occupied in the great café at the corner a little farther on. But it was, of course, deserted at that early hour. A flower-stall at the corner was gay with flowers, and two French peasant women were arranging the blooms. And then the fiacre swung into the Rue Joanne d'Arc, and opposite a gloomy-looking entrance pulled up with a jerk. "Here we are," said Jenks. "It's up an infernal flight of steps."

The officers' club in Rouen was not monstrously attractive, but they got a good wash in a little room that looked out over a tangle of picturesque roofs, and finally some excellent coffee and bacon and eggs.

Jenks lit a cigarette and handed one to Peter. "Better leave your traps," he said. "I'll go up with you; I've nothing to do."

Outside the street was filling with the morning traffic, and the two walked up the slight hill to the accompaniment of a running fire of comments and explanations from Jenks, "That's Cox's—useful place for the first half of a month, but not much use to me, anyway, for the second…. You ought to go to I that shop and buy picture post-cards, padre; there's a topping girl who sells 'em…. Rue de la Grosse Horloge—you can see the clock hanging over the road. The street runs up to the cathedral: rather jolly sometimes, but nothing doing now…. What's that? I don't know. Yes, I do, Palais de Justice or something of that sort. Pretty old, I believe…. In those gardens is the picture gallery; not been in myself, but I believe they've got some good stuff…. That's your show, over there. Don't be long; I'll hang about."

Peter crossed the street, and, following directions ascended some wooden stairs. A door round the corner at the top was inscribed "A.C.G. (C. of E.)," and he went up to it. There he cogitated: ought one to knock, or, being in uniform, walk straight in? He could not think of any reason why one should not knock being in uniform, so he knocked.

- 33 -

"Come in," said a voice.

He opened the door and entered. At a desk before him sat a rather elderly man, clean-shaven, who eyed him keenly. On his left, with his back to him, was a man in uniform pattering away busily on a typewriter, and, for the rest, the room contained a few chairs, a coloured print of the Light of the World over the fireplace, and a torn map. Peter again hesitated. He wondered what was the rank of the officer in the chair, and if he ought to salute. While he hesitated, the other said: "Good-morning. What can I do for you?"

Peter, horribly nervous, made a half-effort at saluting, and stepped forward. "My name's Graham, sir," he said. "I've just come over, and was told in the C.G.'s office in London to report to Colonel Chichester, A.C.G., at Rouen."

The other put him at his ease at once. He rose and held a hand out over the littered desk. "How do you do, Mr. Graham?" he said. "We were expecting you. I am the A.C.G. here, and we've plenty for you to do. Take a seat, won't you? I believe I once heard you preach at my brother's place down in Suffolk. You were at St. Thomas's, weren't you, down by the river?"

Peter warmed to the welcome. It was strangely familiar, after the past twenty-four hours, to hear himself called "Mr." and, despite the uniforms and the surroundings, he felt he might be in the presence of a vicar in England. Some of his old confidence began to return. He replied freely to the questions.

Presently the other glanced at his watch. "Well," he said, "I've got to go over to H.Q., and you had better be getting to your quarters. Where did I place Captain Graham, Martin?"

The orderly at the desk leaned sideways and glanced at a paper pinned on the desk. "No. 5 Rest Camp, sir," he said.

"Ah, yes, I remember now. You can get a tram at the bottom of the street that will take you nearly all the way. It's a pretty place, on the edge of the country. You'll find about one thousand men in camp, and the O.C.'s name is—what is it, Martin?"

"Captain Harold, sir."

"Harold, that's it. A decent chap. The men are constantly coming and going, but there's a good deal to do."

"Is there a chapel in the camp?" asked Peter.

"Oh, no, I don't think so. You'll use the canteen. There's a quiet room there you can borrow for celebrations. There's a P.O.W. camp next door one way and a South African Native Labour Corps lot the other. But they have their own chaplains. We'll let you down easy at first, but you might see if you can fix up a service or so for the men in the forest. There's a Labour Company out there cutting wood. Maybe you'll be able to get a lift out in a car, but get your O.C. to indent for a bicycle if there isn't one. Drop in and see me some day and tell me how you are getting on, I'll find you some more work later on."

Peter got up. The other held out his hand, which Peter took, and then, remembering O.T.C. days at Oxford, firmly and, unblushingly saluted. The Colonel made a little motion. "Good-bye," he said, and Peter found himself outside the door.

"No. 5 Rest. Camp;" said Jenks a moment later: "you're in luck, padre. It's a topping camp, and the skipper is an awfully good sort. Beast of a long way out, though. You'll have to have a taxi now."

"The A.C.G. said a tram would do," said Peter.

"Then he talked through his blooming hat," replied the other. "He's probably never been there in his little life. It's two miles beyond the tram terminus if it's a yard. My place is just across the river, and there's a ferry that pretty well drops you there. Tell you what I'll do. I'll see you down and then skip over."

"What about your stuff, though?" queried Peter.

"Oh? bless you, I can get a lorry to collect that. That's one use in being A.S.C., at any rate."

"It's jolly decent of you," said Peter.

"Not a bit, old dear," returned the other. "You're the right sort, padre, and I'm at a loose end just now. Besides, I'd like to see old Harold. He's one of the best. Come on."

They found a taxi this time, near the Gare du Vert, and ran quickly out, first over cobbles, then down a wide avenue with a macadamised surface which paralleled the river, downstream.

"Main road to Havre," volunteered Jenks. "I've been through once or twice with our stuff. It's a jolly pretty run, and you can lunch in Candebec with a bit of luck, which is one of the beauty-spots of the Seine, you know."

The road gave on open country in a few miles, though there were camps to be seen between it and the river, with wharves and buildings at intervals, and ahead a biggish waterside village. Just short of that they pulled up. A notice-board remarked "No. 5 Rest Camp," and Peter saw he had arrived.

The sun was well up by this time, and his spirits with it. The country smiled in the clear light. Behind the camp fields ran up to a thick wood through which wound a road, and the river was just opposite them. A sentry came to attention as they passed in, sloped arms, and saluted. Peter stared at him. "You ought to take the salute, padre," said Jenks; "you're senior to me, you know."

They passed down a regular street of huts, most of which had little patches of garden before them in which the green of some early spring flowers was already showing, and stopped before the orderly-room. Jenks said he would look in and see if "the skipper" were inside, and in a second or two came out with a red-faced, cheerful-looking man, whom he introduced as Captain Harold. With them was a tall young Scots officer in a kilt, whom Peter learned was Lieutenant Mackay of their mess.

"Glad to see you, padre," said Harold. "Our last man wasn't up to much, and Jenks says you're a sport. I've finished in there, so come on to the mess and let's have a spot for luck. Come on, Scottie. Eleven o'clock's all right for you, isn't it?"

"Shan't say no," said the gentleman addressed, and they passed behind the orderly-room and in at an open door.

Peter glanced curiously round. The place was very cheerful—a fire burning and gay pictures on the wall. "Rather neat, isn't it, padre?" queried Harold. "By the way, you've got to dub up a picture. Everyone in the mess gives one. There's a blank space over there that'll do nicely for a Kirschner, if you're sport enough for that, Jenko'll show you where to get a topper. What's yours, old son?"

"Same as usual, skipper," said Jenks, throwing himself into a chair.

Harold walked across to a little shuttered window and tapped. A man's face appeared in the opening, "Four whiskies, Hunter—that's all right, padre?"

"Yes," said Peter, and walked to the fire, while the talk became general.

"First time over?" queried Mackay.

"Well, how's town?" asked Harold. "Good shows on? I ought to be due next month, but I think I'll! wait a bit. Want to get over in the spring and see a bit of the country too. What do they think of the war over there, Jenko?"

"It's going to be over by summer. There's a big push coming off this spring, and Fritz can't stand much more. He's starving, and has no reserves worth talking of. The East does not matter, though the doings at Salonika have depressed them no end. This show's going to be won on the West, and that quickly. Got it, old bean?"

"Good old Blighty!" ejaculated Harold. "But they don't really believe all that, do they, padre?"

"They do," said Peter. "And, to tell you the truth, I wondered if I'd be over in time myself. Surely the Yanks must come in and make a difference."

"This time next year, perhaps, though I doubt it. What do you think, Scottie?"

"Oh, ask another! I'm sick of it. Say, skipper, what about that run out into the forest you talked of?"

"Good enough. Would you care to go, padre? There's a wood-cuttin' crowd out there, and I want to see 'em about firewood. There's a car possible to-day, and we could all pack in."

"Count me out," said Jenks. "I'll have to toddle over and report. Sorry, all the same."

"I'd love it," said Peter. "Besides, the A.C.G. said I was to look up those people."

"Oh, well done. It isn't a joy-ride at all, then. Have another, padre, and let's get off. No? Well, I will. How's yours, Scottie?"

Ten minutes later the three of them got into a big car and glided smoothly off, first along the river, and then up a steep road into the forest. Peter, fresh from London, lay back and enjoyed it immensely. He had no idea Normandy boasted such woods, and the world looked very good to him. It was all about as different from what he had imagined as it could possibly have been. He just set himself to appreciate it.

The forest was largely fir and pine, and the sunlight glanced down the straight trunks and patterned on the carpet beneath. Hollies gleamed green against the brown background, and in an open space of bare beech trees the littered ground was already pricked with the new green of the wild hyacinth. Now and again the rounded hills gave glimpses of the far Normandy plain across the serpentine river, then would as suddenly close in on them again until the car seemed to dart between the advancing battalions of the forest as though to escape capture. At length, in one such place, they leaped forward up a short rise, then rushed swiftly downhill, swung round a corner, and came out on what had become all but a bare tableland, set high so that one could see distant valleys—Boscherville, Duclair—and yet bare, for the timber had been all but entirely cut down.

Five hundred yards along this road brought them to a small encampment. There were some lines of Nysson huts, a canteen with an inverted triangle for sign, some tents, great stacks of timber and of smaller wood, a few lorries drawn up and silent, and, beyond, two or three buildings of wood set down by themselves, with a garden in front, and a notice "Officers' Quarters." Here, then, Captain Harold stopped the car, and they got out. There were some jovial introductions, and presently the whole party set off across the cleared space to where, in the distance, one could see the edge of the forest.

Peter did not want to talk, and dropped a little behind. Harold and the O.C. of the forestry were on in front, and Mackay, with a junior local officer, were skirmishing about on the right, taking pot-shots with small chunks of wood at the stumps of trees and behaving rather like two school-boys.

The air was all heavy with resinous scent, and the carpet beneath soft with moss and leaves and fragrant slips of pine. Here and there, on a definite plan, a small tree had been spared, and when he joined the men ahead, Peter learned how careful were the French in all this apparently wholesale felling. In the forest, as they saw as they reached it, the lines were numbered and lettered and in some distant office every woodland group was known with its place and age. There are few foresters like the French, and it was cheering to think that this great levelling would, in a score of years, do more good than harm.

Slowly biting into the untouched regiments of trees were the men, helped in their work by a small power engine. The great trunks were lopped and roughly squared here, and then dragged by motor traction to a slide, which they now went to view. It was a fascinating sight. The forest ended abruptly on a high hill, and below, at their feet, wound the river. Far down, working on a wharf that had been constructed of piles driven into the mud, was a Belgian detachment with German prisoners, and near the wharf rough sheds housed the cutting plant. Where they stood was the head of a big slide, with back-up sides, and the forest giants, brought to the top from the place where they were felled, were levered over, to swish down in a cloud of dust to the waiting men beneath.

"Well, skipper, what about the firewood?" asked Harold as they stood gazing.

"How much do you want?" asked the O.C. Forestry.

"Oh, well, what can you let me have? You've got stacks of odd stuff about; surely you can spare a bit."

"It's clean agin regulations, but could you send for it?"

"Rather! There's an A.S.C. camp below us, and the men there promised me a lorry if I'd share the spoils with them. Will that do?"

"All right. When will you send up?"

"What's to-day? Wednesday? How about Sunday? I could put some boys on to load up who'd like the jaunt. How would Sunday do?"

"Capital. My chaps work on all day, of course, and I don't want to give them extra, so send some of yours."

Peter listened, and now cut in.

"Excuse me, sir," he said, "but I was told I ought to try and get a service of some sort out here. Could I come out on the lorry and hold one?"

"Delighted, padre, of course. I'll see what I can do for you. About eleven? Probably you won't get many men as there are usually inspection parades and some extra fatigues on Sunday, but I'll put it in orders. We haven't had a padre for a long time."

"Eleven would suit me," said Peter, "if Captain Harold thinks the lorry can get up here by that time. Will it, sir?"

"Oh, I should think so, and, anyway, an hour or so won't make much difference. If I can, I'll come with you myself. But, I say, we ought to be getting back now. It will be infernally late for luncheon."

"Come and have a drink before you start, anyway," said the O.C.; and he led the way back to the camp and into an enclosure made of bushes and logs in the rear of the mess, where rustic seats and a table had been constructed under the shade of a giant oak. "It's rattling here in summer," he said, "and we have most of our meals out of doors. Sit down, won't you? Orderly!"

"By Jove! you people are comfortable out here," said Harold. "Wish I had a job of this sort."

"Oh, I don't know, skipper; it would feed you up after a while, I think. It's bally lonely in the evening, and we can't always get a car to town. It's a damned nuisance getting out again, too." Then, as the orderly brought glasses and a bottle: "Have a spot. It's Haig and Haig, Mackay, and the right, stuff."

"Jolly good, sir," said that worthy critically. "People think because I don't talk broad Scots I'm no Highlander, but when it comes to the whisky I've got a Scottish thirst. Say when, sir."

Peter had another because he was warm with the sense of good comradeship, and was warmer still when he climbed into the car ten minutes later. Life seemed so simple and easy; and he was struck with the cheeriness of his new friends, and the ready welcome to himself and his duty. He waved to the O.C. "See you Sunday, sir," he called, out, "'bout eleven. You won't forget to put it in orders, will you? Cheerio."

"Let's go round by the lower road, skipper," said Mackay. "We can look in at that toppin' little pub—what's its name, Croix something?—and besides, the surface is capital down there."

"And see Marie, eh? But don't forget you've got a padre aboard."

"Oh, he's all right, and if he's going to be out here, it's time he knew Marie."

Graham laughed. "Carry on," he said. "It's all one to me where we go, skipper."

He lay back more comfortably than ever, and the big car leaped forward through the forest, ever descending towards the river level. Soon the trees thinned, and they were skirting ploughed fields. Presently they ran through a little village, where a German prisoner straightened himself from his work in a garden and saluted. Then through a wood which suddenly gave a vista of an avenue to a stately house, turreted in the French style, a quarter of a mile away; then over a little stream; then round a couple of corners, past a dreamy old church, and a long immemorial wall, and so out into the straight road along the river. The sun gleamed on the water, and there were ships in view, a British and a couple of Norwegian tramps, ploughing slowly down to the sea. On the far bank the level of the land was low, but on this side only some narrow apple-orchards and here and there lush water-meadows separated them from the hills.

The Croix de Guerre stood back from the road in a long garden just where a forest bridle-path wound down through a tiny village to the main road. Their chauffeur backed the car all but out of sight into this path after they climbed out, and the three of them made for a sidedoor in a high wall. Harold opened it and walked in. The pretty trim little garden had a few flowers in bloom, so sheltered was it, and Mackay picked a red rosebud as they walked up the path.

Harold led the way without ceremony into a parlour that opened off a verandah, and, finding it empty, opened a door beyond. "Marie! Marie!" he called.

"Ah, Monsieur le Capitaine, I come," came a girl's voice, and Marie entered. Peter noticed how rapidly she took them all in, and how cold were the eyes that nevertheless sparkled and greeted Harold and Mackay with seeming gaiety. She was short and dark and not particularly good-looking, but she had all the vivacity and charm of the French.

"Oh, monsieur, where have you been for so long? I thought you had forgotten La Croix de Guerre altogether. It's the two weeks—no, *three*—since you come here. The gentlemen will have déjeuner? And perhaps a little aperitif before?"

"Bon jour, Marie," began the Captain in clumsy French, and then abandoned the attempt. "I could not come, Marie, you know. C'est la guerre. Much work each day."

"Ah, non, monsieur cannot cheat me. He had found another cafe and another girl…. Non, non, monsieur, it is not correct;" and the girl drew herself up with a curiously changed air as Harold clumsily reached out towards her, protesting. "And you have a curé here—how do you say, a chapelain?" and Marie beamed on Peter.

The two officers looked at him and laughed. "What can I bring you, Monsieur le Capitaine le Curé?" demanded the girl. "Vermuth? Cognac?"

Mackay slipped from the edge of the table on which he had been sitting and advanced towards her, speaking fluent French, with a curious suggestion of a Scotch accent that never appeared in his English. Peter watched with a smile on his face and a curious medley of feelings, while the Lieutenant explained, that they could not stop to lunch, that they would take three mixed vermuth, and that he would come and help her get them. They went out together, Marie protesting, and Harold, lighting a cigarette and offering one to Peter, said with a laugh: "He's the boy, is Mackay. Wish I could sling the lingo like him. It's a great country, padre."

In a minute or two the pair of them came back, Marie was wearing the rose at the point of the little *décolleté* of her black dress, and was all over smiles. She carried a tray with glasses and a bottle. Mackay carried the other. With a great show, he helped her pour out, and chatted away in French while they drank.

Harold and Peter talked together, but the latter caught scraps of the others' conversation. Mackay wanted to know, apparently, when she would be next in town, and was urging a date on her. Peter caught "Rue Jeanne d'Arc," but little more, and Harold was insistent on a move in a few minutes. They skirmished at the door saying "Good-bye," but it was with an increased feeling of the warmth and jollity of his new life that Peter once more boarded the car. This time Mackay got in front and Harold joined Graham behind. As they sped off, Peter said:

"By Jove, skipper, you do have a good time out here!"

Harold flicked off the ash of his cigarette. "So, so, padre," he said. "But the devil's loose. It's all so easy; I've never met a girl yet who was not out for a spree. Of course, we don't see anything of the real French ladies, though, and this isn't the line. By God! when I think of the boys up there, I feel a beast sometimes. But I can't help it; they won't pass me to go up, and it's no use growling down here because of it."

"I suppose not," said Peter, and leaned back reflecting for the rest of the way. He felt as if he had known these men all his days, and as if his London life had been lived on another planet.

After lunch he was given a cubicle, and spent an hour or two getting unpacked. That done, just as he was about to sit down to a letter, there came a knock at the door, and Mackay looked in.

"You there, padre?" he asked. "There's a lorry going up to town that has just brought a batch of men in: would you care to come? I've got to do some shopping, and we could dine at the club and come back afterwards."

Peter jumped up. "Topping," he said. "I want to get one or two things, and I'd love it."

"Come on, then," said the other. "I'll meet you at the gate in five minutes."

Peter got on his Sam Browne and went out, and after a bit Mackay joined him. They jolted up to town, and went first to the Officers' Store at the E.F.C. Mackay bought some cigarettes, and Peter some flannel collars and a tie. Together the pair of them strolled round town, and put their heads in at the cathedral at Peter's request. He had a vision of old grey stone and coloured glass and wide soaring spaces, but his impatient companion hauled him out. "Of course, you'll want to see round, padre," he said, "but you can do it some other time and with somebody else. I've seen it once, and that's enough for me. Let's get on to the club and book a table; there's usually a fearful crowd."

Peter was immensely impressed with the crowd of men, the easy greetings of acquaintances, and the way in which one was ignored by the rest. He was introduced to several people, who were all very cheerful, and in the long dining-room they eventually sat down to table with two more officers whom the Scotsman knew. Peter was rather taken with a tall man, slightly bald, of the rank of Captain, who was attached to a Labour Corps. He had travelled a great deal, and been badly knocked about in Gallipoli. In a way, he was more serious than the rest, and he told Peter a good deal about the sights of the town—the old houses and churches, and where was the best glass, and so on. Mackay and the fourth made merry, and Mackay, who called the W.A.A.C. waitress by her Christian name, was plainly getting over-excited. Peter's friend was obviously a little scornful. "You'll meet a lot of fools here, padre," he said, "old and young. The other day I was having tea here when two old buffers came in—dug-outs, shoved into some job or another—and they sat down at the table next mine. I couldn't help hearing what they said. The older and fatter, a Colonel, looked out of window, and remarked ponderously:

"'By the way, wasn't Joan of Arc born about here?'

"'No,' said the second; 'down in Alsace-Lorraine, I believe. She was burnt here, and they threw her ashes into the Grand Pont.'"

Peter laughed silently, and the other smiled at him. "Fact," he said. "That's one type of ass, and the second is (dropping his voice) your friend here and his like, if you don't mind my saying so. Look at him with that girl now. Somebody'll spot it, and they'll keep an eye on him. Next time he meets her on the sly he'll be caught out, and be up for it. Damned silly fool, I think! The bally girl's only a waitress from Lyons."

Peter glanced at Mackay. He was leaning back holding the menu, which she, with covert glances at the cashier's desk, was trying to take away from him. "Isobel," he said, "I say, come here—no, I really want to see it—tell me, when do you get out next?"

"We don't get no leave worth talking of, you know," she said. "Besides, you don't mean it. You can't talk to me outside. Oh, shut up! I must go. They'll see us," and she darted away.

"Damned pretty girl, eh?" said Mackay contentedly. "Don't mind me, padre. It's only a bit of a joke. Come on, let's clear out."

The four went down the stairs together and stood in a little group at the entrance-door. "Where you for now, Mac?" asked the second officer, a subaltern of the West Hampshires.

"Don't know, old sport. I'm with the padre. What you for, padre?"

"I should think we had better be getting back," said Peter, glancing at the watch on his wrist. "We've a long way to go."

"Oh, hang it all, not yet! It's a topping evenin'. Let's stroll up the street."

Peter glanced at the Labour Corps Captain, who nodded, and they two turned off together. "There's not much to do," he said. "One gets sick of cinemas, and the music-hall is worse, except when one is really warmed up for a razzle-dazzle. I don't wonder these chaps go after wine and women more than they ought. After all, most of them are just loose from home. You must make allowances, padre. It's human nature, you know."

Peter nodded abstractedly. It was the second time he had heard that. "It's all so jolly different from what I expected," he said meditatively.

"I know," said the other. "Not much danger or poverty or suffering here, seemingly. But you never can tell. Look at those girls: I bet you would probably sum them up altogether wrongly if you tried."

Peter glanced at a couple of French women who were passing. The pair were looking at them, and in the light of a brilliantly lit cinema they showed up clearly. The paint was laid on shamelessly; their costumes, made in one piece, were edged with fur and very gay. Each carried a handbag and one a tasselled stick. "Good-night, chérie," said one, as they passed.

Peter gave a little shudder. "How ghastly!" he said. "How can anyone speak to them? Are there many like that about?" He glanced back again: "Why, good heavens," he cried, "one's Marie!"

"Hullo, padre," said his friend, the ghost of a smile beginning about his lips. "Where have you been? Marie! By Jove! I shall have to report you to the A.C.G."

Peter blushed furiously. "It was at an inn," he said, "this morning, as we were coming back from the forest. But she seemed so much better then, Mackay knew her; why, I heard him say...."

He glanced back at the sudden recollection. The two girls were speaking to the two others, twenty paces or so behind. "Oh," he exclaimed, "look here!..."

The tall Labour man slipped his arm in his and interrupted. "Come on, padre," he said; "you can't do anything. Mackay's had a bit too much as it is, and the other chap is looking for a night out. We'll stroll past the cathedral, and I'll see you a bit of the way home."

"But how damnable, how beastly!" exclaimed Peter. "It makes one sick!..." He broke off, and the two walked on in silence.

"Is there much of that?" Peter demanded suddenly.

The other glanced at him. "You'll find out without my telling you," he said; "but don't be too vehement till you've got your eyes open. There are worse things."

"There can't be," broke in Peter. "Women like that, and men who will go with them, aren't fit to be called men and women. There's no excuse. It's bestial, that's what it is."

"You wouldn't speak to one?" queried the other.

"Good heavens, no! Do you forget what I am?"

"No, I don't, padre, but look here, I'm not a Christian, and I take a common-sense view of these things, but I'm bound to say I think you're on the wrong tack, too. Didn't Christ have compassion on people like that? Didn't He eat and drink with publicans and sinners?"

"Yes, to convert them. You can't name the two things in the same breath. He had compassion on the multitude of hungry women and children and misguided men, but He hated sin. You can't deny that." Peter recalled his sermon; he was rather indignant, unreasonably, that the suggestion should have been made.

"So?" said the other laconically. "Well, you know more about it than I do, I suppose. Come on; we go down here."

They parted at the corner by the river again, and Peter set out for his long walk home alone. It was a lovely evening of stars, cool, but not too cold, and at first the streets were full of people. He kept to the curb or walked in the road till he was out of the town, taking salutes automatically, his thoughts far away. The little *cafés debits* were crowded, largely by Tommies. He was not accosted again, for he walked fast, but he saw enough as he went.

More than an hour later he swung into camp, and went to his room, lit a candle, and shut the door. Tunic off, he sat on the edge of the camp-bed and stared at the light. He seemed to have lived a year in a day, and he felt unclean. He thought of Hilda, and then actually smiled, for Hilda and this life seemed so incredibly far apart. He could not conceive of her even knowing of its existence. Yet, he supposed, she knew, as he had done, that such things were. He had even preached about them…. It suddenly struck him that he had talked rot in the pulpit, talked of things of which he knew nothing. Yet, of course, his attitude had been right.

He wondered if he should speak to Mackay, and, so wondering, fell forward on his knees.

CHAPTER IV

Hilda's religion was, like the religion of a great many Englishwomen of her class, of a very curious sort. She never, of course, analysed it herself, and conceivably she would object very strongly to the description set down here, but in practical fact there is no doubt about the analysis. To begin with, this conventional and charming young lady of Park Lane had in common with Napoleon Bonaparte that Christianity meant more to them both as the secret of social order than as the mystery of the Incarnation. Hilda was convinced that a decent and orderly life rested on certain agreements and conclusions in respect to marriage and class and conduct, and that these agreements and conclusions were admirably stated in the Book of Common Prayer, and most ably and decorously advocated from the pulpit of St. John's. She would have said that she believed the agreements and conclusions because of the Prayer Book, but in fact she had primarily given in her allegiance to a social system, and supported the Prayer Book because of its support of that. Once a month she repeated the Nicene Creed, but only because, in the nature of things, the Nicene Creed was given her once a month to repeat, and she never really conceived that people might worry strenuously about it, any more than she did. Being an intelligent girl, she knew, of course, that people did, and occasionally preachers occupied the pulpit of St. John's who were apparently quite anxious that she and the rest of the congregation should understand that it meant this and not that, or that and not this, according to the particular enthusiasm of the clergyman of the moment. Sentence by sentence she more or less understood what these gentlemen keenly urged upon her; as a whole she understood nothing. She was far too much the child of her environment and age not to perceive that Mr. Lloyd George's experiments in class legislation were vastly more important.

Peter, therefore, had always been a bit of an enigma to her. As a rule he fitted in with the scheme of things perfectly well, for he was a gentleman, he liked nice things, and he was splendidly keen on charity organisation and the reform of abuses on right lines. But now and again he said and did things which perturbed her. It was as if she had gradually become complete mistress of a house, and then had suddenly discovered a new room into which she peeped for a minute before it was lost to her again and the door shut. It was no Bluebeard's chamber into which she looked; it was much more that she had a suspicion that the room contained a live mistress who might come out one day and dispute her own title. She could tell how Peter would act nine times out of ten; she knew by instinct, a great deal better than he did, the conceptions that ruled his life; but now and again he would hesitate perplexedly as if at the thought of something that she did not understand, or act suddenly in response to an overwhelming flood of impulse whose spring was beyond her control or even her surmise. Women mother all their men because men are on the whole such big babies, but from a generation of babies is born occasionally the master. Women get so used to the rule that they forget the exception. When he comes, then, they are troubled.

But this was not all Hilda's religion. For some mysterious reason this product of a highly civilised community had the elemental in her. Men and women both have got to eliminate all trace of sex before they can altogether escape that. In other words, because in her lay latent the power of birth, in which moment she would be cloistered alone in a dark and silent room with infinity, she clung unreasonably and all but unconsciously to certain superstitions which she shared with primitive savages and fetish-worshippers. All of which seems a far cry from the War Intercession Services at wealthy and fashionable St. John's, but it was nothing more or less than this which was causing her to kneel on a high hassock, elbows comfortably on the prayer-rail, and her face in her hands, on a certain Friday evening in the week after Peter's arrival in France, while the senior curate (after suitable pauses, during which her mind was uncontrollably busy with an infinite number of things, ranging from the doings of Peter in France to the increasing difficulty of obtaining silk stockings), intoned the excellent stately English of the Prayers set forth by Authority in Time of War.

Two pews ahead of her knelt Sir Robert Doyle, in uniform. That simple soldier was a bigger child than most men, and was, therefore, still conscious of a number of unfathomable things about him, for the which Hilda, his godchild, adored and loved him as a mother will adore her child who sits in a field of buttercups and sees, not minted, nor botanical, but heavenly gold. He was all the more lovable, because he conceived that he was much bigger and stronger than she, and perfectly capable of looking after her. In that, he was like a plucky boy who gets up from his buttercups to tell his mother not to be frightened when a cow comes into the field.

They went out together, and greeted each other in the porch. "Good-evening, child," said the soldier, with a smile. "And how's Peter?"

Hilda smiled back, but after a rather wintry fashion, which the man was quick to note. "I couldn't have told you fresh news yesterday," she said, "but I had a letter this morning all about his first Sunday. He's at Rouen at a rest camp for the present, though he thinks he's likely to be moved almost at once; and he's quite well."

"And then?" queried the other affectionately.

"Oh, he doesn't know at all, but he says he doesn't think there's any chance of his getting up the line. He'll be sent to another part where there is likely to be a shortage of chaplains soon."

"Well, that's all right, isn't it? He's in no danger at Rouen, at any rate. If we go on as we're going on now, they won't even hear the guns down there soon. Come, little girl, what's worrying you? I can see there's something."

They were in the street now, walking towards the park, and Hilda did not immediately reply. Then she said: "What are you going to do? Can't you come in for a little? Father and mother will be out till late, and you can keep me company."

He glanced at his watch. "I've got to be at the War Office later," he said, "but my man doesn't reach town till after ten, so I will. The club's not over-attractive these days. What with the men who think one knows everything and won't tell, and the men who think they know everything and want to tell, it's a bit trying."

Hilda laughed merrily. "Poor Uncle Bob," she said, giving him her childhood's name that had never been discontinued between them. "You shall come home with me, and sit in father's chair, and have a still decent whisky and a cigar, and if you're very good I'll read you part of Peter's letter."

"What would Peter say?"

"Oh, he wouldn't mind the bits I'll read to you. Indeed, I think he'd like it: he'd like to know what you think. You see, he's awfully depressed; he feels he's not wanted out there, and—though I don't know what he means—that things, religious things, you know, aren't real."

"Not wanted, eh?" queried the old soldier. "Now, I wonder why he resents that. Is it because he feels snubbed? I shouldn't be surprised if he had a bit of a swelled head, your young man, you know, Hilda."

"Sir Robert Doyle, if you're going to be beastly, you can go to your horrid old club, and I only hope you'll be worried to death. Of course it isn't that. Besides, he says everyone is very friendly and welcomes him—only he feels that that makes it worse. He thinks they don't want—well, what he has to give, I suppose."

"What he has to give? But what in the world has he to give? He has to take parade services, and visit hospitals and" (he was just going to say "bury the dead," but thought it hardly sounded pleasant), "make himself generally decent and useful, I suppose. That's what chaplains did when I was a subaltern, and jolly decent fellows they usually were."

"Well, I know. That's what I should feel, and that's what I don't quite understand. I suppose he feels he's responsible for making the men religious—it reads like that. But you shall hear the letter yourself."

Doyle digested this for a while in silence. Then he gave a sort of snort, which is inimitable, but always accompanied his outbursts against things slightly more recent than the sixties. It had the effect of rousing Hilda, at any rate.

"Don't, you dear old thing," she said, clutching his arm. "I know exactly what you're going to say. Young men of your day minded their business and did their duty, and didn't theorise so much. Very likely. But, you see, our young men had the misfortune to be born a little later than you. And they can't help it." She sighed a little. "It *is* trying sometimes…. But they're all right really, and they'll come back to things."

They were at the gate by now. Sir Robert stood aside to let her pass. "I know, dear," he said, "I'm an old fogey. Besides, young Graham has good stuff in him—I always said so. But if he's on the tack of trying to stick his fingers into people's souls, he's made a mistake in going to France. I know Tommy—or I did know him. (The Lord alone knows what's in the Army these days.) He doesn't want that sort of thing. He swears and he grouses and he drinks, but he respects God Almighty more than you'd think, and he serves his Queen—I mean his King. A parade service is a parade, and it's a bore at times, but it's discipline, and it helps in the end. Like that little 'do' to-night, it helps. One comes away feelin' one can stand a bit more for the sake of the decent, clean things of life."

Hilda regarded the fine, straight old man for a second as they stood, on the top of the steps. Then her eyes grew a little misty. "God bless you, Uncle Bob," she said. "You *do* understand." And the two went in together.

Hilda opened the door of the study. "I'm going to make you comfortable myself," she said. She pulled a big armchair round; placed a reading-lamp on a small table and drew it close; and she made the old soldier sit in the chair. Then she unlocked a little cupboard, and got out a decanter and siphon and glass, and a box of cigars. She placed these by his side, and stood back quizzically a second. Then she threw a big leather cushion at his feet and walked to the switches, turning off the main light and leaving only the shaded radiance of the reading-lamp. She turned the shade of it so that the light would fall on the letter while she sat on the cushion, and then she bent down, kissed her godfather, and went to the door. "I won't be a moment, Uncle Bob," she said. "Help yourself, and get comfortable."

Five minutes later the door opened and she came in. As she moved into the circle of light, the man felt an absurd satisfaction, as if he were partly responsible for the dignified figure with its beautifully waved soft, fair hair, of which he was so proud. She smiled on him, and sat down at his feet, leaning back against his chair and placing her left elbow on his knees. He laid a caressing hand on her arm, and then looked steadily in front of him lest he should see more than she wished.

Hilda rustled the sheets. "The first is all about me," she explained, "and I'll skip that. Let me see—yes, here we are. Now listen. It's rather long, but you mustn't say anything till I've finished."

"'Saturday' (Peter's letter ran) I gave up to getting ready for Sunday, though Harold' (he's the O.C. of the camp, Peter says, a jolly decent sort of man) 'wanted me to go up town with him. I had had a talk with him about the services, and had fixed up to have a celebration in the morning in the Y.M.C.A. in camp—they have a quiet room, and there is a table in it that one puts against the wall and uses for an altar—and an evening service in the canteen-hall part of the place. I couldn't have a morning service, as I was to go out to the forest camp, as I have told you.' He said in his first letter how he had been motored out to see a camp in the forest where they are cutting wood for something, and he had fixed up a parade," said Hilda, looking up. Doyle nodded gravely, and she went on reading: "'Harold said he'd like to take Communion, and that I could put up a notice in the anteroom of the Officers' Mess.

"'Well, I spent the morning preparing sermons. I thought I'd preach from "The axe is laid to the root of the tree" in the forest, and make a sort of little parable out of it for the men. I planned to say how Christ was really watching and testing each one of us, especially out here, and to begin by talking a bit about Germany, and how the axe was being laid to that tree because it wouldn't bear good fruit. I couldn't get much for the evening, so I thought I'd leave it, and perhaps say much the same as the morning, only differently introduced. I went and saw the hut manager, a very decent fellow who is a Baptist minister at home, and he said he'd like to come in the morning. Well, I didn't know what to say to that; I hated to hurt him, and, of course, he has no Baptist chapel out here; but I didn't know what the regulations might be, and excused myself on those grounds.

"'Then in the afternoon I went round the camp. Oh, Hilda, I was fearfully nervous—I don't know why exactly, but I was. The men were playing "crown and anchor," and sleeping, and cleaning kit (this is a rest camp you know), and it seemed so cold-blooded somehow. I told them anyone could come in the evening if he wanted to, but that in the morning the service was for Church of England communicants. I must say I was very bucked up over the result. I had no end of promises, and those who were going to be out in the evening said so straight out. Quite thirty said they'd come in the morning, and they were very respectful and decent. Then I wrote out and put up my notices. The mess ragged a bit about it, but quite decently ("Here's the padre actually going to do a bit of work!" and the usual "I shall be a chaplain in the next war!"); and I mentioned to one or two whom I knew to be Church of England that Captain Harold had said he would come to the early service. Someone had told me that if the O.C. of a camp comes, the others often will. After dinner we settled down to bridge, and about ten-thirty I was just going off to bed when Harold came in with two or three other men. Well, I hate to tell you, dear, but I promised I'd write, and, besides, I do want to talk to somebody. Anyway, he was what they call "merry," and he and his friends were full of talk about what they'd done up town. I don't know that it was anything very bad, but it was awful to me to think that this chap was going to communicate next day. I didn't know what to do, but I couldn't say anything then, and I slipped off to bed as soon as I could. They made a huge row in the anteroom for some time, but at last I got to sleep.

"'Next morning I was up early, and got things fixed up nicely. At eight o'clock *one man* came rather sheepishly—a young chap I'd seen the day before—and I waited for some five minutes more. Then I began. About the Creed, Harold came in, and so we finished the service. Neither of them seemed to know the responses at all, and I don't think I have ever felt more miserable. However, I had done all I could do, and I let it go at that. I comforted myself that I would get on better in the forest, where I thought there was to be a parade.

"'We got out about eleven o'clock, and I went to the O.C.'s hut. He was sitting in a deck chair reading a novel. He jumped up when he saw me, and was full of apologies. He'd absolutely forgotten I was coming, and so no notice had been given, and, anyway, apparently it isn't the custom in these camps to have ordered parade services. He sent for the Sergeant-Major, who said the men were mostly cleaning camp, but he thought he could get some together. So I sat and talked for about twenty minutes, and then went over. The canteen had been opened, and there were about twenty men there. They all looked as if they had been forced in, except one, who turned out to be a Wesleyan, and chose the hymns out of the Y.M.C.A. books in the place. They had mission hymns, and the only one that went well was "Throw out the life-line," which is really a rather ghastly thing. We had short Matins, and I preached as I had arranged. The men sat stiffly and looked at me. I don't know why, but I couldn't work up any enthusiasm and it all seemed futile. Afterwards I tried to talk to this Wesleyan corporal. He was great on forming a choir to learn hymns, and then I said straight out that I was new to this sort of work, and I hoped what I had said was all right. He said: "Yes, sir, very nice, I'm sure; but, if you'll excuse me, what the men need is converting."

"'Said I: "What exactly do you mean by that, corporal?"

"'"Well, sir," he said "they want to be led to put their trust in the Lord and get right with God. There's many a rough lad in this camp, sir. If you knew what went on, you'd see it."

"I said that I had told them God was watching them, and that we had to ask His daily help to live clean, honest lives, and truly repent of our sins.

"'"Yes, you did, sir," he said. "That's what I say, sir, it was very nice; only somehow these chaps have heard that before. It don't grip, sir. Now, we had a preacher in our chapel once...." And he went on to tell me of some revival mission.

"'Well, I went back to the O.C. He wanted me to have a drink, and I did, for, to tell you the truth, I felt like it. Then I got back to camp.

"'In the afternoon I went round the lines again. Hilda, I *wish* I could tell you what I felt. Everyone was decent enough, but the men would get up and salute as I came up, and by the very sound of their voices you could tell how their talk changed as soon as they saw me. Mind you, they were much more friendly than men at home, but I felt all the time out of touch. They didn't want me, and somehow Christ and the Gospel seemed a long way off. However, we had the evening service. The hut was fairly full, which pleased me, and I preached a much more "Gospel" address than in the morning. Some officers came, and then afterwards two or three of us went out for a stroll and a talk.

"'Among these officers was a tall chap I had met at the club, named Langton. He had come down to see somebody in our mess, and had come on to service. He is an extraordinarily nice person, different from most, a man who thinks a lot and controls himself. He did most of the talking, and began as we strolled up the hill.

"'"Padre," he said, "how *does* Christ save us?"

"'I said He had died to obtain our forgiveness from God, and that, if we trusted in Him, He would forgive and help us to live nobler and manlier lives. (Of course, I said much more, but I see plainly that that is what it all comes to.)

"'When I had done, he walked on for a bit in silence, and then he said, "Do you think the men understand that?"

"'I said I thought and hoped they might. It was simple enough.

"""Well," he said, "it's hopeless jargon to me. If I try to analyse it, I am knocked out right and left by countless questions; but leave that. It is when I try to take you practically at your word that I find you are mumbling a fetish. Forgive me, but it is so."

"'I was a little annoyed and very troubled. "Do explain," I said.

"""All right, only you mustn't mind if I hurt you," he said. "Take *Trust in Christ*—well, that either means that a man gets intoxicated by an idea which does control his life, just as it would if he were intoxicated by the idea *Trust in Buddha*, or else it comes to nothing. I can't really trust in a dead man, or a man on the right hand of the throne of God. What Tommy wants is a pal to lean on in the canteen and the street. He wants somebody more real and more lovable and more desirable than the girl who tempts him into sin. And he can't be found. Was he in your service to-night? Can he be emotionally conjured up by 'Yield not to temptation' or 'Dare to be a Daniel'? Be honest, padre—the thing is a spectre of the imagination."

"'I was absolutely silent. He went on:

"""You make much talk of sin and forgiveness. Well, Tommy doesn't understand what you mean by sin. He is confused to bits about it; but the main thing that stands out is that a man may break all the Ten Commandments theologically and yet be a rattling good pal, as brave as a lion, as merry as a cricket, and the life and soul and *Christ* of a platoon. That's the fact, and it is the one thing that matters. But there is another thing: if a man sins, how is he to get forgiveness? What sort of a God is it Who will wipe the whole blessed thing out because in a moment of enthusiasm the sinner says he is sorry? If that's all sin is, it isn't worth worrying about, and if that is all God is, He's not got the makings of a decent O.C."

"""Good for you, skipper," said the other man.

"'Langton rounded on him. "It isn't good for me or for anyone," he said. "And I'll tell you what, my boy: all that I've said doesn't justify a man making a beast of himself, which is what the majority of us do. I can see that a man may very wisely get drunk at times, but he's a ——— fool to get himself sodden with drink." (And he went on to more, Hilda, that I can't write to you.)

"'Well, I don't know what I said. I went back utterly miserable. Oh, Hilda, I think I never ought to have come out here. Langton's right in a way. We clergy have said the same thing so often that we forget how it strikes a practical common-sense man. But there must be an answer somewhere, if I only knew it. Meantime I'm like a doctor among the dying who cannot diagnose the disease. I'm like a salesman with a shop full of goods that nobody wants because they don't fulfil the advertisement. And I never felt more utterly alone in my life.

"'These men talk a different language from mine; they belong to another world. They are such jolly good fellows that they are prepared to accept me as a comrade without question, but as for my message, I might as well be trying to cure smallpox by mouthing sonorous Virgil—only it is worse than that, for they no longer even believe that the diagnosis is what I say. And what gets over me is that they are, on the whole, decent chaps. There's Harold—he's probably immoral and he certainly drinks too much, but he's as unselfish as possible, and I feel in my bones he'd do anything to help a friend.

"'Of course, I hate their vices. The sights in the streets make me feel positively sick. I wouldn't touch what they touch with a stick. When I think of you, so honest and upright and clean....' Oh, but I needn't read that, Uncle Bob." She turned over a page or so. "I think that's all. No, just this:

"'I've been made mess secretary, and I serve out coffee in the canteen for a couple of hours every other day. That's about all there is to do. I wish to Heaven I had an ordinary commission!'"

The girl's voice ceased with a suspicious suddenness, and the man's hand tightened on her arm. For a minute they remained so, and then, impulsively and unrestrained, she half-turned and sobbed out against his knees:

"Oh, Uncle Bob, I'm so unhappy! I feel so sorry for him. And—and—the worst is, I don't really understand.... I don't see what worries him. Our religion is good enough, I'm sure. Oh, I *hate* those beasts of men out there! Peter's too good for them. I wish he'd never gone. I feel as if he'd never come back!"

"There, there, my dear," said the old soldier, uncomfortably. "Don't take on so. He'll find his feet, you know. It's not so bad as that. You can trust him, can't you?"

She nodded vigorously. "But what do *you* think of it all?" she demanded.

Sir Robert Doyle cleared his throat. "Well," he began, but stopped. To him it was an extraordinarily hard thing to speak of religion, partly because he cherished so whole-heartedly what he had got, and partly because he had never formulated it, probably for that very reason. Sir Robert could hardly have told his Maker what he believed about Him. When he said the Creed he always said it with lowered voice and bowed head, as one who considered very deeply of the matter, but in fact he practically never considered at all....

"Well," he began again, "you see, dear, it's a strange time out there, and it is a damned unpleasant age, if you'll excuse me. People can't take anything these days without asking an infernal number of questions. Some blessed Socialist'll begin to ask why a man should love his mother next, and, not getting a scientific answer, argue that one shouldn't. As for the men, they're all right, or they used to be. 'Love the Brotherhood. Fear God. Honour the King'—that's about enough for you and me, I take it, and Graham'll find it's enough for him. And he'll play the game, and decent men will like him and get—er—helped, my dear. That's all there is to it. But it's a pity," added the old Victorian Regular, "that these blessed labour corps, and rest camps, and all the rest of it, don't have parade services. The boy's bound to miss that. I'm hanged if I don't speak about it!... And that reminds me.... Good Lord, it's ten o'clock! I must go."

He started up, Hilda rose, smiling a little.

"That's better," said the old fellow; "must be a man, what? It's all a bit of the war, you know."

"Oh, Uncle Bob, you *are* a dear. You do cheer one up, somehow. I wish men were more like you."

"No, you don't, my dear, don't you think it. I'm a back number, and you know it, as well as any."

"You're not, Uncle Bob. I won't have you say it. Give me a kiss and say you don't mean it."

"Well, well, Hilda, there is life in the old dog yet, and I must be off and show it. No, I won't have another, not before duty. Good-night, dear, and don't worry."

Hilda saw him off, and waved her hand from the door. Then she went back slowly to the study and looked round. She stood a few moments and then switched off the lights, and went out and slowly upstairs. The maid was in the bedroom, and she dismissed her, keeping her face turned away. In front of her glass, she held her letter irresolutely a moment, and then folded it and slipped it into a drawer. She lifted a photo from the dressing-table and looked at it for a few minutes earnestly. Then she went to her window, threw it up, and leaned on the sill, staring hard over the dark and empty park.

Outside, the General walked some distance before he found a taxi. He walked fast for a man of his age, and ruminated as he went. It was his way, and the way of his kind. Most of the modern sciences left him unmoved, and although he would vehemently have denied it, he was the most illogical of men. He held fast by a few good, sound, old-fashioned principles, and the process of thought, to him, meant turning over a new thing until he had got it into line with these principles. It was an excellent method as far as it went, and it made him what he was—a thoroughly sound and dependable servant of the State in any routine business.

At the War Office he climbed more slowly up the steps and into the lobby. An officer was just coming out, and they recognised each other under the shaded lights. "Hullo, Chichester, what are you doing here?" demanded Doyle heartily. "Thought you were in France."

"So I was, up to yesterday. I've just arrived. Orders."

"Where have you been?"

"Rouen. It's a big show now. Place full of new troops and mechanics in uniform. To tell you the truth, Doyle, the Army's a different proposition from what it was when you and I were in Egypt and India. But that's a long time ago, old friend."

"Rouen, eh? Now, that's a coincidence. A young chap I know has just gone there, in your department. Graham—Peter Graham. Remember him?"

"Oh, quite well. A very decent chap, I thought. Joined us ten days ago or so. What about it? I forget for the moment where we put him."

"Oh, nothing, nothing. He'll find his feet all right. But what's this about no parade services these days?"

"No parade services? We have 'em all right, when we can. Of course, it depends a bit on the O.C., and in the Labour Corps especially it isn't usually possible. It isn't like the line, old fellow, and even the line isn't what we knew it. You can't have parade services in trenches, and you can't have them much when the men are off-loading bully beef or mending aeroplanes and that sort of thing. This war's a big proposition, and it's got to go on. Why? Young Graham grousing?"

"No, no—oh, no," hastily asserted Doyle, the soul of honour. "No, not at all. Only mentioned not getting a parade, and it seemed to me a pity. There's a lot in the good old established religion."

"Is there?" said the other thoughtfully. "I'm not so sure to-day. The men don't like being ordered to pray. They prefer to come voluntarily."

Doyle got fierce. "Don't like being ordered, don't they? Then what the deuce are they there for? Good Lord, man! the Army isn't a debating society or a mothers' meeting. You might as well have voluntary games at a public school!"

The A.C.G. smiled. "That's it, old headstrong! No, my boy, the Army isn't a mothers' meeting—at any rate, Fritz doesn't think so. But times have changed, and in some ways they're better. I'd sooner have fifty men at a voluntary service than two hundred on a parade."

"Well, I wouldn't," exploded Doyle. "I know your voluntary services— Moody and Sankey hymns on a Sunday night. The men had better be in a decent bar. But turn 'em out in the morning, clean and decent on parade, and give 'em the old service, and it'll tighten 'em up and do 'em good. Voluntary service! You'll have volunteer evangelists instead of Army chaplains next!"

Colonel Chichester still smiled, but a little grimly. "We've got them," he said. "And no doubt there's something in what you say; but times change, and the Church has got to keep abreast of the times. But, look here, I must go. What about a luncheon? I've not got much leave."

"So must I; I've an appointment," said Doyle. "But all right, old friend, to-morrow at the club. But you're younger than I, Chichester, or perhaps you parsons don't get old as quickly!"

They shook hands and parted. Sir Robert was busy for an hour, and came out again with his head full of the proposed plans for the aerial defence of London. "Taxi, sir?" he was asked at the door. "No," he replied; "I'll walk home."

"Best way to think, walking at night," he said to himself as he turned down Whitehall, through the all but empty streets, darkened as they were. The meaning of those great familiar spaces struck him as he walked. Hardly formulating it, he became aware of a sense of pride and responsibility as he passed scene after scene of England's past glory. The old Abbey towered up in the moonlight, solemn and still, but almost as if animate and looking at him. He felt small and old as he passed into Victoria Street. There the Stores by night made him smile at the contrast, but in Ashley Gardens Westminster Cathedral made him frown. If he hated anything, it was that for which it stood. Romanism meant to him something effeminate, sneaking, monstrous.... That there should be Englishmen to build such a place positively angered him. He was not exactly a bigot or a fanatic; he would not have repealed the Emancipation Acts; and he would have said that if anyone wanted to be a Romanist, he had better be one. But he would not have had time for anyone who did so want, and if he should have had to have by any chance dealings with a priest, he would have been so frigidly polite that the poor fellow would probably have been frozen solid. Of course, Irishmen were different, and he had known some capital fellows, Irish priests and chaplains....

And then he saw two men ahead of him. They were privates on leave and drunk, but not hopelessly drunk. They were trying to negotiate the blank of the entrance to the Catholic Soldiers' Hut in the protecting wall which guarded the pavement just beyond the cathedral. As Sir Robert came within earshot, one of them stumbled through it and collapsed profanely. He halted for a second irresolutely, with the officer's hesitancy at meddling with a drunken man.

The fellow on the ground tried to raise himself, and got one elbow on the gravel. This brought him into such a position that he stared straight at the illuminated crucifix across the path, and but little farther in.

"Lor', blimey, Joe," he said, "I'm blasted drunk, I am! Thought I was in old Wipers, I did, and see one of them blessed cru-crushifixes!"

The other, rather less away, pulled at his arm. "So yer did, ole pal," he said. "It's there now. This 'ere's some Cartholic place or other. Come *hon*."

"Strike me dead, so it is, Joe, large as life! Christ! oo'd 'ave thought it? A bloody cru-cru-chifix! Wat's old England comin' to, Joe?" And with drunken solemnity he began to make a sign of the cross, as he had seen it done in Belgium.

The other, in the half-light, plainly started. "Shut your bloody jaw, 'Enery," he said, "It's bad luck to swear near a cruchifix. I saw three chaps blotted out clean next second for it, back behind Lar Basay. Come on, will yer? We carn't stay 'ere all the blasted night."

"You are down on a chap, you are," said the other. "*Hi* don't mean no 'arm. *'E* ought to know that, any'ow." He got unsteadily to his feet. "'E died to save us, 'E did. I 'eard a Y.M.C.A. bloke say them very words, 'E died on the cru-cru-chifix to save us."

"'Ere, cheese it, you fool! We'll have somebody out next. Come away with yer. I've got some Bass in my place, if we git there."

At this the other consented to come. Together they staggered out, not seeing Sir Robert, and went off down the street, "'Enery" talking as they went. The General stood and listened as the man's voice died down.

"Good for yer, old pal. But 'E died to save us *hall*, 'E did. Made a bloomer of it, I reckon. Didn't save us from the bloody trenches—not as I can see, any'ow. If that chap could 'ave told us 'ow to get saved from the blasted rats an' bugs an'...."

Sir Robert pulled himself together and walked away sharply. By the cathedral the carven Christ hung on in the wan yellow light, very still.

CHAPTER V

Peter lay on a home-made bed between the blankets and contemplated the ceiling while he smoked his first cigarette. He had been a fortnight at Rouen, and he was beginning to feel an old soldier—that is to say, he was learning not to worry too much about outside things, and not to show he worried particularly about the interior. He was learning to stand around and smoke endless cigarettes; to stroll in to breakfast and out again, look over a paper, sniff the air, write a letter, read another paper, wander round the camp, talk a lot of rubbish and listen to more, and so do a morning's work. Occasionally he took a service, but his real job was, as mess secretary, to despatch the man to town for the shopping and afterwards go and settle the bills. Just at present he was wondering sleepily whether to continue ordering fish from the big merchants, Biais Frères et Cie, or to go down to the market and choose it for himself. It was a very knotty problem, because solving it in the latter way meant getting up at once. And his batman had not yet brought his tea.

There came a knock at the door, and the tea came in. With it was a folded note. "Came last night, sir, but you was out," said the man. He collected his master's tunic and boots, and departed.

Peter opened the note and swore definitely and unclerically when he had read it. It was from some unknown person, who signed himself as Acting Assistant Chaplain-General, to the effect that he was to be moved to another base, and that as the A.C.G. was temporarily on leave, he had better apply to the Colonel of his own group for the necessary movement order. On the whole this was unintelligible to Peter, but he was already learning that there was no need to worry about that, for somebody would be able to read the riddle. What annoyed him was the fact that he had got to move just as he was settling down. It was certainly a matter for another cigarette, and as he lit it he perceived one gleam of sunshine: he need worry no more about the fish.

Peter waited till Harold had finished his breakfast before he imparted the news to the world a couple of hours or so later. "I say, skipper," he said, "I've got to quit."

"What, padre? Oh, hang it all, no, man! You've only just taken on the mess secretary's job, and you aren't doing it any too badly either. You can't go, old dear."

"I must. Some blighter's written from the A.C.G.'s office, and I've got to get a movement order from the Colonel of the group, whatever that means. But I suppose you can put me straight about that, anyway."

"Sure thing. Come up to the orderly-room 'bout eleven, and you can fill up the chit and I'll fire it in for you. It's only a matter of form. It goes through to Colonel Lear at La Croisset. Where to?"

Peter told him moodily.

"Eh?" said Harold. "Well, you can cheer up about that. Havre's not at all a bad place. There are some decent shows about there and some very decent people. What you got to do?"

"I don't know; I suppose I shall find out when I get there. But I don't care what it's like. It's vile having to leave just now, when I'm getting straight. And what'll you do for a four at bridge?"

Harold got up and fumbled in his pockets. As usual, there was nothing there. "Why that damned batman of mine won't put my case in my pocket I can't think," he said. "I'll have to fire the blighter, though he is T.T. and used to be a P. and O. steward. Give me a fag, somebody. Thanks. Well, padre, it's no use grousing. It's a beastly old war, and you're in the blinkin' British Army, me lad. Drop in at eleven, then. Cheerio till then."

At eleven Peter found Harold signing papers. He glanced up. "Oh, sergeant," he said, "give Captain Graham a Movement Order Application Form, will you? Sit down, padre; there's a pen there."

Peter wrestled with the form, which looked quite pretty when it was done. Harold endorsed it. "Fire this through to the orderly-room, 10th Group, sergeant," he said, and rose wearily. "Come along, padre," he said: "I've got to go round the camp, and you can come too, if you've nothing better to do."

"When'll I have to go, do you think?" asked Peter as they went out.

"Oh, I don't know. In a day or two. You'll have to hang about, for the order may come any time, and I don't know how or when they'll send you."

Peter did hang about, for ten days, with his kit packed. His recently acquired calm forsook him about the sixth day, and on the tenth he was entirely mutinous. At lunch he voiced his grievances to the general mess.

"Look here, you men," he said, "I'm fed up to the back teeth. I've hung round this blessed camp for more than a week waiting for that infernal movement order, and I'm hanged if I'm going to stay in any more. It's a topping afternoon. Who'll come down the river to La Bouille, or whatever it is called?"

Harold volunteered. "That's a good line, padre. I want to go there myself. Are the boats running now?"

"Saw 'em yesterday," volunteered somebody, and it was settled.

The two of them spent a decent afternoon on the river, and at Harold's insistence went on back right up to town. They dined and went to a cinema, and got back to camp about midnight. Graham struck a match and looked at the board in the anteroom. "May as well see if there is anything for me," he said. There was, of course. He tore the envelope open. "Good Lord, skipper!" he said. "Here's my blessed movement order, to report at the Gare du Vert at eight p.m. this very day. I'm only four hours too late. What the dickens shall I do?"

Harold whistled. "Show it me," he said. "'The following personnel to report at Gare du Vert ... at 8 p.m. 28th inst'" he read. "You're for it, old bird," he continued cheerfully. "But what rot! Look here, it was handed in to my orderly-room at six-thirty. You'd have hardly had time to get there at any rate."

Graham looked over his shoulder. "That's so," he said. "But what'll I do now?"

"Haven't a notion," said the other, "except that they'll let you know quick enough. Don't worry—that's the main thing. If they choke you off, tell 'em it came too late to get to the station."

Peter meditated this in silence, and in some dismay. He saw visions of courts-martial, furious strafing, and unholy terrors. He was to be forgiven, for he was new to comic opera; and besides, when a page of *Punch* falls to one in real life, one hardly realises it till too late. But it was plain that nothing could be done that night, and he went to bed with what consolation he could derive from the cheerful Harold.

Next morning his breakfast was hardly over when an orderly came in. Harold had been earlier than usual, and had finished and gone out. "Captain Graham, sir?" queried the man. "Captain Harold's compliments, and a telephone message has just come in that you are to report to H.Q. 10th Group as quickly as possible."

Peter brushed himself up, and outwardly cheerful but inwardly quaking, set off. Half an hour's walk brought him to the place, a little office near a wharf in a tangle of trolley lines. He knocked, went in, came to attention, and saluted.

Colonel Lear was a short, red-faced, boorish fellow, and his Adjutant sat beside him at the desk, for the Colonel was not particularly well up in his job. The Adjutant was tall, slightly bald, and fat-faced, and he leaned back throughout the interview with an air of sneering boredom, only vouchsafing laconic replies to his superior's occasional questions. Peter didn't know which he hated the more; but he concluded that whereas he would like to cut the Colonel in Regent Street, he would enjoy shooting the Adjutant.

"Ah!" said the Colonel. "Are you Captain Graham? Well, sir, what's the meaning of this? You applied for a movement order, and one was sent you, and you did not report at the station. You damned padres think you can do any bally thing you choose! Out here for a picnic, I suppose. What is the meaning of it?"

"Well, sir," said Peter, "I waited ten days for the order and it did not come. At last I went out for the afternoon, and got back too late to execute it. I'm very sorry, but can't I go to-day instead?"

"Good God, sir! do you think the whole British Army is arranged for your benefit? Do you think nobody has anything else to do except to arrange things to suit your convenience? We haven't got troopers with Pullman cars every day for the advantage of you chaplains, though I suppose you think we ought to have. Supposing you did have to wait, what about it? What else have you to do? You'd have waited fast enough if it was an order to go on leave; that's about all you parsons think about. *I* don't know what you can do. What had he better do, Mallony?"

The Adjutant leaned forward leisurely, surveying Peter coolly.

"Probably he'd better report to the R.T.O., sir," he said.

"Oh, very well. It won't be any good, though. Go up to the R.T.O. and ask him what you can do. Here's the order." (He threw it across the table, and Peter picked it up, noting miserably the blue legend, "Failed to Report— R.T.O., Gare du Vert.") "But don't apply to this office again. Haven't you got a blessed department to do your own damned dirty work?"

"The A.C.G.'s away, sir," said Peter.

"On leave, I suppose. Wish to God I were a padre, eh, Mallony? Always on leave or in Paris, and doin' nothing in between.... Got those returns, sergeant?... What in hell are you waiting for, padre?"

For the first time in his life Peter had an idea of what seeing red really means. But he mastered it by an effort, saluted without a word, and passed out.

In a confused whirl he set off for the R.T.O., and with a sinking heart reached the station, crowded with French peasantry, who had apparently come for the day to wait for the train. Big notices made it impossible to miss the Railway Transport Officer. He passed down a passage and into an office. He loathed and hated the whole wide world as he went in.

A young man, smoking a cigarette and reading a magazine, glanced up at him. Peter observed in time that he had two stars only on his shoulder-strap. Before he could speak, the other said cheerily: "Well, padre, and what can I do for you?"

Peter deprecatingly told him. He had waited ten days, etc., and had at last gone out, and the movement order had come with...

The other cut him short: "Oh, you're the chap who failed to report, are you? Blighted rotters they are at these Group H.Q.'s. Chuck us over the chit."

Peter brightened up and obeyed. The other read it. "I know," ventured Peter, "but I got the dickens of a strafe from the Colonel. He said he had no idea when I could get away, and had better see you. What can I do?"

"Silly old ass! You'd better go to-night. There are plenty of trains, and you're all alone, aren't you? I might just alter the date, but I suppose now you had better go to his nibs the Deputy Assistant Officer controlling Transport. He's in the Rue de la Republique, No. 153; you can find it easily enough. Tell him I sent you. He'll probably make you out a new order."

Peter felt enormously relieved. He relaxed, smiled, and got out a cigarette, offering the other one. "Beastly lot of fuss they make over nothing, these chaps," he said.

"I know," said the R.T.O.; "but they're paid for it, my boy, and probably your old dear had been strafed himself this morning. Well, cheerio; see you again to-night. Come in time, and I'll get you a decent place."

The great man's office was up two flights of wooden stairs in what looked like a deserted house. But Peter mounted them with an easy mind. He had forgiven Lear, and the world smiled. He still didn't realise he was acting in *Punch*.

Outside a suitably labelled door he stood a moment, listening to a well-bred voice drawling out sarcastic orders to some unfortunate. Then, with a smile he entered. A Major looked up at him, and heard his story without a word. Peter got less buoyant as he proceeded, and towards the end he was rather lame. A silence followed. The great man scrutinised the order. "Where were you?" he demanded at last, abruptly.

It was an awkward question. Peter hedged. "The O.C. of my camp asked me to go out with him," he said at last, feebly.

The other picked up a blue pencil and scrawled further on the order. "We've had too much of this lately," he said icily. "Officers appear to think they can travel when and how they please. You will report to the D.A.Q.M.G. at Headquarters, 3rd Echelon." He handed the folded order back, and the miserable Peter had a notion that he meant to add: "And God have mercy on your soul."

He ventured a futile remonstrance. "The R.T.O. said you could perhaps alter the date."

The Major leaned back and regarded him in silence as a remarkable phenomenon such as had not previously come his way. Then he sighed, and picked up a pen. "Good-morning," he said.

Peter, in the street, contemplated many things, including suicide. If Colonel Chichester had been in Rouen he would have gone there; as it was, he did not dare to face that unknown any more than this other. In the end he set out slowly for H.Q., was saluted by the sentry under the flag, climbed up to a corridor with many strangely labelled doors, and finally entered the right one, to find himself in a big room in which half a dozen men in uniform were engaged at as many desks with orderlies moving between them. A kind of counter barred his farther passage. He stood at it forlornly for a few minutes.

At last an orderly came to him, and he shortly explained his presence and handed in the much-blued order. The man listened in silence, asked him to wait a moment, and departed. Peter leaned on the counter and tried to look indifferent. With a detached air he studied the Kirschner girls on the walls. These added a certain air to the otherwise forlorn place, but when, a little later, W.A.A.C.'s were installed, a paternal Government ordered their removal. But that then mattered no longer to Peter.

At the last the orderly came back. "Will you please follow me, sir?" he said.

Peter was led round the barrier like a sheep to execution, and in at a small door. He espied a General Officer at a desk by the window, telephone receiver in one hand, the fateful order in the other. He saluted. The other nodded. Peter waited.

"Ah, yes! D.A.Q.M.G. speaking. That 10th Group Headquarters? Oh yes; good-morning, Mallony. About Captain Graham's movement order. When was this order applied for at your end?... What? Eighteenth? Humph! What time did your office receive it?... Eh? Ten a.m.? Then, sir, I should like to know what it was doing in your office till six p.m. This officer did not receive it till six-thirty. What? He was out? Yes, very likely, but it reached his mess at six-thirty: it is so endorsed.... Colonel Lear has had the matter under consideration? Good. Kindly ask Colonel Lear to come to the telephone."

He leaned back, and glanced up at Graham, taking him in with a grave smile. "I understand you waited ten days for this, Captain Graham," he said. "It's disgraceful that it should happen. I am glad to have had an instance brought before me, as we have had too many cases of this sort of thing lately...." He broke off. "Yes? Colonel Lear? Ah, good-morning, Colonel Lear. This case of the movement order of Captain Graham has just been brought to me. This officer was kept waiting ten days for his order, and then given an impossibly short time to report. Well, it won't do, Colonel. There must be something very wrong in your orderly-room; kindly see to it. Chaplains have other things to do than sit around in camps waiting the convenience of Group Headquarters. The application for this order reached us on the 27th, and was sent off early next morning, in ample time for the officer to travel. I am very displeased about it. You will kindly apply at once for a fresh order, and see that it is in Captain Graham's hands at least six hours before he must report. That is all. Good-morning."

Peter could hardly believe his ears, but he could barely keep a straight face either. The D.A.Q.M.G. hung up the receiver and repeated the latter part of the message. Peter thanked him and departed, walking on air. A day later an orderly from the group informed him at 11 a.m. that the order had been applied for and might be expected that day, and at 1 o'clock he received it. Such is the humour of the high gods who control the British Army. But he never saw Colonel Lear again, and was thankful.

Peter reached his new base, then, early in March in a drizzle of rain. He was told his camp and set off to find it, and for an hour walked through endless docks, over innumerable bridges, several of which, being open to admit and let out ships, caused him pretty considerable delay. It was a strange, new experience. The docks presented types of nearly every conceivable nationality and of every sort of shipping. French marines and seamen were, of course everywhere, but so were Chinese, South African natives, Egyptians, Senegalese, types of all European nationalities, a few of the first clean, efficient-looking Americans in tight-fitting uniforms, and individual officers of a score of regiments.

The old town ended in a row of high, disreputable-looking houses that were, however, picturesque enough, and across the *pavé* in front of them commenced the docks. One walked in and out of harbours and waterways, the main stretch of harbour opening up more and more on the right hand, and finally showing two great encircling arms that nearly met, and the grey Channel beyond. Tossing at anchor outside were more than a dozen ships, waiting for dark to attempt the crossing. As he went, a seaplane came humming in from the mists, circled the old town, and took the harbour water in a slither of foam. He had to wait while a big Argentine ship ploughed slowly in up a narrow channel, and then, in the late afternoon, crossed a narrow swing foot-bridge, and found himself on the main outer sea-wall.

Following directions, he turned to the right and walked as if going out to the harbour mouth a mile or so ahead. It seemed impossible that his camp should be here, for on the one hand he was close to the harbour, and on the other, over a high wall and some buildings, was plainly to be espied the sea. A few hundred yards on, however, a crowd of Tommies were lined up and passing embarkation officers for a big trooper, and Peter concluded that this was the leave boat by which he was to mark his camp across the road and more or less beyond it.

He crossed a railway-line, went in at a gate, and was there.

The officers' quarters had a certain fascination. You stepped out of the anteroom and found yourself on a raised concrete platform at the back of which washed the sea. Very extensive harbour works, half completed, ran farther out in a great semicircle across a wide space of leaden water, over which gulls were circling and crying; but the thin black line of this wall hardly interrupted one's sense of looking straight out to sea, and its wide mouth away on the right let in the real invigorating, sea-smelling wind. The camp itself was a mere strip between the railway-line and the water, a camp of R.E.'s to which he was attached. He was also to work a hospital which was said to be close by.

It was pointed out to him later. The railway ran out all but to the harbour mouth, and there ended in a great covered, wide station. Above it, large and airy, with extensive verandahs parallel to the harbour, was the old Customs, and it was this that had been transformed into a hospital. It was an admirable place. The Red Cross trains ran in below, and the men could be quickly swung up into the cool, clean wards above. These, all on one level, had great glass doors giving access to the verandahs, and from the verandahs broad gangways could be placed, running men, at high tide, on to the hospital ship alongside. The nurses' quarters were beyond, and their sitting-room was perched up, as it were, sea on one side and harbour on the other.

At present, of course, Peter did not know all this. He was merely conducted by an orderly in the dusk to the anteroom of the mess, and welcomed by the orderly-officer, who led him into a comfortable room already lit, in a corner of which, near a stove, four officers sat at cards.

"Hearts three," said one as Peter came in.

"Pass me," said another, and it struck Peter that he knew the tone.

The four were fairly absorbed in their game, but the orderly officer led Peter towards the table. At that they looked up, and next minute one had jumped up and was greeting him.

"By all that's wonderful! It's you again," he said.

"Donovan!" exclaimed Peter, "What: are you doing here?"

The South African held out his hand. "I've got attached to one of our nigger outfits," he said, "just up the dock from here. But what are you doing?"

"Oh, I've been moved from Rouen," said Peter, "and told to join up here. Got to look after the hospital and a few camps. And I was told," he added, "I'd live in this camp."

"Good enough," said Donovan. "Let me introduce you. This is Lieutenant Pennell, R.E.—Lieutenant Pennell, Captain Graham. This is a bird of your kidney, mess secretary and a great man, Padre Arnold, and this is one Ferrars, Australian Infantry. He tried to stop a shell," went on Donovan easily, "and is now recovering. The shock left him a little insane, or so his best friends think; hence, as you may have heard, he has just gone three hearts. And that's all anyone can do at present, padre, so have a cigarette and sit down. I hope you haven't changed your old habits, as you are just in time for a sun-downer. Orderly!"

He pulled up a large easy-chair, and Peter subsided into it with a pleasant feeling of welcome. He remembered, now, having heard that Donovan was at Havre, but it was none the less a surprise to meet him.

Donovan played a good hand when he liked, but when he was not meeting his mettle, or perhaps when the conditions were not serious enough, he usually kept up a diverting, unorthodox run of talk the whole time. Peter listened and took in his surroundings lazily. "Come on," said his friend, playing a queen. "Shove on your king, Pennell; everyone knows you've got him. What? Hiding the old gentleman, are you? Why, sure it's myself has him all the time"—gathering up the trick and leading the king. "Perhaps somebody's holding up the ace now...." and so on.

Pennell played well too, but very differently. He was usually bored with his luck or the circumstances, and until you got to know him you were inclined to think he was bored with you. He was a young-looking man of thirty-five, rather good-looking, an engineer in peace-time who had knocked about the world a good deal, but hardly gave you that impression. The Australian played poorly. With curly dark hair and a perpetual pipe, his face was almost sullen in repose, but it lit up eagerly enough at any chance excitement. Arnold was easily the eldest, a short man with iron-grey hair and very kindly eyes, a man master of himself and his circumstances. Peter watched him eagerly. He was likely to see a good deal of him, he thought, and he was glad there would be a padre as well in camp.

Donovan and Ferrars won the game and so the rubber easily, and the former pushed his chair back from the table. "That's enough for me, boys," he said. "I must trek in a minute. Well, padre, and what do you think of the Army now?"

"Mixed biscuits rather," Peter said. "But I had a rum experience getting here. You wouldn't have thought it possible," and he related the story of the movement order. At the close, Pennell nodded gloomily. "Pack of fools they are!" he said. "Hardly one of them knows his job. You can thank your lucky stars that the D.A.Q.M.G. had a down on that Colonel What's-his-name, or it would have taken you another month to get here, probably—eh, Donovan?"

"That's so, old dear," said that worthy, "But I'm hanged if I'd have cared. Some place, Rouen. Better'n this hole."

"Well, at Rouen they said this was better," said Peter.

Arnold laughed. "That's the way of the Army," he said. "It's all much the same, but you would have to go far to beat this camp."

Pennell agreed. "You're right there, padre," he said. "This is as neat a hole as I've struck. If you know the road," he went on to Peter, "you can slip into town in twenty-five minutes or so, and we're much better placed than most camps. There's no mud and cinders here, is there, Donovan? His camp's built on cinders," he added.

"There are not," said that worthy, rising. "And you're very convenient to the hospital here, padre. You better get Arnold to show you round; he's a dog with the nurses."

"What about the acting matron, No. 1 Base?" demanded Arnold. "He has tea there every Sunday," he explained to Peter, "and he a married man, too."

"It's time I went," said Donovan, laughing; "all the same, there's a concert on Tuesday in next week, a good one, I believe, and I've promised to go and take some people. Who'll come? Pennell, will you?"

"Not this child, thanks. Too many nurses, too much tea, and too much talk for me. Now, if you would pick me out a pretty one and fix up a little dinner in town, I'm your man, old bean."

"Well, that might be managed. It's time we had a flutter of some sort. I'll see. What about you, Graham? You game to try the hospital? You'll have to get to know the ropes of them all, you know."

"Yes, I'll come," said Peter—"if I can, that is." He looked inquiringly at Arnold.

"Oh, your time is more or less your own," he replied—"at least, it is our side of the house. Are you C.G. or P.C.?"

"Good God, padre!" said the Australian, getting up too, "what in the world do you mean?"

"Chaplain-General's Department or Principal Chaplain's Department, Church of England or Nonconformist. And it's sixpence a swear in this mess." Arnold held out a hand.

Donovan caught his friend by the arm. "Come on out of it," he said. "You won't get back in time if you don't. The padre's a good sort; you needn't mind him. So long everybody. Keep Tuesday clear, Graham. I'll call for you."

"Well, I'd better fix you up, Graham," said Arnold. "For my sins I'm mess secretary, and as the president's out and likely to be, I'll find a place for you."

He led Peter into the passage, and consulted a board on the wall. "I'd like to put you next me, but I can't," he said. "Both sides occupied. Wait a minute. No. 10 Pennell, and No. 11's free. How would you like that? Pennell," he called through the open door, "what's the next room to yours like? Light all right?"

"Quite decent," said Pennell, coming to the door. "Going to put him there, padre? Let's go and see." Then the three went off together down the passage.

The little room was bare, except for a table under the window, Arnold opened it, and Peter saw he looked out over the sea. Pennell switched on the light and found it working correctly, and then sauntered across the couple of yards or so of the cubicle's width to look at the remains of some coloured pictures pasted on the wooden partition.

"Last man's made a little collection from *La Vie Parisienne* for you, padre," he said, "Not a very bright selection, either. You'll have to cover them up, or it'll never do to bring your A.C.G. or A.P.C., or whatever he is, in here. What a life!" he added, regarding them. "They are a queer people, the French.... Well, is this going to do?"

Graham glanced at Arnold, "Very well," he said, "if it's all right for me to have it."

"Quite all right," said Arnold. "Remember, Pennell is next door left, so keep him in order. Next door right is the English Channel, more or less. Now, what about your traps?"

"I left them outside the orderly-room," said Peter, "except for some that a porter was to bring up. Perhaps they'll be here by now. I've got a stretcher and so on."

"I'll go and see," said Pennell, "and I'll put my man on to get you straight, as you haven't a batman yet." And he strolled off.

"Come to my room a minute," said Arnold, and Peter followed him.

Arnold's room was littered with stuff. The table was spread with mess accounts, and the corners of the little place were stacked up with a gramophone, hymn-books, lantern-slides, footballs, boxing-gloves, and such-like. The chairs were both littered, but Arnold cleared one by the simple expedient of piling all its contents on the other, and motioned his visitor to sit down. "Have a pipe?" he asked, holding out his pouch.

Peter thanked him, filled and handed it back, then lit his pipe, and glanced curiously round the room as he drew on it. "You're pretty full up," he said.

"Fairly," said the other. "There's a Y.M.C.A. here, and I run it more or less, and Tommy likes variety. He's a fine chap, Tommy; don't you think so?"

Peter hesitated a second, and the other glanced at him shrewdly.

"Perhaps you haven't been out long enough," he said.

"Perhaps not," said Peter. "Not but what I do like him. He's a cheerful creature for all his grousing, and has sterling good stuff in him. But religiously I don't get on far. To tell you the truth, I'm awfully worried about it."

The elder man nodded. "I guess I know, lad," he said. "See here. I'm Presbyterian and I reckon you are Anglican, but I expect we're up against much the same sort of thing. Don't worry too much. Do your job and talk straight, and the men'll listen more than you think."

"But I don't think I know what to tell them," said Peter miserably, but drawn out by the other.

Arnold smiled. "The Prayer Book's not much use here, eh? But forgive me; I don't mean to be rude. I know what you mean. To tell you the truth, I think this war is what we padres have been needing. It'll help us to find our feet. Only—this is honest—if you don't take care you may lose them. I have to keep a tight hold of that"—and he laid his hand on a big Bible—"to mind my own."

Peter did not reply for a minute. He could not talk easily to a stranger. But at last he said: "Yes; but it doesn't seem to me to fit the case. Men are different. Times are different. The New Testament people took certain things for granted, and even if they disagreed, they always had a common basis with the Apostles. Men out here seem to me to talk a different language: you don't know where to begin. It seems to me that they have long ago ceased to believe in the authority of anyone or anything in religion, and now to-day they actually deny our very commonplaces. But I don't know how to put it," he added lamely.

Arnold puffed silently for a little. Then he took his pipe out of his mouth and regarded it critically. "God's in the soul of every man still," he said. "They can still hear Him speak, and speak there. And so must we too, Graham."

Peter said nothing. In a minute or so steps sounded in the passage, and Arnold looked up quickly. "Maybe," he said, "our ordinary life prevented us hearing God very plainly ourselves, Graham, and maybe He has sent us here for that purpose. I hope so. I've wondered lately if we haven't come to the kingdom for such a time as this."

Pennell pushed the door open, and looked in. "You there, Graham?" he asked. "Oh, I thought I'd find him here, padre; his stuff's come."

Peter got up. "Excuse me, Arnold," he said; "I must shake in. But I'm jolly glad you said what you did, and I hope you'll say it again, and some more."

The older man smiled an answer, and the door closed. Then he sighed a little, and stretched out his hand again for the Bible.

CHAPTER VI

The great central ward at No. 1 Base Hospital looked as gay as possible. In the centre a Guard's band sat among palms and ferns, and an extemporised stage, draped with flags, was behind, with wings constructed of Japanese-figured material. Pretty well all round were the beds, although many of them had been moved up into a central position, and there was a space for chairs and forms. The green-room had to be outside the ward, and the performers, therefore, came and went in the public gaze. But it was not a critical public, and the men, with a plenitude of cigarettes, did not object to pauses. On the whole, they were extraordinarily quiet and passive. Modern science has made the battlefield a hell, but it has also made the base hospital something approaching a Paradise.

There were women in plenty. The staff had been augmented by visitors from most of the other hospitals in the town, and there was a fair sprinkling of W.A.A.C.'s, Y.M.C.A. workers, and so on, in addition. Jack Donovan and Peter were a little late, and arrived at the time an exceedingly popular subaltern was holding the stage amid roars of laughter. They stood outside one of the many glass doors and peered in.

Once inside, one had to make one's way among beds and chairs, and the nature of things brought one into rather more than the usual share of late-comers' scrutiny, but nothing could abash Donovan. He spotted at once a handsome woman in nurse's indoor staff uniform, and made for her. She, with two others, was sitting on an empty bed, and she promptly made room for Donovan. Graham was introduced, and a quiet girl moved up a bit for him to sit down; but there was not much room, and the girl would not talk, so that he sat uncomfortably and looked about him, listening with one ear to the fire of chaff on his right. Donovan was irrepressible. His laugh and voice, and the fact that he was talking to a hospital personage, attracted a certain amount of attention. Peter tried to smile, but he felt out of it and observed. He stared up towards the band, which was just striking up again.

Suddenly he became conscious, as one will, that someone was particularly looking at him. He glanced back over the chairs, and met a pair of eyes, roguish, laughing, and unquestionably fixed upon him. The moment he saw them, their owner nodded and telegraphed an obvious invitation. Peter glanced at Donovan: he had not apparently seen. He looked back; the eyes called him again. He felt himself getting hot, for, despite the fact that he had a kind of feeling that he had seen those eyes before, he was perfectly certain he did not know the girl. Perhaps she had made a mistake. He turned resolutely to his companion.

"Jolly good band, isn't it?" he said.

"Yes," she replied.

"But I suppose at a hospital like this you're always hearing decent music?" he ventured.

"Not so often," she said.

"This band is just back from touring the front, isn't it? My friend said something to that effect."

"I believe so," she said.

Peter could have cursed her. It was impossible to get anything out of her, though why he had not a notion. The answer was really simple, for she wanted to be next Donovan, and wasn't, and she was all the while scheming how to get there. But Peter did not tumble to that; he felt an ass and very uncomfortable, and he broke into open revolt.

He looked steadily towards the chairs. The back of the girl who had looked at him was towards him now, for she was talking sideways to somebody; but he noted an empty chair just next her, and that her uniform was not that of the nurses of this hospital. He felt confident that she would look again, and he was not disappointed. Instantly he made up his mind, nodded, and reached for his cap. "I see a girl I know over there," he said to his neighbour. "Excuse me, will you?" Then he got up and walked boldly over to the vacant chair. He was fast acclimatising to war conditions.

He sat down on that empty chair and met the girl's eyes fairly. She was entirely at her ease and laughing merrily. "I've lost my bet," she said, "and Tommy's won."

"And you've made me tell a thundering lie," he replied, laughing too, "which you know is the first step towards losing one's soul. Therefore you deserve your share in the loss."

"Why? What did you say?" she demanded.

"I said I saw a girl I knew," he replied. "But I haven't any idea who you are, though I can't help feeling I've seen you before."

She chuckled with amusement, and turned to her companion. "He doesn't remember, Tommy," she said.

The second girl looked past her to Peter. "I should think not," she said. "Nobody would. But he'll probably say in two minutes that he does. You're perfectly shameless, Julie."

Julie swung round to Peter. "You're a beast, Tommy," she said over her shoulder, "and I shan't speak to you again. You see," she went on to Peter, "I could see you had struck a footling girl, and as I don't know a single decent boy here, I thought I'd presume on an acquaintance, and see if it wasn't a lucky one. We've got to know each other, you know. The girl with me on the boat—oh, damn, I've told you!—and I am swearing, and you're a parson, but it can't be helped now—well, the girl told me we should meet again, and that it was probably you who was mixed up with my fate-line. What do you think of that?"

Peter had not an idea, really. He was going through the most amazing set of sensations. He felt heavy and dull, and as if he were utterly at a loss how to deal with a female of so obviously and totally different a kind from any he had met before; but, with it all, he was very conscious of being glad to be there. Underneath everything, too, he felt a bit of a dare-devil, which was a delightful experience for a London curate; and still deeper, much more mysteriously and almost a little terrifyingly, something stranger still, that he had known this girl for ages, although he had not seen her for a long time. "I'm highly privileged, I'm sure," he said, and could have kicked himself for a stupid ass.

"Oh Lord!" said Julie, with a mock expression of horror; "for goodness' sake don't talk like that. That's the worst of a parson: he can't forget the drawing-room. At any rate, I'm not sure that *I'm* highly fortunate, but I thought I ought to give Fate a chance. Do you smoke?"

"Yes," said Peter wonderingly.

"Then for goodness' sake smoke, and you'll feel better. No, I daren't here, but I'm glad you are educated enough to ask me. Nurses aren't supposed to smoke in public, you know, and I take it that even you have observed that I'm a nurse."

She was quite right. Peter drew on his cigarette and felt more at ease. "Well, to be absolutely honest, I had," he said. "And I observe, moreover, that you are not wearing exactly an English nurse's uniform, and that you have what I might venture to call a zoological badge. I therefore conclude that, like my friend Donovan, you hail from South Africa. What hospital are you in?"

"Quai de France," she said. "Know it?"

Peter repressed a start. "Quai de France?" he queried. "Where's that, now?"

At this moment a song started, but his companion dropped her voice to stage whisper and replied: "End of the harbour, near where the leave-boat starts. Know it now?"

He nodded, but was saved a reply.

She looked away toward the platform, and he studied her face surreptitiously. It seemed very young till you looked closely, especially at the eyes, and then you perceived something lurking there. She was twenty-seven or twenty-eight, he concluded. She looked as if she knew the world inside out, and as if there were something hidden below the gaiety. Peter felt curiously and intensely attracted. His shyness vanished. He had, and had had, no intimations of the doings of Providence, and nobody could possibly be more sceptical of fate-lines than he, but it dawned on him as he stared at her that he would fathom that look somehow, somewhere.

"I'm practically not made up at all," she whispered, without turning her head, "so for Heaven's sake don't say there's too much powder on my nose."

Peter shook silently. "No, but a faint trace on the right cheek," he whispered back. She turned then and looked at him, and her eyes challenged his. And yet it is to be supposed that Hilda knew nothing whatever about it.

"'*Right on my mother's knee....*'" sang the platform.

"'*Without a shirt, without a shirt,*'" gagged Peter, *sotto voce*, and marvelled at himself. But he felt that her smothered laughter amply rewarded him.

The song ceased in time, and the encore, which they both rigorously demanded. And immediately she began again.

"I hope to goodness tea isn't far off," she said. "By the way, you'll have to take me to it, now, you know. We go out of that door, and up a flight of steps, and there's the matron's room on the top and a visitor's room next to it, and tea'll be there. It will be a fiendish squash, and I wouldn't go if I hadn't you to get me tea and take me away afterwards as soon as possible."

"I'm highly privileged, I'm sure," said Peter again, quite deliberately. She laughed. "You are," she said. "Look how you're coming on! Ten minutes ago you were a bored curate, and now you're—what are you?"

Peter hesitated perceptibly. He felt he might say many things. Then he said "A trapped padre," and they both laughed.

"Thank goodness you're not sentimental, anyway," she said. "Nor's your friend; but the matron is. I know her sort. Look at them."

Peter looked. Donovan appeared still entirely at his ease, but he was watching Peter, who realised why he had been made to look. He brazened it out, smiled back at him, and turned perfectly deliberately to his companion.

"Julie," he said, "don't look over there any more, for goodness' sake, or we'll have Donovan here. And if he comes he'll sail in and take you to tea without a word. I know him. He's got an unfair advantage over me. I'm just waking up, and he's been awake for years. Please give me a chance."

She leaned, back and regarded him humorously. "You're not doing so badly," she said, "I don't know that a man has ever called me 'Julie' before in the first quarter of an hour. Do you know that, Solomon?"

"It's your fault, I've never been introduced, and I must call you something, so why not the name your friend called you? Julie's very pretty and suits you. Somehow I couldn't call you 'Miss' anything, though it may be convenient to know the rest. Do you think you could call me the Rev. Peter Graham?"

"I couldn't," she confessed, slightly more solemnly. "Queer, isn't it? But don't, talk about it: it isn't lucky. I shall call you Solomon for ever now. And you can only call me Miss Gamelyn when you've got to. See?"

"But why in the world 'Solomon'? It doesn't fit me a bit."

"Oh," she said, "it does, but don't worry why. Perhaps because, as the old man said to the vicar when he heard of Solomon's wives, you are a highly privileged Christian. You can't deny that, since you've said it twice. Praises be, here is tea. Come on; come on, Tommy. Oh, Tommy, this is the Very Reverend Peter Graham. Mr. Graham, this is one Raynard, commonly known as Tommy, my half-section, so try to be polite."

There was a general movement, and Peter shook hands as he got up. The other girl struck him at once as a good sort.

"You're booked to take us to tea, I suppose?" she said. "Julie's far more practical than you'd imagine, padre."

They left the row of chairs together, Julie well in front and apparently forgetful of their existence. As they came abreast of the empty bed, Peter noticed that the assistant matron had gone, and that Donovan was drifting in the stream alongside her in front. But before they were out of the great ward, Julie and he were laughing together. Peter felt absurdly hurt, and hated himself for feeling it. The other girl was talking at his elbow, but he made ridiculous and commonplace replies and hardly noticed her. She broke off at last abruptly, and he roused himself to carry on. He caught her expression, and somehow or other it landed him deeper in the business. He made a deliberate move.

"Where are you going after this?" he asked.

"Down town to do some shopping; then I suppose home, unless a fit seizes Julie and we run a risk once more of being summarily repatriated."

He laughed. "Does that often happen?"

"Quite often. You see ours is an English hospital, though we are South Africans attached to it. I think they're much more strict than Colonial hospitals. But they give us more latitude than the rest, at any rate. Julie had a fearful row once, and simply declared she would do some things, and since then they turn a blind eye occasionally. But there are limits, and one day she'll step over them—I know she will."

"Let's hope not," said Peter; "but now let me get you some tea."

The little room was packed, but Peter got through somehow and made his way to a series of tables spread with cakes and sandwiches. He got a cup and seized a plate, and shouldered his way back. In the crush he saw only the top of Miss Raynard's head, and made for that. "Here you are," he said cheerfully, as he emerged. "Have a sandwich?"

"Thanks," she said as she took it; "but why didn't you bring two cups?"

"Why?" he asked.

She nodded towards a corner and there was Julie, wedged in between people, and refusing tea from a subaltern. "She expects you to bring it," said Miss Raynard.

Peter looked puzzled, "Where's Donovan?" he said. "I thought she came in with him."

The girl smiled. "She did, but she arranged for you to bring her tea, whoever Donovan is, and she'll wait for it. She's that sort. Besides, if Donovan was that officer with the matron, he's probably got other fish to fry."

Peter waited for no more, but plunged into the press again. As he emerged, he crossed the track of his friend, who was steering about with cakes. "Hullo, padre," that individual said; "you're a smart one, you are. Let's take those girls out to dinner. They'll come all right."

Peter mumbled something, and went on with his tea towards the corner. The other's readiness and effrontery staggered him, but he wasn't going to give himself away.

"You're a brute!" said Julie promptly. "Where have you been?"

"It's where have you been, you mean," retorted Peter. "I thought I was to take you in to tea. When last I saw you, you had Donovan in tow."

"And you had Tommy. Don't you like her?"

"Awfully," said Peter; "I think she wants something now. But do come across to our side. Aren't you going soon?"

"Yes, when we can get away. Remember, everyone is watching. You go on out, and we can meet you below."

"Right," said Peter; "I'll collect Donovan."

He found him after a bit, and the two made their adieus and thanks.

As they went down the steps, Jack outlined the campaign. "I just joked to her about dinner," he said, "but I think they'll rise. If they do, we'll go to Travalini's, if they dare. That girl of yours is up to anything: she knows a thing or two. You've some nerve, old thing."

"Nothing to yours," retorted Graham, still not at all sure of himself. "But, look here, what about Travalini's? I don't know that I care to go there."

"Oh, it's all right, old dear. You haven't a vast collar on now, and you ought to see life. I've seen scores of chaplains there, even old Arnold. I'll look after your morals. Come on; let's get out and across the road. We shall see them coming down the steps."

The hospital fronted on to the sea and the promenade that once was so fashionable. The sun was setting, blood red, over the Channel, the ships at anchor looking dark by contrast. But there was still plenty of light, and Peter was inwardly conscious of his badges. Still, he told himself that he was an ass, and the two of them sauntered slowly townwards.

In a few minutes Jack glanced back. "They're coming," he said, and as the girls crossed on to the pavement behind them, turned round. "Good for you," he said. "You got out quicker than I thought you would. Shall we tram or walk?"

"Walk, I think," said Julie; "it's topping here by the sea. I want to get a pair of shoes, and the shop's not too far. Besides, you can buy shoes by artificial light, which won't do for some things. Tommy bought a hat the other night, and she nearly had a fit in the morning. She's keeping it for the next fancy-dress stunt."

She ran on, and, despite Peter, Donovan annexed her. They set off gaily ahead, Julie's clear laugh coming back now and again. Peter felt depressed and angry. He told himself he was being let in for something he did not want, and he had not much to say. To make conversation, he asked about South Africa.

It appeared the girls came from Natal. Miss Raynard was enthusiastic, and he gathered they had been trained together in Pietermaritzburg, but lived somewhere on the coast, where there was tennis all the year and moonlight bathing picnics in the season, and excellent river boating. He could not catch the name, but it was not too far from Durban. He said, in the end, that he had always wanted to visit South Africa, and should certainly come to Natal....

They turned off the promenade into a boulevard lined with the usual avenue of trees. It was dusk now, and looked darker by contrast with the street lamps. Small tram-cars rushed by now and again, with clanging bells and platforms crowded before and behind, and there were plenty of people in the street, Julie turned abruptly.

"I say, Tommy," she said, "Captain Donovan wants us to go out to dinner. What do you say? My shoes can wait, and we needn't be in till eight-thirty. It's not more than six now. It will be a spree."

"I'm game; but where are we going?"

"I suggest Travalini's, padre," said Donovan.

"Not for me;" said Miss Raynard; "it's too public and you seem to forget, Captain' Donovan, that we are forbidden to dine with officers."

"Nobody is likely to give us away, Tommy," said Miss Gamelyn.

"I'm not going to take the risk in uniform. Let's go to a quiet hotel, or else to some very French place. That would be fun."

"A jolly good idea," cried Donovan, "and I know what will just fix us up. Come on."

Tommy smiled. "Probably it *will* fix us up. Tell us about it first."

"It's absolutely safe," Donovan protested. "It's quite French, and we shall get one knife and fork each. There's a cinema on top, and billiards underneath, and practically no officers go. A Belgian Captain I came out with took me. He said you could 'eat well' there, and you can, for the cooking is a treat. I swear it's all right."

"Lead on," said Julie; "we'll trust you," and she manoeuvred so that her half-section was left with Donovan.

The four walked briskly through the dusk. "Don't you love France in the evening?" demanded Julie.

"Yes," said Peter, but dubiously. "I don't know it much yet," he added.

"Oh, I do. Even a girl can almost do what she likes out here. I've had some awful fun in Havre. I think one ought to take one's pleasure when one has the chance, don't you? But some of these girls give me the hump; they're so narrow. They can't see you with a man without imagining all sorts of things, whereas I've had some rattling good pals among men out here. Then they're so afraid of doing things—the girls, I mean. Do you know I went to Paris when I came up here from Boulogne? Had absolutely *the* time. Of course, nobody knows, so don't speak of it—except Tommy, of course."

"How did you do it?" demanded Peter, amused.

"Well, you see, I and another girl, English, were sent over by Boulogne, as you know, because you saw us on the boat, and we were supposed to come straight here. In the train we met a Canadian in the French Air Service, and he put us wise about changing, and so on. But it appeared you have to change at Amiens in the middle of the night, and he said the thing was to sleep in the train and go right on to Paris. Then you got twenty-four hours there, and left next day by the Havre express. The girl was horribly scared, but I said we'd try it. Nothing happened at all. We had a carriage to ourselves, and merely sat still at Amiens. When we got to Paris we simply walked out, bold as brass. I showed our tickets at Havre and told the French inspector we had overslept. He merely told us the time to leave next day. We went to an hotel, and then strolled up the Avenue de l'Opera. And what do you think? Who should I see but an old dear of a General I knew out in South Africa who is in the French Red Cross. He was simply delighted to see us. He motored us out to the Bois in the afternoon, dined us, and took us to the theatre—only, by Jove! I did curse that other girl. She was in a ferment all the time. Next morning he had a job on, but he sent a car for us with a subaltern to put us on the train, and we went to the R.T.O. this time. He couldn't do enough for us when he heard the name of General de Villiers and saw his card. We got into Havre at midday, and nobody was a penny the wiser."

Peter laughed. "You were lucky," he said; "perhaps you always are."

"No, I'm not," she said "but I usually do what I want and get through with it. Hullo, is this the place?"

"I suppose so," said Peter. "Now for it. Look as if you'd been going to such places all your life."

"I've probably been more often than you, anyhow, Solomon," said Julie, and she ran lightly up the steps.

They passed through swing-doors into a larger hall brilliantly lit and heavy with a mixed aroma of smoke and food. There was a sort of hum of sound going on all the time and Peter looked round wonderingly. He perceived immediately that there was an atmosphere about this French restaurant unlike that of any he had been in before. He was, in truth, utterly bewildered by what he saw, but he made an effort not to show it. Julie, on the other hand, was fairly carried away. They seated themselves at a table for four near the end of the partition, and she led the party in gaiety. Donovan hardly took his eyes off her, and cut in with dry, daring remarks with a natural case. Tommy played a good second to Julie, and if she had had any fears they were not visible now.

"What about an appetiser?" demanded Donovan.

"Oh, rather! Mixed vermuth for me; but Tommy must have a very small one: she gets drunk on nothing. Give me a cigarette now, padre; I'm dying to smoke."

Peter produced his case. "Don't call him 'padre' here," said Donovan; "you'll spoil his enjoyment."

"A cigarette, Solomon, then," whispered Julie, as the other turned to beckon a *garçon*, flashing her eyes on him.

Peter resisted no longer. "Don't," he said. "Call me anything but that." It seemed to him that there was something inevitable in it all. He did not formulate his sensations, but it was the lure of the contrast that won him. Ever since he had landed in France he had, as it were, hung on to the old conventional position, and he had felt increasingly that it was impossible to do so. True, there seemed little connection between a dinner with a couple of madcap girls in a French restaurant and religion, but there was one. He had felt out of touch with men and life, and now a new phase of it was offered him. He reached out for it eagerly.

Julie leaned back and blew out a thin stream of smoke, her eyes daring him, picking up the little glass as she did so.

"Here's to the girl with the little grey shoes," she chanted merrily.

"Don't Julie, for Heaven's sake!" pleaded Tommy. "He'll be shocked."

"Oh, go on," said Peter; "what is it?"

"Captain Donovan will finish," laughed Julie.

"'Deed I can't, for I don't know it," he said. "Let's have it, little girl; I'm sure it's a sporting toast."

"Who eats your grub and drinks your booze," continued she.

"Shut up, Julie," said Tommy, leaning over as if to snatch her glass.

"And then goes home to her mother to snooze," called Julie breathlessly, leaning back.

"I don't think," ejaculated Donovan.

Julie tipped down the drink. "You knew it all the time," she said. And they all burst out laughing.

Peter drank, and called for another, his eyes on Julie. He knew that he could not sum her up, but he refused to believe that this was the secret behind the eyes. She was too gay, too insolent. What Donovan thought he could not say, but he almost hated him for the ease with which he kept pace with their companions.

They ordered dinner, and the great dish of *hors d'oeuvres* was brought round by a waiter who seemed to preside over it with a fatherly solicitude. Julie picked up an olive in her fingers, and found it so good that she grumbled at only having taken one.

"Have mine," said Donovan, shooting one on to her plate.

"Thanks," she said. "Oh, heavens! I forgot that patch on my left cheek—or was it my right, Solomon? Let's see."

She dived into her pocket, and produced a tiny satin beaded box, "Isn't it chic?" she demanded, leaning over to show Donovan. "I got it in the Nouvelles Galeries the other day." She took off the lid, which revealed its reverse as a tiny mirror, and scrutinised herself, patting back a stray lock on her forehead.

"Oh, don't," said Donovan, and he slipped the hair out again with his finger.

"Be quiet; but I'll concede that. This won't do, though." Out came a tiny powder-puff. "How's that?" she demanded, smiling up at him.

"Perfect," he said. "But it's not fair to do that here."

"Wait for the taxi then," she said. "Besides, it won't matter so much then."

"What won't matter?" demanded Peter.

"Solomon, dear, you're as innocent as a new-born babe. Isn't he?" she demanded of his friend.

Donovan looked across at him. "Still waters run deep," he said. "I don't know, but excuse me!"

He had been sitting next Julie and opposite Miss Raynard, but he was now on his feet and begging her to change places with him. She consented, laughing, and did so, but Julie pretended to be furious.

"I won't have it. You're a perfect beast, Tommy. Captain Donovan, I'll never come out with you again. Solomon, come and sit here, and you, Tommy, go over there."

Peter hadn't an idea why, but he too got up. Tommy protested. "Look here," she said, "I came for dinner, not for a dance. Oh, look out, Captain

Graham; you'll upset the cutlets!" Peter avoided the waiter by an effort, but came on round her to the other side.

"Get out of it, Tommy," said Julie, leaning over and pushing her. "I will have a man beside me, anyhow."

"I'd sooner be opposite," said Donovan. "I can see you better, and you can't make eyes at the Frenchman at the other table quite so well if I get my head in the way."

"Oh, but he's such a dear," said Julie. "I'd love to flirt with him. Only I must say his hair is a bit greasy."

"You'll make his lady furious if you don't take care," said Donovan, "and it's a shame to spoil her trade."

Peter glanced across. A French officer, sitting opposite a painted girl, was smiling at them. He looked at Julie; she was smiling back.

"Julie, don't for Heaven's sake," said her half-section. "We shall have him over here next, and you remember once before how awkward it was."

Julie laughed. "Give me another drink, then, Captain Donovan," she said, "and I'll be good."

Donovan filled up her glass. She raised it and challenged him. "*Here's to we two in Blighty*," she began.

Miss Raynard rose determinedly and interrupted her. "Come on," she said; "that's a bit too much, Julie. We must go, or we'll never get back, and don't forget you've got to go on duty in the morning, my dear." She pulled out a little watch. "Good heavens!" she cried. "Do you know the time? It's eight-twenty now. We ought to have been in by eight, and eighty-thirty is the latest time that's safe. For any sake, come on."

Julie for once agreed. "Good Lord, yes," she said. "We must have a taxi. Can we get one easily?"

"Oh, I expect so," said Donovan. "Settle up, Graham, will you? while I shepherd them out and get a car. Come on, and take care how you pass the Frenchman."

In a few minutes Peter joined them on the steps outside. The restaurant was in the corner of a square which contained a small public garden, and the three of them were waiting for him on the curb. A taxi stood by them. The broad streets ran away to left and right, gay with lights and passers-by, and the dark trees stood out against a starry sky. A group of British officers went laughing by, and one of them recognised Donovan and hailed him. Two spahis crossed out of the shade into the light, their red and gold a picturesque splash of colour. Behind them glared the staring pictures of the cinema show on a great hoarding by the wall.

"Come on, Graham," called Donovan, "hop in."

The four packed in closely, Peter and Tommy opposite the other two, Julie farthest from Peter. They started, and he caught her profile as the street lights shone in and out with the speed of their passing. She was smoking, puffing quickly at her cigarette, and hardly silent a moment.

"It's been a perfect treat," she said. "You're both dears, aren't they, Tommy? You must come and have tea at the hospital any day: just walk in. Mine's Ward 3. Come about four o'clock, and you'll find me any day this week, Tommy's opposite. There's usually a crush at tea, but you must come. By the way, where's your camp? Aren't you going heaps out of your way? Solomon, where do you live? Tell me."

Peter grinned in the dark, and told her.

"Oh, you perfect beast!" she said, "Then you knew the Quai de France all the time. Well, you're jolly near, anyway." "Oh, Lord!" she exclaimed suddenly, "you aren't the new padre?"

"I am," said Peter.

"Good Lord! what a spree! Then you'll come in on duty. You can come in any hour of the day or night. Tommy, do you hear that? Solomon's our spiritual pastor. He's begun well, hasn't he?"

Peter was silent. It jarred him horribly. But just then the car slowed down.

"What's up now?" demanded Donovan.

"Only the sentry at the swing bridge," said Tommy. "They stop all cars at night. He's your side, dear; give him the glad eye."

The door opened, and a red-cap looked in. "Hospital, corporal; it's all right," said Julie, beaming at him.

"Oh, all right, miss. Good-night," said the man, stepping back and saluting in the light of the big electric standard at the bridgehead. "Carry on, driver!"

"We're just there," said Julie; "I am sorry. It's been rippin'. Stop the car, Solomon, somewhere near the leave-boat; it won't do to drive right up to the hospital; we might be spotted."

Peter leaned out of the window on his side. The lights on the quay glowed steadily across the dark water, and made golden flicking streaks upon it as the tide swelled slowly in. In the distance a great red eye flashed in and out solemnly, and on their side he could see the shaded lights of the hospital ship, getting ready for her night crossing. He judged it was time, and told the man to stop.

"Where's my powder-puff?" demanded Julie. "I believe you've bagged it, Captain Donovan. No, it's here. Skip out, Tommy. Is anyone about?"

"No," said the girl from the step. "But don't wait all night. We'd best run for it."

"Well, good-night," said Julie. "You have both been dears, but whether I'm steady enough to get in safely I don't know. Still, Tommy's a rock. See you again soon. Good-bye-ee!"

She leaned forward. "*Now*, if you're good," she said to Donovan. He kissed her, laughing; and before he knew what she was doing, she reached over to Peter, kissed him twice on the lips, and leaped lightly out. "Be good," she said, "and if you can't, be careful."

CHAPTER VII

Following a delay of some days, there had been a fairly heavy mail, and Peter took his letters to the little terrace by the sea outside the mess, and sat in the sun to read them. While he was so occupied Arnold appeared with a pipe, but, seeing him engaged, went back for a novel and a deck-chair. It was all very peaceful and still, and beyond occasional hammering from, the leisurely construction of the outer harbour wall and once or twice the siren of a signalling steamer entering the docks, there was nothing to disturb them at all. Perhaps half an hour passed, then Peter folded up some sheets, put them in his pocket, and walked moodily to the edge of the concrete, staring down, at the lazy slushing of the tide against: the wall below him.

He kicked a pebble discontentedly into the water, and turned to look, at Arnold. The older man was stretched out: in his chair smoking a pipe and regarding him. A slow smile passed between them.

"No, hang it all," said Peter; "there's nothing to smile about, Arnold, I've pretty well got to the end of my tether."

"Meaning what exactly?" queried the other.

"Oh, well, you know enough already to guess the rest.... Look here, Arnold, you and. I are fairly good pals now, I'd just like to tell you exactly what I feel."

"Sit down then, man, and get it out. There's a chair yonder, and you've got the forenoon before ye. I'm a heretic and all that sort of thing, of course, but perhaps that'll make it easier. I take it it's a kind of heretic you're becoming yourself."

Peter pulled up a chair and got out his own pipe. "Arnold," he said, "I'm too serious to joke, and I don't know that I'm even a Christian heretic. I don't know what I am and where I stand. I wish I did; I wish I even knew how much I disbelieved, for then I'd know what to do. But it's not that my dogmas have been attacked and weakened. I've no new light on the Apostles' Creed and no fresh doubts about it. I could still argue for the Virgin Birth of Christ and the Trinity, and so on. But it's worse than that. I feel ..." He broke off abruptly and pulled at his pipe. The other said nothing. They were friends enough by now to understand each other. In a little while the younger man found the words he wanted.

"Look here, it's like this. I remember once, on the East Coast, coming across a stone breakwater high and dry in a field half a mile from the sea. There was nothing the matter with the breakwater, and it served admirably for certain purposes—a seat, for instance, or a shady place for a picnic. But it was no longer of any vital use in the world, for the sea had receded and left it there. Now, that's just what I feel. I had a religion; I suppose it had its weaknesses and its faults; but most of it was good sound stone, and it certainly had served. But it serves no longer, not because it's damaged, but because the need for it has changed its nature or is no longer there." He trailed off into silence and stopped.

Arnold stirred to get out his pouch. "The sea is shifty, though," he said. "If they keep the breakwater in decent repair, it'll come in handy again."

"Yes," burst out Peter. "But, of course, that's where illustrations are so little good: you can't press them. And in any case no engineer worth his salt would sit down by his breakwater and smoke a pipe till the sea came in handy again. His job is to go after it."

"True for ye, boy. But if the old plan was so good, why not go down to the beach and get on with building operations of the same sort?"

"Arnold," said Peter, "you couldn't have put it better. That's exactly what I came here to do. I knew in London that the sea was receding to some extent, and I thought that there was a jolly good chance to get up with it again out here. But that leads straight to my second problem: I can't build on the old plan, and it doesn't seem any good. It's as if our engineer found quicksands that wouldn't hold his stone, and cross-currents that smashed up all his piles.... I mean, I thought I knew what would save souls. But I find that I can't because my methods are—I don't know, faulty perhaps, out of date maybe possibly worse; and, what is more, the souls don't want my saving. The Lord knows they want something; I can see that fast enough, but what it is I don't know. Heavens! I remember preaching in the beginning of the war from the text 'Jesus had compassion on the multitude.' Well I don't feel that He has changed, and I'm quite sure He still has compassion, but the multitude doesn't want it. I was wrong about the crowd. It's nothing like what I imagined. The crowd isn't interested in Jesus any more. It doesn't believe in Him. It's a different sort of crowd altogether from the one He led."

"I wonder," said Arnold.

Peter moved impatiently. "Well, I don't see how you can," he said. "Do you think Tommy worries about his sins? Are the men in our mess miserable? Does the girl the good books talked about, who flirts and smokes and drinks and laughs, sit down by night on the edge of her little white bed and feel a blank in her life? Does she, Arnold?"

"I'm blest if I know; I haven't been there! You seem to know a precious lot about it," he added dryly.

"Oh, don't rag and don't be facetious. If you do, I shall clear. I'm trying to talk sense, and at any rate it's what I feel. And I believe you know I'm right too." Peter was plainly a bit annoyed.

The elder padre sat up straight at that, and his tone changed. He stared thoughtfully out to sea and did not smoke. But he did not speak all at once. Peter glanced at him, and then lay back in his chair and waited.

Arnold spoke at last: possibly the harbour works inspired him. "Look here, boy," he said, "let's get back to your illustration, which is no such a bad one. What do you suppose your engineer would do when he got down to the new sea-beach and found the conditions you described? It wouldn't do much good if he sat down and cursed the blessed sea and the sands and the currents, would it? It would be mighty little use if he blamed his good stone and sound timber, useless though they appeared. I'm thinking he'd be no much of an engineer either if he chucked his job. What would he do, d'you think?"

"Go on," said Peter, interested.

"Well," said the speaker in parables, "unless I'm mighty mistaken, he'd get down first to studying the new conditions. He'd find they'd got laws governing them, same as the old—different laws maybe, but things you could perhaps reckon with if you knew them. And when he knew them, I reckon he'd have a look at his timber and stone and iron, and get out plans. Maybe, these days, he'd help out with a few tons of reinforced concrete, and get in a bit o' work with some high explosive. I'm no saying. But if he came from north of the Tweed, my lad," he added, with a twinkle in his eye and a touch of accent, "I should be verra surprised if that foreshore hadn't a breakwater that would do its duty in none so long a while."

"And if he came from south of the Tweed, and found himself in France?" queried Peter.

"I reckon he'd get down among the multitude and make a few inquiries," said Arnold, more gravely. "I reckon he wouldn't be in too great a hurry, and he wouldn't believe all he saw and heard without chewing on it a bit, as our Yankee friends say. And he'd know well enough that there was nothing wrong with his Master, and no change in His compassion, only, maybe, that he had perhaps misunderstood both a little."

A big steamer hooted as she came up the river, and the echoes of the siren died out slowly among the houses that climbed up the hill behind them.

Then Peter put his hand up and rested his head upon it, shading his face.

"That's difficult—and dangerous, Arnold" he said.

"It is that, laddie," the other answered quickly. "There was a time when I would have thought it too difficult and too dangerous for a boy of mine. But I've had a lesson or two to learn out here as well as other folks. Up the line men have learnt not to hesitate at things because they are difficult and dangerous. And I'll tell you something else we've learnt—that it is better for half a million to fail in the trying than for the thing not to be tried at all."

"Arnold," said Peter, "what about yourself? Do you mind my asking? Do you feel this sort of thing at all, and, if so, what's your solution?"

The padre from north of the Tweed knocked the ashes out of his pipe and got up, "Young man," he said, "I don't mind your asking, but I'm getting old, and my answering wouldn't do either of us any good, if I have a solution I don't suppose it would be yours. Besides, a man can't save his brother, and not even a father can save his son .... I've nothing to tell ye, except, maybe, this: don't fear and don't falter, and wherever you get to, remember that God is there. David is out of date these days, and very likely it wasn't David at all, but I don't know anything truer in the auld book than yon verse where it says: 'Though I go down into hell, Thou art there also.'"

"I beg your pardon, padre," said a drawling voice behind them. "I caught a word just now which I understand no decent clergyman uses except in the pulpit. If, therefore, you are preaching, I will at once and discreetly withdraw, but if not, for his very morals' sake, I will withdraw your congregation—that is, if he hasn't forgotten his engagement."

Graham jumped up. "Good Heavens, Pennell!" he exclaimed, "I'm blest if I hadn't." He pushed his arm out and glanced at his watch. "Oh, there's plenty of time, anyway. I'm lunching with this blighter down town, padre, at some special restaurant of his," he explained, "and I take it the sum and substance of his unseemly remarks are that he thinks we ought to get a move on."

"Don't let me stand in the way of your youthful pleasures," said Arnold, smiling; "but take care of yourself, Graham. Eat and drink, for to-morrow you die; but don't eat and drink too much in case you live to the day after."

"I'll remember," said Peter, "but I hope it won't be necessary. However, you never know 'among the multitude,' do you?" he added.

Arnold caught up the light chair and lunged out at him. "Ye unseemly creature," he shouted, "get out of it and leave me in peace."

Pennell and Peter left the camp and crossed the swing bridge into the maze of docks. Threading their way along as men who knew it thoroughly they came at length to the main roadway, with its small, rather smelly shops, its narrow side-streets almost like Edinburgh closes, and its succession of sheds and offices between which one glimpsed the water. Just here, the war had made a difference. There was less pleasure traffic up Seine and along Channel, though the Southampton packet ran as regularly as if no submarine had ever been built. Peter liked Pennell. He was an observant creature of considerable decencies, and a good companion. He professed some religion, and although it was neither profound nor apparently particularly vital, it helped to link the two men. As they went on, the shops grew a little better, but no restaurant was visible that offered much expectation.

"Where in the world are you taking me?" demanded Peter. "I don't mind slums in the way of business, but I prefer not to go to lunch in them."

"Wait and see, my boy," returned his companion, "and don't protest till it's called for. Even then wait a bit longer, and your sorrow shall be turned into joy—and that's Scripture. Great Scott! see what comes of fraternising with padres! *Now*."

So saying he dived in to the right down a dark passage, into which the amazed Peter followed him. He had already opened a door at the end of it by the time Peter got there, and was halfway up a flight of wood stairs that curved up in front of them out of what was, obviously, a kitchen. A huge man turned his head as Peter came in, and surveyed him silently, his hands dexterously shaking a frying-pan over a fire as he did so.

"Bon jour, monsieur," said Peter politely.

Monsieur grunted, but not unpleasantly, and Peter gripped the banister and commenced to ascend. Half-way up he was nearly sent flying down again. A rosy-cheeked girl, short and dark, with sparkling eyes, had thrust herself down between him and the rail from a little landing above, and was shouting:

"Une omelette aux champignons. Jambon. Pommes sautes, s'il vous plait."

Peter recovered himself and smiled. "Bon jour, mademoiselle," he said, this time. In point of fact, he could say very little else.

"Bon jour, monsieur," said, the girl, and something else that he could not catch, but by this time he had reached the top in time to witness a little 'business' there. A second girl, taller, older, slower, but equally smiling, was taking Pennell's cap and stick and gloves, making play with her eyes the while. "Merci, chérie," he heard his friend say and then, in a totally different voice: "Ah! Bon jour Marie."

A third girl was before them. In her presence the other two withdrew. She was tall, plain, shrewd of face, with reddish hair, but she smiled even as the others. It was little more than a glance that Peter got, for she called an order (at which the first girl again disappeared down the stairs) greeted Pennell, replied to his question that there were two places, and was out of sight again in the room, seemingly all at once. He too, then, surrendered cap and stick, and followed his companion in.

There were no more than four tables in the little room—two for six, and two for four or five. Most were filled, but he and Pennell secured two seats with their backs to the wall opposite a couple of Australian officers who had apparently just commenced. Peter's was by the window, and he glanced out to see the sunlit street below, the wide sparkling harbour, and right opposite the hospital he had now visited several times and his own camp near it. There was the new green of spring shoots in the window-boxes, snowy linen on the table, a cheerful hum of conversation about him, and an oak-panelled wall behind that had seen the Revolution.

"Pennell," he said, "you're a marvel. The place is perfect."

By the time they had finished Peter was feeling warmed and friendly, the Australians had been joined to their company, and the four spent an idle afternoon cheerfully enough. There was nothing in strolling through the busy streets, joking a little over very French picture post-cards, quizzing the passing girls, standing in a queue at Cox's, and finally drawing a fiver in mixed French notes, or in wandering through a huge shop of many departments to buy some toilet necessities. But it was good fun. There was a comradeship, a youthfulness, carelessness, about it all that gripped Peter. He let himself go, and when he did so he was a good companion.

One little incident in the Grand Magasin completed his abandonment to the day and the hour. They were ostensibly buying a shaving-stick, but at the moment were cheerily wandering through the department devoted to *lingerie*. The attendant girls, entirely at ease, were trying to persuade the taller of the two Australians, whom his friend addressed as "Alex," to buy a flimsy lace nightdress "for his fiancée," readily pointing out that he would find no difficulty in getting rid of it elsewhere if he had not got such a desirable possession, when Peter heard an exclamation behind him.

"Hullo!" said a girl's voice; "fancy finding you here!" He turned quickly and blushed. Julie laughed merrily.

"Caught out," she said, "Tell me what you're buying, and for whom. A blouse, a camisole, or worse?"

"I'm not buying," said Peter, recovering his ease. "We're just strolling round, and that girl insists that my friend the Australian yonder should buy a nightie for his fiancée. He says he hasn't one, so she is persuading him that he can easily pick one up. What do you think?"

She glanced over at the little group. "Easier than some people I know, I should think," she said, smiling, taking in his six feet of bronzed manhood. "But it's no use your buying it. I wear pyjamas, silk, and I prefer Venns'."

"I'll remember," said Peter. "By the way, I'm coming to tea again to-morrow."

"That will make three times this week," she said. "But I suppose you will go round the ward first." Then quickly, for Peter looked slightly unhappy: "Next week I've a whole day off."

"No?" he said eagerly "Oh, do let's fix something up. Will you come out somewhere?"

Her eyes roved across to Pennell, who was bearing down upon them. "We'll fix it up to-morrow," she said. "Bring Donovan, and I'll get Tommy. And now introduce me nicely."

He did so, and she talked for a few minutes, and then went off to join some friends, who had moved on to another department. "By Jove," said Pennell, "that's some girl! I see now why you are so keen on the hospital, old dear. Wish I were a padre."

"I shall be padre in ..." began Alex, but Peter cut him short.

"Oh, Lord," he said, "I'm tired of that! Come on out of it, and let's get a refresher somewhere. What's the club like here?"

"Club's no good," said Pennell. "Let's go to Travalini's and introduce the padre. He's not been there yet."

"I thought everyone knew it," said the other Australian—rather contemptuously, Peter thought. What with one thing and another, he felt suddenly that he'd like to go. He remembered how nearly he had gone there in other company. "Come on, then," he said, and led the way out.

There was nothing in Travalini's to distinguish it from many other such places—indeed, to distinguish it from the restaurant in which Peter, Donovan, and the girls had dined ten days or so before, except that it was bigger, more garish, more expensive, and, consequently, more British in patronage. The restaurant was, however, separated more completely from the drinking-lounge, in which, among palms, a string-band played. There was an hotel above besides, and that helped business, but one could come and go innocently enough, for all that there was "anything a gentleman wants," as the headwaiter, who talked English, called himself a Belgian, and had probably migrated from over the Rhine, said. Everybody, indeed, visited the place now and again. Peter and his friends went in between the evergreen shrubs in their pots, and through the great glass swing-door, with every assurance. The place seemed fairly full. There was a subdued hum of talk and clink of glasses; waiters hurried to and fro; the band was tuning up. British uniforms predominated, but there were many foreign officers and a few civilians. There were perhaps a couple of dozen girls scattered about the place besides.

The friends found a corner with a big plush couch which took three of them, and a chair for Alex. A waiter bustled up and they ordered drinks, which came on little saucers marked with the price. Peter lay back luxuriously.

"Chin-chin," said the other Australian, and the others responded.

"That's good," said Pennell.

"Not so many girls here this afternoon," remarked Alex carelessly. "See, Dick, there's that little Levantine with the thick dark hair. She's caught somebody."

Peter looked across in the direction indicated. The girl, in a cerise costume with a big black hat, short skirt, and dainty bag, was sitting in a chair halfway on to them and leaning over the table before her. As he watched, she threw her head back and laughed softly. He caught the gleam of a white throat and of dark sloe eyes.

"She's a pretty one," said Pennell. "God! but they're queer little bits of fluff, these girls. It beats me how they're always gay, and always easy to get and to leave. And they get rottenly treated sometimes."

"Yes I'm damned if I understand them," said Alex. "Now, padre, I'll tell you something that's more in your way than mine, and you can see what you make of it. I was in a maison tolerée the other day—you know the sort of thing—and there were half a dozen of us in the sitting-room with the girls, drinking fizz. I had a little bit of a thing with fair hair—she couldn't have been more than seventeen at most, I reckon—with a laugh that did you good to hear, and, by gum! we wanted to be cheered just then, for we had had a bit of a gruelling on the Ancre and had been pulled out of the line to refit. She sat there with an angel's face, a chemise transparent except where it was embroidered, and not much else, and some of the women were fair beasts. Well, she moved on my knee, and I spilt some champagne and swore—'Jesus Christ!' I said. Do you know, she pushed back from me as if I had hit her! 'Oh, don't say His Name!' she said. 'Promise me you won't say it again. Do you not know how He loved us?' I was so taken aback that I promised, and to tell you the truth, padre, I haven't said it since. What do you think of that?"

Peter shook his head and drained his glass. He couldn't have spoken at once; the little story, told in such a place, struck him so much. Then he asked: "But is that all? How did she come to be there?"

"Well," Alex said, "that's just as strange. Father was in a French cavalry regiment, and got knocked out on the Marne. They lived in Arras before the war, and you can guess that there wasn't much left of the home. One much older sister was a widow with a big family; the other was a kid of ten or eleven, so this one went into the business to keep the family going. Fact. The mother used to come and see her, and I got to know her. She didn't seem to mind: said the doctors looked after them well, and the girl was making good money. Hullo!" he broke off, "there's Louise," and to Peter's horror he half-rose and smiled across at a girl some few tables away.

She got up and came over, beamed on them all, and took the seat Alex vacated. "Good-evening," she said, in fair English, scrutinising them. "What is it you say, 'How's things'?"

Alex pressed a drink on her and beckoned the waiter. She took a syrup, the rest martinis. Peter sipped his, and watched her talking to Alex and Pennell. The other Australian got up and crossed the room, and sat down with some other men.

The stories he had heard moved him profoundly. He wondered if they were true, but he seemed to see confirmation in the girl before him. Despite some making up, it was a clean face, if one could say so. She was laughing and talking with all the ease in the world, though Peter noticed that her eyes kept straying round the room. Apparently his friends had all her attention, but he could see it was not so. She was on the watch for clients, old or new. He thought how such a girl would have disgusted him a few short weeks ago, but he did not feel disgusted now. He could not. He did not know what he felt. He wondered, as he looked, if she were one of "the multitude," and then the fragment of a text slipped through his brain: "The Friend of publicans and sinners." "*The* Friend": the little adjective struck him as never before. Had they ever had another? He frowned to himself at the thought, and could not help wondering vaguely what his Vicar or the Canon would have done in Travalini's. Then he wondered instantly what that Other would have done, and he found no answer at all.

"Yes, but I do not know your friend yet," he heard the girl say, and saw she was being introduced to Pennell. She held out a decently gloved hand with a gesture that startled him—it was so like Hilda's. Hilda! The comparison dazed him. He fancied he could see her utter disgust, and then he involuntarily shook his head; it would be too great for him to imagine. What would she have made of the story he had just heard? He concluded she would flatly disbelieve it....

But Julie? He smiled to himself, and then, for the first time, suddenly asked himself what he really felt towards Julie. He remembered that first night and the kiss, and how he had half hated it, half liked it. He felt now, chiefly, anger that Donovan had had one too. One? But he, Peter, had had two.... Then he called himself a damned fool; it was all of a piece with her extravagant and utterly unconventional madness. But what, then, would she say to this? Had she anything in common with it?

He played with that awhile, blowing out thoughtful rings of smoke. It struck him that she had, but he was fully aware that that did not disgust him in the least. It almost fascinated him, just as—that *was* it—Hilda's disgust would repel him. Why? He hadn't an idea.

"Monsieur le Capitaine is very dull," said a girl's voice at his elbow. He started: Louise had moved to the sofa and was smiling at him. He glanced towards his companions, Alex was standing, finishing a last drink; Pennell staring at Louise.

He looked back at the girl, straight into her eyes, and could not read them in the least. The darkened eyebrows and the glitter in them baffled him. But he must speak, "Am I?" he said. "Forgive me, mademoiselle; I was thinking."

"Of your fiancée—is it not so? Ah! The Capitaine has his fiancée, then? In England? Ah, well, the girls in England do not suffer like we girls in France.... They are proud, too, the English misses. I know, for I have been there, to—how do you call it?—Folkestone. They walk with the head in the air," and she tilted up her chin so comically that Peter smiled involuntarily.

"No, I do not like them," went on the girl deliberately. "They are only half alive, I think. I almost wish the Boche had been in your land.... They are cold, la! And not so very nice to kiss, eh?"

"They're not all like that," said Pennell.

"Ah, non? But you like the girls of France the best, mon ami; is it not so?" She leaned across towards him significantly.

Pennell laughed. "*Now*, yes, perhaps," he said deliberately; "but after the war ..." and he shrugged his shoulders, like a Frenchman.

A shade passed over the girl's face, and she got up. "It is so," she said lightly. "Monsieur speaks very true—oh, very true! The girls of France now—they are gay, they are alive, they smile, and it is war, and you men want these things. But after—oh, I know you English—you'll go home and be—how do you say?—'respectable,' and marry an English miss, and have—oh! many, many bébés, and wear the top-hat, and go to church. There is no country like England...." She made a little gesture. "What do you believe, you English? In le bon Dieu? Non. In love? Ah, non! In what, then? Je ne sais!" She laughed again. "What 'ave I said? Forgive me, monsieur, and you also, Monsieur le Capitaine. But I do see a friend of mine. See, I go! Bon soir."

She looked deliberately at Peter a moment, then smiled comprehensively and left them. Peter saw that Alex had gone already; he asked no questions, but looked at Pennell inquiringly.

"I think so, padre; I've had enough of it to-night. Let's clear. We can get back in time for mess."

They went out into the darkening streets, crossed an open square, and turned down a busy road to the docks. They walked quickly, but Peter seemed to himself conscious of everyone that passed. He scanned faces, as if to read a riddle in them. There were men who lounged by, gay, reckless, out for fun plainly, but without any other sinister thought, apparently. There were Tommies who saluted and trudged on heavily. There were a couple of Yorkshire boys who did not notice them, flushed, animal, making determinedly for a destination down the street. There was one man at least who passed walking alone, with a tense, greedy, hard face, and Peter all but shuddered.

The lit shops gave way to a railed space, dark by contrast, and a tall building of old blackened stone, here and there chipped white, loomed up. Moved by an impulse, Peter paused, "Let's see if it's open, Pennell," he said. "Do you mind? I won't be a second."

"Not a scrap, old man," said Pennell, "I'll come in too."

Peter walked up to a padded leather-covered door and pushed. It swung open. They stepped in, into a faintly broken silence, and stood still.

Objects loomed up indistinctly—great columns, altars, pews. Far away a light flickered and twinkled, and from the top of the aisle across the church from the door by which they had entered a radiance glowed and lost itself in the black spaces of the high roof and wide nave. Peter crossed towards that side, and his companion followed. They trod softly, like good Englishmen in church, and they moved up the aisle a little to see more clearly; and so, having reached a place from which much was visible, remained standing for a few seconds.

The light streamed from an altar, and from candles above it set around a figure of the Mother of God. In front knelt a priest, and behind him, straggling back in the pews, a score or so of women, some children, and a blue-coated French soldier or two. The priest's voice sounded thin and low: neither could hear what he said; the congregation made rapid responses regularly, but eliding the, to them, familiar words. There was, then, the murmur of repeated prayer, like muffled knocking on a door, and nothing more.

"Let's go," whispered Pennell at last.

They went out, and shut the door softly behind them. As they did so, some other door was opened noisily and banged, while footsteps began to drag slowly across the stone floor and up the aisle they had come down. The new-comer subsided into a pew with a clatter on the boards, but the murmured prayers went on unbroken.

Outside the street engulfed them. The same faces passed by. A street-car banged and clattered up towards the centre of the town, packed with jovial people. Pennell looked towards it half longingly. "Great Scott, Graham! I wish, now, we hadn't come away so soon," he said.

CHAPTER VIII

The lower valley of the Seine is one of the most beautiful and interesting river-stretches in Northern Europe. It was the High Street of old Normandy, and feuda, barons and medieval monks have left their mark upon it. From the castle of Tancarville to the abbey of Jumièges you can read the story of their doings; or when you stand in the Roman circus at Lillebonne, or enter the ancient cloister of M. Maeterlinck's modern residence at St. Wandrille, see plainly enough the writing of a still older legend, such as appeared, once, on the wall of a palace in Babylon. On the left bank steep hills, originally wholly clothed with forest and still thickly wooded, run down to the river with few breaks in them, each break, however, being garrisoned by an ancient town. Of these, Caudebec stands unrivalled. On the right bank the flat plain of Normandy stretches to the sky-line, pink-and-white in spring with miles of apple-orchards. The white clouds chase across its fair blue sky, driven by the winds from the sea, and tall poplars rise in their uniform rows along the river as if to guard a Paradise.

Caudebec can be reached from Le Havre in a few hours, and although cars for hire and petrol were not abundant in France at the time, one could find a chauffeur to make the journey if one was prepared to pay. Given fine weather, it was an ideal place for a day off in the spring. And Peter knew it.

In the Grand Magasin Julie had talked of a day off, and a party of four had been mooted, but when he had leisure to think of it, Peter found himself averse to four, and particularly if one of the four were to be Donovan. He admitted it freely to himself. Donovan was the kind of a man, he thought, that Julie must like, and he was the kind of man, too, to put him, Peter, into the shade. Ordinarily he asked for no better companion, but he hated to see Julie and Jack together. He could not make the girl out, and he wanted to do so. He wanted to know what she thought about many things, and—incidentally, of course—what she thought about him.

He had argued all this over next morning while shaving, and had ended by cutting himself. It was a slight matter, but it argued a certain absent-mindedness, and it brought him back to decency. He perceived that he was scheming to leave his friend out, and he fought resolutely against the idea. Therefore, that afternoon, he went to the hospital, spent a couple of hours chatting with the men, and finally wound up in the nurses' mess-room for tea as usual. It was a little room, long and narrow, at the end of the biggest ward, but its windows looked over the sea and it was convenient to the kitchen. Coloured illustrations cut from magazines and neatly mounted on brown paper decorated the walls, but there was little else by way of furniture or ornament except a long table and chairs. One could get but little talk except of a scrappy kind, for nurses came continually in and out for tea, and, indeed, Julie had only a quarter of an hour to spare. But he got things fixed up for the following Thursday, and he left the place to settle with Donovan.

That gentleman's company of native labour was lodged a mile or so through the docks from Peter's camp, on the banks of the Tancarville Canal. It was enlivened at frequent intervals, day and night, by the sirens of tugs bringing strings of barges to the docks, whence their cargo was borne overseas in the sea-going tramps, or, of course, taking equally long strings to the Seine for Rouen and Paris. It was mud and cinders underfoot, and it was walled off with corrugated-iron sheeting and barbed wire from the attentions of some hundreds of Belgian refugees who lived along the canal and parallel roads in every conceivable kind of resting-place, from ancient bathing-vans to broken-down railway-trucks. But there were trees along the canal and reeds and grass, so that there were worse places than Donovan's camp in Le Havre.

Peter found his friend surveying the endeavours of a gang of boys to construct a raised causeway from the officers' mess to the orderly-room, and he promptly broached his object. Donovan was entranced with the proposal, but he could not go. He was adamant upon it. He could possibly have got off, but it meant leaving his something camp for a whole day, and just at present he couldn't. Peter could get Pennell or anyone. Another time, perhaps, but not now. For thus can the devil trap his victims.

Peter pushed back for home on his bicycle, but stopped at the docks on his way to look up Pennell. That gentleman was bored, weary, and inclined to be blasphemous. It appeared that for the whole, infernal day he had had to watch the off-loading of motor-spares, that he had had no lunch, and that he could not get away for a day next week if he tried. "It isn't everyone can get a day off whenever he wants to, padre," he said. "In the next war I shall be ..." Peter turned hard on his heel, and left him complaining to the derricks.

He was now all but cornered. There was nobody else he particularly cared to ask unless it were Arnold, and he could not imagine Arnold and Julie together. It appeared to him that fate was on his side; it only remained to persuade Julie to come alone. He pedalled back to mess and dinner, and then, about half-past eight, strolled round to the hospital again. It was late, of course, but he was a padre, and the hospital padre, and privileged. He knew exactly what to do, and that he was really as safe as houses in doing it, and yet this intriguing by night made him uncomfortable still. He told himself he was an ass to think so, but he could not get rid of the sensation.

Julie would be on duty till 9.30, and he could easily have a couple of minutes' conversation with her in the ward. He followed the railway-track, then, along the harbour, and went in under the great roof of the empty station. On the far platform a hospital train was being made ready for its return run, but, except for a few cleaners and orderlies, the place was empty.

An iron stairway led up from the platform to the wards above. He ascended, and found himself on a landing with the door of the theatre open before him. There was a light in it, and he caught the sound of water; some pro. was cleaning up. He moved down the passage and cautiously opened the door of the ward.

It was shaded and still. Somewhere a man breathed heavily, and another turned in his sleep. Just beyond the red glow of the stove, with the empty armchairs in a circle before it, were screens from which came a subdued light. He walked softly between the beds towards them, and looked over the top.

Inside was a little sanctum: a desk with a shaded reading-lamp, a chair, a couch, a little table with flowers upon it and a glass and jug, and on the floor by the couch a work-basket. Julie was at the desk writing in a big official book, and he watched her for a moment unobserved. It was almost as if he saw a different person from the girl he knew. She was at work, and a certain hidden sadness showed clearly in her face. But the little brown fringe of hair on her forehead and the dimpled chin were the same....

"Good-evening," he whispered.

She looked up quickly, with a start, and he noticed curiously how rapidly the laughter came back to her face. "You did startle me, Solomon," she said. "What is it?"

"I want to speak to you a minute about Thursday," he said. "Can I come in?"

She got up and came round the screens. "Follow me," she said, "and don't make a noise."

She led him across the ward to the wide verandah, opening the door carefully and leaving it open behind her, and then walked to the balustrade and glanced down. The hospital ship had gone, and there was no one visible on the wharf. The stars were hidden, and there was a suggestion of mist on the harbour, through which the distant lights seemed to flicker.

"You're coming on, Solomon," she said mockingly. "Never tell me you'd have dared to call on the hospital to see a nurse by night a few weeks ago! Suppose matron came round? There is no dangerous case in my ward."

"Not among the men, perhaps," said Peter mischievously. "But, look here, about Thursday; Donovan can't go, nor Pennell, and I don't know anyone else I want to ask."

"Well, I'll see if I can raise a man. One or two of the doctors are fairly decent, or I can get a convalescent out of the officers' hospital."

She had the lights behind her, and he could not see her face, but he knew she was laughing at him, and it spurred him on. "Don't rag, Julie," he said, "You know I want you to come alone."

There was a perceptible pause. Then: "I can't cut Tommy," she said.

"Not for once?" he urged. She turned away from him and looked down at the water. It is curious how there come moments of apprehension in all our lives when we want a thing, but know quite well we are mad to want it. Julie looked into the future for a few seconds, and saw plainly, but would not believe what she saw.

When she turned back she had her old manner completely. "You're a dear old thing," she said, "and I'll do it. But if it gets out that I gadded about for a day with an officer, even though he is a padre, and that we went miles out of town, there'll be some row, my boy. Quick now! I must get back. What's the plan?"

"Thanks awfully," said Peter. "It will be a rag. What time can you get off?"

"Oh, after breakfast easily—say eight-thirty."

"Right. Well, take the tram-car to Harfleur—you know?—as far as it goes. I'll be at the terminus with a car. What time must you be in?"

"I can get late leave till ten, I think," she said.

"Good! That gives us heaps of time. We'll lunch and tea in Caudebec, and have some sandwiches for the road home."

"And if the car breaks down?"

"It won't," said Peter. "You're lucky in love, aren't you?"

She did not laugh. "I don't know," she said. "Good-night."

And then Peter had walked home, thinking of Hilda. And he had sat by the sea, and come to the conclusion that he was a rotter, but in the web of Fate and much to be pitied, which is like a man. And then he had played auction till midnight and lost ten francs, and gone to bed concluding that he was certainly unlucky—at cards.

As Peter sat in his car at the Harfleur terminus that Thursday it must be confessed that he was largely indifferent to the beauties of the Seine Valley that he had professedly come to see. He was nervous, to begin with, lest he should be recognised by anyone, and he was in one of his troubled moods. But he had not long to wait. The tram came out, and he threw away his cigarette and walked to meet the passengers.

Julie looked very smart in the grey with its touch of scarlet, but she was discontented with it. "If only I could put on a few glad rags," she said as she climbed into the car, "this would be perfect. You men can't know how a girl comes to hate uniform. It's not bad occasionally, but if you have to wear it always it spoils chances. But I've got my new shoes and silk stockings on," she added, sticking out a neat ankle, "and my skirt is not vastly long, is it? Besides, underneath, if it's any consolation to you, I've really pretty things. Uniform or not, I see no reason why one should not feel joyful next the skin. What do you think?"

Peter agreed heartily, and tucked a rug round her. "There's the more need for this, then," he said.

"Oh, I don't know: silk always makes me feel so comfortable that I can't be cold. Isn't it a heavenly day? We are lucky, you know; it might have been beastly. Lor', but I'm going to enjoy myself to-day, my dear! I warn you. I've got to forget how Tommy looked when I put her off with excuses. I felt positively mean."

"What did she say?" asked Peter.

"That she didn't mind at all, as she had got to write letters," said Julie, "Solomon, Tommy's a damned good sort!... Give us a cigarette, and don't look blue. We're right out of town."

Peter got out his case. "Don't call me Solomon to-day," he said.

Julie threw herself back in her corner and shrieked with laughter. The French chauffeur glanced round and grimaced appreciatively, and Peter felt a fool. "What am I to call you, then?" she demanded. "You are a funny old thing, and now you look more of a Solomon than ever."

"Call me Peter," he said.

She looked at him, her eyes sparkling with amusement. "I'm really beginning to enjoy myself," she said. "But, look here, you mustn't begin like this. How in the world do you think we shall end up if you do? You'll have nothing left to say, and I shall be worn to a rag and a temper warding off your sentimentality."

"Julie," said Peter, "are you ever serious? I can't help it, you know, I suppose because I am a parson, though I am such a rotten one."

"Who says you're a rotten one?"

"Everybody who tells the truth, and, besides, I know it. I feel an absolute stummer when I go around the wards. I never can say a word to the men."

"They like you awfully. You know little Jimmy, that kiddie who came in the other day who's always such a brick? Well, last night I went and sat with him a bit because he was in such pain. I told him where I was going to-day as a secret. What do you think he said about you?"

"I don't want to know," said Peter hastily.

"Well, you shall. He said if more parsons were like you, more men would go to church. What do you make of that, old Solomon?"

"It isn't true to start with. A few might come for a little, but they would soon fall off. And if they didn't, they'd get no good. I don't know what to say to them."

Julie threw away her cigarette-stump. "One sees a lot of human nature in hospitals, my boy," she said, "and it doesn't leave one with many illusions. But from what I've seen, I should say nobody does much good by talking."

"You don't understand," said Peter. "Look here, I shouldn't call you religious in a way at all Don't be angry. I don't *know*, but I don't think so, and I don't think you can possibly know what I mean."

"I used to do the flowers in church regularly at home," she said. "I believe in God, though you think I don't."

Peter sighed. "Let's change the subject," he said. "Have you seen any more of that Australian chap lately?"

"Rather! He's engaged to a girl I know, and I reckon I'm doing her a good turn by sticking to him. He's a bit of a devil, you know, but I think I can keep him off the French girls a bit."

Peter looked at her curiously. "You know what he is, and you don't mind then?" he said.

"Good Lord, no!" she replied. "My dear boy, I know what men are. It isn't in their nature to stick to one girl only. He loves Edie all right, and he'll make her a good husband one day, if she isn't too particular and inquisitive. If I were married, I'd give my husband absolute liberty—and I'd expect it in return. But I shall never marry. There isn't a man who can play fair. They'll take their own pleasures, but they are all as jealous as possible. I've seen it hundreds of times."

"You amaze me," said Peter. "Let's talk straight. Do you mean to say that if you were married and your husband ran up to Paris for a fortnight, and you knew exactly what he'd gone for, you wouldn't mind?"

"No," she declared roundly. "I wouldn't. He'd come back all the more fond of me, I'd know I'd be a fool to expect anything else."

Peter stared at her. She was unlike anything he had ever seen. Her moral standards, if she had any, he added mentally, were so different from his own that he was absolutely floored. He thought grimly that alone in a motor-car he had got among the multitude with a vengeance. "Have you ever been in love?" he demanded.

She laughed. "Solomon, you're the quaintest creature. Do you think I'd tell you if I had been? You never ought to ask anyone that. But if you want to know, I've been in love hundreds of times. It's a queer disease, but not serious—at least, not if you don't take it too seriously."

"You don't know what love is at all," he said.

She faced him fairly and unashamed. "I do," she said, "It's an animal passion for the purpose of populating the earth. And if you ask me, I think it is rather a dirty trick on the part of God."

"You don't mean that," he said, distressed.

She laughed again merrily, and slipped her hand into his under the rug. "Peter," she said—"there, am I not good? You aren't made to worry about these things. I don't know that anyone is. We can't help ourselves, and the best thing is to take our pleasures when we can find them. I suppose you'll be shocked at me, but I'm not going to pretend. I wasn't built that way. If this were a closed car I'd give you a kiss."

"I don't want that sort of a kiss," he said. "That was what you gave me the other night. I want...."

"You don't know what you want, my dear, though you think you do. You shouldn't be so serious. I'm sure I kiss very nicely—plenty of men think so? anyway, and if there is nothing in that sort of kiss, why not kiss? Is there a Commandment against it? I suppose our grandmothers thought so, but we don't. Besides, I've been east of Suez, where there ain't no ten Commandments. There's only one real rule left in life for most of us, Peter, and that's this: 'Be a good pal, and don't worry.'"

Peter sighed. "You and I were turned out differently, Julie," he said. "But I like you awfully. You attract me so much that I don't know how to express it. There's nothing mean about you, and nothing sham. And I admire your pluck beyond words. It seems to me that you've looked life in the face and laughed. Anybody can laugh at death, but very few of us at life. I think I'm terrified of it. And that's the awful part about it all, for I ought to know the secret, and I don't. I feel an absolute hypocrite at times—when I take a service, for example. I talk about things I don't understand in the least, even about God, and I begin to think I know nothing about Him...." He broke off, utterly miserable.

"Poor old boy," she said softly; "is it as bad as that?"

He turned to her fiercely. "You darling!" he said, carried away by her tone. "I believe I'd rather have you than—than God!"

She did not move in her corner, nor did she smile now. "I wonder," she said slowly. "Peter, it's you that hate shams, not I. It's you that are brave, not I. I play with shams because I know they're shams, but I like playing with them. But you are greater than I. You are not content with playing. One of these days—oh, I don't know...." She broke off and looked away.

Peter gripped her hand tightly. "Don't, little girl," he said. "Let's forget for to-day. Look at those primroses; they're the first I've seen. Aren't they heavenly?"

They ran into Caudebec in good time, and lunched at an hotel overlooking the river, with great enthusiasm. To Peter it was utterly delicious to have her by him. She was as gay as she could possibly be, and made fun over everything. Sitting daintily before him, her daring, unconventional talk carried him away. She chose the wine, and after *déjeuner* sat with her elbows on the table, puffing at a cigarette, her brown eyes alight with mischief, apparently without a thought for to-morrow.

"Oh, I say," she said, "do look at that party in the corner. The old Major's well away, and the girl'll have a job to keep him in hand, I wonder where they're from? Rouen, perhaps; there was a car at the door. What do you think of the girl?"

Peter glanced back. "No better than she ought to be," he said.

"No, I don't suppose so, but they are gay, these French girls. I don't wonder men like them. And they have a hard time. I'd give them a leg up any day if I could. I can't, though, so if ever you get a chance do it for me, will you?"

Peter assented. "Come on," he said. "Finish that glass if you think you can, and let's get out."

"Here's the best, then, I've done. What are we going to see?"

For a couple of hours they wandered round the old town, with its narrow streets and even fifteenth-century houses, whose backs actually leaned over the swift little river that ran all but under the place to the Seine. They penetrated through an old mill to its back premises, and climbed precariously round the water-wheel to reach a little moss-grown platform from which the few remaining massive stones of the Norman wall and castle could still be seen. The old abbey kept them a good while, Julie interested Peter enormously as they walked about its cool aisles, and tried to make out the legends of its ancient glass. She had nothing of that curious kind of shyness most people have in a church, and that he would certainly have expected of her. She joked and laughed a little in it—at a queer row of mutilated statues packed into a kind of chapel to keep quiet out of the way till wanted, at the vivid red of the Red Sea engulfing Pharaoh and all his host—but not in the least irreverently. He recalled a saying of a book he had once read in which a Roman Catholic priest had defended the homeliness of an Italian congregation by saying that it was right for them to be at home in their Father's House. It was almost as if Julie were at home, yet he shrank from the inference.

She was entirely ignorant of everything, except perhaps, of a little biblical history, but she made a most interested audience. Once he thought she was perhaps egging him on for his own pleasure, but when he grew more silent she urged him to explain. "It's ripping going round with somebody who knows something," she said. "Most of the men one meets know absolutely nothing. They're very jolly, but one gets tired. I could listen to you for ages."

Peter assured her that he was almost as ignorant as they, but she was shrewdly insistent. "You read more, and you understand what you read," she said. "Most people don't. I know."

They bought picture post-cards off a queer old woman in a peasant head-dress, and then came back to the river and sat under the shade of a line of great trees to wait for the tea the hotel had guaranteed them. Julie now did all the talking—of South Africa, of gay adventures in France and on the voyage, and of the men she had met. She was as frank as possible, but Peter wondered how far he was getting to know the real girl.

Tea was an unusual success for France. It was real tea, but then there was reason for that, for Julie had insisted on going into the big kitchen, to madame's amusement and monsieur's open admiration, and making it herself. But the chocolate cakes, the white bread and proper butter, and the cream, were a miracle. Peter wondered if you could get such things in England now, and Julie gaily told him that the French made laws only to break them, with several instances thereof. She declared that if a food-ration officer existed in Caudebec he must be in love with the landlady's daughter and that she only wished she could get to know such an official in Havre. The daughter in question waited on them, and Julie and she chummed up immensely. Finally she was despatched to produce a collection of Army badges and buttons—scalps Julie called them. When they came they turned them over. All ranks were represented, or nearly so, and most regiments that either could remember. There were Canadian, Australian, and South African badges, and at last Julie declared that only one was wanting.

"What will you give for this officer's badge?" she demanded, seizing hold of one of Peter's Maltese crosses.

The girl looked at it curiously. "What is it?" she said.

"It's the badge of the Sacred Legion," said Julie gravely. "You know Malta? Well, that's part of the British Empire, of course, and the English used to have a regiment there to defend it from the Turks. It was a great honour to join, and so it was called the Sacred Legion. This officer is a Captain in it."

"Shut up Julie," said Peter, *sotto voce.*

But nothing would stop her. "Come now," she said. "What will you give? You'll give her one for a kiss, won't you, Solomon?"

The girl laughed and blushed "Not before mademoiselle," she said, looking at Peter.

"Oh, I'm off," cried Julie, "I'll spare you one, but only one, remember." and she deliberately got up and left them.

Mademoiselle was "tres jolie," said the girl, collecting her badges. Peter detached a cross and gave it her, and she demurely put up her mouth. He kissed her lightly, and walked leisurely out to settle the bill and call the car. He had entirely forgotten his depression, and the world seemed good to him. He hummed a little song by the water's edge as he waited, and thought over the day. He could never remember having had such a one in his life. Then he recollected that one badge was gone, and he abstracted the other. Without his badges he would not be known as a chaplain.

When Julie appeared, she made no remark, as he had half-expected. They got in, and started off back in the cooling evening. Near Tancarville they stopped the car to have the hood put up, and strolled up into the grounds of the old castle while they waited.

"Extraordinary it must have been to have lived in a place like this," said Peter.

"Rather," said Julie, "and beyond words awful to the women. I cannot imagine what they must have been like, but I think they must have been something like native African women."

"Why?" queried Peter.

"Oh, because a native woman never reads and hardly goes five miles from her village. She is a human animal, who bears children and keeps the house of her master, that's all. That's what these women must have done."

"The Church produced some different types," said Peter; "but they had no chance elsewhere, perhaps. Still, I expect they were as happy as we, perhaps happier."

"And their cows were happier still, I should think," laughed Julie. "No, you can't persuade me. I wouldn't have been a woman in those days for the world."

"And now?" asked Peter.

"Rather! We have much the best time on the whole. We can do what we like pretty well. If we want to be men, we can. We can put on riding-breeches, even, and run a farm. But if we like, we can wear glad rags and nice undies, and be more women than ever."

"And in the end thereof?" Peter couldn't help asking.

"Oh," said Julie lightly, "one can settle down and have babies if one wants to. And sit in a drawing-room and talk scandal as much as one likes. Not that I shall do either, thank you. I shall—oh, I don't know what I shall do. Solomon, you are at your worst. Pick me some of those primroses, and let's be going. You never can tell: we may have to walk home yet."

Peter plucked a few of the early blooms, and she pushed them into her waist-belt. Then they went back to the car, and got in again.

"Cold?" he asked, after a little.

"A bit," she said. "Tuck me up, and don't sit in that far corner all the time. You make me feel chilly to look at you. I hate sentimental people, but if you tried hard and were nice I could work up quite a lot of sentiment just now."

He laughed, and tucked her up as required. Then he lit a cigarette and slipped his arm round her waist. "Is that better?" he said.

"Much. But you can't have had much practice. Now tell me stories."

Peter had a mind to tell her several, but he refrained, and they grew silent, "Do you think we shall have another day like this?" he demanded, after a little.

"I don't see why not," she said. "But one never knows, does one? The chances are we shan't. It's a queer old world."

"Let's try, anyway; I've loved it," he said.

"So have I," said Julie. "It's the best day I've had for a long time, Peter. You're a nice person to go out with, you know, though I mustn't flatter you too much. You should develop the gift; it's not everyone that has it."

"I've no wish to," he said.

"You are an old bear," she laughed; "but you don't mean all you say, or rather you do, for you will say what you mean. You shouldn't, Peter. It's not done nowadays, and it gives one away. If you were like me, now, you could say and do anything and nobody would mind. They'd never know what you meant, and of course all the time you'd mean nothing."

"So you mean nothing all the time?" he queried.

"Of course," she said merrily. "What do you think?"

That jarred Peter a little, so he said nothing and silence fell on them, and at the Hôtel de Ville in the city he asked if she would mind finishing alone.

"Not a bit, old thing, if you want to go anywhere," she said.

He apologised. "Arnold—he's our padre—is likely to be at the club, and I promised I'd walk home with him," he lied remorselessly. "It's beastly rude, I know, but I thought you'd understand."

She looked at him, and laughed. "I believe I do," she said.

He stopped the car and got out, settling with the man, and glancing up at a clock. "You'll be in at nine-forty-five," he said, "as proper as possible. And thank you so much for coming."

"Thank you, Solomon," she replied. "It's been just topping. Thanks awfully for taking me. And come in to tea soon, won't you?" He promised and held out his hand. She pressed it, and waved out of the window as the car drove off. And no sooner was it in motion than he cursed himself for a fool. Yet he knew why he had done as he had, there, in the middle of the town. He knew that he feared she would kiss him again—as before.

Not noticing where he went, he set off through the streets, making, unconsciously almost, for the sea, and the dark boulevards that led from the gaily lit centre of the city towards it. He walked slowly, his mind a chaos of thoughts, and so ran into a curious adventure.

As he passed a side-street he heard a man's uneven steps on the pavement, a girl's voice, a curse, and the sound of a fall. Then followed an exclamation in another woman's voice, and a quick sentence in French.

Peter hesitated a minute, and then turned down the road to where a small group was faintly visible. As he reached it, he saw that a couple of street girls were bending over a man who lay sprawling on the ground, and he quickened his steps to a run. His boots were rubber-soled, and all but noiseless. "Here, I say," he said as he came up. "Let that man alone. What are you doing?" he added in halting French. One of the two girls gave a little scream, but the other straightened herself, and Peter perceived that he knew her. It was Louise, of Travalini's.

"What are you doing?" he demanded again in English. "Is he hurt?"

"Non, non, monsieur," said Louise. "He is but 'zig-zag.' We found him a little way down the street, and he cannot walk easily. So we help him. If the gendarme—how do you call him?—the red-cap, see him, maybe he will get into trouble. But now you come. You will doubtless help him. Vraiment, he is in luck. We go now, monsieur."

Peter bent over the fallen man. He did not know him, but saw he was a subaltern, though a middle-aged man. The fellow was very drunk, and did little else than stutter curses in which the name of our Lord was frequent.

Peter pulled at his arm, and Louise stooped to help him. Once up, he got his arm round him, and demanded where he lived.

The man stared at them foolishly. Peter gave him a bit of a shake, and demanded the address again, "Come on," he said. "Pull yourself together, for the Lord's sake. We shall end before the A.P.M. if you don't. What's your camp, you fool?"

At that the man told him, stammeringly, and Peter sighed his relief. "I know," he said to Louise. "It's not far. I'll maybe get a taxi at the corner." She pushed him towards a doorway: "Wait a minute," she said. "I live here; it's all right. I will get a fiacre. I know where to find one."

She darted away. It seemed long to Peter, but in a few minutes a horn tooted and a cab came round the corner. Between them, they got the subaltern in, and Peter gave the address. Then he pulled out his purse before stepping in himself, opened it, found a ten-franc note, and offered it to Louise.

The girl of the street and the tavern pushed it away. "La!" she exclaimed. "Vite! Get in. Bon Dieu! Should I be paid for a kindness? Poor boy! he does not know what he does. He will 'ave a head—ah! terrible—in the morning. And see, he has fought for la patrie." She pointed to a gold wound-stripe on his arm. "Bon soir, monsieur."

She stepped back and spoke quickly to the driver, who was watching sardonically. He nodded. "Bon soir, monsieur," she said again, and disappeared in the doorway.

CHAPTER IX

A few weeks later the War Office—if it was the War Office, but one gets into the habit of attributing these things to the War Office—had one of its regular spasms. It woke up suddenly with a touch of nightmare, and it got fearfully busy for a few weeks before going to sleep again. All manner of innocent people were dragged into the vortex of its activities, and blameless lives were disturbed and terrorised. This particular enthusiasm involved even such placid and contented souls as the Chaplain-General, the Principal Chaplain, their entire staffs and a great many of their rank and file. It created a new department, acquired many additional offices for the B.E.F., dragged from their comfortable billets a certain number of high-principled base officers, and then (by the mercy of Providence) flickered out almost as soon as the said officers bad made themselves a little more comfortable than before in their new posts.

It was so widespread a disturbance that even Peter Graham, most harmless of men, with plenty of his own fish to fry, was dragged into it, as some leaf, floating placidly downstream, may be caught and whirled away in an excited eddy. More definitely, it removed him from Havre and Julie just when he was beginning to want most definitely to stay there, and of course, when it happened, he could hardly know that it was to be but a temporary separation.

He was summoned, then, one fine morning, to his A.C.G.'s office in town, and he departed on a bicycle, turning over in his mind such indiscretions of which he had been guilty and wondering which of them was about to trip him. Pennell had been confident, indeed, and particular.

"You're for it, old bean," he had said. "There's a limit to the patience even of the Church. They are going to say that there is no need for you to visit hospitals after dark, and that their padres mustn't be seen out with nurses who smoke in public. And all power to their elbow, I say."

Peter's reply was certainly not in the Prayer-Book, and would probably have scandalised its compilers, but he thought, secretly, that there might be something in what his friend said. Consequently he rode his bicycle carelessly, and was indifferent to tram-lines and some six inches of nice sticky mud on parts of the *pavé*. In the ordinary course, therefore, these things revenged themselves upon him. He came off neatly and conveniently opposite a small *café debit* at a turn in the dock road, and the mud prevented the *pavé* from seriously hurting him.

A Frenchman, minding the cross-lines, picked him up, and he, madame, her assistant, and a customer, carried him into the kitchen off the bar and washed and dried him. The least he could do was a glass of French beer all round, with a franc to the dock labourer who straightened his handle-bars and tucked in a loose spoke, and for all this the War Office—if it was the War Office, for it may, quite possibly, have been Lord Northcliffe or Mr. Bottomley, or some other controller of our national life—was directly responsible. When one thinks that in a hundred places just such disturbances were in progress in ten times as many innocent lives, one is appalled at their effrontery. They ought to eat and drink more carefully, or take liver pills.

However, in due time Peter sailed up to the office of his immediate chief but little the worse for wear, and was ushered in. He was prepared for a solitary interview, but he found a council of some two dozen persons, who included an itinerant Bishop, an Oxford Professor, a few Y.M.C.A. ladies, and—triumph of the A.C.G.—a Labour member. Peter could not conceive that so great a weight of intellect could be involved in his affairs, and took comfort. He seated himself on a wooden chair, and put on his most intelligent appearance; and if it was slightly marred by a mud streak at the back of his ear, overlooked by madame's kindly assistant who had attended to that side of him, he was not really to blame. Again, it was the fault of Lord Northcliffe or—or any of the rest of them.

It transpired that he was slightly late: the Bishop had been speaking. He was a good Bishop and eloquent, and, as the A.C.G. who now rose to take the matter in hand remarked, he had struck the right note. In all probability it was due to Peter's having missed that note that he was so critical of the scheme. The note would have toned him up. He would have felt a more generous sympathy for the lads in the field, and would have been more definitely convinced that something must be done. If not plainly stated in the Holy Scriptures, his lordship had at least found it indicated there, but Peter was not aware of this. He only observed that the note had made everyone solemn and intense except the Labour member. That gentleman, indeed, interrupted the A.C.G. before he was fairly on his legs with the remark: "Beggin' your pardon, sir, but as this is an informal conference, does anyone mind if I smoke?"...

Peter's A.C.G. was anything but a fool, and the nightmare from Headquarters had genuinely communicated itself to him. He felt all he said, and he said it ably. He lacked only in one regard: he had never been down among the multitude. He knew exactly what would have to have been in his own mind for him to act as he believed some of them were acting, and he knew exactly how he would, in so deplorable a condition of affairs, have set about remedying it. These things, then, he stated boldly and clearly. As he proceeded, the Y.M.C.A. ladies got out notebooks, the Professor allowed himself occasional applause, and the Labour member lit another pipe.

It appeared that there was extreme unrest and agitation among the troops, or at least a section of the troops, for no one could say that the armies in the field were not magnificent. They had got to remember that the Tommy of to-day was not as the Tommy of yesterday—not that he suffered by comparison, but that he was far better educated and far more inclined to think for himself. They were well aware that a little knowledge was a dangerous thing, or, again, as his friend the Bishop would have doubtless put it, how great a matter a little fire kindleth. There was no escaping it: foreign propaganda, certain undesirable books and papers—books and papers, he need hardly say, outside the control of the reputable Press—and even Socialistic agitators, were abroad in the Army. He did not wish to say too much; it was enough to remind them of what, possibly, they already knew, that certain depots on certain occasions had refused to sing the National Anthem, and were not content with their wages. Insignificant as these things might be in detail, G.H.Q. had felt there was justifiable cause for alarm. This meeting had gathered to consider plans for a remedy.

Now he thanked God that they were not Prussians. There must be no attempt at coercion. A war for liberty must be won by free people. One had, of course, to have discipline in the Army, but theirs was to-day a citizen Army. His friend who had left his parliamentary duties to visit France might rest assured that the organizations represented there that morning would not forget that. In a word, Tommy had a vote, and he was entitled to it, and should keep it. One day he should even use it; and although no one could wish to change horses crossing a stream, still, they hoped that day would speedily come—the day of peace and victory.

But meantime, what was to be done? As the Bishop had rightly said, something must be done. Resolute on this point, H.Q. had called in the C.G. and the P.C. and, he believed, expert opinion on both sides the House of Commons; and the general opinion agreed upon was that Tommy should be educated to vote correctly when the time came, and to wait peacefully for that time. The Professor could tell them of schemes even now in process of formation at home in order that the land they loved might be cleaner, sweeter, better and happier, in the days to come. But Tommy, meantime, did not know of these things. He was apparently under the delusion that he must work out his own salvation, whereas, in point of fact, it was being worked out for him scientifically and religiously. If these things were clearly laid before him, H.Q. was convinced that agitation, dissatisfaction, and even revolution—for there were those who thought they were actually trending in that direction—would be nipped in the bud.

The scheme was simple and far-reaching. Lectures would be given all over the areas occupied by British troops. Every base would be organised in such a way that such lectures and even detailed courses of study should be available for everyone. Every chaplain, hutworker, and social entertainer must do his or her bit. They must know how to speak wisely and well—not all in public, but, everyone as the occasion offered, privately, in hut or camp, to inquiring and dissatisfied Tommies. They would doubtless feel themselves insufficient for these things, but study-circles were to be formed and literature obtained which would completely furnish them with information. He would conclude by merely laying on the table a bundle of the splendid papers and tracts already prepared for this work. The Professor would now outline what was being attempted at home, and then the meeting would be open for discussion.

The Professor was given half an hour, and he made an excellent speech for a cornered and academic theorist. The first ten minutes he devoted to explaining that he could not explain in the time; in the second, tempering the wind to the shorn lamb, he pointed out that it was no use his outlining schemes not yet completed, or that they could read for themselves, or that, possibly, without some groundwork, they could not understand; and in the third ten minutes he outlined the committees dealing with the work and containing such well-known names as Robert Smiley, Mr. Button, and Clydens. He sat down. Everyone applauded—the M.P., and possibly the A.C.G., because they honestly knew and respected these gentlemen, and the rest because they felt they ought to do so. The meeting was then opened for discussion.

Peter took no part in what followed, and, indeed, nothing over-illuminating was said save one remark, cast upon the waters by the Labour member, which was destined to be found after many days. They were talking of the lectures, and one of the ladies (Peter understood a Girton lecturer) was apparently eager to begin without delay. The M.P. begged to ask a question: Were there to be questions and a discussion?

The A.C.G. glanced at a paper before him, and rose. He apologised for omitting to mention it before, but H.Q. thought it would be subverse of all discipline if, let us say, privates should be allowed to get up and argue with the officers who might have addressed them. They all knew what might be said in the heat of argument. Also, if he might venture to say so, some of their lecturers, though primed with the right lecture, might not be such experts that they could answer every question, and plainly failure to satisfy a questioner might be disastrous. But questions could be written and replies given at the next lecture. He thought, smiling, that some of them would perhaps find that convenient.

The M.P. leaned back in his chair. "Well, sir," he said, "I'm sorry to be a wet-blanket, but if that is so, the scheme is wrecked from the start. You don't know the men; I do. They're not going to line up, like the pupils of Dotheboys Academy, for a spoonful of brimstone and treacle."

The meeting was slightly scandalised. The chairman, however, rose to the occasion. That, he said, was a matter for H.Q. They were there to do their duty. And, being an able person, he did his. In ten minutes they were formed into study-bands and were pledged to study, with which conclusion the meeting adjourned.

Peter was almost out of the door when he heard his name called, and turning, saw the A.C.G. beckoning him. He went up to the table and shook hands.

"Do you know the Professor?" asked his superior. "Professor, this is Mr. Graham."

"How do you do?" said the man of science. "You are Graham of Balliol, aren't you? You read Political Science and Economics a little at Oxford, I think? You ought to be the very man for us, especially as you know how to speak."

Peter was confused, but, being human, a little flattered. He confessed to the sins enumerated, and waited for more.

"Well," said the A.C.G., "I've sent in your name already, Graham, and they want you to go to Abbeville for a few weeks. A gathering is to be made there of the more promising material, and you are to get down to the work of making a syllabus, and so on. You will meet other officers from all branches of the Service, and it should be interesting and useful. I presume you will be willing to go? Of course it is entirely optional, but I may say that the men who volunteer will not be forgotten."

"Quite so," said the Professor. "They will render extremely valuable service. I shall hope to be there part of the time myself."

Peter thought quickly of a number of things, as one does at such a moment. Some of them were serious things, and some quite frivolous—like Julie. But he could hardly do otherwise than consent. He asked when he should have to go.

"In a few days. You'll have plenty of time to get ready. I should advise you to write for some books, and begin to read up a little, for I expect you are a bit rusty, like the rest of us. And I shall hope to have you back lecturing in this Army area before long."

So to speak, bowed out, Peter made his way home. In the Rue de Paris Julie passed him, sitting with a couple of other nurses in an ambulance motor-lorry, and she waved her hand to him. The incident served to depress him still more, and he was a bit petulant as he entered the mess. He flung his cap on the table, and threw himself into a chair.

"Well," said Pennell, who was there, "on the peg all right?"

"Don't be a fool!" said Peter sarcastically. "I'm wanted on the Staff. Haig can't manage without me. I've got to leave this perishing suburb and skip up to H.Q., and don't you forget it, old dear. I shall probably be a Major-General before you get your third pip. Got that?"

Pennell took his pipe from his mouth. "What's in the wind now?" he demanded.

"Well, you might not have noticed it, but I'm a political and economic expert, and Haig's fed up that you boys don't tumble to the wisdom of the centuries as you ought. Consequently I've got to instruct you. I'm going to waltz around in a motor-car, probably with tabs up, and lecture. And there aren't to be any questions asked, for that's subversive of discipline."

"Good Lord, man, do talk sense! What in the world do you mean?"

"I mean jolly well what I say, if you want to know, or something precious like it. The blinking Army's got dry-rot and revolutionary fever, and we may all be murdered in our little beds unless I put a shoulder to the wheel. That's a bit mixed, but it'll stand. I shall be churning out this thing by the yard in a little."

"Any extra pay?" demanded Pennell anxiously. "I can lecture on engineering, and would do for an extra sixpence. Whisky's going up, and I haven't paid my last mess bill."

"You haven't, old son," said Arnold, coming in, "and you've jolly well got to. Here's a letter for you, Graham."

Peter glanced at the envelope and tore it open. Pennell knocked his pipe out with feigned dejection. "The fellow makes me sick, padre," he said. "He gets billets-doux every hour of the blessed day."

Peter jumped up excitedly. "This is better," he said. "It's a letter from Langton at Rouen, a chap I met there who writes occasionally. He's been hauled in for this stunt himself, and is to go to Abbeville as well. By Jove, I'll go up with him if I can. Give me some paper, somebody. I'll have to write to him at once, or we'll boss it."

"And make a will, and write to a dozen girls, I should think," said Pennell. "I don't know what the blooming Army's coming to. Might as well chuck it and have peace, I think. But meantime I've got to leave you blighted slackers to gad about the place, and go and do an honest day's work. *I* don't get Staff jobs and red tabs. No; I help win the ruddy war, that's all. See you before you go, Graham, I suppose? They'll likely run the show for a day or two more without you. There'll be time for you to stand a dinner on the strength of it yet."

A week later Peter met Langton by appointment in the Rouen club, the two of them being booked to travel that evening via Amiens to Abbeville. His tall friend was drinking a whisky-and-soda in the smoke-room and talking with a somewhat bored expression to no less a person than Jenks of the A.S.C.

Peter greeted them. "Hullo!" he said to the latter. "Fancy meeting you here again. Don't say you're going to lecture as well?"

"The good God preserve us!" exclaimed Jenks blasphemously. "But I am off in your train to Boulogne. Been transferred to our show there, and between ourselves, I'm not sorry to go. It's a decent hole in some ways, Boulogne, and it's time I got out of Rouen. You're a lucky man, padre, not to be led into temptation by every damned girl you meet. I don't know what they see in me," he continued mournfully, "and, at this hour of the afternoon, I don't know what I see in them."

"Nor do I," said Langton. "Have a drink, Graham? There'll be no getting anything on the ruddy train. We leave at six-thirty, and get in somewhere about four a.m. next morning, so far as I can make out."

"You don't sound over-cheerful," said Graham.

"I'm not. I'm fed up over this damned lecture stunt! The thing's condemned to failure from the start, and at any rate it's no time for it. Fritz means more by this push than the idiots about here allow. He may not get through; but, on the other hand, he may. If he does, it's UP with us all. And here we are to go lecturing on economics and industrial problems while the damned house is on fire!"

Peter took his drink and sat down. "What's your particular subject?" he asked.

"The Empire. Colonies. South Africa. Canada. And why? Because I took a degree in History in Cambridge, and have done surveying on the C.P.R. Lor'! Finish that drink and have another."

They went together to the station, and got a first to themselves, in which they were fortunate. They spread their kit about the place, suborned an official to warn everyone else off, and then Peter and Langton strolled up and down the platform for half an hour, as the train was not now to start till seven. Somebody told them there was a row on up the line, though it was not plain how that would affect them. Jenks departed on business of his own. A girl lived somewhere in the neighbourhood.

"How're you getting on now, padre?" asked Langton.

"I'm not getting on," said Peter. "I'm doing my job as best I can, and I'm seeing all there is to see, but I'm more in a fog than ever. I've got a hospital at Havre, and I distribute cigarettes and the news of the day. That's about all. I get on all right with the men socially, and now and again I meet a keen Nonconformist who wants me to pray with him, or an Anglican who wants Holy Communion, but not many. When I preach I rebuke vice, as the Apostle says, but I'm hanged if I really know why."

Langton laughed. "That's a little humorous, padre," he said. "What about the Ten Commandments?"

Peter thought of Julie. He kicked a stone viciously. "Commandments are no use," he said—"not out here."

"Nor anywhere," said Langton, "nor ever, I think, too. Why do you suppose I keep moderately moral? Chiefly because I fear natural consequences and have a wife and kiddies that I love. Why does Jenks do the opposite? Because he's more of a fool or less of a coward, and chiefly loves himself. That's all, and that's all there is in it for most of us."

"You don't fear God at all, then?" demanded Peter.

"Oh that I knew where I might find him!" quoted Langton. "I don't believe He thundered on Sinai, at any rate."

"Nor spoke in the Sermon on the Mount?"

"Ah, I'm not so sure but it seems to me that He said too much or He said too little there, Graham. One can't help 'looking on' a woman occasionally. And in any case it doesn't seem to me that the Sermon is anything like the Commandments. Brotherly love is behind the first, fear of a tribal God behind the second. So far as I can see, Christ's creed was to love and to go on loving and never to despair of love. Love, according to Him, was stronger than hate, or commandments or preaching, or the devil himself. If He saved souls at all, He saved them by loving them whatever they were, and I reckon He meant us to do the same. What do you make of the woman taken in adultery, and the woman who wiped His feet with her hair? Or of Peter? or of Judas? He saved Peter by loving him when he thought he ought to have the Ten Commandments and hell fire thrown at his head and I reckon He'd have saved Judas by giving him that sop-token of love if he hadn't had a soul that could love nothing but himself."

"What is love, Langton?" asked Peter, after a pause.

The other looked at him curiously, and laughed. "Ask the Bishops," he said. "Don't ask me. I don't know. Living with the woman to whom you're married because you fear to leave her, or because you get on all right, is not love at any rate. I can't see that marriage has got much to do with it. It's a decent convention of society at this stage of development perhaps, and it may sign and seal love for some people. But I reckon love's love—a big positive thing that's bigger than sin, and bigger than the devil. I reckon that if God sees that anywhere, He's satisfied. I don't think Cranmer's marriage service affects Him much, nor the laws of the State. If a man cares to do without either, he runs a risk, of course. Society's hard on a woman, and man's meant to be a gregarious creature. But that's all there is in it."

"But how can you tell lust from love?" demanded Peter.

"You can't, I think," said Langton. "Most men can't, anyway. Women may do, but I don't know. I reckon that what they lust after mostly is babies and a home. I don't think they know it any more than men know that what they're after is the gratification of a passion; but there it is. We're sewer rats crawling up a damned long drain, if you ask me, padre! I don't know who said it, but it's true."

They turned in their walk, and Peter looked out over the old town. In the glow of sunset the thin iron modern spire of the cathedral had a grace not its own, and the roofs below it showed strong and almost sentient. One could imagine that the distant cathedral brooding over the city heard, saw, and spoke, if in another language than the language of men.

"If that were all, Langton," said Peter suddenly, "I'd shoot myself."

"You're a queer fellow, Graham," said Langton. "I almost think you might. I'd like to know what becomes of you, anyway. Forgive me—I don't mean to be rude—but you may make a parson yet. But don't found a new religion for Heaven's sake, and don't muddle up man-made laws and God-made instincts—if they are God-made," he added.

Peter said nothing, until they were waiting at the carriage-door for Jenks. Then he said: "Then you think out here men have simply abandoned conventions, and because there is no authority or fear or faith left to them, they do as they please?"

Langton settled himself in a corner. "Yes," he said, "that's right in a way. But that's negatively. I'd go farther than that. Of course, there are a lot of Judas Iscariots about for whom I shouldn't imagine the devil himself has much time, though I suppose we ought not to judge 'em, but there are also a lot of fine fellows—and fine women. They are men and women, if I understand it, who have sloughed off the conventions, that are conventions simply for convention's sake, and who are reaching out towards the realities. Most of them haven't an idea what those are, but dumbly they know. Tommy knows, for instance, who is a good chum and who isn't; that is, he knows that sincerity and unselfishness and pluck are realities. He doesn't care a damn if a chap drinks and swears and commits what the Statute-Book and the Prayer-Book call fornication. And he certainly doesn't think there is an ascending scale of sins, or at any rate that you parsons have got the scale right."

"I shouldn't be surprised if we haven't," said Peter. "The Bible lumps liars and drunkards and murderers and adulterers and dogs—whatever that may mean—into hell altogether."

"That's so," said Langton, sticking a candle on the window-sill; "but I reckon that's not so much because they lie or drink or murder or lust or— or grin about the city like our friend Jenks, who'll likely miss the boat for that very reason, but because of something else they all have in common."

"What's that?" demanded Peter.

"I haven't the faintest idea," said Langton.

At this moment the French guard, an R.T.O., and Jenks appeared in sight simultaneously, the two former urging the latter along. He caught sight of them, and waved.

"Help him in," said the R.T.O., a jovial-looking subaltern, genially—"and keep him there," he added under his voice. "He's had all he can carry, and if he gets loose again he'll be for the high jump. The wonder is he ever got back in time."

Peter helped him up. The subaltern glanced at his badges and smiled. "He's in good company anyway, padre," he said. "If you're leaving the ninety-and-nine in the wilderness, here's one to bring home rejoicing." He slammed the door. "Right-o!" he said to the guard; "they're all aboard now." The man comprehended the action, and waved a flag. The train started after the manner of French trains told off for the use of British soldiers, and Jenks collapsed on the seat.

"Damned near thing that!" he said unsteadily; "might have missed the bloody boat! I saw my little bit, though. She's a jolly good sort, she is. Blasted strong stuff that French brandy, though! Whiskies at the club first, yer know. Give us a hand, padre; I reckon I'll just lie down a bit.... Jolly good sort of padre, eh, skipper? What?"

Peter helped him into his place, and then came and sat at his feet, opposite Langton, who smiled askance at him. "I'll read a bit," he said. "Jenks won't trouble us further; he'll sleep it off. I know his sort. Got a book, padre?"

Peter said he had, but that he wouldn't read for a little, and he sat still looking at the country as they jolted past in the dusk. After a while Langton lit his candle, and contrived a wind-screen, for the centre window was broken, of a newspaper. Peter watched him drowsily. He had been up early and travelled already that day. The motion helped, too, and in half an hour or so he was asleep.

He dreamt that he was preaching Langton's views on the Sermon on the Mount in the pulpit of St. John's, and that the Canon, from his place beside the credence-table within the altar-rails, was shouting at him to stop. In his dream he persisted, however, until that irate dignitary seized the famous and massive offertory-dish by his side and hurled it in the direction of the pulpit. The clatter that it made on the stone floor awoke him.

He was first aware that the train was no longer in motion, and next that Langton's tall form was leaning half out of the window. Then confused noises penetrated his consciousness, and he perceived that light flickered in the otherwise darkened compartment. "Where are we?" he demanded, now fully awake. "What's up?"

Langton answered over his shoulder. "Some where outside of a biggish town," he said; "and there's the devil of a strafe on. The whole sky-line's lit up, but that may be twenty miles off. However, Fritz must have advanced some."

He was interrupted by a series of much louder explosions and the rattle of machine-gun fire. "That's near," he said. "Over the town, I should say—an air-raid, though it may be long-distance firing. Come and see for yourself."

He pulled himself back into the carriage, and Peter leaned out of the window in his turn. It was as the other had said. Flares and sudden flashes, that came and went more like summer-lightning than anything else, lit up the whole sky-line, but nearer at hand a steady glow from one or two places showed in the sky. One could distinguish flights of illuminated tracer bullets, and now and again what he took to be Very lights exposed the countryside. Peter saw that they were in a siding, the banks of which reached just above the top of the compartments. It was only by craning that he could see fields and what looked like a house beyond. Men were leaning out of all the windows, mostly in silence. In the compartment next them a man cursed the Huns for spoiling his beauty sleep. It was slightly overdone, Peter thought.

"Good God!" said, his companion behind him. "Listen!"

It was difficult, but between the louder explosions Peter concentrated his senses on listening. In a minute he heard something new, a faint buzz in the air.

"Aeroplanes," said Langton coolly. "I hope they don't spot us. Let me see. Maybe it's our planes." He craned out in Peter's place. "I can't see anything," he said, "and you can hear they're flying high."

Down the train everyone was staring upwards now. "Christ!" exclaimed Langton suddenly, "some fool's lighting a pipe! Put that match out there," he called.

Other voices took him up. "That's better," he said in a minute. "Forgive my swearing, padre, but a match might give us away."

Peter was silent, and, truth to tell, terrified. He tried hard not to feel it, and glanced at Jenks. He was still asleep, and breathing heavily. He pressed his face against the pane, and tried to stare up too.

"They're coming," said Langton suddenly and quickly. "There they are, too—Hun planes. They may not see us, of course, but they may...." He brought his head in again and sat down.

"Is there anything we can do?" said Peter.

"Nothing," said Langton, "unless you like to get under the seat. But that's no real good. It's on the knees of the gods, padre, whatever gods there be."

Just then Peter saw one. Sailing obliquely towards them and lit by the light of a flare, the plane looked serene and beautiful. He watched it, fascinated.

"It's very low—two hundred feet, I should say," said Langton behind him. "Hope he's no pills left. I wonder whether there's another. Let's have a look the other side."

He had scarcely got up to cross the compartment when the rattle of a machine-gun very near broke out. "Our fellows, likely," he exclaimed excitedly, struggling with the sash, but they knew the truth almost as he spoke.

Langton ducked back. A plane on the other side was deliberately flying up the train, machine-gunning. "Down, padre, for God's sake!" he exclaimed, and threw himself on the floor.

Peter couldn't move. He heard the splintering of glass and a rending of woodwork, some oaths, and a sudden cry. The whirr of an engine filled his ears and seemed, as it were, on top of them. Then there was a crash all but at his side, and next instant a half-smothered groan and a dreadful gasp for breath.

He couldn't speak. He heard Langton say, "Hit, anyone?" and then Jenks' "They've got me, skipper," in a muffled whisper, and he noticed that the hard breathing had ceased. At that he found strength and voice and jumped up. He bent over Jenks. "Where have you got it, old man?" he said, and hardly realised that it was himself speaking.

The other was lying just as before, on his back, but he had pulled his knees up convulsively and a rug had slipped off. In a flare Peter saw beads of sweat on his forehead and a white, twisted face.

He choked back panic and knelt down. He had imagined it all before, and yet not quite like this. He knew what he ought to say, but for a minute he could not formulate it. "Where are you hit, Jenks?" was all he said.

The other turned his head a little and looked at him. "Body—lungs, I think," he whispered. "I'm done, padre; I've seen chaps before."

The words trailed off. Peter gripped himself mentally, and steadied his voice. "Jenks, old man," he said. "Just a minute. Think about God—you are going to Him, you know. Trust Him, will you? 'The blood of Jesus Christ, God's Son, saveth us from all sin.'"

The dying man, moved his hand convulsively. "Don't you worry, padre," he said faintly; "I've been—confirmed." The lips tightened a second with pain, and then: "Reckon I won't—shirk. Have you—got—a cigarette?"

Peter felt quickly for his case, fumbled and dropped one, then got another into his fingers. He hesitated a second, and then, put it to his own lips, struck a match, and puffed at it. He was in the act of holding it to the other when Langton spoke behind him:

"It's no good now, padre," he said quietly; "it's all over."

And Peter saw that it was.

The planes did not come back. The officer in charge of the train came down it with a lantern, and looked in. "That makes three," he said. "We can do nothing now, but we'll be in the station in a bit. Don't show any lights; they may come back. Where the hell were our machines, I'd like to know?"

He went on, and Peter sat down in his corner. Langton picked up the rug, and covered up the body. Then he glanced at Peter. "Here," he said, holding out a flask, "have some of this."

Peter shook his head. Langton came over to him. "You must," he said; "it'll pull you together. Don't go under now, Graham. You kept your nerve just now—come on."

At that Peter took it, and drained the little cup the other poured out for him. Then he handed it back, without a word.

"Feel better?" queried the other, a trifle curiously, staring at him.

"Yes, thanks," said Peter—"a damned sight better! Poor old Jenks! What blasted luck that he should have got it!... Langton, I wish to God it had been me!"

PART II

"And the Lord turned and looked upon Peter."
ST. LUKE'S GOSPEL.

CHAPTER I

The charm of the little towns of Northern France is very difficult to imprison on paper. It is not exactly that they are old, although there is scarcely one which has not a church or a château or a quaint medieval street worth coming far to see; nor that they are particularly picturesque, for the ground is fairly flat, and they are all but always set among the fields, since it is by agriculture far more than by manufacture that they live. But they are clean and cheerful; one thinks of them under the sun; and they are very homely. In them the folk smile simply at you, but not inquisitively as in England, for each bustles gaily about his own affairs, and will let you do what you please, with a shrug of the shoulders. Abbeville is very typical of all this. It has its church, and from the bridge over the Somme the backs of ancient houses can be seen leaning half over the river, which has sung beneath them for five hundred years; and it is set in the midst of memories of stirring days. Yet it is not for these that one would revisit the little town, but rather that one might walk by the still canal under the high trees in spring, or loiter in the market-place round what the Hun has left of the statue of the famous Admiral with his attendant nymphs, or wander down the winding streets that skirt the ancient church and give glimpses of its unfinished tower.

Peter found it very good to be there in the days that followed the death of Jenks. True, it was now nearer to the seat of war than it had been for years, and air-raids began to be common, but in a sense the sound of the guns fitted in with his mood. So great a battle was being fought within him that the world could not in any case have seemed wholly at peace, and yet in the quiet fields, or sauntering of an afternoon by the river, he found it easier than at Havre to think. Langton was almost his sole companion, and a considerable intimacy had grown up between them. Peter found that his friend seemed to understand a great deal of his thoughts without explanation. He neither condoled nor exhorted; rather he watched with an almost shy interest the other's inward battle.

They lodged at the Hôtel de l'Angleterre, that hostelry in the street that leads up and out of the town towards Saint Riquier, which you enter from a courtyard that opens on the road and has rooms that you reach by means of narrow, rickety flights of stairs and balconies overhanging the court. The big dining-room wore an air of gloomy festivity. Its chandeliers swathed in brown paper, its faded paint, and its covered upholstery, suggested that it awaited a day yet to be when it should blossom forth once more in glory as in the days of old. Till then it was as merry as it could be. Its little tables filled up of an evening with the new cosmopolitan population of the town, and old Jacques bustled round with the good wine, and dropped no hint that the choice brands were nearly at an end in the cellar.

Peter and Langton would have their war-time apology for *petit déjeuner* in bed or alone. Peter, as a rule, was up early, and used to wander out a little and sometimes into church, coming back to coffee as good as ever, but war-time bread instead of rolls on a small table under a low balcony in the courtyard if it were fine. He would linger over it, and have chance conversation with passing strangers of all sorts, from clerical personages belonging to the Church Army or the Y.M.C.A. to officers who came and went usually on unrevealed affairs. Then Langton would come down, and they would stroll round to the newly-fitted-up office which had been prepared for the lecture campaign and glance at maps of districts, and exchange news with the officer in charge, who, having done all he could, had now nothing to do but stand by and wait for the next move from a War Office that had either forgotten his existence or discovered some hitch in its plans. They had a couple of lectures from people who were alleged to know all about such topics as the food shortage at home or the new plans for housing, but who invariably turned out to be waiting themselves for the precise information that was necessary for successful lectures. After such they would stroll out through the town into the fields, and Langton would criticise the thing in lurid but humorous language, and they would come back to the club and sit or read till lunch.

The club was one of the best in France, it was an old house with lovely furniture, and not too much of it, which stood well back from the street and boasted an old-fashioned garden of shady trees and spring flowers and green lawns. Peter could both read and write in its rooms, and it was there that he finally wrote to Hilda, but not until after much thought.

After his day with Julie at Caudebec one might have supposed that there was nothing left for him to do but break off his engagement to Hilda. But it did not strike him so. For one thing, he was not engaged to Julie or anything like it, and he could not imagine such a situation, even if Julie had not positively repudiated any desire to be either engaged or married. He had certainly declared, in a fit of enthusiasm, that he loved her, but he had not asked if she loved him. He had seen her since, but although they were very good friends, nothing more exciting had passed between them. Peter was conscious that when he was with Julie she fascinated him, but that when he was away—ah! that was it, when he was away? It certainly was not that Hilda came back and took her place; it was rather that the other things in his mind dominated him. It was a curious state of affairs. He was less like an orthodox parson than he had ever been, and yet he had never thought so much about religion. He agonised over it now. At times his thoughts were almost more than he could bear.

It came, then, to this, that he had not so much changed towards Hilda as changed towards life. Whether he had really fundamentally changed in such a way that a break with the old was inevitable he did not know. Till then Hilda was part of the old, and if he went back to it she naturally took her old place in it. If he did not—well, there he invariably came to the end of thought. Curiously enough, it was when faced with a mental blank that Julie's image began to rise in his mind. If he admitted her, he found himself abandoning himself to her. He felt sometimes that if he could but take her in his arms he could let the world go by, and God with it. Her kisses were at least a reality. There was neither convention nor subterfuge nor divided allegiance there. She was passion, naked and unashamed, and at least real.

And then he would remember that much of this was problematical after all, for they had never kissed as that passion demanded, or at least that he had never so kissed her. He was not sure of the first. He knew that he did not understand Julie, but he felt, if he did kiss her, it would be a kiss of surrender, of finality. He feared to look beyond that, and he could not if he would.

He wrote, then, to Hilda, and he told of the death of Jenks, and of their arrival in Abbeville, "You must understand, dear," he said, "that all this has had a tremendous effect upon me. In that train all that I had begun to feel about the uselessness of my old religion came to a head. I could do no more for that soul than light a cigarette.... Possibly no one could have done any more, but I cannot, I will not believe it. Jenks was not fundamentally evil, or at least I don't think so. He was rather a selfish fool who had no control, that is all. He did not serve the devil; it was much more that he had never seen any master to serve. And I could do nothing. I had no master to show him.

"You may say that that is absurd: that Christ is my Master, and I could have shown Him. Hilda, so He is: I cling passionately to that. But listen: I can't express Him, I don't understand Him. I no longer feel that He was animating and ordering the form of religion I administered. It is not that I feel Anglicanism to be untrue, and something else—say Wesleyanism—to be true; it is much more that I feel them all to be out of touch with reality. *That's* it. I don't think you can possibly see it, but that is the main trouble.

"That, too, brings me to my next point, and this I find harder still to express. I want you to realise that I feel as if I had never seen life before. I feel as if I had been shown all my days a certain number of pictures and told that they were the real thing, or given certain descriptions and told that they were true. I had always accepted that they were. But, Hilda, they are not. Wickedness is not wicked in the way that I was told it was wicked, and what I was told was salvation is not the salvation men and women want. I have been playing in a fool's paradise all these years, and I've got outside the gate. I am distressed and terrified, I think, but underneath it all I am very glad....

"You will say, 'What are you going to do?' and I can only reply, I don't know. I'm not going to make any vast change, if you mean that. A padre I am, and a padre I shall stay for the war at least, and none of us can see beyond that at present. But what I do mean to do is just this: I mean to try and get down to reality myself and try to weigh it up. I am going to eat and drink with publicans and sinners; maybe I shall find my Master still there."

Peter stopped and looked up. Langton was stretched out in a chair beside him, reading a novel, a pipe in his mouth. Moved by an impulse, he interrupted him.

"Old man," he said, "I want you to let me read you a bit of this letter. It's to my girl, but there's nothing rotten in reading it. May I?"

Langton did not move. "Carry on," he said shortly.

Peter finished and put down the sheet. The other smoked placidly and said nothing. "Well?" demanded Peter impatiently.

"I should cut out that last sentence," pronounced the judge.

"Why? It's true."

"Maybe, but it isn't pretty."

"Langton," burst out Peter, "I'm sick of prettinesses! I've been stuffed up with them all my life, and so has she. I want to break with them."

"Very likely, and I don't say that it won't be the best thing for you to try for a little to do so, but she hasn't been where you've been or seen what you've seen. You can't expect her wholly to understand. And more than that, maybe she is meant for prettinesses. After all, they're pretty."

Peter stabbed the blotting-paper with his pen. "Then she isn't meant for me," he said.

"I'm not so sure," said Langton. "I don't know that you've stuff enough in you to get on without those same prettinesses yourself. Most of us haven't. And at any rate I wouldn't burn my boats yet awhile. You may want to escape yet."

Peter considered this in silence. Then he drew the sheets to him and added a few more words, folded the paper, put it in the envelope, and stuck it down. "Come on," he said, "let's go and post this and have a walk."

Langton got up and looked at him curiously, as he sometimes did. "Peter," he said, "you're a weird blighter, but there's something damned gritty in you. You take life too strenuously. Why can't you saunter through it like I do?"

Peter reached for this cap. "Come on," he said again, "and don't talk rot."

Out in the street, they strolled aimlessly on, more or less in silence. The big book-shop at the corner detained them for a little, and they regarded its variegated contents through the glass. It contained a few good prints, and many more poorly executed coloured pictures of ruined places in France and Belgium, of which a few, however, were not bad. Cheek by jowl with some religious works, a statue of Notre Dame d'Albert, and some more of Jeanne d'Arc, were a line of pornographic novels and beyond packets of picture post-cards entitled *Théâtreuses, Le Bain de la Parisienne, Les Seins des Marbre,* and so on. Then Langton drew Graham's attention to one or two other books, one of which had a gaudy cover representing a mistress with a birch-rod in her hands and a number of canes hung up beside her, while a girl of fifteen or so, with very red cheeks, was apparently about to be whipped. "Good Lord," said Langton, "the French are beyond me. This window is a study for you, Graham, in itself. I should take it that it means that there is nothing real in life. It is utterly cynical.

"'And if the Wine you drink, the Lip you press,
End in what All begins and ends in—Yes;
Think then you are To-day what Yesterday
You were—To-morrow you shall not be less,'"

he quoted.

"Yes," said Peter. "Or else it means that there are only two realities, and that the excellent person who keeps this establishment regards both in a detached way, and conceives it her business to cater for each. Let's go on."

They turned the corner, and presently found themselves outside the famous carven door of the church. "Have you ever been round?" asked Peter.

"No," said Langton; "let's go in."

They passed through the door into the old church, which, in contrast to that at Le Havre, was bathed in the daylight that streamed through many clear windows. Together they wandered round it, saying little. They inspected an eighteenth-century statue of St. Roch, who was pulling up his robe to expose a wound and looking upwards at the same time seraphically—or, at least, after the manner that the artist of that age had regarded as seraphic. A number of white ribbons and some wax figures of feet and hands and other parts of the body were tied to him. They stood before a wonderful coloured alabaster reredos of the fourteenth century, in which shepherds and kings and beasts came to worship at the manger. They had a little conversation as to the architectural periods of the nave, choir, and transepts, and Langton was enthusiastic over a noble pillar and arch. Beyond they gazed in silence at a statue of Our Lady Immaculate in modern coloured plaster, so arranged that the daylight fell through an unseen opening upon her. Among the objects in front were a pair of Renaissance candlesticks of great beauty. A French officer came up and arranged and lit a votive candle as they watched, and then went back to stand in silence by a pillar. The church door banged and two peasants came in, one obviously from the market, with a huge basket of carrots and cabbages and some long, thin French loaves. She deposited this just inside the door, took holy water, clattered up towards the high altar, dropped a curtsy, and made her way to an altar of the Sacred Heart, at which she knelt. Peter sighed. "Come on," he said; "let's get out."

Langton marched on before him, and held the door back as they stepped into the street. "Well, philosopher," he demanded, "what do you make of that?"

Peter smiled. "What do you?" he said.

"Well," said Langton, "it leaves me unmoved, except when I'm annoyed by the way their wretched images spoil the church, but it is plain that they like it. I should say one of your two realities is there. But I find it hard to forgive the bad art."

"Do you?" said Peter, "I don't. It reminds me of those appalling enlargements of family groups that you see, for example, in any Yorkshire cottage. They are unutterably hideous, but they stand for a real thing that is honest and beautiful—the love of home and family. And by the same token, when the photographs got exchanged, as they do in Mayfair, for modern French pictures of nude women, or some incredible Futurist extravagance, that love has usually flown out of the window."

"Humph!" said Langton—"not always. Besides, why can't a family group be made artistically, and so keep both art and love? I should think we ought to aim at that."

"I suppose we ought," said Peter, "but in our age the two don't seem to go together. Goodness alone knows why. Why, hullo!" he broke off.

"What's up now?" demanded Langton.

"Why, there, across the street, if that isn't a nurse I know from Havre, I don't know who it is. Wait a tick."

He crossed the road, and saw, as he got near, that it was indeed Julie. He came up behind her as she examined a shop-window. "By all that's wonderful, what are you doing here?" he asked.

She turned quickly, her eyes dancing. "I wondered if I should meet you," she said. "You see, your letter told me you were coming here, but I haven't heard from you since you came, and I didn't know if you had started your tour or not. *I* came simply enough. There's a big South African hospital here, and we had to send up a batch of men by motor. As they knew I was from South Africa, they gave me the chance to come with them."

"Well, I *am* glad," said Peter, devouring the sight of her. "Wait a minute; I must introduce you to Langton. He and I are together, and he's a jolly good chap."

He turned and beckoned Langton, who came over and was introduced. They walked up the street a little way together. "Where are you going now?" asked Peter.

"Back to the hospital," said Julie. "A car starts from the square at twelve-forty-five, and I have to be in for lunch."

"Have you much to do up there?" asked Peter.

"Oh no," she said, "my job's done. I clear off the day after to-morrow. We only got in last night, so I get a couple of days' holiday. What are you doing? You don't look any too busy."

Peter glanced across at Langton and laughed. "We aren't," he said. "The whole stunt's a wash-out, if you ask me, and we're really expecting to be sent back any day. There's too much doing now for lectures. Is the hospital full?"

"Packed," said Julie gravely. "The papers say we're falling back steadily so as not to lose men, but the facts don't bear it out. We're crammed out. It's ghastly; I've never known it so bad."

Peter had hardly ever seen her grave before, and her face showed a new aspect of her. He felt a glow of warmth steal over him. "I say," he said, "couldn't you dine with us to-night? We're at the Angleterre, and its tremendously respectable."

She laughed, her gravity vanishing in a minute. "I must say," she said, "that I'd love to see you anywhere really respectable. He's a terrible person for a padre—don't you think so, Captain Langton?"

"Terrible," said Langton. "But really the Angleterre is quite proper. You don't get any too bad a dinner, either. Do come, Miss Gamelyn."

She appeared to consider. "I might manage it," she said at last, stopping just short of entering the square; "but I haven't the nerve to burst in and ask for you. Nor will it do for you to see me all the way to that car, or we shall have a dozen girls talking. If you will meet me somewhere," she added, looking at Peter, "I'll risk it. I'll have a headache and not go to first dinner; then the first will think I'm at the second, and the second at the first. Besides, I've no duty, and the hospital's not like Havre. It's all spread out in huts and tents, and it's easy enough to get in. Last, but not least, it's Colonial, and the matron is a brick. Yes, I'll come."

"Hurrah!" said Peter. "I tell you what: I'll meet you at the cross-roads below the hospital and bring you on. Will that do? What time? Five-thirty?"

"Heavens! do you dine at five-thirty?" demanded Julie.

"Well, not quite, but we've got to get down," said Peter, laughing.

"All right," said Julie, "five-thirty, and the saints preserve us. Look here, I shall chance it and come in mufti if possible. No one knows me here."

"Splendid!" said Peter. "Good-bye, five-thirty."

"Good-bye," said Langton; "we'll go and arrange our menu."

"There must be champagne," called Julie merrily over her shoulder, and catching his eye.

The two men watched her make for the car across the sunlit square, then they strolled round it towards a café. "Come on," said Langton; "let's have an appetiser."

From the little marble-topped table Peter watched the car drive away. Julie was laughing over something with another girl. It seemed to conclude the morning, somehow. He raised his glass and looked at Langton.
"Well," he said, "here's to reality, wherever it is."

"And here's to getting along without too much of it," said Langton, smiling at him.

* * * * *

The dinner was a great success—at least, in the beginning. Julie wore a frock of some soft brown stuff, and Peter could hardly keep his eyes off her. He had never seen her out of uniform before, and although she was gay enough, she said and did nothing very exciting. If Hilda had been there she need hardly have behaved differently, and for a while Peter was wholly delighted. Then it began to dawn on him that she was playing up to Langton, and that set in train irritating thoughts. He watched the other jealously, and noticed how the girl drew him out to speak of his travels, and how excellently he did it, leaning back at coffee with his cigarette, polite, pleasant, attractive. Julie, who usually smoked cigarette after cigarette furiously, only, however, getting through about half of each, now refused a second, and glanced at the clock about 8.30.

"Oh," she said, "I must go."

Peter remonstrated. "If you can stay out later at Havre," he said, "why not here?"

She laughed lightly. "I'm reforming," she said, "in the absence of bad companions. Besides, they are used to my being later at Havre, but here I might be spotted, and then there would be trouble. Would you fetch my coat, Captain Graham?"

Peter went obediently, and they all three moved out into the court.

"Come along and see her home, Langton," he said, though he hardly knew why he included the other.

"Thanks," said his friend; "but if Miss Gamelyn will excuse me, I ought not. I've got some reading I must do for to-morrow, and I want to write a letter or two as well. You'll be an admirable escort, Graham."

"Good-night," said Julie, holding out her hand; "perhaps we shall meet again some time. One is always running up against people in France. And thank you so much for your share of the entertainment."

In a few seconds Peter and she were outside. The street was much darkened, and there was no moon. They walked in silence for a little. Suddenly he stopped. "Wouldn't you like a cab?" he said; "we might be able to get one."

Julie laughed mischievously, and Peter gave a little start in the dark. It struck him that this was the old laugh and that he had not heard it that night before. "It's convenient, of course," she said mockingly. "Do get one by all means. But last time I came home with you in a cab, you let me finish alone. I thought that was to be an invariable rule."

"Oh, don't Julie," said Peter.

Her tone changed. "Why not?" she demanded. "Solomon, what's made you so glum to-night? You were cheerful enough when you met me, and when we began; then you got silent. What's the matter?"

"Nothing," he said.

She slipped her hand in his arm. "There is something," she said. "Do tell me."

"Do you like Langton?" he asked.

"Oh, immensely—why? Oh, Lord, Solomon, what do you mean?"

"You were different in his presence, Julie, from anything you've been before."

They took a few paces in silence; then Peter had an idea, and glanced at her. She was laughing silently to herself. He let her hand fall from his arm, and looked away. He knew he was behaving like an ass, but he could not help it.

She stopped suddenly. "Peter," she said, "I want to talk to you. Take me somewhere where it's possible."

"At this hour of the evening? What about being late?"

She gave a little stamp with her foot, then laughed again. "What a boy it is!" she said. "Don't you know anywhere to go?"

Peter hesitated; then he made up his mind. There was an hotel he knew of, out of the main street, of none too good a reputation. Some men had taken Langton and him there, once, in the afternoon, between the hours in which drinks were legally sold, and they had gone through the hall into a little back-room that was apparently partly a sitting-room, partly part of the private rooms of the landlord, and had been served there. He recalled the description of one of the men: "It's a place to know. You can always get a drink, and take in anyone you please."

"Come on, then," he said, and turned down a back-street.

"Where in the world are you taking me?" demanded Julie. "I shall have no reputation left if this gets out."

"Nor shall I," said Peter.

"Nor you will; what a spree! Do you think it's worth it, Peter?"

Under a shaded lamp they were passing at the moment, he glanced at her, and his pulses raced! "Good God, Julie!" he said, "you could do anything with me."

She chuckled with laughter, her brown eyes dancing. "Maybe," she said, "but I'm out to talk to you for your good now."

They turned another corner, into an old street, and under an arch. Peter walked forward to the hotel entrance, and entered. There was a woman in the office, who glanced up, and looked, first at Peter, then at Julie. On seeing her behind him, she came forward. "What can I do for monsieur?" she asked.

"Good-evening, madame," said Peter. "I was here the other day. Give us a bottle of wine in that little room at the back, will you?"

"Why, certainly, monsieur," said she. "Will madame follow me? It is this way."

She opened, the door, and switched on the light, "Shall I light the fire, madame?" she demanded.

Julie beamed on her. "Ah, yes; that would be jolly," she said. "And the wine, madame—Beaune."

The woman smiled and bowed. "Let madame but seat herself and it shall come," she said, and went out.

Julie took off her hat, and walked to the glass, patting her hair. "Give me a cigarette, my dear," she said. "It was jolly hard only to smoke one to-night."

Peter opened and handed her his case in silence, then pulled up a big chair. There was a knock at the door, and a girl came in with the wine and glasses, which she set on the table, and, then knelt down to light the fire. She withdrew and shut the door. They were alone.

Peter was still standing. Julie glanced at him, and pointed to a chair opposite. "Give me a drink, and then go and sit there," she said.

He obeyed. She pulled her skirts up high to the blaze and pushed one foot out to the logs, and sat there, provocative, sipping her wine and puffing little puffs of smoke from her cigarette. "Now, then," she said, "what did I do wrong to-night?"

Peter was horribly uncomfortable. He felt how little he knew this girl, and he felt also how much he loved her.

"Nothing, dear," he said; "I was a beast."

"Well," she said, "if you won't tell me, I'll tell you. I was quite proper to-night, immensely and intensely proper, and you didn't like it. You had never seen me so. You thought, too, that I was making up to your friend. Isn't that so?"

Peter nodded. He marvelled that she should know so well, and he wondered what was coming.

"I wonder what you really think of me, Peter," she went on. "I suppose you think I never can be serious—no, I won't say serious—conventional. But you're very stupid; we all of us can be, and must be sometimes. You asked me just now what I thought of your friend—well, I'll tell you. He is as different from you as possible. He has his thoughts, no doubt, but he prefers to be very tidy. He takes refuge in the things you throw overboard.

He's not at all my sort, and he's not yours either, in a way. Goodness knows what will happen to either of us, but he'll be Captain Langton to the end of his days. I envy that sort of person intensely, and when I meet him I put on armour. See?"

Peter stared at her. "How is he different from Donovan?" he asked.

"Donovan! Oh, Lord, Peter, how dull you are! Donovan has hardly a thought in his head about anything except Donovan. He was born a jolly good sort, and he's sampled pretty well everything. He's cool as a cucumber, though he has his passions like everyone else. If you keep your head, you can say or do anything with Donovan. But Langton is deliberate. He knows about things, and he refuses and chooses. I didn't want ..." She broke off. "Peter," she said savagely, "in two minutes that man would know more about me than you do, if I let him."

He had never seen her so. The childish brown eyes had a look in them that reminded him of an animal caught in a trap. He sprang up and dropped on his knees by her side, catching her hand.

"Oh, Julie, don't," he said. "What do you mean? What is there about you that I don't know? How are you different from either of them?"

She threw her cigarette away, and ran her fingers through his hair, then made a gesture, almost as if pushing something away, Peter thought, and laughed her old ringing trill of laughter.

"Lor', Peter, was I tragic? I didn't mean to be, my dear. There's a lot about me that you don't know, but something that you've guessed. I can't abide shams and conventions really. Let's have life, I say, whatever it is. Heavens! I've seen street girls with more in them than I pretended to your friend to have in me to-night. They at least deal with human nature in the raw. But that's why I love you; there's no need to pretend to you, partly because, at bottom, you like real things as much as I, and partly because—oh, never mind."

"Julie, I do mind—tell me," he insisted.

Her face changed again. "Not now, Peter," she said. "Perhaps one day—who can say? Meantime, go on liking me, will you?"

"Like you!" he exclaimed, springing up, "Why, I adore you! I love you! Oh, Julie, I love you! Kiss me, darling, now, quick!"

She pushed him off. "Not now," she cried; "I've got to have my revenge. I know why you wouldn't come home in the cab! Come! we'll clink glasses, but that's all there is to be done to-night!" She sprang up, flushed and glowing, and held out an empty glass.

Peter filled hers and his, and they stood opposite to each other. She looked across the wine at him, and it seemed to him that he read a longing and a passion in her eyes, deep down below the merriness that was there now. "Cheerio, old boy," she said, raising hers. "And 'here's to the day when your big boots and my little shoes lie outside the same closed door!'"

"Julie!" he said, "you don't mean it!"

"Don't I? How do you know, old sober-sides. Come, buck up, Solomon; we've been sentimental long enough. I'd like to go to a music-hall now or do a skirt-dance. But neither's really possible; certainly not the first, and you'd be shocked at the second. I'm half a mind to shock you, though, only my skirt's not long and wide enough, and I've not enough lace underneath. I'll spare you. Come on!"

She seized her hat and put it on. They went out into the hall. There was a man in uniform there, at the office, and a girl, French and unmistakable, who glanced at Julie, and then turned away. Julie nodded to madame, and did not glance at the man, but as she passed the girl she said distinctly, "Bon soir, mademoiselle." The girl started and turned towards her. Julie smiled sweetly and passed on.

Peter took her arm in the street, for it was quite dark and deserted.

"Why did you do that?" he said.

"What?" she demanded.

"Speak to that girl. You know what she is?"

"I do—a poor devil that's playing with Fate for the sake of a laugh and a bit of ribbon. I'm jolly sorry for her, for they are both worth a great deal, and it's hard to be cheated into thinking you've got them when Fate is really winning the deal. And I saw her face before she turned away. Why do you think she turned away, Peter? Not because she was ashamed, but because she is beginning to know that Fate wins. Oh, la! la! what a world! Let's be more cheerful. *There's a long, long trail a-winding.*" she hummed.

Peter laughed. "Oh, my dear," he said, "was there ever anyone like you?"

Langton was reading in his room when Peter looked in to say good-night.

"Hullo!" he said. "See her home?"

"Yes," said Peter. "What did you think of her?"

"She's fathoms deep, I should say. But I should take care if I were you, my boy. It's all very well to eat and drink with publicans and sinners, though, as I told you, it's better no one should know. But they are dangerous company."

"Why especially?" demanded Peter.

Langton stretched himself. "Oh, I don't know," he said. "Perhaps because society's agin 'em."

"Look here, Langton," said Peter. "Do you hear what I say? *Damn* society! Besides, do you think your description applies to that girl?"

Langton smiled. "No," he said, "I shouldn't think so, but she's not your sort, Peter. When you take that tunic off, you've got to put on a black coat. Whatever conclusions you come to, don't forget that."

"Have I?" said Peter; "I wonder."

Langton got up. "Of course you have," he said. "Life's a bit of a farce, but one's got to play it. See here, I believe in facing facts and getting one's eyes open, but not in making oneself a fool. Nothing's worth that."

"Isn't it?" said Peter; and again, "I wonder."

"Well, I don't, and at any rate I'm for bed. Good-night."

"Good-night," said Peter; "I'm off too. But I don't agree with you. I'm inclined to think exactly the opposite—that anything worth having is worth making oneself a fool over. What is a fool, anyway? Good-night."

He closed the door, and Langton walked over to the window to open it. He stood there a few minutes listening to the silence. Then a cock crew somewhere, and was answered far away by another. "Yes," said Langton to himself, "what is a fool, anyway?"

CHAPTER II

The Lessing family sat at dinner, and it was to be observed that some of those incredible wonders at which Peter Graham had once hinted to Hilda had come about. There were only three courses, and Mr. Lessing had but one glass of wine, for one thing; for another he was actually in uniform, and was far more proud of his corporal's stripes than he had previously been of his churchwarden's staff of office. Nor was he only in the Volunteers; he was actually in training to some extent, and the war had at any rate done him good. His wife was not dressed for dinner either; she had just come in from a war committee of some sort. A solitary maid waited on them, and they had already given up fires in the dining-room. Not that Mr. Lessing's income had appreciably diminished, but, quite honestly, he and his were out to win the war. He had come to the conclusion at last that business could not go on as usual, but, routed out of that stronghold, he had made for himself another. The war was now to him a business. He viewed it in that light.

"We must stop them," he was saying. "Mark my words, they'll never get to Amiens. Did you see Haig's last order to the troops? Not another inch was to be given at any cost. We shan't give either. We've *got* to win this war; there's too much at stake for us to lose. Whoever has to foot the bill for this business is ruined, and it's not going to be Great Britain. They were saying in the Hall to-night that the Army is as cheerful as possible: that's the best sign. I doubt the German Army is. Doesn't Graham say anything about it, Hilda?"

"No, father," said Hilda shortly, and bent over her plate.

"'Xtraordinary thing. He's a smart chap, and I should have thought he'd have been full of it. Perhaps he's too far back."

"He was in a big town he doesn't name the other day, in an air-raid, and a man was killed in his carriage."

"Good Lord! you don't say so? When did you hear that? I thought we had command of the air."

"I got a letter to-night, father. He just mentioned that, but he doesn't say much else about it. He's at Abbeville now, on the Somme, and he says the Germans come over fairly often by night."

"Impossible!" snorted the old man, "I have it on the best possible authority that our air service is completely up to date now, and far better than the

German. He must be exaggerating. They would never allow the enemy to out-distance us in so important a department. What else does he say?"

"Oh, nothing;" said Hilda, "or at least nothing about the war in a way. It's full of—of his work." She stopped abruptly.

"Well, well," said Mr. Lessing, "I was against his going at first; but it's all shoulders to the wheel now, and it was plain he ought to see a little life out there. A young man who doesn't won't have much of a look in afterwards—that's how *I* reasoned it. And he works hard, does Graham; I've always said that for him, I expect he's of great service to them. Eh, Hilda?"

"I don't know," said the girl; "he doesn't say. But he's been chosen for some special work, lecturing or something, and that's why he's at Abbeville."

"Ah! Good! Special work, eh? He'll go far yet, that fellow. I don't know that I'd have chosen him for you, Hilda, at first, but this business has shaken us all up, and I shouldn't be surprised if Graham comes to the front over it." He stopped as the maid came in, "I think I'll have my coffee in the study, my dear," he said to Mrs. Lessing; "I have some reading to do."

When the two women were once more alone Mrs. Lessing put her cup down, and spoke. "What is it, dear?" she questioned.

Hilda did not look at her. The two, indeed, understood each other very well. "I can't tell you here, mother," she said.

"Come, then, dear," said Mrs. Lessing, rising. "Let's go to my room. Your father will be busy for some time, and we shall not be disturbed there."

She led the way, and lit a small gas fire. "I can't be cold in my bedroom," she said; "and though I hate these things, they are better than nothing. Now, dear, what is it?"

Hilda seated herself on a footstool on the other side of the fire, and stared into it. The light shone on her fair skin and hair, and Mrs. Lessing contemplated her with satisfaction from several points of view. For one thing, Hilda was so sensible....

"What is it?" she asked again. "Your father saw nothing—men don't; but you can't hide from me, dear, that your letter has troubled you. Is Peter in trouble?"

Hilda shook her head. Then she said: "Well, at least, mother, not that sort of trouble. I told father truly; he's been picked for special service."

"Well, then, what is it?" Mrs. Lessing was a trifle impatient.

"Mother," said Hilda, "I've known that he has not been happy ever since his arrival in France, but I've never properly understood why. Peter is queer in some ways, you know. You remember that sermon of his? He won't be content with things; he's always worrying. And now he writes dreadfully. He says…" She hesitated. Then, suddenly, she pulled out the letter. "Listen, mother," she said, and read what Peter had written in the club until the end. "'I am going to eat and drink with publicans and sinners; maybe I shall find my Master still there.'"

If Langton could have seen Mrs. Lessing he would have smiled that cynical smile of his with much satisfaction. She was frankly horrified—rendered, in fact, almost speechless.

"Hilda!" she exclaimed. "What a thing to write to you! But what does he mean? Has he forgotten that he is a clergyman? Why, it's positively blasphemous! He is speaking of Christ, I suppose. My poor girl, he must be mad. Surely you see that, dear."

Hilda stared on into the fire, and made no reply. Her mother hardly needed one, "Has he met another woman, Hilda?" she demanded.

"I don't know; he doesn't say so," said Hilda miserably. "But anyhow, I don't see that that matters."

"Not matter, girl! Are you mad too? He is your fiancé, isn't he? Really, I think I must speak to your father."

Hilda turned her head slowly, and mother and daughter looked at each other. Mrs. Lessing was a woman of the world, but she was a good mother, and she read in her daughter's eyes what every mother has to read sooner or later. It was as one woman to another, and not as mother to daughter, that she continued lamely: "Well, Hilda, what do you make of it all? What are you going to do?"

The girl looked away again, and a silence fell between them. Then she said, speaking in short, slow sentences:

"I will tell you what I make of it, mother. Peter's gone beyond me, I think, now, that I have always feared a little that he might. Of course, he's impetuous and headstrong, but it is more than that. He feels differently from me, from all of us. I can see that, though I don't understand him a bit. I thought" (her voice faltered) "he loved me more. He knows how I wanted him to get on in the Church, and how I would have helped him. But that's nothing to him, or next to nothing. I think he doesn't love me at all, mother, and never really did."

Mrs. Lessing threw her head back. "Then he's a fool, my dear," she said emphatically. "You're worth loving; you know it. I should think no more about him, Hilda."

Hilda's hands tightened round her knees. "I can't do that," she said.

Mrs. Lessing was impatient again. "Do you mean, Hilda, that if he persists in this—this madness, if he gives up the Church, for example, you will not break off the engagement? Mind you, that is the point. Every young man must have a bit of a fling, possibly even clergymen, I suppose, and they get over it. A sensible girl knows that. But if he ruins his prospects—surely, Hilda, you are not going to be a fool?"

The word had been spoken again. Peter had had something to say on it, and now the gods gave Hilda her chance. She stretched her fine hands out to the fire, and a new note came into her voice.

"A fool, mother? Oh no, I shan't be a fool. A fool would follow him to the end of the world. A fool of a woman would give him all he wants for the sake of giving, and be content with nothing in return. I see that. But I'm not made for that sort of foolery.... No, I shan't be a fool."

Mrs. Lessing could not conceal her satisfaction. "Well, I am sure I am very glad to hear you say it, and so would your father be. We have not brought you up carefully for nothing, Hilda. You are a woman now, and I don't believe in trying to force a woman against her will, but I am heartily glad, my dear, that you are so sensible. When you are as old as I am and have a daughter of your own, you will be glad that you have behaved so to-night."

Hilda got up, and put her hands behind her head, which was a favourite posture of hers. She stood looking down at her mother with a curious expression on her face. Mrs. Lessing could make nothing of it; she merely thought Hilda "queer"; she had travelled farther than she knew from youth.

"Shall I, mother?" said Hilda. "Yes, I expect I shall. I have been carefully brought up, as you say, so carefully that even now I can only just see what a fool might do, and I know quite well that I can't do it. After a while I shall no more see it than you do. I shall even probably forget that I ever did. So that is all. And because I love him, really, I don't think I can even say 'poor Peter!' That's curious, isn't it, mother?... Well, I think I'll go to my room for a little. I won't come in again. Good-night."

She bent and kissed Mrs. Lessing. Her mother held her arms a moment more.
"Then, what are you going to do?" she demanded.

Hilda freed herself, "Write and try to persuade him not to be a fool either, I think. Not that it's any good. And then—wait and see." She walked to the floor, "Of course, this is just between us two, isn't it, dear?" she said, playing with the handle.

"Of course," said her mother. "But do be sensible, dear, and don't wait too long. It is much better not to play with these things—much better. And do tell me how things go, darling, won't you?"

"Oh yes," said Hilda slowly, "Oh yes I'll tell you…. Good-night."

She passed out and closed the door gently "I wonder why I can't cry to-night?" she asked herself as she went to her room, and quite honestly she did not know.

Across the water Peter's affairs were speeding up. If Hilda could have seen him that night she would probably have wept without difficulty, but for a much more superficial reason than the reason why she could not weep in London. And it came about in this way.

On the morning after the dinner Peter was moody, and declared he would not go down to the office, but would take a novel out to the canal. He was in half a mind to go up and call at the hospital, but something held him back. Reflection showed him how near he had been to the fatal kiss the night before, and he did not wish, or, with the morning, he thought he did not wish, to see Julie so soon again. So he got his novel and went out to the canal, finding a place where last year's leaves still lay thick, and one could lie at ease and read. We do these things all our days, and never learn the lesson.

Half-way through the morning he looked up to see Langton striding along towards him. He was walking quickly, with the air of one who brings news, and he delivered his message as soon as they were within earshot of each other. "Good news, Graham," he called out. "This tomfoolery is over. They've heard from H.Q. that the whole stunt is postponed, and we've all to go back to our bases. Isn't it like 'em?" he demanded, as he came up. "Old Jackson in the office is swearing like blazes. He's had all his maps made and plans drawn up, etcetera and etcetera, and now they're so much waste-paper. Jolly fortunate, any road." He sat down and got out a pipe.

Peter shut his book. "I'm glad," he said. "I'm sick of foolin' round here. Not but what it isn't a decent enough place, but I prefer the other. There's more doing. When do we go?"

"To-morrow. They're getting our movement orders, yours to Havre, mine to Rouen. I put in a spoke for you, to get one via Rouen, but I don't know if you will. It's a vile journey otherwise."

"By Jove!" cried Peter. "I've an idea! Miss Gamelyn's troop of motor-buses goes back to Havre to-morrow empty. Why shouldn't I travel on them? Think I could work it?"

Langton puffed solemnly. "Sure, I should think," he said, "being a padre, anyway."

"What had I best do?"

"Oh, I should go and see Jackson and get him to 'phone the hospital for you—that is, if you really want to go that way."

"It's far better than that vile train," said Peter. "Besides, one can see the country, which I love. And I've never been in Dieppe, and they're to go through there and pick up some casualties."

"Just so," said Langton, still smoking.

"Well," said Peter, "reckon I'll go and see about it. Jackson's a decent old stick, but I'd best do it before he tackles the R.T.O. Coming?"

"No," said Langton. "Leave that novel, and come back for me. You won't be long."

"Right-o," said Peter, and set off.

It was easily done. Jackson had no objections, and rang up the hospital while Peter waited. Oh yes, certainly they could do it. What was the name? Captain. Graham, C.F. certainly. He must be at the hospital early—eight-thirty the next morning. That all right? Thank you.

"Thank you," said Peter. "Motoring's a long sight better than the train these days, and I'll get in quicker, too, as a matter of fact, or at any rate just as quickly." He turned to go, but a thought struck him. "Have you an orderly to spare?" he asked.

"Any quantity," said the other bitterly. "They've been detailed for weeks, and done nothing. You can have one with pleasure. It'll give the perisher something to do."

"Thanks," said Peter; "I want to send a note, that's all. May I write it here?"

He was given pen and paper, and scribbled a little note to Julie. He did not know who else might be on the lorry, or if she would want to appear to know him. The orderly was called and despatched and he left the place for the last time.

Langton and he walked out to St. Riquier in the afternoon, had tea there, and got back to dinner. A note was waiting for Peter, a characteristic one.

"DEAREST SOLOMON (it ran),

"You are really waking up! There will be three of us nurses in one lorry, and they're sure to start you off in another. We lunch at Eu, and I'll be delighted to see you. Then you can go on in our car. Dieppe's on the knees of the gods, as you say, but probably we can pull off something.

"JULIE."

He smiled and put it in his pocket. Langton said nothing till the coffee and liqueurs came in. Then he lit a cigarette and held the match out to Peter. "Wonder if we shall meet again?" he said.

"Oh, I expect so," said Peter. "Write, anyway, won't you? I'll likely get a chance to come to Rouen."

"And I likely won't be there. I'm putting in again for another job. They're short of men now, and want equipment officers for the R.A.F. It's a stunt for which engineering's useful, and I may get in. I don't suppose I'll see much of the fun, but it's better than bossing up a labour company, any road."

"Sportsman," said Peter. "I envy you. Why didn't you tell me? I've half a mind to put in too. Do you think I'd have a chance?"

"No," said Langton brutally. "Besides, it's not your line. You know what yours is; stick to it."

"And you know that I'm not so sure that I can," said Peter.

"Rot!" said the other. "You can if you like. You won't gain by running away. Only I give you this bit of advice, old son: go slow. You're so damned hot-headed! You can't remake the world to order in five minutes; and if you could, I bet it wouldn't be a much better old world. We've worried along for some time moderately well. Don't be too ready to turn down the things that have worked with some success, at any rate, for the things that have never been tried."

Peter smoked in silence. Then he said: "Langton you're a bit different from what you were. In a way, it's you who have set me out on this racket, and it's you who encouraged me to try and get down to rock-bottom. You've always been a cautious old rotter, but you're more than cautious now. Why?"

Langton leaned over and touched the other's tunic pocket in which lay Julie's note. Then he leaned back and went on with his cigarette.

Peter flushed. "It's too late," he said judicially, flicking off his ash.

"So? Well, I'm sorry, frankly—sorry for her and sorry for you. But if it is, I'll remember my own wisdom: it's no use meddling with such things. For all that, you're a fool, Peter, as I told you last night."

"Just so. And I asked what was a fool."

"And I didn't answer. I reckon fools can be of many sorts. Your sort of fool chucks the world over for the quest of an ideal."

"Thank you," said Peter quietly.

"You needn't. That fool is a real fool, and bigger than most. Ideals are ideals, and one can't realise them. It's waste of time to try."

"Is it?" said Peter. "Well, at any rate, I don't know that I'm out after them much. I don't see any. All I know is that I've looked in the likely places, and now I'll look in the unlikely."

Langton ground his cigarette-end in his coffee-cup. "You will," he said, "whatever I say.... Have another drink? After all, there's no need to 'turn down the empty glass' yet."

They did not see each other in the morning, and Peter made his way early to the hospital as arranged. The P.M.O. met him, and he was put in nominal charge of the three Red-Cross ambulance-cars. While he was talking to the doctor the three nurses came out and got in, Julie not looking in his direction; then he climbed up next the driver of the first car. "Cheerio," said the P.M.O., and they were off.

It was a dull day, and mists hung over the water-meadows by the Somme. For all that Peter enjoyed himself immensely. They ran swiftly through the little villages, under the sweeping trees all new-budded into green, and soon had vistas of the distant sea. The driver of Peter's car was an observant fellow, and he knew something of gardening. It was he who pointed out that the fruit-trees had been indifferently pruned or not pruned at all, and that there were fields no longer under the plough that had been plainly so not long before. In a word, the country bore its war scars, although it needed a clever eye to see them.

But Peter had little thought for this. Now and again, at a corner, he would glance back, his mind on Julie in the following car, while every church tower gave him pause for thought. He tried to draw the man beside him on religion, but without any success, though he talked freely enough of other things. He was for the Colonies after the war, he said. He'd knocked about a good deal in France, and the taste for travel had come to him. Canada appeared a land of promise; one could get a farm easily, and his motor knowledge would be useful on a farm these days. Yes, he had a pal out there, a Canadian who had done his bit and been invalided out of it. They corresponded, and he expected to get in with him, the one's local knowledge eking out the other's technical. No, he wasn't for marrying yet awhile; he'd wait till he'd got a place for the wife and kiddies. Then he would. The thought made him expand a bit, and Peter smiled to himself as he thought of his conversation with Langton over the family group. It struck him to test the man, and as they passed a wayside Calvary, rudely painted, he drew his attention to it. "What do you think of that?" he asked.

The man glanced at it, and then away. "It's all right for them as like it," he said. "Religion's best in a church, it seems to me. I've seen chaps mock at them crucifixes, sir, same as they wouldn't if they'd only been in church."

"Yes," said Peter; "but I suppose some men have been helped by them who never would have been if they had only been in church. But don't you think they're rather gaudy?"

"Gaudy, sir? Meanin' 'ighly painted? No, not as I knows on. They're more like what happened, I reckon, than them brass crosses we have in our churches."

They ran into Eu for lunch, and drew up in the market-square. Peter went round to the girls' car, greeted Julie, and was introduced. He led them to an old inn in the square, and they sat down to luncheon in very good humour. The other girls were ordinary enough, and Julie rather subdued for her. Afterwards they spent an hour in the church and a picture-postcard shop, and it was there that Julie whispered: "Go on in your own car. At Dieppe, go to the Hôtel Trois Poissons and wait for me. I found out yesterday that a woman I know is a doctor in Dieppe, and she lives there. I'll get leave easily to call. Then I can see you. If we travel together these girls'll talk; they're just the sort."

Peter nodded understanding, and they drifted apart. He went out to see if the cars were ready and returned to call the nurses, and in a few minutes they were off again.

The road now ran through forests nearly all the way, except where villages had cleared a space around them, as was plain to see. They crossed little streams, and finally came downhill through the forest into the river valley that leads to Dieppe. It was still early, and Peter stopped the cars to suggest that they might have a look at the castle of Arques-le-Bataille. The grand old pile kept them nearly an hour, and they wandered about the ruins to their hearts' content. Julie would climb a buttress of the ancient keep when their guide had gone on with the others, and Peter went up after her. She was as lissom as a boy and seemingly as strong, swinging up by roots of ivy and the branches of a near tree, in no wise impeded by her short skirts. From the top one had, indeed, a glorious view. The weather had cleared somewhat, and one could see every bit of the old castle below, the village at its feet, and the forest across the little stream out of which the Duke of Mayenne's infantry had debouched that day of battle from which the village took its name.

"They had some of the first guns in the castle, which was held for Henry of Navarre," explained Peter, "and they did great execution. I suppose they fired one stone shot in about every five minutes, and killed a man about every half-hour. The enemy were more frightened than hurt, I should think. Anyway, Henry won."

"Wasn't he the King who thought Paris worth more than a Mass?" she demanded.

"Yes," said Peter, watching her brown eyes as she stared out over the plain.

"I wonder what he thinks now," she said.

He laughed. "You're likely to wonder," he said.

"Funny old days," said Julie. "I suppose there were girls in this castle watching the fight. I expect they cared more for the one man each half-hour the cannon hit than for either Paris or the Mass. That's the way of women, Peter, and a damned silly way it is! Come on, let's go. I'll get down first, if you please."

On the short road remaining Peter asked his chauffeur if he knew the Trois Poissons, and, finding that he did, had the direction pointed out. They ran through the town to the hospital, and Peter handed his cars over. "I'll sleep in town," he said. "What time ought we to start in the morning?" He was told, and walked away. Julie had disappeared.

He found the Trois Poissons without difficulty, and made his way to the sitting-room, a queer room opening from the pavement direct on the one side, and from the hall of the hotel on the other. It had a table down the middle, a weird selection of chairs, and a piano. A small woman was sitting in a chair reading the *Tatler* and smoking. An empty glass stood beside her.

She looked up as he came in, and he noticed R.A.M.C. badges. "Good-evening," he said cheerily.

"Good-evening, padre," she replied, plainly willing to talk. "Where have you sprung from?"

"Abbeville via Eu in a convoy of Red Cross cars," he said, "and I feel like a sun-downer. Won't you have another with me?"

"Sure thing," she said, and he ordered a couple from the French maid who came in answer to his ring. "Do you live here?" he asked.

"For my sins I do," she said. "I doctor Waac's, and I don't think much of it. A finer, heartier lot of women I never saw. Epsom salts is all they want. A child could do it."

Peter laughed. "Well, I don't see why you should grumble," he said.

"Don't you? Where's the practice? This business out here is the best chance for doctors in a lifetime, and I have to strip strapping girls hopelessly and endlessly."

"You do, do you?" said a voice in the doorway, and there stood Julie. "Well, at any rate you oughtn't to talk about it like that to my gentleman friends, especially padres. How do you do, my dear?"

"Julie, by all that's holy! Where have you sprung from?"

She glanced from one to the other. "From Abbeville via Eu in a convoy of Red Cross cars, I dare bet," she said.

"Julie, you're beyond me. If you weren't so strong I'd smack you, but as it is, give me another kiss. *And* introduce us. There may as well be propriety somewhere."

They sorted themselves out and sat down. "What do you think of my rig?" demanded Dr. Melville (as Julie had introduced her).

"Toppin'," said Julie critically. "But what in the world is it? Chiefly Waac, with three pukka stars and an R.A.M.C. badge. Teanie, how dare you do it?"

"I dare do all that doth become a woman," she answered complacently. "And it doth, doth it not? Skirt's a trifle short, perhaps," she added, sticking out a leg and examining the effect critically, "but upper's eminently satisfactory."

Julie leaned over and prodded her. "No corsets?" she inquired innocently.

"Julie, you're positively indecent. You must have tamed your padre completely. You're not married by any chance?" she added suddenly.

Julie screamed with laughter. "Oh, Teanie, you'll be the death of me," she said at last. "Solomon, are we married? I don't think so, Teanie. There's never no telling these days, but I can't recollect it."

"Well, it strikes me you ought to be if you're jogging round the country together," said the other, her eyes twinkling. "But if you're not, take warning, padre. A girl that talks about corsets in public isn't respectable, especially as she doesn't wear them herself, except in the evening, for the sake of other things. Or she used not to. But perhaps you know?"

Peter tried to look comfortable, but he was completely out of his depth. He finished his drink with a happy inspiration, and ordered another. That down, he began to feel more capable of entering into the spirit of these two. They were the sort he wanted to know, both of them, women about as different from those he had met as they could possibly be.

Another man dropped in after a while, so the talk became general. The atmosphere was very free and easy, bantering, careless, jolly, and Peter expanded in it. Julie led them all. She was never at a loss, and apparently had no care in the world.

The two girls and Peter went together to dinner and sat at the same table. They talked a good deal together, and Peter gathered they had come to know each other at a hospital in England. They were full of reminiscences.

"Do you remember ducking Pockett?" Teanie asked Julie.

"Lor', I should think I do! Tell Peter. He won't be horrified unless you go into details. If I cough, Solomon, you're to change the subject. Carry on, Teanie."

"Well, Pockett was a nurse of about the last limit. She was fearfully snobby, which nobody of that name ought to be, and she ruled her pros. with a rod of iron. I expect that was good for them, and I say nothing as to that, but she was a beast to the boys. We had some poor chaps in who were damnably knocked about, and one could do a lot for them in roundabout ways. Regulations are made to be broken in some cases, I think. But she was a holy terror. Sooner than call her, the boys would endure anything, but some of us knew, and once she caught Julie here..."

"It wasn't—it was you, Teanie."

"Oh, well, one of us, anyway, in her ward when she was on night duty, sitting with a poor chap who pegged out a few days after. It soothed him to sit and hold her hand. Well, anyway, she was furious and reported it. There was a bit of a row—had to be, I suppose, as it was against regulations—but thank God the P.M.O. knew his job, so there was only a strafe with the tongue in the cheek. However, we swore revenge, and we had it—eh, Julie?"

"We did. Go on. It was you who thought of it."

"Well, we filled a bath with tepid water and then went to her room one night. She was asleep, and never heard us. We had a towel round her head in two twinks, and carried her by the legs and arms to the bathroom. Julie had her legs, and held 'em well up, so that down went her head under water. She couldn't yell then. When we let her up, I douched her with cold water, and then we bolted. We saw to it that there wasn't a towel in the bathroom, and we locked her bedroom door. Oh, lor', poor soul, but it was funny! She met an orderly in the corridor, and he nearly had a fit, and I don't wonder, for her wet nightie clung to her figure like a skin. She had to try half a dozen rooms before she got anyone to help her, and then, when she got back, we'd ragged her room to blazes. She never said a word, and left soon after. Ever hear of her again, Julie?"

"No," said she, looking more innocent than ever, Peter thought; "but I expect she's made good somewhere. She must have had something in her or she'd have kicked up a row."

Miss Melville was laughing silently. "You innocent babe unborn," she said; "never shall I forget how you held...."

"Come on, Captain Graham," said Julie, getting up; "you've got to see me home, and I want a nice walk by the sea-front."

They went out together, and stood at the hotel door in the little street. There was a bit of a moon, with clouds scurrying by, and when it shone the road was damp and glistening in the moonlight. "What a heavenly night!" said Julie. "Come on with us along the sea-front, Teanie—do!"

Miss Melville smiled up at them. "I reckon you'd prefer to be alone," she said.

Peter glanced at Julie, and then protested. "No," he said; "do come on," and Julie rewarded him with a smile.

So they set out together. On the front the wind was higher, lashing the waves, and the moonlight shone fitfully on the distant cliffs, the harbour mouth, and the sea. The two girls clung together, and as Peter walked by Julie she took his arm. Conversation was difficult as they battled their way along the promenade. There was hardly a soul about, and Peter felt the night to fit his mood.

They went up once and down again, and at the Casino grounds Teanie stopped them. "'Nough," she said; "I'm for home and bed. You two dears can finish up without me."

"Oh, we must see you home," said Peter.

The doctor laughed. "Think I shall get stolen?" she demanded. "Someone would have to get up pretty early for that. No, padre, I'm past the need of being escorted, thanks. Good-night. Be good, Julie. We'll meet again sometime, I hope. If not, keep smiling. Cheerio."

She waved her hand and was gone in the night. "If there was ever a plucky, unselfish, rattling good woman, there she goes," said Julie. "I've known her sit up night after night with wounded men when she was working like a horse all day. I've known her to help a drunken Tommy into a cab and get him home, and quiet his wife into the bargain. I saw her once walk off out of the Monico with a boy of a subaltern, who didn't know what he was doing, and take him to her own flat, and put him to bed, and get him on to the leave-train in time in the morning. She'd give away her last penny, and you wouldn't know she'd done it. And yet she's not the sort of woman you'd choose to run a mother's meeting, would you, Solomon?"

"Sure thing I wouldn't," said Peter, "not in my old parish, but I'm not so sure I wouldn't in my new one."

"What's your new one?" asked Julie curiously.

"Oh, it hasn't a name," said Peter, "but it's pretty big. Something after the style of John Wesley's parish, I reckon. And I'm gradually getting it sized up."

"Where do I come in, Solomon?" demanded Julie.

They were passing by the big Calvary at the harbour gates, and there was a light there. He stopped and turned so that the light fell on her. She looked up at him, and so they stood a minute. He could hear the lash of the waves, and the wind drumming in the rigging of the flagstaff near them. Then, deliberately, he bent down, and kissed her on the lips. "I don't know, Julie," he said, "but I believe you have the biggest part, somehow."

CHAPTER III

All that it is necessary to know of Hilda's return letter to Peter ran as follows:

"My Dear Boy,

"Your letter from Abbeville reached me the day before yesterday, and I have thought about nothing else since. It is plain to me that it is no use arguing with you and no good reproaching you, for once you get an idea into your head nothing but bitter experience will drive it out. But, Peter, you must see that so far as I am concerned you are asking me to choose between you and your strange ideas and all that is familiar and dear in my life. You can't honestly expect me to believe that my Church and my parents and my teachers are all wrong, and that, to put it mildly, the very strange people you appear to be meeting in France are all right. My dear Peter, do try and look at it sensibly. The story you told me of the death of Lieutenant Jenks was terrible—terrible; it brings the war home in all its ghastly reality; but really, you know, it was his fault and not yours, and still less the fault of the Church of England, that he did not want you when he came to die. If a man lives without God, he can hardly expect to find Him at the point of sudden death. What you say about Christ, too, utterly bewilders me. Surely our Church's teachings in the Catechism and the Prayer-Book is Christian teaching, isn't it? Nothing is perfect on earth, and the Church is human, but our Church is certainly the best I know of. It is liberal, active, moderate, and—I don't like the word, but after all it is a good one—respectable. I don't know much about these things, but surely you of all people don't want to go shouting in the street like a Salvation Army Captain. I can't see that that is more 'in touch with reality.' Peter, what do you mean? Are not St. John's, and the Canon, and my people, and myself, real? Surely, Peter, our love is real, isn't it? Oh, how can you doubt that?

"Darling boy, don't you think you are over-strained and over-worried? You are in a strange country, among strange people, at a very peculiar time. War always upsets everything and makes things abnormal. London, even, isn't normal, but, as the Canon said the other day, a great many of the things people do just now are due to reaction against strain and anxiety. Can't you see this? Isn't there any clergyman you can go and talk to? Your Presbyterian and other new friends and your visits to Roman Catholic churches can't be any real help.

"Peter, dear, for my sake, do, *do* try to see things like this. I *hate* that bit in your letter about publicans and sinners. How can a clergyman expect *them* to help *him*? Surely you ought to avoid such people, not seek their company. It is so like you to get hold of a text or two and run it to death. It's not that I don't *trust* you, but you are so easily influenced, and you may equally easily go and do something that will separate us and ruin your life. Peter, I hate to write like this, but I can't help it...."

Peter let the sheets fall from his hands and stared out of the little window. The gulls were screaming and fighting over some refuse in the harbour, and he watched the beat of their wings, fascinated. If only he, too, could catch the wind and be up and away like that!

He jumped up and paced up and down the floor restlessly, and he told himself that Hilda was right and he was a cad and worse. Julie's kiss on his lips burned there yet. That at any rate was wrong; by any standards he had no right to behave so. How could he kiss her when he was pledged to Hilda—Hilda to whom everyone had looked up, the capable, lady-like, irreproachable Hilda, the Hilda to whom Park Lane and St. John's were such admirable setting. And who was he, after all, to set aside all that for which both those things stood?

And yet.... He sat down by the little table and groaned.

"What the dickens is the matter with you, padre?"

Peter started and looked round. In the doorway stood Pennell, regarding him with amusement. "Here am I trying to read, and you pacing up and down like a wild beast. What the devil's up?"

"The devil himself, that's what's up," said Peter savagely. "Look here, Pen, come on down town and let's have a spree. I hate this place and this infernal camp. It gets on my nerves. I must have a change. Will you come? It's my do."

"I'm with you, old thing. I know what you feel like; I get like that myself sometimes. It's a pleasure to see that you're so human. We'll go down town and razzle-dazzle for once. I'm off duty till to-night. I ought to sleep, I suppose, but I can't, so come away with you. I won't be a second."

He disappeared. Peter stood for a moment, then slipped his tunic off and put on another less distinctive of his office. He crossed to the desk, unlocked it, and reached for a roll of notes, shoving them into his pocket. Then he put on his cap, took a stick from the corner, and went out into the passage. But there he remembered, and came quickly back. He folded Hilda's letter and put it away in a drawer; then he went out again. "Are you ready, Pennell?" he called.

The two of them left camp and set out across the docks. As they crossed a bridge a one-horse cab came into the road from a side-street and turned in their direction. "Come on," said Peter. "Anything is better than this infernal walk over this *pavé* always. Let's hop in."

They stopped the man, who asked where to drive to.

"Let's go to the Bretagne first and get a drink," said Pennell.

"Right," said Peter—"any old thing. Hôtel de la Bretagne," he called to the driver.

They set off at some sort of a pace, and Pennell leaned back with a laugh. "It's a funny old world, Graham," he said. "One does get fed-up at times. Why sitting in a funeral show like this cab and having a drink in a second-rate pub should be any amusement, I don't know. But it is. You're infectious, my boy. I begin to feel like a rag myself. What shall we do?"

"The great thing," said Peter judiciously, "is not to know what one is going to do, but just to take anything that comes along. I remember at the 'Varsity one never set out to rag anything definitely. You went out and you saw a bobby and you took his hat, let us say. You cleared, and he after you. Anything might happen then."

"I should think so," said Pennell.

"I remember once walking home with a couple of men, and one of them suggested dousing all the street lamps in the road, which was a residential one leading into town. There wasn't anything in it, but we did it. One man put his back against a post, while the second went on to the next post. Then the third man mounted the first man's back, shoved out the light, jumped clear, and ran on past the next lamp-post to the third. The first man jumped on No. 2's back and doused his lamp, and so on. We did the street in a few minutes, and then a constable came into it at the top. He probably thought he was drunk, then he spotted lights going out, and like an ass he blew his whistle. We were round a corner in no time, and then turned and ran back to see if we could offer assistance!"

"Some gag!" chuckled Pennell; "but I hope you won't go on that sort of racket to-night. It would be a little more serious if we were caught.... Also, these blighted gendarmes would probably start firing, or some other damned thing."

"They would," said Peter; "besides, that doesn't appeal to me now. I'm getting too old, or else my tastes have become depraved."

The one-horse cab stopped with a jerk. "Hop out," said Peter. He settled the score, and the two of them entered the hotel and passed through into the private bar.

"What is it to be?" demanded Pennell.

"Cocktails to-day, old son," said Peter; "I want bucking up. What do you say to martinis?"

The other agreed, and they moved over to the bar. A monstrously fat woman stood behind it, like some bloated spider, and a thin, weedy-looking girl assisted her. A couple of men were already there. It was too early for official drinks, but the Bretagne knew no law.

They ordered their drinks, and stood there while madame compounded them and put in the cherries. Another man came in, and Peter recognised the Australian Ferrars, whom he had met before. He introduced Pennell and called for another martini.

"So you frequent this poison-shop, do you?" said Ferrars.

"Not much," laughed Peter, "but it's convenient."

"It is, and it's a good sign when a man like you wants a drink. I'd sooner listen to your sermons any day than some chaps' I know."

"Subject barred here," said Pennell. "But here's the very best to you, Graham, for all that."

"Same here," said Ferrars, and put down his empty glass.

The talk became general. There was nothing whatever in it—mild chaffing, a yarn or two, a guarded description by Peter of his motor drive from Abbeville, and then more drinks. And so on. The atmosphere was warm and genial, but Peter wondered inwardly why he liked it, and he did not like it so much that Pennell's "Well, what about it? Let's go on, Graham, shall we?" found him unready. The two said a general good-bye, promised madame to look in again, and sauntered out.

They crossed the square in front of Travalini's, lingered at the flower-stalls, refused the girls' pressure to buy, and strolled on. "I'm sick of Travalini's," said Pennell. "Don't let's go in there."

"So am I," said Peter. "Let's stroll down towards the sea."

They turned down a side-street, and stood for a few minutes looking into a picture and book shop. At that moment quick footsteps sounded on the pavement, and Pennell glanced round.

Two girls passed them, obviously sisters. They were not flashily dressed exactly, but there was something in their furs and their high-heeled, high-laced boots that told its own story. "By Jove, that's a pretty girl!" exclaimed Pennell; "let's follow them."

Peter laughed; he was reckless, but not utterly so. "If you like," he said. "I'm on for any rag. We'll take them for a drink, but I stop at that, mind, Pen."

"Sure thing," said Pennell. "But come on; we'll miss them."

They set out after the girls, who, after one glance back, walked on as if they did not know they were being followed. But they walked slowly, and it was easy for the two men to catch them up.

Peter slackened a few paces behind. "Look here, Pen," he said, "what the deuce are we going to do? They'll expect more than a drink, you know."

"Oh no, they won't, not so early as this. It's all in the way of business to them, too. Let's pass them first," he suggested, "and then slacken down and wait for them to speak."

Peter acquiesced, feeling rather more than an ass, but the drinks had gone slightly to his head. They executed their share of the maneuver, Pennell looking at the girls and smiling as he did so. But the two quickened their pace and passed the officers without a word.

"If you ask me, this is damned silly," said Peter. "Let's chuck it."

"No, no; wait a bit," said Pennell excitedly. "You'll see what they'll do. It's really an amusing study in human nature. Look! I told you so. They live there."

The girls had crossed the street, and were entering a house. One of them unlocked the door, and they both disappeared. "There," said Peter, "that finishes it. We've lost them."

"Have we?" said his companion. "Come on over."

They crossed the street and walked up to the door. It was open and perhaps a foot ajar. Pennell pushed it wide and walked in. "Come on," he said again. Peter followed reluctantly, but curious. He was seeing a new side of life, he thought grimly.

Before them a flight of stairs led straight up to a landing, but there was no sign of the girls. "What's next?" demanded Peter. "We'll be fired out in two twos if nothing worse happens. Suppose they're decent girls after all; what would you say?"

"I'd ask if Mlle. Lucienne lived here," said Pennell, "and apologise profusely when I found she didn't. But you can't make a mistake in this street, Graham. I'm going up. It's the obvious thing, and probably what they wanted. Coming?"

He set off to mount the stairs, and Peter, reassured, followed him, at a few paces. When he reached the top, Pennell was already entering an open door.

"How do you do, ma chérie?" said one of the girls, smiling, and holding out a hand.

Peter looked round curiously. The room was fairly decently furnished in a foreign middle-class fashion, half bedroom, half sitting-room. One of the girls sat on the arm of a big chair, the other was greeting his friend. She was the one he had fancied, but a quick glance attracted Peter to the other and elder. He was in for it now, and he was determined to play up. He crossed the floor, and smiled down at the girl on the arm of the chair.

"So you 'ave come," she said in broken English. "I told Lucienne that you would not."

"Lucienne!" exclaimed Peter, and looked back at Pennell.

That traitor laughed, and seated himself on the edge of the bed, drawing the other girl to him. "I'm awfully sorry, Graham," he said; "but I couldn't help it. You wanted to see life, and you'd have shied off if I hadn't played a game. I do just know this little girl, and jolly nice she is too. Give me a kiss, Lulu."

The girl obeyed, her eyes sparkling. "It's not proper before monsieur," she said. "'E is—how do you say?—shocked?"

She seated herself on Pennell's knee, and, putting an arm round his neck, kissed him again, looking across at Peter mischievously. "We show 'im French kiss," she added to Pennell, and pouted out her lips to his.

"Well, now you 'ave come, what do you want?" demanded the girl on the arm of Peter's chair. "Sit down," she said imperiously, patting the seat, "and talk to me."

Peter laughed more lightly than he felt. "Well, I want a drink," he said, at random. "Pen," he called across the room, "what about that drink?" The girl by him reached over and touched a bell. As she did so, Peter saw the curls that clustered on her neck and caught the perfume of her hair. It was penetrating and peculiar, but not distasteful, and it did all that it was meant to do. He bent, and kissed the back of her neck, still marvelling at himself.

She straightened herself, smiling. "That is better. You aren't so cold as you pretended, chérie. Now kiss me properly," and she held up her face.

Peter kissed her lips. Before he knew it, a pair of arms were thrown about his neck, and he was being half-suffocated with kisses. He tore himself away, disgusted and ashamed.

"No!" he cried sharply, but knowing that it was too late.

The girl threw herself back, laughing merrily, "Oh, you are funny!" she said. "Lucienne, take your boy away; I want to talk to mine."

Before he could think of a remonstrance, it was done. Pennell and the other girl got up from the bed where they had been whispering together, and left the room. "Pennell!" called Peter, too late again, jumping up. The girl ran round him, pushed the door to, locked it, and dropped the key down the neck of her dress. "Voila!" she said gaily.

There came a knock on the door. "Non, non!" she cried in French. "Take the wine to Mlle. Lucienne; I am busy."

Peter walked across the room to her. "Give me the key," he said, holding out his hand, and changing his tactics. "Please do. I won't go till my friend comes back. I promise."

The girl looked at him. "You promise? But you will 'ave to find it."

He smiled and nodded, and she walked deliberately to the bed, undid the front of her costume, and slipped it off. Bare necked and armed, she turned to him, holding open the front of her chemise. "Down there," she said.

It was a strange moment and a strange thing, but a curious courage came back to Peter in that second. Without hesitation, he put his hand down and sought for the key against her warm body. He found it, and help it up, smiling. Then he moved to the door, pushed the key in the keyhole, and turned again to the girl. "There!" he said simply.

With a gesture of abandon, she threw herself on the bed, propping her cheek on her hand and staring at him. He sat down where Pennell had sat, but made no attempt to touch her, leaning, instead, back and away against the iron bed-post. She pulled up her knees, flung her arms back, and laughed. "And now, monsieur?" she said.

Peter had never felt so cool in his life. His thoughts raced, but steadily, as if he had dived into cold, clear water. He smiled again, unhesitatingly, but sadly. "Dear," he said deliberately, "listen to me. I have cheated you by coming here to-day, though you shan't suffer for it. I did not want anything, and I don't now. But I'm glad I've come, even though you do not understand. I don't want to do a bit what my friend is doing. I don't know why, but I don't. I'm engaged to a girl in England, but it's not because of that. I'm a chaplain too—a curé, you know—in the English Army; but it's not because of that."

"Protestant?" demanded the girl on the bed.

He nodded. "Ah, well," she said, "the Protestant ministers have wives. They are men; it is different with priests. If your fiancée is wise, she wouldn't mind if you love me a little. She is in England; I am here—is it not so? You love me now; again, perhaps, once or twice. Then it is finished. You do not tell your fiancée and she does not know. It is no matter. Come on, chérie!"

She held out her hands and threw her head back on the pillow.

Peter smiled again. "You do not understand," he said. "And nor do I, but I must be different from some men. I do not want to."

"Ah, well," she exclaimed brightly, sitting up, "another time! Give me my dress, monsieur le curé."

He got up and handed it to her. "Tell me," he said, "do you like this sort of life?"

She shrugged her white shoulders indifferently. "Sometimes," she said—"sometimes not. There are good boys and bad boys. Some are rough, cruel, mean; some are kind, and remember that it costs much to live these days, and one must dress nicely. See," she said deliberately, showing him, "it is lace, fine lace; I pay fifty francs in Paris!"

"I will give you that," said Peter, and he placed the note on the bed.

She stared at it and at him. "Oh, I love you!" she cried. "You are kind! Ah, now, if I could but love you always!"

"Always?" he demanded.

"Yes, always, always, while you are here, in Le Havre. I would have no other boy but you. Ah, if you would! You do not know how one tires of the music-hall, the drinks, the smiles! I would do just all you please—be gay, be solemn, talk, be silent, just as you please! Oh, if you would!"

Half in and half out of her dress, she stood there, pleading. Peter looked closely at the little face with its rouge and powder.

"You hate that!" she exclaimed, with quick intuition. "See, it is gone. I use it no more, only a leetle, leetle, for the night." And she ran across to the basin, dipped a little sponge in water, passed it over her face, and turned to him triumphantly.

Peter sighed. "Little girl," he said sadly, hardly knowing that he spoke. "I cannot save myself: how can I save you?"

"Pouf!" she cried. "Save! What do you mean?" She drew herself up with an absurd gesture. "You think me a bad girl? No, I am not bad; I go to church. Le bon Dieu made us as we are; it is nécessaire."

They stood before each other, a strange pair, the product of a strange age. God knows what the angels made of it. But at any rate Peter was honest. He thought of Julie, and he would not cast a stone.

There came a light knock at the door. The girl disregarded it, and ran to him. "You will come again?" she said in low tones. "Promise me that you will! I will not ask you for anything; you can do as you please; but come again! Do come again!"

Peter passed his hand over her hair. "I will come if I can," he said; "but the Lord knows why."

The knock came again, a little louder. The girl smiled and held her face up. "Kiss me," she demanded.

He complied, and she darted away, fumbling with her dress. "I come," she called, and opened the door. Lucienne and Pennell came in, and the two men exchanged glances. Then Pennell looked away. Lucienne glanced at them and shrugged her shoulders. "Come, Graham," said Pennell; "let's get out! Good-bye, you two."

The pair of them went down and out in silence. No one had seen them come, and there was no one to see them go. Peter glanced at the number and made a mental note of it, and they set off down the street.

Presently Pennell laughed, "I played you a dirty trick, Graham," he said, "I'm sorry."

"You needn't be," said Peter; "I'm very glad I went."

"Why?" said Pennell curiously, glancing sideways at him. "You *are* a queer fellow, Graham." But there was a note of relief in his tone.

Peter said nothing, but walked on. "Where next?" demanded Pennell.

"It looks as if you are directing this outfit," said Peter; "I'm in your hands."

"All right," said Pennell; "I know."

They took a street running parallel to the docks, and entered an American bar. Peter glanced round curiously. "I've never been here before," he said.

"Probably not," said Pennell. "It's not much at this time of the year, but jolly cool in the summer. And you can get first-class cocktails. I want something now; what's yours?"

"I'll leave it to you," said Peter.

He sat down at a little table rather in the corner and lit a cigarette. The place was well lighted, and by means of mirrors, coloured-glass ornaments, paper decorations, and a few palms, it looked in its own way smart. Two or three officers were drinking at the bar, sitting on high stools, and Pennell went up to give his order. He brought two glasses to Peter's table and sat down. "What fools we are, padre!" he said. "I sometimes think that the man who gets simply and definitely tight when he feels he wants a breather is wiser than most of us. We drink till we're excited, and then we drink to get over it. And I suppose the devil sits and grins. Well, it's a weary world, and there isn't any good road out of it. I sometimes wish I'd stopped a bullet earlier on in the day. And yet I don't know. We do get some excitement. Let's go to a music-hall to-night."

"What about dinner?"

"Oh, get a quiet one in a decent hotel. I'll have to clear out at half-time if you don't mind."

"Not a bit," said Peter. "Half will be enough for me, I think. But let's have dinner before we've had more of these things."

The bar was filling up. A few girls came and went. Pennell nodded to a man or two, and finished his glass. And they went off to dinner.

The music-hall was not much of a show, but it glittered, and people obviously enjoyed it. Peter watched the audience as much as the stage. Quite respectable French families were there, and there was nothing done that might not have been done on an English stage—perhaps less, but the words were different. The women as well as the men screamed with laughter, flushed of face, but an old fellow, with his wife and daughter, obviously from the country, sat as stiffly as an English farmer through it all. The daughter glanced once at the two officers, but then looked away; she was well brought up. A half-caste Algerian, probably, came on and danced really extraordinarily well, and a negro from the States, equally ready in French and English, sang songs which the audience demanded. He was entirely master, however, and, conscious of his power, used it. No one in the place seemed to have heard of the colour-bar, except a couple of Americans, who got up and walked out when the comedian clasped a white girl round the waist in one of his songs. The negro made some remark that Peter couldn't catch, and the place shook with laughter.

At half-time everyone flocked into a queer kind of semi-underground hall whose walls were painted to represent a cave, dingy cork festoons and "rocks" adding to the illusion. Here, at long tables, everyone drank innocuous French beer, that was really quite cool and good. It was rather like part of an English bank holiday. Everybody spoke to everybody else, and there were no classes and distinctions. You could only get one glass of beer, for the simple reason that there were too many drinking and too few supplying the drinks for more in the time.

"I must go," said Pennell, "but don't you bother to come."

"Oh yes, I will," said Peter, and they got up together.

In the entrance-hall, however, a girl was apparently waiting for someone, and as they passed Peter recognised her. "Louise!" he exclaimed.

She smiled and held out her hand. Peter took it, and Pennell after him.

"Do you go now?" she asked them. "The concert is not half finished."

"I've got to get back to work," said Pennell, "worse luck. It is la guerre, you know!"

"Poor boy!" said she gaily. "And you?" turning to Peter.

Moved by an impulse, he shook his head. "No," he said, "I was only seeing him home."

"Bien! See me home instead, then," said Louise.

"Nothing doing," said Peter, using a familiar phrase.

She laughed. "Bah! cannot a girl have friends without that, eh? You have a fiancée, 'ave you not? Oh yes, I remember—I remember very well. Come! I have done for to-day; I am tired. I will make you some coffee, and we shall talk. Is it not so?"

Peter looked at Pennell. "Do you mind, Pen?" he asked. "I'd rather like to."

"Not a scrap," said the other cheerfully; "wish I could come too. Ask me another day, Louise, will you?"

She regarded him with her head a little on one side. "I do not know," she said. "I do not think you would talk with me as he will. You like what you can get from the girls of France now; but after, no more. Monsieur, 'e is different. He want not quite the same. Oh, I know! Allons."

Pennell shrugged his shoulders. "One for me," he said. "Well, good-night. I hope you both enjoy yourselves."

In five minutes Peter and Louise were walking together down the street. A few passers-by glanced at them, or especially at her, but she took no notice, and Peter, in a little, felt the strangeness of it all much less. He deliberately crossed once or twice to get between her and the road, as he would have done with a lady, and moved slightly in front of her when they encountered two drunken men. She chatted about nothing in particular, and Peter thought to himself that he might almost have been escorting Hilda home. But if Hilda had seen him!

She ushered him into her flat. It was cosy and nicely furnished, very different from that of the afternoon. A photograph or two stood about in silver frames, a few easy-chairs, a little table, a bookshelf, and a cupboard. A fire was alight in the grate; Louise knelt down and poked it into a flame.

"You shall have French coffee," she said. "And I have even lait for you." She put a copper kettle on the fire, and busied herself with cups and saucers. These she arranged on the little table, and drew it near the fire. Then she offered him a cigarette from a gold case, and took one herself. "Ah!" she said, sinking back into a chair. "Now we are, as you say, comfy, is it not so? We can talk. Tell me how you like la France, and what you do."

Peter tried, but failed rather miserably, and the shrewd French girl noticed it easily enough. She all but interrupted him as he talked of Abbeville and the raid. "Mon ami," she said, "you have something on your mind. You do not want to talk of these things. Tell me."

Peter looked into the kindly keen eyes. "You are right, Louise," he said. "This is a day of trouble for me."

She nodded. "Tell me," she said again. "But first, what is your name, mon ami? It is hard to talk if one does not know even the name."

He hardly hesitated. It seemed natural to say it. "Peter," he said.

She smiled, rolling the "r." "Peterr. Well, Peterr, go on."

"I'll tell you about to-day first," he said, and, once launched, did so easily. He told the little story well, and presently forgot the strange surroundings. It was all but a confession, and surely one was never more strangely made. And from the story he spoke of Julie, but concealed her identity, and then he spoke of God. Louise hardly said a word. She poured out coffee in the middle, but that was all. At last he finished.

"Louise," he said, "it comes to this: I've nothing left but Julie. It was she restrained me this afternoon, I think. I'm mad for her; I want her and nothing else. But with her, somehow, I lose everything else I possess or ever thought I possessed." And he stopped abruptly, for she did not know his business in life, and he had almost given it away.

When he had finished she slipped a hand into his, and said no word. Suddenly she looked up. "Peterr, mon ami," she said, "listen to me. I will tell you the story of Louise, of me. My father, he lived—oh, it matters not; but he had some money, he was not poor. I went to a good school, and I came home for the holidays. I had one sister older than me. Presently I grew up; I learnt much; I noticed. I saw there were terrible things, chez nous. My mother did not care, but I—I cared. I was mad. I spoke to my sister: it was no good. I spoke to my father, and, truly, I thought he would kill me. He beat me—ah, terrible—and I ran from the house. I wept under the hedges: I said I would no more go 'ome. I come to a big city. I found work in a big shop—much work, little money—ah, how little! Then I met a friend: he persuade me, at last he keep me—two months, three, or more; then comes the war. He is an officer, and he goes. We kiss, we part—oui, he love me, that officer. I pray for him: I think I nevair leave the church; but it is no good. He is dead. Then I curse le bon Dieu. They know me in that place: I can do nothing unless I will go to an 'otel—to be for the officers, you understand? I say, Non. I sell my things and I come here. Here I do well—you understand? I am careful; I have now my home. But this is what I tell you, Peterr: one does wrong to curse le bon Dieu. He is wise— ah, how wise!—it is not for me to say. And good—ah, Jesu! how good! You think I do not know; I, how should I know? But I know. I do not understand. For me, I am caught; I am like the bird in the cage. I cannot get out. So I smile, I laugh—and I wait."

She ceased. Peter was strangely moved, and he pressed the hand he held almost fiercely. The tragedy of her life seemed so great that he hardly dare speak of his own. But: "What has it to do with me?" he demanded.

She gave a little laugh. "'Ow should I say?" she said. "But you think God not remember you, and, Peterr, He remember all the time."

"And Julie?" quizzed Peter after a moment.

Louise shrugged her shoulders. "This love," she said, "it is one great thing. For us women it is perhaps the only great thing, though your English women are blind, are dead, they do not see. Julie, she is as us, I think. She is French inside. La pauvre petite, she is French in the heart."

"Well?" demanded Peter again.

"C'est tout, mon ami. But I am sorry for Julie."

"Louise," said Peter impulsively, "you're better than I—a thousand times. I don't know how to thank you." And he lifted her hand to his lips.

He hardly touched it. She sprang up, withdrawing it. "Ah, non, non," she cried. "You must not. You forget. It is easy for you, for you are good—yes, so good. You think I did not notice in the street, but I see. You treat me like a lady, and now you kiss my hand, the hand of the girl of the street.... Non, non!" she protested vehemently, her eyes alight. "I would kiss your feet!"

Outside, in the darkened street, Peter walked slowly home. At the gate of the camp he met Arnold, returning from a visit to another mess. "Hullo!" he called to Peter, "and where have you been?"

Peter looked at him for a moment without replying. "*I'm* not sure, but seeing for the first time a little of what Christ saw, Arnold, I think," he said at last, with a catch in his voice.

CHAPTER IV

Looking back on them afterwards, Peter saw the months that followed as a time of waiting between two periods of stress. Not, of course, that anyone can ever stand still, for even if one does but sit by a fire and warm one's hands, things happen, and one is imperceptibly led forward. It was so in this case, but, not unnaturally, Graham hardly noticed in what way his mind was moving. He had been through a period of storm, and he had to a certain extent emerged from it. The men he had met, and above all Julie, had been responsible for the opening of his eyes to facts that he had before passed over, and it was entirely to his credit that he would not refuse to accept them and act upon them. But once he had resolved to do so things, as it were, slowed down. He went about his work in a new spirit, the spirit not of the teacher, but of the learner, and ever since his talk with Louise he thought—or tried to think—more of what love might mean to Julie than to himself. The result was a curious change in their relations, of which the girl was more immediately and continually conscious than Peter. She puzzled over it, but could not get the clue, and her quest irritated her. Peter had always been the least little bit nervous in her presence. She had known that he never knew what she would do or say next, and her knowledge had amused and carried her away. But now he was so self-possessed. Very friendly they were, and they met often—in the ward for a few sentences that meant much to each of them; down town by arrangement in a cafe, or once or twice for dinner; and once for a day in the country, though not alone; and he was always the same. Sometimes, on night duty, she would grope for an adjective to fit him, and could only think of "tender." He was that. And she hated it, or all but hated it. She did not want tenderness from him, for it seemed to her that tenderness meant that he was, as it were, standing aloof from her, considering, helping when he could. She demanded the fierce rush of passion with which he would seize and shrine her in the centre of his heart, deaf to her entreaties, careless of her pain. She would love then, she thought, and sometimes, going to the window of the ward and staring out over the harbour at the twinkling lights, she would bite her lip with the pain of it. He had thought she dismissed love lightly when she called it animal passion. Good God, if he only knew!...

Peter, for his part, did not realise so completely the change that had come over him. For one thing, he saw himself all the time, and she did not. She did not see him when he lay on his bed in a tense agony of desire for her. She did not see him when life looked like a tumbled heap of ruins to him and she smiled beyond. She all but only saw him when he was staring at the images that had been presented to him during the past months, or hearing in imagination Louise's quaintly accepted English and her quick and vivid "La pauvre petite!"

For it was Louise, curiously enough, who affected him most in these days. A friendship sprang up between them of which no one knew. Pennell and Donovan, with whom he went everywhere, did not speak of it either to him or to one another, with that real chivalry that is in most men, but if they had they would have blundered, misunderstanding. Arnold, of whom Peter saw a good deal, did not know, or, if he knew, Peter never knew that he knew. Julie, who was well aware of his friendship with the two first men, knew that he saw French girls, and, indeed, openly chaffed him about it. But under her chaff was an anxiety, typical of her. She did not know how far he went in their company, and she would have given anything to know. She guessed that, despite everything, he had had no physical relationship with any one of them, and she almost wished it might be otherwise. She knew well that if he fell to them, he would the more readily turn to her. There was a strength about him now that she dreaded.

Whatever Louise thought she kept wonderfully hidden. He took her out to dinner in quiet places, and she would take him home to coffee, and they would chat, and there was an end. She was seemingly well content. She did her business, and they would even speak of it. "I cannot come to-night, mon ami," she would say; "I am busy." She would nod to him as she passed out of the restaurant with someone else, and he would smile back at her. Nor did he ever remonstrate or urge her to change her ways. And she knew why. He had no key with which to open her cage.

Once, truly, he attempted it, and it was she who refused the glittering thing. He rarely came uninvited to her flat, for obvious reasons; but one night she heard him on the stairs as she got ready for bed. He was walking unsteadily, and she thought at first that he had been drinking. She opened to him with the carelessness her life had taught her, her costume off, and her black hair all about her shoulders. "Go in and wait, Peterr," she said; "I come."

She had slipped on a coloured silk wrap, and gone in to the sitting-room to find him pacing up and down. She smiled. "Sit down, mon ami," she said; "I will make the coffee. See, it is ready. Mais vraiment, you shall drink café noir to-night. And one leetle glass of this—is it not so?" and she took a green bottle of peppermint liqueur from the cupboard.

"Coffee, Louise," he said, "but not the other. I don't want it."

She turned and looked more closely at him then. "Non," she said, "pardon. But sit you down. Am I to have the wild beast prowling up and down in my place?"

"That's just it, Louise," he cried; "I am a wild beast to-night. I can't stand it any longer. Kiss me."

He put his arms round her, and bent her head back, studying her French and rather inscrutable eyes, her dark lashes, her mobile mouth, her long white throat. He put his hand caressingly upon it, and slid his fingers beneath the loose lace that the open wrap exposed. "Dear," he said, "I want you to-night."

"To-night, chérie?" she questioned.

"Yes, now," he said hotly. "And why not? You give to other men—why not to me, Louise?"

She freed herself with a quick gesture, and, brave heart, she laughed merrily. The devil must have started at that laugh, and the angels of God sung for joy. "Ah, non," she cried, "It is the mistake you make. I *sell* myself to other men. But you—you are my friend; I cannot sell myself to you."

He did not understand altogether why she quibbled; how should he have done? But lie was ashamed. He slid into the familiar chair and ran his fingers through his hair. "Forgive me, dear," he muttered. "I think I am mad to-night, but I am not drunk, as you thought, except with worrying. I feel lost, unclean, body and soul, and I thought you would help me to forget—no, more than that, help me to feel a man. Can't you, won't you?" he demanded, looking up. "I am tired of play-acting. I've a body, like other men. Let me plunge down deep to-night, Louise. It will do me good, and it doesn't matter. That girl was right after all. Oh, what a fool I am!"

Then did the girl of the streets set out to play her chosen part. She did not preach at all—how could she? Besides, neither had she any use for the Ten Commandments. But if ever Magdalene broke an alabaster-box of very precious ointment, Louise did so that night. She was worldly wise, and she did not disdain to use her wisdom. And when he had gone she got calmly into bed, and slept—not all at once, it is true, but as resolutely as she had laughed and talked. It was only when she woke in the morning that she found her pillow wet with tears.

It was a few days later that Louise took Peter to church. His ignorance of her religion greatly amused her, or so at least she pretended, and when he asked her to come out of town to lunch one morning, and she refused because it was Corpus Christi, and she wanted to go to the sung Mass, it was he who suggested that he should go with her. She looked at him queerly a moment, and then agreed. They met outside the church and went in together, as strange a pair as ever the meshes of that ancient net which gathers of all kinds had ever drawn towards the shore.

Louise led him to a central seat, and found the place for him in her Prayer-Book. The building was full, and Peter glanced about him curiously. The detachment of the worshippers impressed him immensely. There did not appear to be any proscribed procedure among them, and even when the Mass began he was one of the few who stood and knelt as the rubrics of the service directed. Louise made no attempt to do so. For the most part she knelt, and her beads trickled ceaselessly through her fingers.

Peter was, if anything, bored by the Mass, though he would not admit it to himself. It struck him as being a ratherly poorly played performance. True, the officiating ministers moved and spoke with a calm regularity which impressed him, familiar as he was with clergymen who gave out hymns and notices, and with his own solicitude at home that the singing should go well or that the choirboys should not fidget. But there was a terrible confusion with chairs, and a hideous kind of clapper that was used, apparently, to warn the boys to sit and rise. The service, moreover, as a reverential congregational act of worship such as he was used to hope for, was marred by innumerable collections, and especially by the old woman who came round even during the *Sanctus* to collect the rent of the chairs they occupied, and changed money or announced prices with all the zest of the market-place.

But at the close there was a procession which is worth considerable description. Six men with censers of silver lined up before the high altar, and stood there, slowly swinging the fragrant bowls at the end of their long chains. The music died down. One could hear the rhythmical, faint clangour of the metal. And then, intensely sudden, away in the west gallery, but almost as if from the battlements of heaven, pealed out silver trumpets in a fanfare. The censers flew high in time with it, and the sweet clouds of smoke, caught by the coloured sunlight of the rich painted windows, unfolded in the air of the sanctuary. Lights moved and danced, and the space before the altar filled with the white of the men and boys who should move in the procession. Again and again those trumpets rang out, and hardly had the last echoes died away than the organ thundered the *Pange Lingua*, as a priest in cloth of gold turned from the altar with the glittering monstrance in his hand. Even from where he stood Peter could see the white centre of the Host for Whom all this was enacted. Then the canopy, borne by four French laymen in frock-coats and white gloves, hid It from his sight; and the high gold cross, and its attendant tapers, swung round a great buttress into view.

Peter had never heard a hymn sung so before. First the organ would peal alone; then the men's voices unaided would take up the refrain; then the organ again; then the clear treble of the boys; then, like waves breaking on immemorial cliffs, organ, trumpets, boys, men, and congregation would thunder out together till the blood raced in his veins and his eyes were too dim to see.

Down the central aisle at last they came, and Peter knelt with the rest. He saw how the boys went before throwing flowers; how in pairs, as the censers were recharged, the thurifers walked backward before the three beneath the canopy, of whom one, white-haired and old, bore That in the monstrance which all adored. In music and light and colour and scent the Host went by, as It had gone for centuries in that ancient place, and Peter knew, all bewildered as he was, there, by the side of the girl, that a new vista was opening before his eyes.

It was not that he understood as yet, or scarcely so. In a few minutes all had passed them, and he rose and turned to see the end. He watched while, amid the splendour of that court, with singers and ministers and thurifers arranged before, the priest ascended to enthrone the Sacrament in the place prepared for It. With banks of flowers behind, and the glitter of electric as well as of candle light, the jewelled rays of the monstrance gleaming and the organ pealing note on note in a triumphant ecstasy, the old, bent priest placed That he carried there, and sank down before It. Then all sound of singing and of movement died away, and from that kneeling crowd one lone, thin voice, but all unshaken, cried to Heaven of the need of men. It was a short prayer and he could not understand it, but it seemed to Peter to voice his every need, and to go on and on till it reached the Throne. The "Amen" beat gently about him, and he sank his face in his hands.

But only for a second. The next he was lifted to his feet. All that had gone before was as nothing to this volume of praise that shook, it seemed to him, the very carven roof above and swept the ancient walls in waves of sound.

Adoremus in aeternum Sanctissimum Sacramentum, cried men on earth, and, as it seemed to him, the very angels of God.

But outside he collected his thoughts. "Well," he said. "I'm glad I've been, but I shan't go again."

"Why not?" demanded Louise. "It was most beautiful. I have never 'eard it better."

"Oh yes, it was," said Peter; "the music and singing were wonderful, but—forgive me if I hurt you, but I can't help saying it—I see now what our people mean when they say it is nothing less than idolatry."

"Idolatry?" queried Louise, stumblingly and bewildered. "But what do you mean?"

"Well," said Peter, "the Sacrament is, of course, a holy thing, a very holy thing, the sign and symbol of Christ Himself, but in that church sign and symbol were forgotten; the Sacrament was worshipped as if it were very God."

"Oui, oui," protested Louise vehemently, "It is. It is le bon Jesu. It is He who is there. He passed by us among them all, as we read He went through the crowds of Jerusalem in the holy Gospel. And there was not one
He did not see, either," she added, with a little break in her voice.

Peter all but stopped in the road. It was absurd that so simple a thing should have seemed to him new, but it is so with us all. We know in a way, but we do not understand, and then there comes the moment of illumination—sometimes.

"Jesus Himself!" he exclaimed, and broke off abruptly. He recalled a fragment of speech: "Not a dead man, not a man on the right hand of the throne of God." But "He can't be found," Langton had said. Was it so? He walked on in silence. What if Louise, with her pitiful story and her caged, earthy life, had after all found what the other had missed? He pulled himself together; it was too good to be true.

One day Louise asked him abruptly if he had been to see the girl in the house which he had visited with Pennell. He told her no, and she said—they had met by chance in the town—"Well, go you immediately, then, or you will not see her."

"What do you mean?" he asked. "Is she ill—dying?"

"Ah, non, not dying, but she is ill. They will take her to a 'ospital to-morrow. But this afternoon she will be in bed. She like to see you, I think."

Peter left her and made for the house. On his way he thought of something, and took a turning which led to the market-place of flowers. There, at a stall, he bought a big bunch of roses and some sprays of asparagus fern, and set off again. Arriving, he found the door shut. It was a dilemma, for he did not even know the girl's name, but he knocked.

A grim-faced woman opened the door and stared at him and his flowers. "I think there is a girl sick here," said Peter. "May I see her?"

The woman stared still harder, and he thought she was going to refuse him admission, but at length she gave way. "Entrez," she said. "Je pense que vous savez le chambre. Mais, le bouquet—c'est incroyable."

Peter went up the stairs and knocked at the door. A voice asked who was there, and he smiled because he could not say. The girl did not know his name, either. "A friend," he said: "May I come in?"

A note of curiosity sounded in her voice. "Oui, certainement. Entrez," she called. Peter turned the handle and entered the remembered room.

The girl was sitting up in bed in her nightdress, her hair in disorder, and the room felt hot and stuffy and looked more tawdry than ever. She exclaimed at the sight of his flowers. He deposited the big bunch by the side of her, and seated himself on the edge of the bed. She had been reading a book, and he noticed it was the sort of book that Langton and he had seen so prominently in the book-shop at Abbeville.

If he had expected to find her depressed or ashamed, he was entirely mistaken. "Oh, you darling," she cried in clipped English. "Kiss me, quick, or I will forget the orders of the doctor and jump out of bed and catch you. Oh, that you should bring me the rose so beautiful! Hélas! I may not wear one this night in the café! See, are they not beautiful here?"

She pulled her nightdress open considerably more than the average evening dress is cut away and put two or three of the blooms on her white bosom, putting her head on one side to see the result. "Oui," she exclaimed, "je suis exquise! To-night I 'ave so many boys I do not know what to do! But I forget: I cannot go. Je suis malade, très malade. You knew? You are angry with me—is it not so?"

He laughed; there was nothing else to do. "No," he said; "why should I be? But I am very sorry."

She shrugged her shoulders. "It is nothing," she said. "C'est la guerre for me. I shall not be long, and when I come out you will come to see me again, will you not? And bring me more flowers? And you shall not let me 'ave the danger any more, and if I do wrong you shall smack me 'ard. Per'aps you will like that. In the books men like it much. Would you like to whip me?" she demanded, her eyes sparkling as she threw herself over in the bed and looked up at him.

Peter got up and moved away to the window. "No," he said shortly, staring out. He had a sensation of physical nausea, and it was as much as he could do to restrain himself. He realised, suddenly, that he was in the presence of the world, the flesh, and the devil's final handiwork. Only his new knowledge kept him quiet. Even she might be little to blame. He remembered all that she had said to him before, and suddenly his disgust was turned into overwhelming pity. This child before him—for she was little more than a child—had bottomed degradation. For the temporary protection and favour of a man that she guessed to be kind there was nothing in earth or in hell that she would not do. And in her already were the seeds of the disease that was all but certain to slay her.

He turned again to the bed, and knelt beside it. "Poor little girl," he said, and lightly brushed her hair. He certainly never expected the result.

She pushed him from her. "Oh, go, go!" she cried. "Quick go! You pretend, but you do not love me. Why you give me money, the flowers, if you do not want me? Go quick. Come never to see me again!"

Peter did the only thing he could do; he went. "Good-bye," he said cheerfully at the door. "I hope you will be better soon. I didn't mean to be a beast to you. Give the flowers to Lucienne if you don't want them; she will be able to wear them to-night. Cheerio. Good-bye-ee!"

"Good-bye-ee!" she echoed after him. And he closed the door on her life.

In front of the Hôtel de Ville he met Arnold, returning from the club, and the two men walked off together. In a moment of impulse he related the whole story to him. "Now," he said, "what do you make of all that?"

Arnold was very moved. It was not his way to say much, but he walked on silently for a long time. Then he said: "The Potter makes many vessels, but never one needlessly. I hold on to that. And He can remake the broken clay."

"Are you sure?" asked Peter.

"I am," said Arnold. "It's not in the Westminster Confession, nor in the Book of Common Prayer, nor, for all I know, in the Penny Catechism, but I believe it. God Almighty must be stronger than the devil, Graham."

Peter considered this. Then he shook his head. "That won't wash, Arnold," he said. "If God is stronger than the devil, so that the devil is never ultimately going to succeed, I can see no use in letting him have his fling at all. And I've more respect for the devil than to think he'd take it. It's childish to suppose the existence of two such forces at a perpetual game of cheat. Either there is no devil and there is no hell—in which case I reckon that there is no heaven either, for a heaven would not be a heaven if it were not attained, and there would be no true attainment if there were no possibility of failure—or else there are all three. And if there are all three, the devil wins out, sometimes, in the end."

"Then, God is not almighty?"

Peter shrugged his shoulders. "If I breed white mice, I don't lessen my potential power if I choose to let some loose in the garden to see if the cat will get them. Besides, in the end I could annihilate the cat if I wanted to."

"You can't think of God so," cried Arnold sharply.

"Can't I?" demanded Peter. "Well, maybe not, Arnold; I don't know that I can think of Him at all. But I can face the facts of life, and if I'm not a coward, I shan't run away from them. That's what I've been doing these days, and that's what I do not think even a man like yourself does fairly. You think, I take it, that a girl like that is damned utterly by all the canons of theology, and then, forced on by pity and tenderness, you cry out against them all that she is God's making and He will not throw her away. Is that it?"

Arnold slightly evaded an answer. "How can you save her, Graham?" he asked.

"I can't. I don't pretend I can. I've nothing to say or do. I see only one flicker of hope, and that lies in the fact that she doesn't understand what love is. No shadow of the truth has ever come her way. If now, by any chance, she could see for one instant—in *fact*, mind you—the face of God.... If God is Love," he added. They walked a dozen paces. "And even then she might refuse," he said.

"Whose fault would that be?" demanded the older man.

Peter answered quickly, "Whose fault? Why, all our faults—yours and mine, and the fault of men like Pennell and Donovan, as well as her own, too, as like as not. We've all helped build up the scheme of things as they are, and we are all responsible. We curse the Germans for making this damned war, and it is the war that has done most to make that girl; but they didn't make it. No Kaiser made it, and no Nietzsche. The only person who had no hand in it that I know of was Jesus Christ."

"And those who have left all and followed Him," said Arnold softly.

"Precious few," retorted Peter.

The other had nothing to say.

* * * * *

During these months Peter wrote often to Hilda, and with increasing frankness. Her replies grew shorter as his letters grew longer. It was strange, perhaps, that he should continue to write, but the explanation was not far to seek. It was by her that he gauged the extent of his separation from the old outlook, and in her that he still clung, desperately, as it were, to the past. Against reason he elevated her into a kind of test position, and if her replies gave him no encouragement, they at least served to make him feel the inevitableness and the reality of his present position. It would have been easy to get into the swim and let it carry him carelessly on—moderately easy, at any rate. But with Hilda to refer to he was forced to take notice, and it was she, therefore, that hastened the end. Just after Christmas, in a fit of temporary boldness, he told her about Louise, so that it was Louise again who was the responsible person during these months. Hilda's reply was delayed, nor had she written immediately. When he got it, it was brief but to the point. She did not doubt, she said, but that what he had written was strictly true, and she did not doubt his honour. But he must see that their relationship was impossible. She couldn't marry the man who appeared actually to like the company of such a woman, nor could she do other than feel that the end would seem to him as plain as it did to her, and that he would leave the Church, or at any rate such a ministry in it as she could share. She had told her people that she was no longer engaged in order that he should feel free, but she would ever remember the man as she had known him, whom she had loved, and whom she loved still.

It was in the afternoon that Peter got the letter, and he was just setting off for the hospital. When he had read it, he put on his cap and set off in the opposite direction. There was a walk along the sea-wall a few feet wide, where the wind blew strongly laden with the Channel breezes, and on the other side was a waste of sand and stone. In some places water was on both sides of the wall, and here one could feel more alone than anywhere else in the town.

Peter set off, his head in a mad whirl. He had felt that such a letter would come for weeks, but that did not, in a way, lessen the blow when it came. He had known, too, that Hilda was not to him what she had been, but he had not altogether felt that she never could be so again. Now he knew that he had gone too far to turn back. He felt, he could not help it, released in a sense, with almost a sense of exhilaration behind it, for the unknown lay before. And yet, since we are all so human, he was intensely unhappy below all this. He called to mind little scenes and bits of scenes: their first meeting; the sight of her in church as he preached; how she had looked at the dining-table in Park Lane; her walk as she came to meet him in the park. And he knew well enough how he had hurt her, and the thought maddened him. He told himself that God was a devil to treat him so; that he had tried to follow the right; and that the way had led him down towards nothing but despair. He was no nearer answering the problems that beset him. He might have been in a fool's paradise before, but what was the use of coming out to see the devil as he was and men and women as they were if he could see no more than that? The throne of his heart was empty, and there was none to fill it.

Julie?

CHAPTER V

The sea-wall ended not far from Donovan's camp of mud and cinders, and having got there, Peter thought he would go on and get a cup of tea. He crossed the railway-lines, steered through a great American rest camp, crossed the canal, and entered the camp. It was a cheerless place in winter, and the day was drawing in early with a damp fog. A great French airship was cruising around overhead and dropping down towards her resting-place in the great hangar near by. She looked cold and ghostly up aloft, the more so when her engines were shut off, and Peter thought how chilly her crew must be. He had a hankering after Donovan's cheery humour, especially as he had not seen him for some time. He crossed the camp and made for the mess-room.

It was lit and the curtains were drawn, and, at the door, he stopped dead at the sound of laughter. Then he walked quickly in. "Caught out, by Jove!" said Donovan's voice. "You're for it, Julie."

A merry party sat round the stove, taking tea. Julie and Miss Raynard were both there, with Pennell and another man from Donovan's camp. Julie wore furs and had plainly just come in, for her cheeks were glowing with exercise. Pennell was sitting next Miss Raynard, but Donovan, on a wooden camp-seat, just beyond where Julie sat in a big cushioned chair, looked out at him from almost under Julie's arm, as he bent forward. The other man was standing by the table, teapot in hand.

One thinks quickly at such a time, and Peter's mind raced. Something of the old envy and almost fear of Donovan that he had had first that day in the hospital came back to him. He had not seen the two together for so long that it struck him like a blow to hear Donovan call her by her Christian name. It flashed across his mind also that she knew that it was his day at the hospital, and that she had deliberately gone out; but it dawned on him equally quickly that he must hide all that.

"I should jolly well think so," he said, laughing. "How do you do, Miss Raynard? Donovan, can you give me some tea? I've come along the sea-wall, and picked up a regular appetite. Are you in the habit of taking tea here, Julie? I thought nurses were not allowed in camps."

She looked at him quickly, but he missed the meaning of her glance. "Rather," she said; "I come here for tea about once a week, don't I, Jack? No, nurses are not allowed in camps, but I always do what's not allowed as far as possible. And this is so snug and out of the way. Mr. Pennell, you can give me a cigarette now."

The other man offered Peter tea, which he took. "And how did the festivities go off at Christmas?" he asked.

"Oh, topping," said Julie. "Let me see, you were at the play, so I needn't talk about that; but you thought it good, didn't you?"

"Rippin'" said Peter.

"Well," said Julie, "then there was the dance on Boxing Night. We had glorious fun. Jack, here, behaved perfectly abominably. He sat out about half the dances, and I should think he kissed every pretty girl in the room. Then we went down to the nurses' quarters of the officers' hospital and made cocoa of all things, and had a few more dances on our own. They made me dance a skirt dance on the table, and as I had enough laces on this time, I did. After that—but I don't think I'll tell you what we did after that. Why didn't you come?"

Peter had been at a big Boxing Night entertainment for the troops in the Y.M.C.A. Central Hall, but he did not say so. "Oh," he said, "I had to go to another stunt, but I must say I wish I'd been at yours. May I have another cup of tea?"

The third man gave it to him again, and then, apologizing, left the room. Donovan exchanged glances with Julie, and she nodded.

"I say, Graham," said Donovan, "I'll tell you what we've really met here for to-day. We were going to fix it up and then ask you; but as you've dropped in, we'll take it as a dispensation of Providence and let you into the know. What do you say to a really sporting dinner at the New Year?"

"Who's to be asked?" queried Peter, looking round. "Fives into a dinner won't go."

"I should think not," cried Julie gaily. "Jack, here, is taking me, aren't you?" Donovan said "I am" with great emphasis, and made as if he would kiss her, and she pushed him off, laughing, holding her muff to his face. Then she went on: "You're to take Tommy. It is Tommy's own particular desire, and you ought to feel flattered. She says your auras blend, whatever that may be; and as to Mr. Pennell, he's got a girl elsewhere whom he will ask. Three and three make six; what do you think of that?"

"Julie," said Tommy Raynard composedly, "you're the most fearful liar I've ever met. But I trust Captain Graham knows you well enough by now."

"I do," said Peter, but a trifle grimly, though he tried not to show it—"I do. I must say I'm jolly glad Donovan will be responsible for you. It's going to be 'some' evening, I can see, and what you'll do if you get excited I don't know. Flirt with the proprietor and have his wife down on us, as like as not.

- 182 -

In which event it's Donovan who'll have to make the explanations. But come on, what are the details?"

"Tell him, Jack," said Julie. "He's a perfect beast, and I shan't speak to him again."

Peter laughed. "Pas possible," he said. "But come on, Donovan; do as you're told."

"Well, old bird," said Donovan, "first we meet here. Got that? It's safer than any other camp, and we don't want to meet in town. We'll have tea and a chat and then clear off. We'll order dinner in a private room at the Grand, and it'll be a dinner fit for the occasion. They've got some priceless sherry there, and some old white port. Cognac fine champagne for the liqueur, and what date do you think?—1835 as I'm alive. I saw some the other day, and spoke about it. That gave me the idea of the dinner really, and I put it to the old horse that that brandy was worthy of a dinner to introduce it. He tumbled at once. Veuve Cliquot as the main wine. What about it?"

Peter balanced himself on the back of his chair and blew out cigarette-smoke.

"What time are you ordering the ambulances?" he demanded.

"The beds, you mean," cried Julie, entirely forgetting her last words. "That's what I say. *I* shall never be able to walk to a taxi even."

"I'll carry you," said Donovan.

"You won't be able, not after such a night; besides, I don't believe you could, anyhow. You're getting flabby from lack of exercise."

"Am I?" cried Donovan. "Let's see, anyway."

He darted at her, slipped an arm under her skirts and another under her arms, and lifted her bodily from the chair.

"Jack," she shrieked, "put me down! Oh, you beast! Tommy, help, help! Peter, make him put me down and I'll forgive you all you've said."

Tommy Raynard sprang up, laughing, and ran after Donovan, who could not escape her. She threw an arm round his neck and bent his head backwards. "I shall drop her," he shouted. Peter leaped forward, and Julie landed in his arms.

For a second she lay still, and Peter stared down at her. With her quick intuition she read something new in his eyes, and instantly looked away, scrambling out and standing there flushed and breathing hard, her hands at her hair. "You perfect brute!" she said to Donovan, laughing. "I'll pay you out, see if I don't. All my hair's coming down."

"Capital!" said Donovan. "I've never seen it down, and I'd love to. Here, let me help."

He darted at her; she dodged behind Peter; he adroitly put out a foot, and Donovan collapsed into the big chair.

Julie clapped her hands and rushed at him, seizing a cushion, and the two struggled there till Tommy Raynard pulled Julie forcibly away.

"Julie," she said, "this is a positive bear-garden. You must behave."

"And I," said Pennell, who had not moved, "would like to know a little more about the dinner." He spoke so dryly that they all laughed, and order was restored. Donovan, however, refused to get out of the big chair, and Julie deliberately sat on his knee, smiling provocatively at him.

Peter felt savage and bitter. Like a man, he was easily deceived, and he had been taken by surprise at a bad moment. But he did his best to hide it, and merely threw any remnants of caution he had left at all to the winds.

"I suppose this is the best we can hope for, Captain Graham," said Miss Raynard placidly. "Perhaps now you'll give us your views. Captain Donovan never gets beyond the drinks, but I agree with Mr. Pennell we want something substantial."

"I'm blest if I don't think you all confoundedly ungrateful," said Donovan. "I worked that fine champagne for you beautifully. Anyone would think you could walk in and order it any day. If we get it at all, it'll be due to me and my blarney. Not but what it does deserve a good introduction," he added. "I don't suppose there's another bottle in the town."

Tommy sighed. "He's off again, or he will be," she said. "Do be quick, Captain Graham."

"Well," said Peter. "I suggest, first, that you leave the ordering of the room to me, and the decorations. I've most time, and I'd like to choose the flowers. And the smokes and crackers. And I'll worry round and get some menu-cards, and have 'em printed in style. And, if you like, I'll interview the chef and see what he can give us. It's not much use our discussing details without him."

"'A Daniel come to judgment,'" said Pennell. "Padre, I didn't know you had it in you."

"A Solomon," said Julie mischievously.

"A Peter Graham," said Miss Raynard. "I always knew he had more sense in his little finger than all the rest of you in your heads."

Donovan sighed from the depths of the chair. "Graham," he said, "for Heaven's sake remember those..."

Julie clapped her hand over his mouth. He kissed it. She withdrew it with a scream.

"...Drinks," finished Donovan. "The chef must suggest accordin'."

"Well," said Pennell, "I reckon that's settled satisfactorily. I'll get out my invitation. In fact, I think, if I may be excused, I'll go and do it now." He got up and reached for his cap.

They all laughed. "We'll see to it that there's mistletoe," cried Julie.

"Ah, thanks!" said Pennell; "that will be jolly, though some people I know seem to get on well enough without it. So long. See you later, padre."

He avoided Julie's flung cushion and stepped through the door. Miss Raynard got up. "We ought to get a move on too, my dear," she said to Julie.

"Oh, not yet," protested Donovan. "Let's have some bridge. There are just four of us."

"You can never have played bridge with Julie, Captain Donovan," said Miss Raynard. "She usually flings the cards at you half way through the rubber. And she never counts. The other night she played a diamond instead of a heart, when hearts were trumps, and she had the last and all the rest of the tricks in her hand."

"Ah, well," said Donovan, "women are like that. They often mistake diamonds for hearts."

"Jack," said Julie, "you're really clever. How do you do it? I had no idea. Does it hurt? But don't do it again; you might break something. Peter, you've been praised this evening, but you'd never think of that."

"He would not," said Miss Raynard.... "Come on, Julie."

Peter hesitated a second. Then he said: "You're going my way. May I see you home?"

"Thanks," said Miss Raynard, and they all made a move.

"It's deuced dark," said Donovan. "Here, let me. I'll go first with a candle so that you shan't miss the duck-boards."

He passed out, Tommy Raynard after him. Peter stood back to let Julie pass, and as she did so she said: "You're very glum and very polite to-night, Solomon. What's the matter?"

"Am I?" said Peter; "I didn't know it. And in any case Donovan is all right, isn't he?"

He could have bitten his tongue out the next minute. She looked at him and then began to laugh silently, and, still laughing, went out before him. Peter followed miserably. At the gate Donovan said good-bye, and the three set out for the hospital. Miss Raynard walked between Peter and Julie, and did most of the talking, but the ground was rough and the path narrow, and it was not until they got on to the dock road that much could be said.

"This is the best Christmas I've ever had," declared Miss Raynard. "I'm feeling positively done up. There was something on every afternoon and evening last week, and then Julie sits on my bed till daybreak, more or less, and smokes cigarettes. We've a bottle of benedictine, too, and it always goes to her head. The other night she did a Salome dance on the strength of it."

"It was really fine," said Julie. "You ought to have seen me."

"Till the towel slipped off: not then, I hope," said Tommy dryly.

"I don't suppose he'd have minded—would you, Peter?"

"Not a bit," said Peter cheerfully—"on the contrary."

"I don't know if you two are aware that you are positively indecent," said Tommy. "Let's change the subject. What's your news, Captain Graham?"

Peter smiled in the dark to himself. "Well," he said, "not much, but I'm hoping for leave soon. I've pushed in for it, and our Adjutant told me this morning he thought it would go through."

"Lucky man! I've got to wait three months. But yours ought to be about now, Julie."

"I think it ought," said Julie shortly. Then: "What about the menu-cards, Peter? Would you like me to help you choose them?"

"Would you?" said he eagerly. "To-morrow?"

"I'm on duty at five o'clock, but I can get off for an hour in the afternoon. Could you come, Tommy?"

"No. Sorry; but I must write letters. I haven't written one for ages."

"Nor have I," said Julie, "but I don't mean to. I hate letters. Well, what about it, Peter?"

"I should think we had better try that stationer's in the Rue Thiers," he said. "If that won't do, the Nouvelles Galeries might. What do you think?"

"Let's try the Galeries first. We could meet there. Say at three, eh? I want to get some baby-ribbon, too."

Tommy sighed audibly. "She's off again," she said.

"Thank God, here's the hospital! Good-night, Captain Graham. You mustn't cross the Rubicon to-night."

"You oughtn't to swear before him," said Julie in mock severity. "And what in the world is the Rubicon?"

"Materially, to-night, it's the railway-line between his camp and the hospital," said Tommy Raynard. "What else it is I'll leave him to decide."

She held out her hand, and Peter saw a quizzical look on her face. He turned rather hopelessly to Julie. "I say," he said, "didn't you *know* it was my afternoon at the hospital?"

"Yes," said Julie, "and I knew you didn't come. At least, I couldn't see you in any of the wards."

"Oh," he exclaimed, "I thought you'd been out all the afternoon. I'm sorry. I am a damned fool, Julie!"

She laughed in the darkness. "I've known worse, Peter," she said, and was gone.

* * * * *

Next day Julie was in her most provocative of moods. Peter, eminently respectable in his best tunic, waited ten minutes for her outside the Nouvelles Galeries, and, like most men in his condition, considered that she was never coming, and that he was the cynosure of neighbouring eyes. When she did come, she was not apparently aware that she was late. She ran her eyes over him, and gave a pretended gasp of surprise. "You're looking wonderful, Padre Graham," she said. "Really, you're hard to live up to. I never know what to expect or how to behave. Those black buttons terrorise me. Come on."

She insisted on getting her ribbon first, and turned over everything there was to be seen at that counter. The French girl who served them was highly amused.

"Isn't that chic?" Julie demanded of Peter, holding up a lacy camisole and deliberately putting it to her shoulders. "Wouldn't you love to see me in it?"

"I would," he said, without the ghost of a smile.

"Well, you never will, of course," she said. "I shall never marry or be given in marriage, and in any case, in that uniform, you've nothing whatever to hope for.... Yes, I'll take that ribbon, thank you, ma'm'selle. Peter, I suppose you can't carry it for me. Your pocket? Not a bad idea; but let me put it in."

Peter stood while she undid his breast-pocket and stuffed it inside.

"Anything more?" demanded the French saleswoman interrogatively.

"Not to-day, merci," said Julie. "You see, Peter, you couldn't carry undies for me, even in your pocket; it wouldn't be respectable. *Do* come on. You will keep us here the entire day."

They passed the smoking department, and she stopped suddenly. "Peter," she said, "I'm going to give you a pipe. Those chocolates you gave me at Christmas were too delicious for anything. What sort do you like? A briar? Let me see if it blows nicely." She put it to her lips. "I swear I shall start a pipe soon, in my old age. By the way, I don't believe you have any idea how old I am—have you, Peter? Guess."

She was quick to note the return to his old manner. He was nervous with her, not sure of himself, and so not sure of her either. And she traded on it. At the stationery department she made eyes at a couple of officers, and insisted on examining Kirschner picture-postcards, some of which she would not show him. "You can't possibly be seen looking at them with those badges up," she whispered. "Dear me, if only Donovan were here! He wouldn't mind, and I don't know which packet I like best. These have got very little on, Peter—*very* little, but I'm not sure that they are not more decent than those. It's *much* worse than a camisole, you know...."

Peter was horribly conscious that the men were smiling at her. "Julie," he said desperately, "*do* be sensible, just for a minute. We must get those menu-cards."

"Well, you go and find the books," she said merrily. "I told you you ought not to watch me buy these. I'll take the best care of myself," and she looked past him towards the men.

Peter gave it up. "Julie," he said savagely, "if you make eyes any more, I'll kiss you here and now—I swear I will."

Julie laughed her little nearly silent chuckle, and looked at him. "I believe you would, Peter," she said, "and I certainly mustn't risk that. I'll be good. Are those the books? Fetch me a chair, then, and I'll look through them."

He bent over her as she turned the leaves. She wore a little toque that had some relation to a nurse's uniform, but was distinctive of Julie. Her fringe of brown hair lay along her forehead, and the thick masses of the rest of it tempted him almost beyond endurance. "How will that do?" she demanded, her eyes dancing. "Oh, do look at the cards and not at me! You're a terrible person to bring shopping, Peter!"

The card selected, she had a bright idea. "What about candle-shades?" she queried. "We can't trust the hotel. I want some with violets on them: I love violets."

"Do you?" he said eagerly. "That's just what I wanted to know. Yes, it's a fine idea; let's go and get them."

Outside, she gave a sigh of relief, and looked at the little gold wrist-watch on her arm. "We've time," she said. "Take me to tea."

"You must know it's not possible," he said. "They're enforcing the order, and one can't get tea anywhere."

She shook her head at him. "I think, Peter," she said, "you'll never learn the ropes. Follow me."

Not literally, but metaphorically, he followed her. She led him to a big confectioner's with two doors and several windows, in each of which was a big notice of the new law forbidding teas or the purchase of chocolates. Inside, she walked up to a girl who was standing by a counter, and who greeted her with a smile. "It is cold outside," she said. "May I have a warm by the fire?"

"Certainly, mademoiselle," said the girl. "And monsieur also. Will it please you to come round here?"

They went behind the counter and in at a little door. There was a fire in the grate of the small kitchen, and a kettle singing on the hob. Julie sat down on a chair at the wooden table and looked round with satisfaction.

"Why, it's all ready for us!" she exclaimed. "Chocolate cakes, Suzanne, please, *and* hot buttered scones. I'll butter them, if you bring the scones."

They came, and she went to the fire, splitting them open and spreading the butter lavishly. "I love France," she said. "All laws are made to be broken, which is all that laws are good for, don't you think?"

"Yes," he said deliberately, glancing at the closed door, and bent and kissed her neck. She looked up imperiously. "Again," she said; and he kissed her on the lips. At that she jumped up with a quick return to the old manner: "Peter! For a parson you are the outside edge. Go and sit down over there and recollect yourself. To begin with, if we're found, here, there'll be a row, and if you're caught kissing me, who knows what will happen?"

He obeyed gaily. "Chaff away, Julie," he said, "but I shan't wear black buttons at the dinner. You'll have to look out that night."

She put the scones on the table, and sat down. "And if I don't?" she queried. Peter said nothing. He had suddenly thought of something. He looked at her, and for the first time she would not meet his eyes.

It was thought better on New Year's Eve that they should go separately to Donovan's camp, so Peter and Pennell set out for it alone. By the canal Pennell left his friend to go and meet Elsie Harding, the third girl. Peter went on alone, and found Donovan, giving some orders in the camp. He stood with him till they saw the other four, who had met on the tow-path, coming in together.

"He's a dark horse," called Julie, almost before they had come up, "and so's she. Fancy Elsie being the third! I didn't know they knew each other. We're a Colonial party to-night, Jack—all except Peter, that is, for Mr. Pennell is more Canadian than English. We'll teach them. By the way, I can't go on saying 'Mr. Pennell' all night. What shall I call him, Elsie?"

Peter saw that the new-comer wore an Australian brooch, and caught the unmistakable but charming accent in her reply. "He's 'Trevor' to me, and he can be to you, if you like, Julie," she said.

Tommy sighed audibly. "They're beginning early," she said; "but I suppose the rest of us had better follow the general example—eh, Peter?"

In the anteroom, where tea was ready, Peter saw that Elsie was likely to play Julie a good second. She was tall, taller than Pennell himself, and dark skinned, with black hair and full red lips, and rather bigly built. It appeared that her great gift was a set of double joints that allowed her to play the contortionist with great effect. "You should just see her in tights," said Julie. "Trevor, why didn't you say whom you were bringing, and I'd have made her put them on. Then we could have had an exhibition, but, as it is, I suppose we can't."

"I didn't know you knew her," he said.

"You never have time to talk of other people when you're together, I suppose," she retorted. "Well, I've no doubt you make the most of your opportunities, and you're very wise. But to-night you've got to behave, more or less—at least, till after the coffee. Otherwise all our preparations will be wasted—won't they, Peter?"

After tea they set off together for the tram-car that ran into town. It was Julie who had decided this. She said she liked to see the people, and the cars were so perfectly absurd, which was true. Also, that it would be too early to enjoy taxis, the which was very like her. So they walked in a body to the terminus, where a crowd of Tommies and French workmen and factory girls were waiting. The night was cloudy and a little damp, but it had the effect of adding mystery to the otherwise ugly street, and to the great ships under repair in the dockyards close by. The lights of the tram appeared at length round the corner, an engine-car and two trailers. There was a bolt for them. They were packed on the steps, and the men had to use elbows freely to get the whole party in, but the soldiers and the workmen were in excellent humour, and the French girls openly admiring of Julie. In the result, then, they were all hunched up in the end of a "first" compartment, and Peter found himself with his back to the glass door, Julie on his right, Elsie on his left.

"Every rib I have is broken," said the former.

"The natural or the artificial?" demanded Elsie. "Personally, I think I broke a few of other people's."

They started, and the rattling of the ramshackle cars stopped conversation. Julie drew Peter's attention to a little scene on the platform outside, and he looked through the glass to see a big French linesman with his girl. The man had got her into a corner, and then, coolly putting his arms out on either side to the hand-rail and to the knob of their door, he was facing his amorata, indifferent to the world. Peter looked at the girl's coarse face. She was a factory hand, bareheaded, and her sleeves were rolled up at her elbows. For all that, she was neat, as a Frenchwoman invariably is. The girl caught his gaze, and smiled. The linesman followed the direction of her eyes and glanced friendly at Peter too. Then he saw Julie. A look of admiration came over his face, and he put one hand comically to his heart. The girl slapped it in a pretended fury, and Julie doubled up with laughter in her corner. Peter bent over her. "*'Everybody's doing it, doing it, doing it,'*" he quoted merrily.

The tram stopped, in the square before the Hôtel de Ville. There was a great air of festivity and bustle about as they stepped out, for the New Year is a great time in France. Lights twinkled in the misty dark; taxis sprinted across the open spaces; and people greeted each other gaily by the brightly-lit shops. Somehow or another the whole thing went to Peter's head like wine. The world was good and merry, he thought exultantly, and he, after all, a citizen of it. He caught Julie's arm, "Come on," he called to the others. "I know the way," And to her: "Isn't it topping? Do you feel gloriously exhilarated? I don't know why, Julie, but I could do anything to-night."

She slipped her fingers down into his hand. "I'm so glad," she said. "So could I."

They whirled across the road, the others after them, round the little park in the centre of the square, and down an empty side-street. Peter had reconnoitred all approaches, he said, and this was the best way. Begging him to give her time to breathe, Tommy came along with Donovan, and it suddenly struck Peter that the latter seemed happy enough. He pressed Julie's hand: "Donovan's dropped into step with Tommy very easily," he said. "Do you mind?"

She laughed happily and glanced back. "You're as blind as a bat, Peter, when all's said and done," she said; "but oh, my dear, I can't play with you to-night. There's only one person I want to walk with Peter."

Peter all but shouted. He drew her to him, and for once Julie was honestly alarmed.

"Not now, you mad boy!" she exclaimed, but her eyes were enough for him.

"All right," he laughed at her; "wait a bit. There's time yet."

In the little entrance-hail the *maître d'hôtel* greeted them. They were the party of importance that night. He ushered them upstairs and opened a door. The mademoiselles might make the toilette there. Another door: they would eat here.

The men deposited their caps and sticks and coats on pegs outside, and the girls, who had had to come in uniform also, were ready as soon as they. They went in together. Elsie gave a little whistle of surprise.

Peter had certainly done well. Holly and mistletoe were round the walls, and a big bunch of the latter was placed in such a way that it would hang over the party as they sat afterwards by the fire. In the centre a silver bowl held glorious roses, white and red, and at each girl's place was a bunch of Parma violets and a few sprigs of flowering mimosa. Bon-bons were spread over the white cloth. Julie's candle-shades looked perfect, and so did the menu-cards.

"I trust that monsieur is satisfied," said the *maître d'hôtel*, bowing towards the man who had had the dealings with him. He got his answer, but not from Peter, and, being a Frenchman, smiled, bowed again, and discreetly left the room; for Elsie, turning to Peter cried: "Did you do it—even the wattle?" and kissed him heartily. He kissed her back, and caught hold of Julie. "Tit for tat," he said to her under his breath, holding her arms; "do you remember our first taxi?" Then, louder: "Julie is responsible for most of it," and he kissed her too.

They sorted themselves out at last, and the dinner, that two of them at least who were there that night were never to forget, began. They were uproariously merry, and the two girls who waited came and went wreathed in smiles.

With the champagne came a discussion over the cork. "Give it to me" cried Julie; "I want to wear it for luck."

"So do I," said Elsie; "we must toss for it."

Julie agreed, and they spun a coin solemnly.

"It's mine," cried Elsie, and pounced for it.

Julie snatched it away, "No, you don't," she said. "A man must put it in, or there's no luck in it. Here you are, Trevor."

Pennell took it, laughing, and pushed back his chair. The others stood up and craned over to see. Elsie drew up her skirt and Trevor pushed it down her stocking amid screams of laughter, and the rattle of chaff.

"No higher or I faint," said Tommy.

Trevor stood up, a little flushed. "Here," said Peter, filling his glass with what was left in the bottle, "drink this, Pen. You sure want it."

"It's your turn next," said Trevor, "and, by Jove, the bottle's empty! Encore le vin," he called.

"Good idea. It's Julie's next cork, and Graham's the man to do it." said Jack Donovan. "And then it'll be your turn, Tommy."

"And yours," she said, glancing at him.

"Bet you won't dare," said Elsie.

"Who won't?" retorted Julie.

"Peter, of course."

"My dear, you don't know Peter. Here you are, Peter; let's show them."

She tossed the cork to him and stood up coolly, put up her foot on the edge of the table, and lifted her skirt. Peter pushed the cork into its traditional place amid cheers, but he hardly heard. His fingers had touched her skin, and he had seen the look in her eyes. No wine could have intoxicated him so. He raised his glass. "Toasts!" he shouted.

They took him up and everyone rose to their feet.

"'Here's   to   all   those   that   I   love;
Here's   to   all   those   that   love   me;
Here's   to   all   those   that   love   them   that   love   those
That love those that love them that love me!'"

he chanted.

"Julie's turn," cried Elsie.

"No," she said; "they know all my toasts."

"Not all," said Donovan; "there was one you never finished—something about Blighty."

"Rhymes with nighty," put in Tommy coolly; "don't you remember, Julie?"

It seemed to Peter that he and Julie stood there looking at each other for seconds, but probably no one but Tommy noticed. "Take it as read," cried Peter boisterously, and emptied his glass. His example was infectious, and they all followed suit, but Donovan remarked across the table to him:

"You spoiled a humorous situation, old dear."

Dinner over, they pushed the table against the wall, and pulled chairs round the fire. Dessert, crackers, chocolates and cigarettes were piled on a small table, and the famous liqueur came in with the coffee. They filled the little glasses. "This is a great occasion," said Donovan; "let's celebrate it properly. Julie, give us a dance first."

She sprang up at once. "Right-o," she said. "Clear the table."

They pushed everything to one side, and Peter held out his hand. Just touching his fingers, she leaped up, and next minute circled there in a whirl of skirts. A piano stood in a corner of the room, and Elsie ran to it. Looking over her shoulder, she caught the pace, and the notes rang out merrily.

Julie was the very spirit of devilment and fun. So light that she seemed hardly to touch the table, she danced as if born to it. It was such an incarnation of grace and music that a little silence fell on them all. To Peter she appeared to dance to him. He could not take his eyes off her; he cared nothing what others thought or saw. There was a mist before him and thunder in his ears. He saw only her flushed, childlike face and sparkling brown eyes, and a wave of her loosened hair that slipped across them....

The music ceased. Panting for breath, she leaped down amid a chorus of "Bravo's!" and held out her hand for the liqueur-glass. Peter put it in her fingers, and he was trembling more than she, and spilt a little of it. "Well, here's the best," she cried, and raised the glass. Then, with a gay laugh, she put her moistened fingers to his mouth and he kissed them, the spirit on his lips.

And now Elsie must show herself off. They sat down to watch her, and a more insidious feeling crept over Peter as he did so. The girl bent her body this way and that; arched herself over and looked at them between her feet; twisted herself awry and made faces at them. They laughed, but there was a new note in the laughter. An intense look had come into Pennell's face, and Donovan was lolling back, his head on one side, smiling evilly.

She finished and straightened herself, and they had more of the liqueur. Then Tommy, as usual, remembered herself. "Girls," she said, "we must go. It's fearfully late."

Donovan sat up. "What about taxis?" he demanded.

Peter went to the door. "They'll fetch them," he said. "I've made an arrangement."

He went a little unsteadily to find the *maître d'hôtel*, and a boy was despatched, while he settled the bill. They were tramping down the stairs as he came out of the little office, Julie leading and laughing uproariously at some joke. Donovan and Tommy were the steadiest, and they came down together. It seemed to Peter that it was natural for them to do so.

Pennell and Elsie got into one taxi. She leaned out of the window and waved her hand. "We're the luckiest," she called; "we've the farthest to go. Good-night everyone, and thanks ever so much."

A second taxi came up. "Jump in, Julie," said Tommy.

She got in, and Peter put his hand on the door. "I've settled everything, Donovan," he said. "See you to-morrow. Good-night, Tommy."

"Good-night," she called back, and he got in. And next minute he was alone with Julie.

In the closed and darkened taxi he put his arm round her and drew her to him. "Oh, my darling," he murmured. "Julie, do you love me as I love you? I can't live without you." He covered her face with hot kisses, and she kissed him back.

"Julie," he said at length, breathlessly, "listen. My leave's come. I knew this morning. Couldn't you possibly be in England when I am? I saw you first on the boat coming over—remember? And you're due again."

"When do you go?" she queried.

"Fourteenth," he answered.

She considered. "I couldn't get off by then," she said, "but I might the twenty-first or thereabouts. I'm due, as you say, and I think it could be managed."

"Would you?" he demanded, and hung on her words.

She turned her face up to him, and even in the dark he could see her glowing eyes. "It would be heaven, Peter," she whispered.

He kissed her passionately.

"I could meet you in town easily," he said.

"Not the leave-boat train," she replied; "it's not safe. Anyone might be there. But I'll run down for a day or two to some friends in Sussex, and then come up to visit more in town. I know very few people, of course, and all my relations are in South Africa. No one would know to whom I went, and if I didn't go to them, Peter, why nobody would know either."

"Splendid!" he answered, the blood pounding in his temples. "I'll make all the arrangements. Shall I take a flat, or shall we go to an hotel? An hotel's more fun, perhaps, and we can have a suite."

She leaned over against him and caught his hand to her breast, with a little intake of breath.

"I'll leave it all to you, my darling," she whispered.

The taxi swung into the clearing before the hospital. "Peter," said Julie, "Tommy's so sharp; I believe she'll suspect something."

"I don't care a damn for anyone!" said Peter fiercely; "let her. I only want you."

CHAPTER VI

Peter secured his leave for Monday the 21st from Boulogne, which necessitated his leaving Le Havre at least twenty-four hours before that day. There were two ways of travelling—across country in a troop-train, or by French expresses via Paris. He had heard so much of the latter plan that he determined to try it. It had appeared to belong to the reputation of the Church.

His movement order was simply from the one port to the other, and was probably good enough either way round with French officials; but there was a paper attached to it indicating that the personnel in question would report at such a time to the R.T.O. at such a station, and the time and the station spelt troop-train unmistakably. Now, the troop-train set out on its devious journey an hour later than the Paris express from the same station, and the hour of the Paris express corresponded with the time that all decent officers go to dinner. Peter therefore removed the first paper, folded it up thoughtfully, and put it in his pocket. He then reported to the R.T.O. a quarter of an hour before the Paris train started, and found, as he expected, a N.C.O. in sole charge. The man took his paper and read it. He turned it over; there was no indication of route anywhere. "Which train are you going by, sir?" he asked.

"Paris mail," said Peter coolly. "Will you please put my stuff in a first?"

"Certainly, sir," said the man, endorsed the order to that effect, and shouldered a suit-case. Peter followed him. He was given a first to himself, and the Deputy R.T.O. saw the French inspector and showed him the paper. Peter strolled off and collected a bottle of wine, some sandwiches, and some newspapers; then he made himself comfortable. The train left punctually. Peter lay back in his corner and watched the country slip by contentedly. He had grown up, had this young man.

He arrived in Paris with the dawn of Sunday morning, and looked out cautiously. There was no English official visible. However, his papers were entirely correct, and he climbed up the stairs and wandered along a corridor in which hands and letters from time to time indicated the lair of the R.T.O. Arriving, he found another officer waiting, but no R.T.O. The other was "bored stiff," he said; he had sat there an hour, but had seen no sign of the Transport Officer. Peter smiled, and replied that he had no intention whatever of waiting; he only wanted to know the times of the Boulogne trains. These he discovered by the aid of a railway guide on the table, and selected the midnight train, which would land him in Boulogne in time for the first leave-boat, if the train were punctual and the leave-boat not too early. In any case, he could take the second, which would only mean Victoria a few hours later that same day. And these details settled, he left his luggage in a corner and strolled off into the city.

A big city, seen for the first time by oneself alone when one does not know a soul in it, may be intensely boring or intensely interesting. It depends on oneself. Peter was in the mood to be interested. He was introspective. It pleased him to watch the early morning stir; to see the women come out in shawls and slipshod slippers and swill down their bit of pavement; to see sleepy shopkeepers take down their shutters and street-vendors set up their stalls; to try to gauge the thoughts and doings of the place from the shop-windows and the advertisements. His first need was a wash and a shave, and he got both at a little barber's in which monsieur attended to him, while madame, in considerable *négligée*, made her toilette before the next glass. His second was breakfast, and he got it, *à l'anglaise*, with an omelette and jam, in a just-stirring hotel; and then, set up, he strolled off for the centre of things. Many Masses were in progress at the Madeleine, and he heard one or two with a curious contentment, but they had no lesson for him, probably because of the foreign element in the atmosphere, and he did not pray. Still, he sat, chiefly, and watched, until he felt how entirely he was a stranger here, and went out into the sun.

He made his way to the river, and lingered there long. The great cathedral, with its bare January trees silhouetted to the last twig against the clear sky, its massive buttresses, and its cluster of smaller buildings, held his imagination. He went in, but they were beginning to sing Mass, and he soon came out. He crossed to the farther bank and found a seat and lit a pipe. Sitting there, his imagination awoke. He conceived the pageant of faith that had raised those walls. Kings and lords and knights, all the glitter and gold of the Middle Ages, had come there—and gone; Bishops and Archbishops, and even Popes, had had their day of splendour there—and gone; the humbler sort, in the peasant dress of the period, speaking quaint tongues, had brought their sorrows there and their joys—and gone; yet it seemed to him that they had not so surely gone. The great have their individual day and disappear, but the poor, in their corporate indistinguishableness remain. The multitude, petty in their trivial wants and griefs, find no historian and leave no monument. Yet, ultimately, it was because of the Christian faith in the compassion of God for such that Notre-Dame lifted her towers to the sky. The stage for the mighty doings of Kings, it was the home of the people. As he had seen them just now, creeping about the aisles, lighting little tapers, crouched in a corner, so had they always been. Kings and Bishops figured for a moment in pomp before the altar, and then monuments must be erected to their memory. But it was not so with the poor. Peter, in a glow of warmth, considered that he was in truth one of them. And Jesus had had compassion on the multitude, he remembered. The text recalled him, and he frowned to himself.

He knocked out his pipe, and set out leisurely to find luncheon. The famous book-boxes held him, and he bought a print or two. In a restaurant near the Châtelet he got *déjeuner*, and then, remembering Julie, bought and wrote a picture-postcard, and took a taxi for the Bois. He was driven about for an hour or more, and watched the people lured out by the sun, watched the troops of all the armies, watched an aeroplane swing high over the trees and soar off towards Versailles. He discharged his car at the Arc de Triomphe, and set about deciphering the carven pictures. Then, he walked up the great Avenue, made his way to the Place de la République, wandered through the gardens of the Louvre, and, as dusk fell, found himself in the Avenue de l'Opéra. It was very gay. He had a bock at a little marble table, and courteously declined the invitations of a lady of considerable age painted to look young. He at first simply refused, and finally cursed into silence, a weedy, flash youth who offered to show him the sights of the city in an apparently ascending scale till he reached the final lure of a *cancan*, and he dined greatly at a palace of a restaurant. Then, tired, he did not know what to do.

A girl passing, smiled at him, and he smiled back. She came and sat down. He looked bored, she told him, which was a thing one should not be in Paris, and she offered to assist him to get rid of the plague.

"What do you suggest?" he demanded.

She shrugged her shoulders—anything that he pleased.

"But I don't know what I want," he objected.

"Ah, well, I have a flat near," she said—"a charming flat. We need not be bored there."

Peter demurred. He had to catch the midnight train. She made a little gesture; there was plenty of time.

He regarded her attentively. "See, mademoiselle," he said, "I do not want that. But I am alone and I want company. Will you not stroll about Paris with me for an hour or two, and talk?"

She smiled. Monsieur was unreasonable. She had her time to consider; she could not waste it.

Peter took his case from his pocket and selected a note, folded it, and handed it to her, without a word. She slipped it into her bag. "Give me a cigarette," she said. "Let us have one little glass here, and then we will go on to an 'otel I know, and hear the band and see the dresses, and talk—is it not so?"

He could not have found a better companion. In the great lounge, later on, leaning back by his side, she chatted shrewdly and with merriment. She described dresses and laughed at his ignorance. She acclaimed certain pieces, and showed a real knowledge of music. She told him of life in Paris when the Hun had all but knocked at the gates, of the gaiety of relief, of things big and little, of the flowers in the Bois in the spring. He said little, but enjoyed himself. Much later she went with him to the station, and they stood outside to say good-bye.

"Well, little girl," he said, "you have given me a good evening, and I am very grateful. But I do not even know your name. Tell it me, that I may remember."

"Mariette," she said. "And will monsieur not take my card? He may be in Paris again. He is très agréable; I should like much to content him. One meets many, but there are few one would care to see again."

Peter smiled sadly. For the first time a wistful note had crept into her voice. He thought of others like her that he knew, and he spoke very tenderly. "No, Mariette," he said. "If I came back I might spoil a memory. Good-bye. God bless you!" and he held out his hand. She hesitated a second. Then she turned back to the taxi.

"Where would you like to go?" he demanded.

She leaned out and glanced up at the clock. "L'Avenue de l'Opéra," she said, "s'il vous plait."

The man thrust in the clutch with his foot, and Mariette was lost to Peter for ever in the multitude.

In Boulogne he heard that he was late for the first boat, but caught the second easily. Remembering Donovan's advice, he got his ticket for the Pullman at once, and was soon rolling luxuriously to town. The station was bustling as it had done what seemed to him an age before, but he stepped out with the feeling that he was no longer a fresher in the world's or any other university. Declining assistance, he walked over to the Grosvenor and engaged a room, dined, and then strolled out into Victoria Street.

It was all so familiar and it was all so different. He stood aloof and looked at himself, and played with the thought. It was incredible that he was the Peter Graham of less than a year before, and that he walked where he had walked a score of times. He went up Whitehall, and across the Square, and hesitated whether or not he should take the Strand. Deciding against it, he made his way to Piccadilly Circus and chose a music-hall that advertised a world-famous comedian. He heard him and came out, still laughing to himself, and then he walked down Piccadilly to Hyde Park Corner, and stood for a minute looking up Park Lane. Hilda ought to come down, he said to himself amusedly. Then, marvelling that he could be amused at all at the thought, he turned off for his hotel.

It is nothing to write down, but to Peter it was very much. Everything was old, but everything was new to him. At his hotel he smoked a cigarette in the lounge just to watch the men and women who came and went, and then he declined the lift and ascended the big staircase to his room. As he went, it struck him why it was that he felt so much wiser than he had been; that he looked on London from the inside, whereas he had used to look from the outside only; that he looked with a charity of which he had never dreamed, and that he was amazingly content. And as he got into bed he thought that when next he slept in town he would not be alone. He would have crossed Tommy's Rubicon.

Next morning he went down into the country to relations who did not interest him at all; but he walked and rode and enjoyed the English countryside with zest. He went to the little country church on the Sunday twice, to Matins and Evensong, and he came home and read that chapter of Mr. Wells' book in which Mr. Britling expounds the domestication of God. And he had some fierce moments in which he thought of Louise, and of Lucienne's sister, and of Mariette, and of Pennell, and, last of all, of Jenks, and asked himself of what use a domesticated God could be to any of them. And then on the Thursday he came up to meet Julie.

It thrilled him that she was in England somewhere and preparing to come to him. His pulses beat so as he thought of it that every other consideration was temporarily driven from his mind; but presently he caught himself thinking what ought to be done, and of what she would be like. He turned it over in his mind. He had known her in France, in uniform, when he was not sure of her; but now, what would she be like? He could not conceive, and he banished the idea. It would be more splendid when it occurred if he had made no imaginary construction of it.

His station was King's Cross, and he took a taxi to a big central hotel in the neighbourhood of Regent Street. And as he passed its doors they closed irrevocably on his past.

The girl at the bureau looked up and smiled. "Good-morning," she said. "What can I do for you? We are very full."

"Good-morning," he replied. "I expect you are, but my wife is coming up to town this afternoon, and we have only a few days together. We want to be as central as possible. Have you a small suite over the week-end?"

"I don't know," she said, and pulled the big book toward her. She ran a finger down the page. "Four-twenty," she said—"double bedroom, sitting-room, and bathroom, how would that do?"

"It sounds capital," said Peter. "May I go and see it?"

She turned in her seat, reached for a key, and touched a button. A man appeared, soundlessly on the thick, rich carpet. "Show this officer four-twenty, will you?" she said, and turned to someone else. What means so much to some of us is everyday business to others.

Peter followed across the hall and into a lift. They went up high, got out in a corridor, took a turn to the right, and stopped before a door numbered 420. The man opened it. Peter was led into a little hall, with two doors leading from it. The first room was the sitting-room. It was charmingly furnished and very cosy, a couple of good prints on the walls, wide fireplace, a tall standard lamp, some delightfully easy chairs—all this he took in at a glance. He walked to the window and looked out. Far below was the great thoroughfare, and beyond a wilderness of roofs and spires. He stood and gazed at it. London seemed a different place up there. He felt remote, and looked again into the street. Its business rolled on indifferent to him, and unaware. He glanced back into the snug pretty little room. How easy it all was, how secure! "This is excellent," he said, "Show me the bedroom."

"This way, sir," said, the man.

The bedroom was large and airy. A pretty light paper covered the walls, and two beds stood against one of them, side by side. The sun shone in at the big double windows and fell on the white paint of the woodwork, the plate-glass tops of the toilet-tables, and the thick cream-coloured carpet. A door was open on his right. He walked across, and looked in there too. A tiled bathroom, he saw it was, the clean towels on the highly polished brass rail heated by steam, the cork-mat against the wall, the shower, douche, and spray all complete, even the big cake of delicious-looking soap on its sliding rack across the bath. He looked as a man in a fairy-story might look. It was as if an enchanted palace, with the princess just round the corner, had been offered him. Smiling at the conceit, he turned to the man. "I didn't notice the telephone," he said; "I suppose it is installed?"

"In each room, sir," said the man.

"That will do," said Peter. "It will suit me admirably. Have my baggage sent up, will you, and say that I engage the suite. I will be down presently."

"Yes, sir," said the man, and departed.

Peter went back to the sitting-room, and threw himself into a chair. Then he had an idea, got up, went to the telephone, ordered a bottle of whisky to be sent up, and a siphon, and went back to his seat. Presently he was pouring himself out a drink and smoking a cigarette on his own (temporary) hearth-rug. The little incident increased his satisfaction. He was reassuring himself. Here he was really safe and remote and master, with a thousand servants and a huge palace at his beck and call, and all for a few pounds! It was absurd, but he thought to himself that he was feeling civilised for the first time, perhaps.

He looked round, and considered Julie. What would she want? Flowers to begin with, heaps of them; she liked violets for one thing, and by hook or by crook he would get a little wattle or mimosa to remind her of Africa. Then chocolates and cigarettes, both must never be lacking, and a few books—no, not books, magazines; and he would have some wine sent up. What else? Biscuits; after the theatre they might be jolly. Ah, the theatre! he must book seats. Well, a box would be better; they did not want to run too great a risk of being seen. Donovan was quite possibly in town, to say nothing of—older friends. Possibly, considering the run on the theatres, he had better book up fairly completely for the days they had together. But what would she like? Julie would never want to go if she did not spontaneously fancy a play. It was a portentous question, and he considered it long. Finally he decided on half-and-half measures, leaving some time free.... Time! how did it go? By Jove! he ought to make a move. Luncheon first; his last meal alone for some time; then order the things; and Victoria at 5.30. He poured himself another short drink and went out.

He lunched in a big public grill-room, and chatted with a naval officer at his table who was engaged in mine-sweeping with a steam-tramp. The latter was not vastly enthusiastic over things, but was chiefly depressed because he had to report at a naval base that night, and his short London leave was all but run out.

"Tell you what," he said, "I've seen a good many cities one way and another, from San Francisco to Singapore, and I know Paris and Brussels and Berlin, but you can take my word for it, there's no better place for ten days' leave than this same old blessed London. You can have some spree out East if you want it, but you can get much the same, if not better, here. If a fellow wants a bit of a skirt, he can get as good a pick in London as anywhere. If you want a good show, there isn't another spot in the universe that can beat it, whatever it is you feel like. If you want to slip out of sight for a bit, give me a big hotel like this in London. They don't damn-well worry about identification papers much here—too little, p'raps, these days. Did you hear of those German submarine officers who lived in an hotel in Southampton?"

Peter had; there were few people who hadn't, seeing that the same officers lived in most of the coast towns in England that year; but it is a pity to damp enthusiasm. He said he had heard a little.

"Walked in and out cool as you please. When they were drowned and picked up at sea, they had bills and theatre tickets in their pockets, and a letter acknowledging the booking of rooms for the next week! Fact. Had it from the fellow who got 'em. And I ask you, what is there to prevent it? You come here: 'Will you write your name and regiment, please.' You write the damned thing—any old thing, in fact—and what happens? Nothing. They don't refer to them. In France the lists go to a central bureau every day, but here—Lord bless you, the Kaiser himself might put up anywhere if he shaved his moustache!"

Peter heard him, well content. He offered a cigarette, feeling warmly disposed towards the world at large. The naval officer took it. "Thanks," he said. "You in town for long?"

"No," said Peter—"a week end. I've only just happened. What's worth seeing?"

"First and last all the way, *Carminetta*. It's a dream. Wonderful. By Gad, I don't know how that girl does it! Then I'd try *Zigzag*—oh! and go to *You Never Know, You Know*, at the Cri. Absolutely toppin'. A perfect scream all through. The thing at Daly's' good too; but all the shows are good, though, I reckon. Lumme, you wouldn't think the war was on, 'cept they all touch it a bit! *The Better 'Ole* I like, but you mightn't, knowing the real thing. But don't miss *Carminetta* if you have to stand all day for a seat in the gods. Well, I must be going. Damned rough luck, but no help for it. Let's have a last spot, eh?"

Peter agreed, and the drinks were ordered. "Chin-chin," said his acquaintance. "And here's to old London town, and the Good Lord let me see it again. It's less than even chances," he added reflectively.

"Here's luck," said Peter; then, for he couldn't help it: "It's you chaps, by God, that are winning this war!"

"Oh, I don't know," said the other, rising. "We get more leave than you fellows, and I'd sooner be on my tramp than in the trenches. The sea's good and clean to die in, anyway. Cheerio."

Peter followed him out in a few minutes, and set about his shopping. He found a florist's in Regent Street and bought lavishly. The girl smiled at him, and suggested this and that. "Having a dinner somewhere to-night?" she queried. "But I have no violets."

"Got my girl comin' up," said Peter expansively; "that's why there must be violets. See if you can get me some and send them over, will you?" he asked, naming his hotel. She promised to do her best, and he departed.

He went into a chocolate shop. "Got some really decent chocolates?" he demanded.

The girl smiled and dived under the counter. "These are the best," she said, holding out a shovelful for Peter to taste. He tried one. "They'll do," he said. "Give me a couple of pounds, in a pretty box if you've got one."

"Two pounds!" she exclaimed. "What are you thinking of? We can only sell a quarter."

"Only a quarter!" said Peter. "That's no good. Come on, make up the two pounds."

"If my boss comes in or finds out I'll be fired," said the girl; "can't be done."

"Well, that doesn't matter," said Peter innocently, "You'll easily get a job— something better and easier, I expect."

"It's easy enough, perhaps," said the girl, "but you never can tell. *And* it's dangerous, *and* uncertain."

Peter stared at her. When he bought chocolates as a parson, he never had talks like this. He wondered if London had changed since he knew it. Then he played up: "You're pretty enough to knock that last out, anyway?" he said.

"Am I?" she demanded. "Do you mean you'd like to keep me?"

"I've got one week-end left of leave," said Peter. "What about the chocolates?"

"Poor boy!" she said. "Well, I'll risk it." And she made up the two pounds.

He wandered into a tobacconist's, and bought cigarettes which Julie's soul loved, and then he made for a theatre booking-office.

Outside and his business done, he looked at his watch, and found he had a bit of time to spare. He walked down Shaftesbury Avenue, and thought he would get himself spruced up at a hairdresser's. He saw a little place with a foreigner at the door, and he went in. It was a tiny room with three seats all empty. The man seated him in one and began.

Peter discovered that his hair needed this and that, and being in a good temper and an idle mood acquiesced. Presently a girl came in. Peter smelt her enter, and then saw her in the glass. She was short and dark and foreign, too, and she wore a blouse that appeared to have remarkably little beneath it, and to be about to slip off her shoulders. She came forward and stood between him and the glass, smiling. "Wouldn't you like your nails manicured?" she demanded.

"Oh, I don't know," said Peter; "I had not meant to ..." and was lost.

"Second thoughts are best," she said; "but let me look at your hands. Oh, I should think you did need it! Whatever will your girl say to you to-night if you have hands like this?"

Peter, humiliated, looked at his hands. They did not appear to him to differ much from the hands Julie and others had seen without visible consternation before, but he had no time to say so. The young lady was now seated by his side with a basin of hot water, and was dabbling his hand in it. "Nice? Not too hot?" she inquired brightly.

Peter watched her as she bent over her work and kept up a running fire of talk. He gathered that many officers habitually were manicured by her, many of them in their own rooms. It was lucky for him that she was not out. Possibly he would like to make an appointment; she could come early or late. No? Then she thought his own manicure-set must be a poor one, judging from these hands, and perhaps she could sell him another. No? Well, a little cream. Not to-day? He would look in to-morrow? He hadn't a chance? She would tell him what: where was he staying? (Peter, for the fun of it, told her he had a private suite in the hotel.) Well, that was splendid. She would call in with a new set at any time, before breakfast, after the theatre, as he pleased; bring the cream and do his hands once with it to show him how. How would that suit him?

Peter was not required to say, for at that minute the shop-bell rang and a priest came in, a little old man, tired-looking, in a black cassock. He was apparently known, though he seemed to take no notice of anyone. The man was all civility, but put on an expression meant to indicate amusement, to Peter, behind the clerical back. The girl put one of Peter's fingers on her own lips by way of directing caution, and continued more or less in silence. The room became all but silent save for the sound of scissors and the noise of the traffic outside, and Peter reflected again on many things. When he had had his hair cut previously, for instance, had people made faces behind his back? Had young ladies ceased from tempting offers that seemed to include more than manicuring?

He got up to pay. "Well," she demanded, *sotto voce*, "what of the arrangement? She could do him easily at any..."

He cut her short. No; it was really impossible. His wife was coming up that afternoon. It was plain that she now regarded it as impossible also. He paid an enormous sum wonderingly, and departed.

Outside it struck him that he had forgotten one thing. He walked briskly to the hotel, and went up to his rooms. In the sitting-room was the big bunch of flowers and a maid unwrapping it. She turned and smiled at him. "These have just come for you, sir," she said. "Shall I arrange them for you?"

"No, thank you," said Peter. "I'd rather do them myself. I love arranging flowers, and I know just what my wife likes. I expect you'd do them better, but I'll have a shot, if you don't mind. Would you fill the glasses and get me a few more? We haven't enough here."

"Certainly, sir. There was a gentleman here once who did flowers beautifully, he did. But most likes us to do it for them."

She departed for the glasses. Peter saw that the florist had secured his violets, and took them first and filled a bowl. Then he walked into the bedroom and contemplated for a minute. Then he put the violets critically on the little table by the bed nearest the window, and stood back to see the result. Finding it good, he departed. When next he came in, it was to place a great bunch of roses on the mantelshelf, and a few sprays of the soft yellow and green mimosa on the dressing-table. For the sitting-room he had carnations and delphiniums, and he placed a high towering cluster of the latter on the writing-table, and a vase of the former on the mantelpiece. A few roses, left over, went on the small table that carried the reading-lamp, and he and the chambermaid surveyed the results.

"Lovely, I do think," she said; "any lady would love them. I likes flowers myself, I do. I come from the country, sir, where there's a many, and the wild flowers that Jack and I liked best of all. Specially primroses, sir." There was a sound in her voice as she turned away, and Peter heard it.

"Jack?" he queried softly.

"'E's been missing since last July, sir," she said, stopping by the door.

"Has he?" said Peter. "Well, you must not give up hope, you know; he may be a prisoner."

She shook her head. "He's dead," she said, with an air of finality. "I oughtn't to have spoke a word, but them flowers reminded me. I'm glad as how I have to do these rooms, sir. Most of them don't bother with flowers. Is there anything else you might be wanting, sir?"

"Light fires in both the grates, please," he said. "I'm so sorry about Jack," he added.

She gave him a look, and passed out.

Peter wandered about touching this and that. Suddenly he remembered the magazines. He ran out and caught a lift about to descend, and was once more in the street. Near Leicester Square was a big foreign shop, and he entered it, and gathered of all kinds. As he went to pay, he saw *La Vie Parisienne*, and added that also to the bundle; Julie used to say she loved it. Back in the hotel, he sent them to his room, and glanced at his watch. He had time for tea. He went out into the lounge and ordered it, sitting back under the palms. It came, and he was in the act of pouring out a cup when he saw Donovan.

Donovan was with a girl, but so were most men; Peter could not be sure of her. It was only a glimpse he had, for the two had finished and were passing out. Donovan stood back to let her first through the great swing-doors, and then, pulling on his gloves, followed. They both disappeared.

Peter sat on, in a tumult. He had been too busy all day to reflect much, but now just what he was about to do began to overwhelm him. If Donovan met him with Julie? Well, they could pretend they had just met, they could even part, and meet again. Could they? Would Donovan be deceived for a minute? It seemed to him impossible. And he might be staying there. Suppose he met someone else. Langton? Sir Robert Doyle? His late Vicar? Hilda? Mr. Lessing? And Julie would have acquaintances too. He shook himself mentally, and lit a cigarette. Well, suppose they did; he was finished with them. Finished? Then, what lay ahead—what, after this, if he were discovered? And if he were not discovered? God knew....

His mind took a new train of thought: he was now just such a one as Donovan. Or as Pennell. As Langton? He wasn't sure; no, he thought not; Langton kept straight because he had a wife and kids. He had a centre. Donovan and Pennell had not, apparently. Well, he, Peter Graham, would have a centre; he would marry Julie. It would be heavenly. They had not spoken of it, of course, that night of the dinner, but surely Julie would. There could be no doubt after the week-end.... "I shan't marry or be given in marriage," she had said. It was like her to speak so, but of course she didn't mean it. No, he would marry; and then?

He blew out smoke. The Colonies, South Africa; he would get a job schoolmastering? He hated the idea; it didn't interest him. A farm? He knew nothing about it—besides, one wanted capital. What would he do? What did he want to do? *Want*—that was it; how did he want to spend his life? Well, he wanted Julie; everything else would fit round her, everything else would be secondary beside her. Of course. And as he got old it would still be the same, though he could not imagine either of them old. But still, when they did get old, his work would seem more important, and what was it to be? Probably it would have to be schoolmastering. Teaching Latin to little boys—History, Geography, Mathematics. He smiled ruefully; even factors worried him. They would hardly want Latin and Greek much in the Colonies, either. Perhaps at home; but would Julie stop at home? What *would* Julie do? He must ask her, sometime before Monday. Not that night—no, not *that* night....

He ground his cigarette into his cup, and pushed his hands into his pockets, his feet out before him. That night! He saw the sitting-room upstairs; they would go there first. Then he would suggest a dinner to her, in Soho; he knew a place that Pennell had told him of, Bohemian, but one could take anyone—at least, take Julie. It would be jolly watching the people, and watching Julie. He saw her, mentally, opposite him, and her eyes sparkling and alluring. And afterwards, warmed and fed—why, back to the hotel, to the sitting-room, by the fire. They would have a little supper, and then....

He pictured the bedroom. He would let Julie go first. He remembered reading in a novel how some newly married wife said to the fellow: "You'll come up in half an hour or so, won't you, dear?" He could all but see the words in print. And so, in half an hour or so, he would go in, and Julie would be in bed, by the violets, and he—he would know what men talked about, sometimes, in the anteroom.... He recalled a red-faced, coarse Colonel: "No man's a man till he's been all the way, I say...."

And he was a chaplain, a priest. Was he? The past months spun before him, his sermons, his talks to the wounded at the hospital, the things he had seen, the stories he had heard. He sighed. It was all a dream, a sham. There was no reality in it all. Where and what was Christ? An ideal, yes, but no more than an ideal, and unrealisable—a vision of the beautiful. He thought he had seen that once, but not now. The beautiful! Ah! What place had His Beauty in Travalini's, in the shattered railway-carriage, in the dinner at the Grand in Havre with Julie?

Julie. He dwelt on her, eyes, hair, face, skin, and lithe figure. He felt her kisses again on his lips, those last burning kisses of New Year's Night, and they were all to be his, as never before.... Julie. What, then, was she? She was his bride, his wife, coming to him consecrate—not by any State convention, not by any ceremony of man-made religion, but by the pure passion of human love, virginal, clean. It was human passion, perhaps, but where was higher love or greater sacrifice? Was this not worthy of all his careful preparation, worthy of the one centre of his being? Donovan, indeed! He wished he had stopped and told him the whole story, and that he expected Julie that night.

He jumped up, and walked out in the steps of Donovan, but with never another thought of him. A boy in uniform questioned him: "Taxi, sir?" He nodded, and the commissionaire pushed back the great swing-door. He stood on the steps, and watched the passers-by, and the lights all shaded as they were, that began to usher in a night of mystery. His taxi rolled up, and the man held the door open. "Victoria!" cried Peter, and to himself, as he sank back on the seat, "Julie!"

CHAPTER VII

"Julie!" exclaimed Peter, "I should hardly have known you; you do look topping!"

"Glad rags make all that difference, old boy? Well, I am glad you did know me, anyhow. How are you? Had long to wait?"

"Only ten minutes or so, and I'm very fit, and just dying for you, Julie."

She smiled up at him and blushed a little. "Are you, Peter? It's much the same here, my dear. But don't you think we had better get a move on, and not stop here talking all night?"

Peter laughed excitedly. "Rather," he said. "But I'm so excited at seeing you that I hardly know if I'm on my head or my heels. What about your luggage? What have you? Have you any idea where it is? There's a taxi waiting."

"I haven't much: a big suit-case, most important because it holds an evening dress—it's marked with my initials; a small leather trunk, borrowed, with a big star on it; and my dressing-case, which is here. And I *think* they're behind, but I wouldn't swear, because we've seemed to turn round three times in the course of the journey, but it may have been four!"

Peter chuckled. She was just the old Julie, but yet with a touch of something more shining in her eyes, and underlying even the simplest words.

"Well, you stand aside just a moment and I'll go and see," he said, and he hurried off in the crowd.

Julie stood waiting patiently by a lamp-stand while the world bustled about her. She wore a little hat with a gay pheasant's wing in it, a dark green travelling dress and neat brown shoes, and brown silk stockings. Most people looked at her as they passed, including several officers, but there was a different look in her brown eyes from that usually there, and they all passed on unhesitatingly.

It seemed to her a good while before Peter came up again, in his wake a railway Amazon with the trunk on her shoulder and the suit-case in her hand. "Sorry to keep you, dear," he said. "But there was a huge crush and next to no porters, if these *are* porters. It feels rotten to have a woman carrying one's luggage, but I suppose it can't be helped. Come on. Aren't you tired? Don't you want tea?"

"I am a little," she said "And I do a bit. Where are we going to get it? Do they sell teas in London, Peter, or have you taken a leaf out of my book?"

They laughed at the reminiscence. "Julie," said Peter, "this is my outfit, and you shall see what you think of it. Give me your ticket, will you? I want to see you through myself."

She handed him a little purse without a word, and they set off together. She was indulging in the feeling of surrender as if it were not a victory she had won, and he was glowing with the sense of acquisition, as if he had really acquired something.

Julie got into the taxi while Peter settled the luggage, gave directions, and paid the Amazon. Then he climbed in and pulled the door to, and they slipped out of the crowded station-yard into the roar of London. Julie put her hand in his. "Peter," she said, "do tell me where we're going. I'm dying to know. What arrangements have you made? Is it safe?"

He leaned over her, his eyes sparkling. "A kiss, first, Julie: no one will see and it doesn't matter a damn if they do. That's the best of London. My dear, I can hardly believe we're both here at last, and that I've really got you." Their lips met.

Julie flung herself back with a laugh. "Oh, Peter," she said, "I shall never forget that first taxi. If you could have seen your own face! Really it was too comic, but I must say you've changed since then."

"I was a fool and a beast," he said, more gravely; "I'm only just beginning to realise how much of a fool. But don't rub it in, Julie, or not just now. I'm starting to live at last, and I don't want to be reminded of the past."

She pressed his hand and looked out of window. "Where are we, Peter? Whitehall? Where are we off to?"

"I've got the snuggest little suite in all London, darling," he said, "with a fairy palace at our beck and call. I've been revelling in it all day—not exactly in it, you know, but in the thought of it. I've been too busy shopping to be in much; and Julie, I hope you notice my hands: I've had a special manicure in preparation for you. And the girl is coming round to-morrow before breakfast to do me again—or at least she wanted to."

"What are you talking about? Peter, what have you been doing to-day?" She sighed a mock sigh. "Really, you're getting beyond me; it's rather trying."

Peter launched out into the story to fill up time. He really did not want to speak of the rooms, that they might give her the greater surprise. So he kept going till the taxi stopped before the hotel. He jumped out gaily as the commissionaire opened the door.

"Come on," he said, "as quick as ever you can." Then, to the man: "Have these sent up to No. 420, will you, please?" And he took Julie's arm.

They went in at the great door, and crossed the wide entrance-hall. Everyone glanced at Julie, Peter noted proudly, even the girls behind the sweet-counter, and the people waiting about as always. Julie held her head high and walked more sedately than usual. She *was* a bit different, thought Peter, but even nicer. He glowed at the thought.

He led her to the lift and gave his landing number. They walked down the corridor in silence and in at their door. Peter opened the door on the left and stood back. Julie went in. He followed and shut the door behind them.

The maid had lit a fire, which blazed merrily. Julie took it all in—the flowers, the pile of magazines, even the open box of cigarettes, and she turned enthusiastically to him and flung her arms round his neck, kissing him again and again. "Oh, Peter darling," she cried, "I can't tell you how I love you! I could hardly sit still in the railway carriage, and the train seemed worse than a French one. But now I have you at last, and all to myself. Oh, Peter, my darling Peter!"

There came a knock at the door. Julie disengaged her arms from his neck, but slipped her hand in his, and he said, "Come in."

The maid entered, carrying tea. She smiled at them. "I thought madame might like tea at once, sir," she said, and placed the tray on the little table.

"Thank you ever so much," said Julie impulsively; "that is good of you. I'm longing for it. One gets so tired in the train." Then she walked to the glass. "I'll take off my hat, Peter," she said, "and my coat, and then we'll have tea comfortably. I do want it, and a cigarette. You're an angel to have thought of my own De Reszke."

She threw herself into a big basket chair, and leaned over to the table. "Milk and sugar for you, Peter? By the way, I ought to know these things; not that it much matters; ours was a war marriage, and I've hardly seen you at all!"

Peter sat opposite, and watched her pour out. She leaned back with a piece of toast in her hands, her eyes on him, and they smiled across at each other. Suddenly he could bear it no longer. He put his cup down and knelt forward at her feet, his arms on her knees, devouring her. "Oh, Julie," he said, "I want to worship you—I do indeed. I can't believe my luck. I can't think that *you* love *me*."

Her white teeth bit into the toast. "You old silly," she said. "But I don't want to be worshipped; I *won't* be worshipped; I want to be loved, Peter."

He put his arms up, and pulled her head down to his, kissing her again and again, stroking her arm, murmuring foolish words that meant nothing and meant everything. It was she who stopped him. "Go and sit down," she said, "and tell me all the plans."

"Well," he said, "I do hope you'll like them. First, I've not booked up anything for to-night. I thought we'd go out to dinner to a place I know and sit over it, and enjoy ourselves. It's a place in Soho, and quite humorous, I think. Then we might walk back: London's so perfect at night, isn't it? To-morrow I've got seats for the Coliseum matinee. You know it, of course; it's a jolly place where one can talk if one wants to, and smoke; and then I've seats in the evening for *Zigzag*. Saturday night we're going to see *Carminetta*, which they say is the best show in town, and Saturday morning we can go anywhere you please, or do anything. And we can cut out any of them if you like," he added.

She let her arms lie along the chair, and drew a breath of delight. "You're truly wonderful," she said. "What a blessing not having to worry what's to be done! It's a perfect programme. I only wish we could be in Paris for Sunday; it's so slow here."

He smiled. "You're sure you're not bored about to-night?" he asked. She looked him full in the eyes and said nothing. He sprang up and rushed towards her. She laughed her old gay laugh, and avoided him, jumping up and getting round the table. "No," she warned; "no more now. Come and show me the rest of the establishment."

Arm in arm they made the tour of inspection. In the bathroom Julie's eyes danced. "Thank the Lord for that bath, Peter," she said. "I shall revel in it. That's one thing I loathe about France, that one can't get decent baths, and in the country here it's no better. I had two inches of water in a foot-bath down in Sussex, and when you sit in the beastly thing only about three inches of yourself get wet and those the least important inches. I shall lie in this for hours and smoke, and you shall feed me with chocolates and read to me. How will you like that?"

Peter made the only possible answer, and they went back to the bedroom. The man was bringing up her luggage, and he deposited it on the luggage-stool. "Heavens!" said Julie, "where are my keys? Oh, I know, in my purse. I hope you haven't lost it. Do give it to me. The suit-case is beautifully packed, but the trunk is in an appalling mess. I had to throw my things in anyhow. By the way, I wonder what they'll make of different initials on all our luggage? Not that it matters a scrap, especially these days. Besides, I don't suppose they noticed."

She was on her knees by the trunk, and had undone it. She lifted the lid, and Peter saw the confusion inside, and caught sight of the unfamiliar clothes, Julie was rummaging everywhere. "I know I've left them behind!" she exclaimed. "Whatever shall I do? My scent and powder-puff! Peter, it's terrible! I can't go to Soho to dinner without them."

"Let's go and get some," he suggested; "there's time."

"No, I can't," she said. "You go. Don't be long. I want to sit in front of the fire and be cosy."

Peter set off on the unfamiliar errand, smiling grimly to himself. He got the scent easily enough, and then inquired for a powder-puff. In the old days he would scarcely have dared; but he had been in France. He selected a little French box with a mirror in the lid and a pretty rosebud pattern, and paid for it unblushingly. Then he returned.

He opened the door of their sitting-room, and stood transfixed for a minute. The shaded reading-lamp was on, the other lights off. The fire glowed red, and Julie lay stretched out in a big chair, smoking a cigarette. She turned and looked up at him over her shoulder. She had taken off her dress and slipped on a silk kimono, letting her hair down, which fell in thick tumbled masses about her. The arm that held the cigarette was stretched up above her, and the wide, loose sleeve of the kimono had slipped back, leaving it bare to her shoulder. Her white frilled petticoat showed beneath, as she had pushed her feet out before her to the warmth of the fire. Peter's blood pounded in his temples.

"Good boy," she said; "you haven't been long. Come and show me. I had to get comfortable: I hope you don't mind."

He came slowly forward without a word and bent over her. The scent of her rose intoxicatingly around him as he bent down for a kiss. Their lips clung together, and the wide world stood still.

Julie made room for him beside her. "You dear old thing," she exclaimed at the sight of the powder-puff. "It's a gem. You couldn't have bettered it in Paris." She opened it, took out the little puff, and dabbed her open throat. Then, laughing, she dabbed at him: "Don't look so solemn," she said, "Solomon!"

Peter slipped one arm round her beneath the kimono, and felt her warm relaxed waist. Then he pushed his other hand, unresisted, in where her white throat gleamed bare and open to him, and laid his lips on her hair. "Oh, Julie," he said, "I had no idea one could love so. It is almost more than I can bear."

The clock on the mantelpiece struck a half-hour, and Julie stirred in his arms and glanced up. "Good Lord, Peter!" she exclaimed, "do you know what the time is? Half-past seven! I shall never be dressed, and we shall get no dinner. Let me up, for goodness sake, and give me a drink if you've got such a thing. If not, ring for it. I shall never have energy enough to get into my things otherwise."

Peter opened the little door of the sideboard and got out decanter, siphon, and glasses. Julie, sitting up and arranging herself, smiled at him. "Is there a single thing you haven't thought of, you old dear?" she said.

"Say when," said Peter, coming towards her. Then he poured himself out a tumbler and stood by the fire, looking at her.

"It's a pity we have to go out at all," he said, "for I suppose you can't go like that."

"A pity? It's a jolly good thing. You wait till you've seen my frock, my dear. But, Peter, do you think there's likely to be anyone there that we know?"

He shook his head. "Not there, at any rate," he said.

"Here?"

"More likely, but it's such a big place we're not likely to meet them, even so. But if you feel nervous, do you know the best cure? Come down into the lounge, and see the crowd of people. You sit there and people stream by, and you don't know a face. It's the most comfortable, feeling in the world. One's more alone than on a desert island. You might be a ghost that no one sees."

Julie shuddered. "Peter don't! You make me feel creepy." She got up "Go and find that maid, will you? I want her to help me dress."

Peter walked to the bell and rang it, "Where do I come in?" he asked.

"Well, you can go and wash in the bathroom, and if you're frightened of her you can dress there!" And she walked to the door laughing.

"I'll just finish my drink," he said. "You will be heaps longer than I."

Five minutes later, having had no answer to his ring, he switched off the light, and walked out into the hall He hesitated at Julie's door, then he tapped. "Come in," she said.

She was standing half-dressed in front of the glass doing her hair, "Oh, it's you, is it?" she said. "Wherever is that maid? I can't wait all night for her; you'll have to help."

Peter sat down and began to change. Half-surreptitiously he watched Julie moving about, and envied her careless abandon. He was much the more nervous of the two.

Presently she called him from the bathroom to fasten her dress. When it was done, she stood back for him to examine her.

"That all right?" she demanded, putting a touch here and there.

Not every woman could have worn her gown. It was a rose pink with some rich flame-coloured material in front, and was held by two of the narrowest bands on her shoulders. In the deep *décolleté* she pushed two rosebuds from the big bunch, and hung round her neck a pendant of mother-of-pearl and silver. She wore no other jewellery, and she needed none. She faced him, a vision of loveliness.

They went down the stairs together and out into the crush of people, some of the women in evening dress, but few of the men. The many uniforms looked better, Peter thought, despite the drab khaki. They had to stand for awhile while a taxi was found, Julie laughing and chatting vivaciously. She had a wrap for her shoulders that she had bought in Port Said, set with small metallic points, and it sparkled about her in the blaze of light. She flattered him by seeming unconscious of anyone else, and put her hand on his arm as they went out.

They drove swiftly through back-streets to the restaurant that Peter had selected, and stopped in a quiet, dark, narrow road off Greek Street. Julie got out and looked around with pretended fear. "Where in the world have you brought me?" she demanded. "However did you find the place? It's worse than some of your favourite places in Havre."

Inside, however, she looked round appreciatively. "Really, Peter, it's splendid," she said under her breath—"just the place," and smiled sweetly on the padrone who came forward, bowing. Peter had engaged a table, and they were led to it.

"I had almost given you up, sir," said the man, "but by good fortune, some of our patrons are late too."

They sat down opposite to each other, and studied the menu held out to them by a waiter. "I don't know the meaning of half the dishes," laughed Julie. "You order. It'll be more fun if I don't know what's coming."

"We must drink Chianti," said Peter, and ordered a bottle. "You can think you are in Italy."

Elbows on the table as she waited, Julie looked round. In the far corner a gay party of four were halfway through dinner. Two officers, an elderly lady and a young one, she found rather hard to place, but Julie decided the girl was the fiancée of one who had brought his friend to meet her. At other tables were mostly couples, and across the room from her, with an elderly officer, sat a well-made-up woman, very plainly *demimonde*. Immediately before her were four men, two of them foreigners, in morning dress, talking and eating hare. It was evidently a professional party, and one of the four now and again hummed out a little air to the rest, and once jotted down some notes on the back of a programme. They took no notice of anyone, but the eyes of the woman with the officer, who hardly spoke to her, searched Julie unblushingly.

Julie, gave a little sigh of happiness. "This is lovely, Peter," she said. "We'll be ages over dinner. It's such fun to be in nice clothes just for dinner sometimes and not to have to worry about the time, and going on elsewhere. But I do wish my friends could see me, I must say. They'd be horrified. They thought I was going to a stodgy place in West Kensington. I was must careful to be vague, but that was the idea. Peter, how would you like to live in a suburb and have heaps of children, and dine out with city men and their wives once or twice a month for a treat?"

Peter grimaced. Then he looked thoughtful. "It wouldn't have been any so remarkable for me at one time, Julie," he said.

She shook her head. "It would, my dear. You're not made for it."

"What am I made for, then?"

She regarded him solemnly, and then relaxed into a smile. "I haven't a notion, but not that. The thing is never to worry. You get what you're made for in the end, I think."

"I wonder," said Peter. "Perhaps, but not always. The world's full of square pegs in round holes."

"Then they're stodgy pegs, without anything in them. If I was a square peg I'd never go into a round hole."

"Suppose there was no other hole to go into," demanded Peter.

"Then I'd fall out, or I wouldn't go into any hole at all. I'd sooner be anything in the world than stodgy, Peter. I'd sooner be like that woman over there who is staring at me so!"

Peter glanced to one side, and then back at Julie. He was rather grave. "Would you really?" he questioned.

The waiter brought the Chianti and poured out glasses. Julie waited till he had gone, and then lifted hers and looked at Peter across it. "I would," she said. "I couldn't live without wine and excitement and song. I'm made that way. Cheerio, Solomon!"

They drank to each other. Then: "And love?" queried Peter softly.

Julie did not reply for a minute. She set her wine-glass down and toyed with the stem. Then she looked up at him under her eyelashes with that old daring look of hers, and repeated: "And love, Peter. But real love, not stodgy humdrum liking, Peter. I want the love that's like the hot sun, and the wide, tossing blue sea east of Suez, and the nights under the moon where the real world wakes up and doesn't go to sleep, like it does in the country in the cold, hard North. Do you know," she went on, "though I love the cities, and bands, and restaurants, and theatres, and taxis, and nice clothes, I love best of all the places where one has none of these things. I once went with a shooting-party to East Africa, Peter, and that's what I love. I shall never forget the nights at Kilindini, with the fireflies dancing among the bushes, and the moon glistening on the palms as if they were wet, and the insects shrilling in the grass, and the hot, damp air. Or by day, up in the forest, camped under the great trees, with the strange few flowers and the silence, while the sun trickled through the leaves and made pools of light on the ground. Do you know, I saw the most beautiful thing I've ever seen or, I think, shall see in that forest."

"What was that?" asked Peter, under her spell, for she was speaking like a woman in a dream.

"It was one day when we were marching. We came on a glade among the trees, and at the end of it, a little depression of damp green grass, only the grass was quite hidden beneath a sheet of blue—such blue, I can't describe it—that quivered and moved in the sun. We stood quite still, and then a boy threw a little stone. And the blue all rose in the air, silently, like magic. It was a swarm of hundreds and hundreds of blue butterflies, Peter. Do you know what I did? I cried—I couldn't help it. It was too beautiful to see, Peter."

A little silence fell between them. She broke it in another tone.

"And the natives—I love the natives. I just love the all but naked girls carrying the water up to the village in the evening, tall and straight, like Greek statues; and the men, in a string of beads and a spear. I wanted to go naked myself there—at least, I did till one day I tried it, and the sun skinned me in no time. But at least one needn't wear much—cool loose things, and it doesn't matter what one does or says."

Peter laughed. "Who was with you when you tried the experiment?" he demanded.

Julie threw her head back, and even the professional four glanced up and looked at her. "Ah, wouldn't you like to know?" she laughed. "Well, I won't tease you—two native girls if you want to know, that was all. The rest of the party were having a midday sleep. But I never can sleep at midday. I don't mind lying in a hammock or a deck-chair, and reading, but I can't sleep. One feels so beastly when one wakes up, doesn't one?"

Peter nodded, but steered her back. "Tell me more," he said. "You wake something up in me; I feel as if I was born to be there."

"Well," she said reflectively, "I don't know that anything can beat the great range that runs along our border in Natal. It's different, of course, but it's very wonderful. There's one pass I know—see here, you go up a wide valley with a stream that runs in and out, and that you have to cross again and again until it narrows and narrows to a small footpath between great kranzes. At first there are queer stunted trees and bushes about, with the stream, that's now a tiny thing of clear water, singing among them, and there the trees stop, and you climb up and up among the boulders, until you think you can do no more, and at the last you come out on the top."

"And then?"

"You're in wonderland. Before you lies peak on peak, grass-grown and rocky, so clear in the rare, still air. There is nothing there but mountain and rock and grass, and the blue sky, with perhaps little clouds being blown across it, and a wind that's cool and vast—you feel it fills everything. And you look down the way you've come, and there's all Natal spread out at your feet like a tiny picture, lands and woods and rivers, till it's lost in the mist of the distance."

She ceased, staring at her wine-glass. At last the chatter of the place broke in on Peter. "My dear," he exclaimed, "one can see it. But what do you do there?"

She laughed and broke the spell. "What would one do?" she demanded. "Eat and drink and sleep, and make love, Peter, if there's anybody to make love to."

"But you couldn't do that all your life," he objected.

"Why not? Why do anything else? I never can see. And when you're tired—for you *do* get tired at last—back to Durban for a razzle-dazzle, or back farther still, to London or Paris for a bit. That's the life for me, Peter!"

He smiled: "Provided somebody is there with the necessary, I suppose?" he said.

"Solomon," she mocked, "Solomon, Solomon! Why do you spoil it all? But you're right, of course, Peter, though I hate to think of that."

"I see how we're like, and how we're unlike, Julie," said Peter suddenly, "You like real things, and so do I. You hate to feel stuffy and tied up in conventions, and so do I. But you're content with just that, and I'm not."

"Am I?" she queried, looking at him a little strangely.

Peter did not notice; he was bent on pursuing his argument. "Yes, you are," he said. "When you're in the grip of real vital things—nature naked and unashamed—you have all you want. You don't stop to think of to-morrow. You live. But I, I feel that there is something round the corner all the time. I feel as if there must be something bigger than just that. I'd love your forest and your range and your natives, I think, but only because one is nearer something else with them than here. I don't know how to put it, but when you think of those things you feel *full*, and I still feel *empty*."

"Peter," said Julie softly, "do you remember Caudebec?"

He looked up at her then. "I shall never forget it, dear," he said.

"Then you'll remember our talk in the car?"

He nodded. "When you talked about marriage and human nature and men, and so on," he said.

"No, I don't mean that. I did talk of those things, and I gave you a little rather bitter philosophy that is more true than you think; but I don't mean that. Afterwards, when we spoke about shams and playing. Do you remember, I hinted that a big thing might come along—do you remember?"

He nodded again, but he did not speak.

"Well," she said, "it's come—that's all."

"Another bottle of Chianti, sir?" queried the padrone at his elbow.

Peter started. "What? Oh, yes, please," he said. "We can manage another bottle, Julie? And bring on the dessert now, will you? Julie, have a cigarette."

"If we have another bottle you must drink most of it," she laughed, almost as if they had not been interrupted, but with a little vivid colour in her cheeks. "Otherwise, my dear, you'll have to carry me upstairs, which won't look any too well. But I want another glass. Oh, Peter, do look at that woman now!"

Peter looked. The elderly officer had dined to repletion and drank well too. The woman had roused herself; she was plainly urging him to come on out; and as Peter glanced over, she made an all but imperceptible sign to a waiter, who bustled forward with the man's cap and stick. He took them stupidly, and the woman helped him up, but not too noticeably. Together they made for the door, which the waiter held wide open. The woman tipped him, and he bowed. The door closed, and the pair disappeared into the street.

"A damned plucky sort," said Julie; "I don't care what anyone says."

"I didn't think so once, Julie," said Peter, "but I believe you're right now. It's a topsy-turvy world, little girl, and one never knows where one is in it."

"Men often don't," said Julie, "but women make fewer mistakes. Come, Peter, let's get back. I want the walk, and I want that cosy little room."

He drained his glass and got up. Suddenly the thought of the physical Julie ran through him like fire. "Rather!" he said gaily. "So do I, little girl."

The waiter pulled back the chairs. The padrone came up all bows and smiles. He hoped the Captain would come again—any time. It was better to ring up, as they were often very full. A taxi? No? Well, the walk through the streets was enjoyable after dinner, even now, when the lights were so few. Good-evening, madame; he hoped everything had been to her liking.

Julie sauntered across the now half-empty little room, and took Peter's arm in the street. "Do you know the way?" she demanded.

"We can't miss it," he said. "Up here will lead us to Shaftesbury Avenue somewhere, and then we go down. Sure you want to walk, darling?"

"Yes, and see the people, Peter, I love seeing them. Somehow by night they're more natural than they are by day. I hate seeing people going to work in droves, and men rushing about the city with dollars written all across their faces. At night that's mostly finished with. One can see ugly things, but some rather beautiful ones as well. Let's cross over. There are more people that side."

They passed together down the big street. Even the theatres were darkened to some extent, but taxis were about, and kept depositing their loads of men and smiling women. The street-walks held Tommies, often plainly with a sweet-heart from down east; men who sauntered along and scanned the faces of the women; a newsboy or two; a few loungers waiting to pick up odd coppers; and here and there a woman by herself. It was the usual crowd, but they were in the mood to see the unusual in usual things.

In the Circus they lingered a little. Shrouded as it was, an atmosphere of mystery hung over everything. Little groups that talked for a while at the corners or made appointments, or met and broke up again, had the air of conspirators in some great affair. The rush of cars down Regent Street, and then this way and that, lent colour to the thought, and it affected both of them. "What's brooding over it all, Julie?" Peter half-whispered. "Can't you feel that there is something?"

She shrugged her shoulders, and then gave a little shiver. "Love, or what men take for love," she said.

He clasped the hand that lay along his arm passionately. "Come along," he said.

"Oh, this *is* good, Peter," said Julie a few minutes later. She had thrown off her wrap, and was standing by the fire while he arranged the cigarettes, the biscuits, and a couple of drinks on the little table with its shaded light. "Did you lock the door? Are we quite alone, we two, at last, with all the world shut out?"

He came swiftly over to her, and took her in his arms for answer. He pressed kisses on her hair, her lips, her neck, and she responded to them.

"Oh, love, love," he said, "let's sit down and forget that there is anything but you and I."

She broke from him with a little laugh of excitement. "We will, Peter," she said; "but I'm going to take off this dress and one or two other things, and let my hair down. Then I'll come back."

"Take them off here," he said; "you needn't go away."

She looked at him and laughed again. "Help me, then," she said, and turned her back for him to loosen her dress.

Clumsily he obeyed. He helped her off with the shimmering beautiful thing, and put it carefully over a chair. With deft fingers she loosened her hair, and he ran his fingers through it, and buried his face in the thick growth of it. She untied a ribbon at her waist, and threw from her one or two of her mysterious woman's things. Then, with a sigh of utter abandonment, she threw herself into his arms.

They sat long over the fire. Outside the dull roar of the sleepless city came faintly up to them, and now and again a coal fell in the grate. At long last Peter pushed her back a little from him. "Little girl," he said, "I must ask one thing. Will you forgive me? That night at Abbeville, after we left Langton, what was it you wouldn't tell me? What was it you thought he would have known about you, but not I? Julie, I thought, to-night—was it anything to do with East Africa—those tropical nights under the moon? Oh, tell me, Julie!"

The girl raised her eyes to his. That look of pain and knowledge that he had seen from the beginning was in them again. Her hand clasped the lappet of his tunic convulsively, and she seemed to him indeed but a little girl.

"Peter! could you not have asked? But no, you couldn't, not you.... But you guess now, don't you? Oh, Peter, I was so young, and I thought—oh, I thought: the big thing had come, and since then life's been all one big mockery. I've laughed at it, Peter: it was the only way. And then you came along. I haven't dared to think, but there's something about you—oh, I don't know what! But you don't play tricks, do you, Peter? And you've given me all, at last, without a question.... Oh, Peter, tell me you love me still! It's your love, Peter, that can make me clean and save my soul—if I've any soul to save," she added brokenly.

Peter caught her to him. He crushed her so that she caught her breath with the pain of it, and he wound his hand all but savagely in her hair. He got up—and she never guessed he had the strength—and carried her out in his arms, and into the other room.

And hours later, staring into the blackness while she slept as softly as a child by his side, he could not help smiling a little to himself. It was all so different from what he had imagined.

CHAPTER VIII

Peter awoke, and wondered where he was. Then his eye fell on a half-shut, unfamiliar trunk across the room, and he heard splashing through the open door of the bathroom. "Julie!" he called.

A gurgle of laughter came from the same direction and the splashing ceased. Almost the next second Julie appeared in the doorway. She was still half-wet from the water, and her sole dress was a rosebud which she had just tucked into her hair. She stood there, laughing, a perfect vision of unblushing natural loveliness, splendidly made from her little head poised lightly on her white shoulders to her slim feet. "You lazy creature!" she exclaimed; "you're awake at last, are you? Get up at once," and she ran over to him just as she was, seizing the bed-clothes and attempting to strip them off. Peter protested vehemently. "You're a shameless baggage," he said, "and I don't want to get up yet. I want some tea and a cigarette in bed. Go away!"

"You won't get up, won't you?" she said. "All right; I'll get into bed, then," and she made as if to do so.

"Get away!" he shouted. "You're streaming wet! You'll soak everything."

"I don't care," she retorted, laughing and struggling at the same time, and she succeeded in getting a foot between the sheets. Peter slipped out on the other side, and she ran round to him. "Come on," she said; "now for your bath. Not another moment. My water's steaming hot, and it's quite good enough for you. You can smoke in your bath or after it. Come on!"

She dragged him into the bathroom and into that bath, and then she filled a sponge with cold water and trickled it on him, until he threatened to jump out and give her a cold douche. Then, panting with her exertions and dry now, she collapsed on the chair and began to fumble with her hair and its solitary rose. It was exactly Julie who sat there unashamed in her nakedness, Peter thought. She had kept the soul of a child through everything, and it could burst through the outer covering of the woman who had tasted of the tree of knowledge of good and evil and laugh in the sun.

"Peter," she said, "wouldn't you love to live in the Fiji—no, not the Fiji, because I expect that's civilised these days, but on an almost desert island?—though not desert, of course. Why does one call Robinson Crusoe sort of islands *desert*? Oh, I know, because it means deserted, I suppose. But I don't want it quite deserted, for I want you, and three or four huts of nice savages to cut up wood for the fire and that sort of thing. And I should wear a rose—no, a hibiscus—in my hair all day long, and nothing else at all. And you should wear—well, I don't know what you should wear, but something picturesque that covered you up a bit, because you're by no means so good-looking as I am, Peter." She jumped up and stretched out her arms, "Am I not good-looking, Peter? Why isn't there a good mirror in this horrid old bathroom? It's more necessary in a bathroom than anywhere, I think."

"Well, I can see you without it," said Peter. "And I quite agree, Julie, you're divine. You are like Aphrodite, sprung from the foam."

She laughed. "Well, spring from the foam yourself, old dear, and come and dress. I'm getting cold. I'm going to put on the most thrilling set of undies this morning that you ever saw. The cami-... "

Peter put his fingers in his ears. "Julie," he said, "in one minute I shall blush for shame. Go and put on something, if you must, but don't talk about it. You're like a Greek goddess just now, but if you begin to quote advertisements you'll be like—well, I don't know what you'll be like, but I won't have it, anyway. Go on; get away with you. I shall throw the sponge at you if you don't."

She departed merrily, singing to herself, and Peter lay a little longer in the soft warm water. He dwelt lovingly on the girl in the other room; he told himself he was the happiest man alive; and yet he got out of the bath, without apparent rhyme or reason, with a little sigh. But he was only a little quicker than most men in that. Julie had attained and was radiant; Peter had attained—and sighed.

She was entirely respectable by contrast when he rejoined her, shaven and half-dressed, a little later, but just as delectable, as she stood in soft white things putting up her hair with her bare arms. He went over and kissed her. "You never said good-morning at all, you wretch," he said.

She flung her arms round his neck and kissed him again many times. "Purposely," she said. "I shall never say good-morning to you while you're horribly unshaven—never. You can't help waking up like it, I know, but it's your duty to get clean and decent as quickly as possible. See?"

"I'll try *always* to remember," said Peter, and stressed the word.

She held him for an appreciable second at that; then loosed him with a quick movement. "Go, now," she said, "and order breakfast to be brought up to our sitting-room. It must be a very nice breakfast. There must be kippers and an omelette. Go quick; I'll be ready in half a minute."

"I believe that girl is sweeping the room," said Peter. "Am I to appear like this? You must remember that we're not in France."

"Put on a dressing-gown then. You haven't got one here? Then put on my kimono; you'll look exceedingly beautiful.... Really, Peter, you do. Our island will have to be Japan, because kimonos suit you. But I shall never live to reach it if you don't order that breakfast."

Peter departed, and had a satisfactory interview with the telephone in the presence of the maid. He returned with a cigarette between his lips, smiling, and Julie turned to survey him.

"Peter, come here. Have you kissed that girl? I believe you have! How dare you? Talk about being shameless, with me here in the next room!"

"I thought you never minded such things, Julie. You've told me to kiss girls before now. *And* you said that you'd always allow your husband complete liberty—now, didn't you?"

Julie sat down on the bed and heaved a mock sigh. "What incredible creatures are men!" she exclaimed. "Must I mean everything I say, Solomon? Is there no difference between this flat and that miserable old hotel in Caudebec? And last, but not least, have you promised to forsake all other and cleave unto me as long as we both shall live? If you had promised it, I'd know you couldn't possibly keep it; but as it is, I have hopes."

This was too much for Peter. He dropped into the position that she had grown to love to see him in, and he put his arms round her waist, looking up at her laughingly. "But you will marry me, Julie, won't you?" he demanded.

Before his eyes, a lingering trace of that old look crept back into her face. She put her hands beneath his chin, and said no word, till he could stand it no longer.

"Julie, Julie, my darling," he said, "you must."

"Must, Peter?" she queried, a little wistfully he thought.

"Yes, must; but say you want to, say you will, Julie!"

"I want to, Peter," she said—"oh, my dear, you don't know, you can't know, how much. The form is nothing to me, but I want *you*—if I can keep you."

"If you can keep me!" echoed Peter, and it was as if an ice-cold finger had suddenly been laid on his heart. For one second he saw what might be. But he banished it. "What!" he exclaimed. "Cannot you trust me, Julie? Don't you know I love you? Don't you know I want to make you the very centre of my being, Julie?"

"I know, dearest," she whispered, and he had never heard her speak so before. "You want, that is one thing; you can, that is another."

Peter stared up at her. He felt like a little child who kneels at the feet of a mother whom it sees as infinitely loving, infinitely wise, infinitely old. And, like a child, he buried his head in her lap. "Oh, Julie," he said, "you must marry me. I want you so that I can't tell you how much. I don't know what you mean. Say," he said, looking up again and clasping her tightly—"say you'll marry me, Julie!"

She sprang up with a laugh. "Peter," she said, "you're Mid-Victorian. You are actually proposing to me upon your knees. If I could curtsy or faint I would, but I can't. Every scrap of me is modern, down to Venns' cami-knickers that you wouldn't let me talk about. Let's go and eat kippers; I'm dying for them. Come on, old Solomon."

He got up more slowly, half-smiling, for who could resist Julie in that mood? But he made one more effort. He caught her hand. "But just say 'Yes' Julie," he said—"just 'Yes.'"

She snatched her hand away. "Maybe I will tell you on Monday morning," she said, and ran out of the room.

As he finished dressing, he heard her singing in the next room, and then talking to the maid. When he entered the sitting-room the girl came out, and he saw that there were tears in her eyes. He went in and looked sharply at Julie; there was a suspicion of moisture in hers also. "Oh, Peter," she said, and took him by the arm as the door closed, "why didn't you tell me about Jack? I'm going out immediately after breakfast to buy her the best silver photo-frame I can find, see? And now come and eat your kippers. They're half-cold, I expect. I thought you were never coming."

So began a dream-like day to Peter. Julie was the centre of it. He followed her into shops, and paid for her purchases and carried her parcels: he climbed with her on to buses, which she said she preferred to taxis in the day-time; he listened to her talk, and he did his best to find out what she wanted and get just that for her. They lunched, at her request, at an old-fashioned, sober restaurant in Regent Street, that gave one the impression of eating luncheon in a Georgian dining-room, in some private house of great stolidity and decorum. When Julie had said that she wanted such a place Peter had been tickled to think how she would behave in it. But she speedily enlightened him. She drew off her gloves with an air. She did not laugh once. She did not chat to the waiter. She did not hurry in, nor demand the wine-list, nor call him Solomon. She did not commit one single Colonial solecism at table, as Peter had hated himself for half thinking that she might. Yet she never had looked prettier, he thought, and even there he caught glances which suggested that others might think so too. And if she talked less than usual, so did he, for his mind was very busy. In the old days it was almost just such a wife as Julie now that he would have wanted. But did he want the old days? Could he go back to them? Could he don the clerical frock coat and with it the clerical system and outlook of St. John's? He knew, as he sat there, that not only he could not, but that he would not. What, then? It was almost as if Julie suggested that the alternative was madcap days, such as that little scene in the bathroom suggested. He looked at her, and thought of it again, and smiled at the incongruity of it, there. But even as he smiled the cold whisper of dread insinuated itself again, small and slight as it was. Would such days fill his life? Could they offer that which should seize on his heart, and hold it?

He roused himself with an effort of will, poured himself another glass of wine, and drank it down. The generous, full-bodied stuff warmed him, and he glanced at his wrist-watch. "I say," he said, "we shall be late, Julie, and I don't want to miss one scrap of this show. Have you finished? A little more wine?"

Julie was watching him, he thought, as he spoke, and she, too, seemed to him to make a little effort. "I will, Peter," she said, not at all as she had spoken there before—"a full glass too. One wants to be in a good mood for the Coliseum. Well, dear old thing, cheerio!"

Outside he demanded a taxi. "I must have it, Julie," he said. "I want to drive up, and have the old buffer in gold braid open the door for me. Have a cigarette?"

She took one, and laughed as they settled into the car. "I know the feeling, my dear," she said. "And you want to stroll languidly up the red carpet, and pass by the pictures of chorus-girls as if you were so accustomed to the real thing that really the pictures were rather borin', don't you know. And you want to make eyes at the programme-girl, and give a half-crown tip when they open the box, and take off your British warm in full view of the audience, and...."

"Kiss you," said Peter uproariously, suiting the action to the word. "Good Lord, Julie, you're a marvel! No more of those old restaurants for me. We dine at our hotel to-night, in the big public room near the band, and we drink champagne."

"And you put the cork in my stocking?" she queried, stretching out her foot.

He pushed his hand up her skirt and down to the warm place beneath the gay garter that she indicated, and he kissed her passionately again. "It doesn't matter now," he said. "I have more of you than that. Why, that's nothing to me now, Julie. Oh, how I love you!"

She pushed him off, and snatched her foot away also, laughing gaily. "I'm getting cheap, am I?" she said. "We'll see. You're going to have a damned rotten time in the theatre, my dear. Not another kiss, and I shall be as prim as a Quaker."

The car stopped. "You couldn't," he laughed, helping her out. "And what is more, I shan't let you be. I've got you, old darling, and I propose to keep you, what's more." He took her arm resolutely. "Come along. We're going to be confoundedly late."

Theirs was a snug little box, one of the new ones, placed as in a French theatre. The great place was nearly dark as they entered, except for the blaze of light that shone through the curtain. The odour of cigarette-smoke and scent greeted them, with the rustle of dresses and the subdued sound of gay talk. The band struck up. Then, after the rolling overture, the curtain ran swiftly up, and a smart young person tripped on the stage in the limelight and made great play of swinging petticoats.

Julie had no remembrance of her promised severity at any rate. She hummed airs, and sang choruses, and laughed, and was thrilled, exactly as she should have been, while the music and the panorama went on and wrapped them round with glamour, as it was meant to do. She cheered the patriotic pictures and Peter with her, till he felt no end of a fellow to be in uniform. The people in front of them glanced round amusedly now and again, and as like as not Julie would be discovered sitting there demurely, her child's face all innocence, and a big chocolate held between her fingers at her mouth. Peter would lean back in his corner convulsed at her, and without moving a muscle of her face she would put her leg tip on his seat and push him. One scene they watched well back in their dark box, his arm round her waist. It was a little pathetic love-play and well done, and in the gloom he played with the curls at her ears and neck with his lips, and held her hand.

When it was over they went out with the crowd. The January day was done, but it was bewildering for all that to come out into real life. There was no romance for the moment on the stained street, and in the passing traffic. The gold braid of the hall commissionaire looked tawdry, and the pictures of ballet-girls but vulgar. It is the common experience, but each time one feels it there is a new surprise. Julie had her own remedy:

"The liveliest tea-room you can find, Peter," she demanded.

"It will be hard to beat our own," said Peter.

"Well, away there, then; let's get back to a band again, anyhow."

The great palm-lounge was full of people, and for a few minutes it did not seem as if they would find seats; but then Julie espied a half-empty table, and they made for it. It stood away back in a corner, with two wicker armchairs before it, and, behind, a stationary lounge against the wall overhung by a huge palm. The lounge was occupied. "We'll get in there presently," whispered Peter, and they took the chairs, thankful in the crowded place to get seated at all.

"Oh, it was topping, Peter," said Julie. "I love a great place like that. I almost wish we had had dress-circle seats or stalls out amongst the people. But I don't know; that box was delicious. Did you see how that old fossil in front kept looking round? I made eyes at him once, deliberately—you know, like this," and she looked sideways at Peter with subtle invitation just hinted in her eyes. "I thought he would have apoplexy—I did, really."

"It's a good thing I didn't notice, Julie. Even now I should hate to see you look like that, say, at Donovan. You do it too well. Oh, here's the tea. Praise the Lord! I'm dying for a cup. You can have all the cakes; I've smoked too much."

"Wouldn't you prefer a whisky?"

"No, not now—afterwards. What's that they're playing?"

They listened, Julie seemingly intent, and Peter, who soon gave up the attempt to recognise the piece, glanced sideways at the couple on the lounge. They did not notice him. He took them both in and caught—he could not help it—a few words.

She was thirty-five, he guessed, slightly made-up, but handsome and full figured, a woman of whom any man might have been proud. He was an officer, in Major's uniform, and he was smoking a cigarette impatiently and staring down the lounge. She, on the other hand, had her eyes fixed on him as if to read every expression on his face, which was heavy and sullen and mutinous.

"Is that final, then, George?" she said.

"I tell you I can't help it; I promised I'd dine with Carstairs to-night."

A look swept across her face. Peter could not altogether read it. It was not merely anger, or pique, or disappointment; it certainly was not merely grief. There was all that in it, but there was more. And she said—he only just caught the sentence of any of their words, but there was the world of bitter meaning in it:

"Quite alone, I suppose? And there will be no necessity for me to sit up?"

"Peter," said Julie suddenly, "the tea's cold. Take me upstairs, will you? we can have better sent up."

He turned to her in surprise, and then saw that she too had heard and seen.

"Right, dear," he said, "It is beastly stuff. I think, after all, I'd prefer a spot, and I believe you would too."

He rose carefully, not looking towards the lounge, like a man; and Julie got up too, glancing at that other couple with such an ordinary merely interested look that Peter smiled to himself to see it. They threaded their way in necessary silence through the tables and chairs to the doors, and said hardly a word in the lift. But in their sitting-room, cosy as ever, Julie turned to him in a passion of emotion such as he had scarcely dreamed could exist even in her.

"Oh, you darling," she said, "pick me up, and sit me in that chair on your knee. Love me, Peter, love me as you've never loved me before. Hold me tight, tight, Peter hurt me, kiss me, love me, say you love me..." and she choked her own utterance, and buried her face on his shoulder, straining her body to his, twining her slim foot and leg round his ankle. In a moment she was up again, however, and glanced at the clock. "Peter, we must dress early and dine early, mustn't we? The thing begins at seven-forty-five. Now I know what we'll do. First, give me a drink, a long one, Solomon, and take one yourself. Thanks. That'll do. Here's the best.... Oh, that's good, Peter. Can't you feel it running through you and electrifying you? Now, come"— she seized him by the arm—"come on! I'll tell you what you've got to do."

Smiling, though a little astonished at this outburst, Peter allowed himself to be pulled into the bedroom. She sat down on the bed and pushed out a foot. "Take it off, you darling, while I take down my hair," she said.

He knelt and undid the laces and took off the brown shoes one by one, feeling her little foot through the silk as he did so. Then he looked up. She had pulled out a comb or two, and her hair was hanging down. With swift fingers she finished her work, and was waiting for him. He caught her in his arms, and she buried her face again. "Oh, Peter, love me, love me! Undress me, will you? I want you to. Play with me, own me, Peter. See, I am yours, yours, Peter, all yours. Am I worth having, Peter? Do you want more than me?" And she flung herself back on the bed in her disorder, the little ribbons heaving at her breast, her eyes afire, her cheeks aflame.

"Well," said Peter, an hour or two later, "we've got to get this dinner through as quickly as we've ever eaten anything. You'll have to digest like one of your South African ostriches. I say," he said to the waitress in a confidential tone and with a smile, "do you think you can get us stuff in ten minutes all told? We're late as it is, and we'll miss half the theatre else."

"It depends what you order," said the girl, rather sharply. Then, after a glance at them both: "See, if you'll have what I say, I'll get you through quick. I know what's on easiest. Do you mind?"

"The very thing," said Peter; "and send the wine-man over on your way, will you? How will that do?" he added to Julie.

"I'll risk everything to-night, Peter, except your smiling at the waitress," she said. "But I must have that champagne. There's something about champagne that inspires confidence. When a man gives you the gold bottle you know that he is really serious, or as serious as he can be, which isn't saying much for most men. And not half a bottle; I've had half-bottles heaps of times at tête-à-tête dinners. It always means indecision, which is a beastly thing in anyone, and especially in a man. It's insulting, for one thing.... Oh, Peter, do look at that girl over there. Do you suppose she has anything on underneath? I suppose I couldn't ask her, but you might, you know, if you put on that smile of yours. Do walk over, beg her pardon, and say very nicely: 'Excuse me, but I'm a chaplain, and it's my business to know these things. I see you've no stays on, but have you a bathing costume?'"

"Julie, do be quiet; someone will hear you. You must remember we're in England, and that you're talking English."

"I don't care a damn if they do, Peter! Oh, here's the champagne, at any rate. Oh, and some soup. Well, that's something."

"I've got the fish coming," said the girl, "if you can be ready at once."

Julie seized her spoon. "I suppose I mustn't drink it?" she said. "I don't see why I shouldn't, as a matter of fact, but it might reflect on you, Peter, and you're looking so immaculate to-night. By the way, you've never had that manicure. Do send a note for the girl. I'd hide in the bathroom. I'd love to hear you. Peter, if I only thought you would do it, I'd like it better than the play. What is the play, by the way? *Zigzag*? Oh, *Zigzag*" (She mimicked in a French accent.) "Well, it will be all too sadly true if I leave you to that bottle of fizz all by yourself. Give me another glass, please."

"What about you?" demanded Peter. "If you're like this now, Heaven knows what you'll be by the time you've had half of this."

"Peter, you're an ignoramus. Girls like me never take too much. We began early for one thing, and we're used to it. For another, the more a girl talks, the soberer she is. She talks because she's thinking, and because she doesn't want the man to talk. Now, if you talked to-night, I don't know what you might not say. You'd probably be enormously sentimental, and I hate sentimental people. I do, really. Sentiment is wishy-washy, isn't it? I always associate it with comedians on the stage. Look over there. Do you see that girl in the big droopy hat and the thin hands? And the boy—one must say 'boy,' I suppose? He's a little fat and slightly bald, and he's got three pips up, and has had them for a long time. Well, look at them. He's searching her eyes, he is, Peter, really. That's how it's done: you just watch. And he doesn't know if he's eating pea-soup or oyster-sauce. And she's hoping her hat is drooping just right, and that he'll notice her ring is on the wrong finger, and how nice one would look in the right place. To do her justice, she isn't thinking much about dinner, either; but that's sinful waste, Peter, in the first place, and bad for one's tummy in the second. However, they're sentimental, they are, and there's a fortune in it. If they could only bring themselves to do just that for fifteen minutes at the Alhambra every night, they'd be the most popular turn in London."

"That's all very well," said he; "but if you eat so fast and talk at the same time, you'll pay for it very much as you think they will. Have you finished?"

"No, I haven't. I want cheese-straws, and I shall sit here till I get them or till the whole of London zigzags round me."

"I say," said Peter to their waitress, "if you possibly can, fetch us cheese-straws now. Not too many, but quickly. Can you? The lady won't go without them, and something must be done."

"Wouldn't the management wait if you telephoned, Peter dear?" inquired Julie sarcastically. "Just say who you are, and they sure will. If the chorus only knew, they'd go on strike against appearing before you came, or tear their tights or something dreadful like that, so that they couldn't come on. Yes, now I am ready. One wee last little drop of the bubbly—I see it there—and I'll sacrifice coffee for your sake. Give me a cigarette, though. Thanks. And now my wrap."

She rose, the cigarette in her fingers, smiling at him. Peter hastily followed, walking on air. He was beginning to realise how often he failed to understand Julie, and to see how completely she controlled her apparently more frivolous moods; but he loved her in them. He little knew, as he followed her out, the tumult of thoughts that raced through that little head with its wealth of brown hair. He little guessed how bravely she was already counting the fleeting minutes, how resolutely keeping grip of herself in the flood which threatened to sweep her—how gladly!—away.

A good revue must be a pageant of music, colour, scenery, song, dance, humour, and the impossible. There must be good songs in it, but one does not go for the songs, any more than one goes to see the working out of a plot. Strung-up men, forty-eight hours out of the trenches, with every nerve on edge, must come away with a smile of satisfaction on their faces, to have a last drink at home and sleep like babies. Women who have been on nervous tension for months must be able to go there, and allow their tired senses to drink in the feast of it all, so that they too may go home and sleep. And in a sense their evening meant all this to Peter and Julie; but only in a sense.

They both of them bathed in the performance. The possible and impossible scenes came and went in a bewildering variety, till one had the feeling that one was asleep and dreaming the incomprehensible jumble of a dream, and, as in a nice dream, one knew it was absurd, but did not care. The magnificent, brilliant staging dazzled till one lay back in one's chair and refused to name the colours to oneself or admire their blending any more. The chorus-girls trooped on and off till they seemed countless, and one abandoned any wish to pick the prettiest and follow her through. And the gay palace of luxury, with its hundreds of splendidly dressed women, its men in uniform, its height and width and gold and painting, and its great arching roof, where, high above, the stirring of human hearts still went on, took to itself an atmosphere and became sentient with humanity.

Julie and Peter were both emotional and imaginative, and they were spellbound till the notes of the National Anthem roused them. Then, with the commonplaces of departure, they left the place. "It's so near," said Julie in the crowd outside; "let's walk again."

"The other pavement, then," said Peter, and they crossed. It was cold, and Julie clung to him, and they walked swiftly.

At the entrance Peter suggested an hour under the palms, but Julie pleaded against it. "Why, dear?" she said. "It's so cosy upstairs, and we have all we want. Besides, the lounge would be an anti-climax; let's go up."

They went up, and Julie dropped into her chair while Peter knelt to poke the fire. Then he lit a cigarette, and she refused one for once, and he stood there looking into the flame.

Julie drew a deep sigh. "Wasn't it gorgeous, Peter?" she said. "I can't help it, but I always feel I want it to go on for ever and ever. Did you ever see *Kismet?* That was worse even than this. I wanted to get up and walk into the play. These modern things are too clever; you know they're unreal, and yet they seem to be real. You know you're dreaming, but you hate to wake up. I could let all that music and dancing and colour go on round me till I floated away and away, for ever."

Peter said nothing. He continued to stare into the fire.

"What do you feel?" demanded Julie.

Peter drew hard on his cigarette, and then he blew out the smoke. "I don't know," he said. "Yes, I do," he added quickly; "I feel I want to get up and preach a sermon."

"Good Lord, Peter! what a dreadful sensation that must be! Don't begin now, will you? I'm beginning to wish we'd gone into the lounge after all; you surely couldn't have preached there."

Peter did not smile. He went on as if she had not spoken, "Or write a great novel, or, better still, a great play," he said.

"What would be the subject, then, you Solomon, or the title, anyway?"

"I don't know," said Peter dreamily. "*All Men are Grass, The Way of all Flesh*—no, neither of those is good, and besides, one at least is taken. I know," he added suddenly, "I would call it *Exchange*, that's all. My word, Julie, I believe I could do it." He straightened himself, and walked across the room and back again, once or twice. "I believe I could: I feel it tingling in me; but it's all formless, if you understand; I've no plot. It's just what I feel as I sit there in a theatre, as we did just now."

Julie leaned forward and took the cigarette she had just refused. She lit it herself with a half-burnt match, and Peter stood and watched her, but hardly saw what she was doing. She was as conscious of his preoccupation as if it were something physical about him.

"Explain, my dear," she said, leaning back and staring into the fire.

"I don't know that I can," he replied, and she felt as if he did not speak to her. "It's the bigness of it all, the beauty, the triumphant success. It's drawn that great house full, lured them in, the thousands of them, and it does so night after night. Tired people go there to be refreshed, and sad people to be made gay, and people sick of life to laugh and forget it. It's the world's big anodyne. It offers a great exchange. And all for a few shillings, Julie, and for a few hours. The sensation lingers, but one has to go again and again. It tricks one into thinking, almost, that it's the real thing, that one can dance like mayflies in the sun. Only, Julie, there comes an hour when down sinks the sun, and what of the mayflies then?"

Julie shifted her head ever so little. "Go on," she said, looking up intently at him.

He did not notice her, but her words roused him. He began to pace up and down again, and her eyes followed him. "Why," he said excitedly, "don't you see that it's a fraudulent exchange? It's a fraudulent exchange that it offers, and it itself is an exchange as fraudulent as that which our modern world is making. No, not our modern world only. We talk so big of our modernity, when it's all less than the dust—this year's leaves, no better than last year's, and fallen to-morrow. Rome offered the same exchange, and even a better one, I think—the blood and lust and conflict of the amphitheatre. But they're both exchanges, offered instead of the great thing, the only great thing."

"Which is, Peter?"

"God, of course—Almighty God; Jesus, if you will, but I'm not in a mood for the tenderness of that. It's God Himself Who offers tired and sad people, and people sick of life, no anodyne, no mere rest, but stir and fight and the thrill of things nobly done—nobly tried, Julie, even if nobly failed. Can't you see it? And you and I to-night have been looking at what the world offers—in exchange."

He ceased and dropped into a chair the other side of the fire. A silence fell on them. Then Julie gave a little shiver. "Peter, dear," she said tenderly, "I'm a little tired and cold."

He was up at once and bending over her. "My darling, what a beast I am! I clean forgot you for a minute. What will you have? What about a hot toddy? Shall I make one?" he demanded, smiling. "Donovan taught me how, and I'm really rather good at it."

She smiled back at him, and put her hand up to smooth his hair. "That would be another exchange, Peter," she said, "and I don't want it. Only one thing can warm me to-night and give me rest."

He read what she meant in her eyes, and knelt beside the chair to put his arms around her. She leaned her face on his shoulder, and returned the kisses that he showered upon her. "Poor mayflies," she said to herself, "how they love to dance in the sun!"

CHAPTER IX

Ever after that next day, the Saturday, will remain in Peter's memory as a time by itself, of special significance, but a significance, except for one incident, very hard to place. It began, indeed, very quietly, and very happily. They breakfasted again in their own room, and Julie was in one of her subdued moods, if one ever could say she was subdued. Afterwards Peter lit a cigarette and strolled over to the window. "It's a beastly day," he said, "cloudy, cold, windy, and going to rain, I think. What shall we do? Snow up in the hotel all the time?"

"No," said Julie emphatically, "something quite different. You shall show me some of the real London sights, Westminster Abbey to begin with. Then we'll drive along the Embankment and you shall tell me what everything is, and we'll go and see anything else you suggest. I don't suppose you realise, Peter, that I'm all but absolutely ignorant of London."

He turned and smiled on her. "And you really *want* to see these things?" he said.

"Yes, of course I do. You don't think I suggested it for your benefit? But if it will make you any happier, I'll flatter you a bit. I want to see those things now, with you, partly because I'm never likely to find anyone who can show me them better. Now then. Aren't you pleased?"

At that, then, they started. Westminster came first, and they wandered all over it and saw as much as the conditions of war had left for the public to see. It amused Peter to show Julie the things that seemed to him to have a particular interest—the Chapter House, St. Faith's Chapel, the tomb of the Confessor, and so on. She made odd comments. In St. Faith's she said: "I don't say many prayers, Peter, but here I couldn't say one."

"Why not?" he demanded.

"Because it's too private," she said quaintly. "I should think I was pretending to be a saint if I went past everybody else and the vergers and things into a little place like this all by myself. Everyone would know that I was doing something which most people don't do. See? Why don't people pray all over the church, as they do in France in a cathedral, Peter?"

He shrugged his shoulders. "Come on," he said; "your notions are all topsy-turvy, Julie. Come and look at the monuments."

They wandered down the transept, and observed the majesty of England in stone, robed in togas, declaiming to the Almighty, and obviously convinced

- 238 -

that He would be intensely interested; or perhaps dying in the arms of a semi-dressed female, with funeral urns or ships or cannon in the background; or, at least in one case, crouching hopelessly, before the dart of a triumphant death. Julie was certainly impressed, "They are all like ancient Romans, Peter," she said, "and much more striking than those Cardinals and Bishops and Kings, kneeling at prayer, in Rouen Cathedral. But, still, they were *not* ancient Romans, were they? They were all Christians, I suppose. Is there a Christian monument anywhere about?"

"I don't know," said Peter, "but we'll walk round and see."

They made a lengthy pilgrimage, and finally Peter arrested her. "Here's one," he said.

A Georgian Bishop in bas-relief looked down on them, fat and comfortable. In front of him was a monstrous cup, and a plate piled with biggish squares of stone. Julie did not realise what it was. "What's he doing with all that lump-sugar?" she demanded.

Peter was really a bit horrified. "You're an appalling pagan," he said. "Come away!" And they came.

They roamed along the Embankment. Julie was as curious as a child, and wanted to know all about everything, from Boadicea, Cleopatra's Needle, and the Temple Church, to Dewar's Whisky Works and the Hotel Cecil. Thereabouts, Julie asked the name of the squat tower and old red-brick buildings opposite, and when she heard it was Lambeth Palace instantly demanded to visit it. Peter was doubtful if they could, but they crossed to see, and they were shown a good deal by the courtesy of the authorities. The Archbishop was away, to Peter's great relief, for as likely as not Julie would have insisted on an introduction, but they saw the chapel and the dining-hall amongst other things. The long line of portraits fascinated her, but not as it fascinated Peter. The significance of the change in the costumes of the portraits struck him for the first time—first the cope and mitre and cross, then the skull-cap and the tippet, then the balloon-sleeves and the wig, then the coat and breeches and white cravat, then the academic robes, and then a purple cassock. Its interest to Julie was other, however. "Peter," she whispered, "perhaps you'll be there one day."

He looked at her sharply, but she was not mocking him, and, marvelling at her simplicity and honest innocence, he relaxed into a smile. "Not very likely, my dear," he said. "In other days a pleasant underground cell in the Lollards' Tower would have been more likely."

Then, of course, Julie must see the famous tower, and see a little of it they did. She wanted to know what Lollardy was; their guide attempted an explanation. Julie was soon bored. "I can't see why people make such a bother about such things," she said. "A man's religion is his own business, surely, and he must settle it for himself. Don't you think so, Peter?"

"Is it his own business only?" he asked gravely.

"Whose else should it be?" she demanded.

"God's," said Peter simply.

Julie stared at him and sighed. "You're very odd, Peter," she said, "but you do say things that strike one as being true. Go on."

"Oh, there's no more to say," said Peter, "except, perhaps, this: if anyone or any Church honestly believed that God had committed His share in the business to them—well, then he might justifiably feel that he or it had a good deal to do with the settling of another man's religion. Hence this tower, Julie, and as a matter of fact, my dear, hence me, past and present. But come on."

She took his arm with a little shiver which he was beginning to notice from time to time in her. "It's a horrible idea, Peter," she said. "Yes, let's go."

So their taxi took them to Buckingham Palace and thereabouts, and by chance they saw the King and Queen. Their Majesties drove by smartly in morning dress with a couple of policemen ahead, and a few women waved handkerchiefs, and Peter came to the salute, and Julie cheered. The Queen turned towards where she was standing, and bowed, and Peter noticed, amazed, that the eyes of the Colonial girl were wet, and that she did not attempt to hide it.

He had to question her. "I shouldn't have thought you'd have felt about royalty like that, Julie," he said.

"Well, I do," she said, "and I don't care what you say. Only I wish they'd go about with the Life Guards. The King's a King to me. I suppose he is only a man, but I don't want to think of him so. He stands for the Empire and for the Flag, and he stands for England too. I'd obey that man almost in anything, right or wrong, but I don't know that I'd obey anyone else."

"Then you're a survival of the Dark Ages," he said.

"Don't be a beast!" said Julie.

"All right, you're not, and indeed I don't know if I am right. Very likely you're the very embodiment of the spirit of the Present Day. Having lost every authority, you crave for one."

Julie considered this. "There may be something in that," she said. "But I don't like you when you're clever. It was the King, and that's enough for me. And I don't want to see anything more. I'm hungry; take me to lunch."

Peter laughed. "That's it," he said—"like the follower of Prince Charlie who shook hands once with his Prince and then vowed he would never shake hands with anyone again. So you've seen the King, and you won't see anything else, only your impression won't last twelve hours, fortunately."

"I don't suppose the other man kept his vow," said Julie. "For one thing, no man ever does. Come on!"

And so they drifted down the hours until the evening theatre and *Carminetta*. They said and did nothing in particular, but they just enjoyed themselves. In point of fact, they were emotionally tired, and, besides, they wanted to forget how the time sped by. The quiet day was, in its own way too, a preparation for the evening feast, and they were both in the mood to enjoy the piece intensely when it came. The magnificence of the new theatre in which it was staged all helped. Its wide, easy stairways, its many conveniences, its stupendous auditorium, its packed house, ushered it well in. Even the audience seemed different from that of last night.

Julie settled herself with a sigh of satisfaction to listen and watch. And they both grew silent as the opera proceeded. At first Julie could not contain her delight. "Oh, she's perfect, Peter," she exclaimed—"a little bit of life! Look how she shakes her hair back and how impudent she is—just like one of those French girls you know too much about! And she's boiling passion too. And a regular devil. I love her, Peter!"

"She's very like you, Julie," said Peter.

Julie flashed a look at him. "Rubbish!" she said, but was silent.

They watched while Carminetta set herself to win her bet and steal the heart of the hero from the Governor's daughter. They watched her force the palace ballroom, and forgot the obvious foolishness of a great deal of it in the sense of the drama that was being worked out. The whole house grew still. The English girl, with her beauty, her civilisation, her rank and place, made her appeal to her fiancé; and the Spanish bastard dancer, with her daring, her passion, her naked humanity, so coarse and so intensely human, made her appeal also. And they watched while the young conventionally-bred officer hesitated; they watched till Carminetta won.

Julie, leaning forward, held her breath and gazed at the beautiful fashionable room on the stage, gazed through the open French windows to the moonlit garden and the night beyond, and gazed, though at last she could hardly see, at the Spanish girl. That great renunciation held them both entranced. So bitter-sweet, so humanly divine, the passionate, heart-broken, heroic song of farewell, swelled and thrilled about them. And with the last notes the child of the gutter reached up and up till she made the supreme self-sacrifice, and stepped out of the gay room into the dark night for the sake of the man she loved too much to love.

Then Julie bowed her head into her hands, and in the silence and darkness of their box burst into tears. And so, for the first and last time, Peter heard her really weep.

He said foolish man-things to comfort her. She looked up at last, smiling, her brown eyes challengingly brave through her tears, "Peter, forgive me," she said. "I shouldn't be such a damned fool! You never thought I could be like that, did you? But it was so superbly done, I couldn't help it. It's all over now—all over, Peter," she added soberly. "I want to sit in the lounge to-night for a little, if you don't mind. Could you possibly get a taxi? I don't want to walk."

It was difficult to find one. Finally Peter and another officer made a bolt simultaneously and each got hold of a door of a car that was just coming up. Both claimed it, and the chauffeur looked round good-humouredly at the disputants. "Settle it which-hever way you like, gents," he said. "Hi don't care, but settle it soon."

"Let's toss," said Peter.

"Right-o," said the other man, and produced a coin.

"Tails," whispered Julie behind Peter, and "Tails!" he called.

The coin spun while the little crowd looked on in amusement, and tails it was. "Damn!" said the other, and turned away.

"A bad loser, Peter," said Julie; "and he's just been seeing *Carminetta*, too! But am I not lucky! I almost always win."

In the palm lounge Julie was very cheerful. "Coffee, Peter," she said, "and liqueurs."

"No drinks after nine-thirty," said the waiter. "Sorry, sir."

Julie laughed. "I nearly swore, Peter," she said, "but I remembered in time. If one can't get what one wants, one has to go without singing. But I'll have a cigarette, not to say two, before we've finished. And I'm in no hurry; I want to sit on here and pretend it's not Saturday night. And I want to go very slowly to bed, and I don't want to sleep."

"Is that the effect of the theatre?" asked Peter. "And why so different from last night?"

Julie evaded. "Don't you feel really different?" she demanded.

"Yes," he said.

"How?"

"Well, I don't want to preach any sermon to-night. It's been preached."

Julie drew hard on her cigarette, and blew out a cloud of smoke. "It has, Peter," she said merrily, "and thank the Lord I am therefore spared another."

"You're very gay about it now, Julie, but you weren't at first. That play made me feel rather miserable too. No, I think it made me feel small. Carminetta was great, wasn't she? I don't know that there is anything greater than that sort of sacrifice. And it's far beyond me," said Peter.

Julie leaned back and hummed a bar or two that Peter recognised from the last great song of the dancer. "Well, my dear, I was sad, wasn't I?" she said. "But it's over. There's no use in sadness, is there?"

Peter did not reply, and started as Julie suddenly laughed. "Oh, good Lord, Peter!" she exclaimed, "to what *are* you bringing me? Do you know that I'm about to quote Scripture? And I damn-well shall if we sit on here! Let's walk up Regent Street; I can't sit still. Come on." She jumped up.

"Just now," he said, "you wanted to sit still for ages, and now you want to walk. What is the matter with you, Julie? And what was the text?"

"That would be telling!" she laughed. "But can't I do anything I like, Peter?" she demanded. "Can't I go and get drunk if I like, Peter, or sit still, or dance down Regent Street, or send you off to bed and pick up a nice boy? It would be easy enough here. Can't I, Peter?"

Her mood bewildered him, and, without in the least understanding why, he resented her levity. But he tried to hide it. "Of course you can," he said lightly; "but you don't really want to do those things, do you—especially the last, Julie?"

She stood there looking at him, and then, in a moment, the excitement died out of her voice and eyes. She dropped into a chair again. "No, Peter," she said, "I don't. That's the marvel of it. I expect I shall, one of these days, do most of those things, and the last as well, but I don't think I'll ever *want* to do them again. And that's what you've done to me, my dear."

Peter was very moved. He slipped his hand out and took hers under cover of her dress. "My darling," he whispered, "I owe you everything. You have given me all, and I won't hold back all from you. Do you remember, Julie, that once I said I thought I loved you more than God? Well, I know now— oh yes, I believe I do know now. But I choose you, Julie."

Her eyes shone up at him very brightly, and he could not read them altogether. But her lips whispered, and he thought he understood.

"Oh, Peter, my dearest," she said, "thank God I have at least heard you say that. I wouldn't have missed you saying those words for anything, Peter."

So might the serving-girl in Pilate's courtyard have been glad, had she been in love.

CHAPTER X

Part at least of Julie's programme was fulfilled to the letter, for they lay long in bed talking—desultory, reminiscent talk, which sent Peter's mind back over the months and the last few days, even after Julie was asleep in the bed next his. Like a pageant, he passed, in review scene after scene, turning it over, and wondering at significances that he had not before, imagined. He recalled their first meeting, that instantaneous attraction, and he asked himself what had caused it. Her spontaneity, freshness, and utter lack of conventionality, he supposed, but that did not seem to explain all. He wondered at the change that had even then come about in himself that he should have been so entranced by her, He went over his early hopes and fears; he thought again of conversations with Langton; and he realised afresh how true it was that the old authorities had dwindled away; that no allegiance had been left; that his had been a citadel without a master. And then Julie moved through his days again—Julie at Caudebec, daring, iconoclastic, free; Julie at Abbeville, mysterious, passionate, dominant; Julie at Dieppe—ah, Julie at Dieppe! He marvelled that he had held out so long after Dieppe, and then Louise rose before him. He understood Louise less than Julie, perhaps, and with all the threads in his hand he failed to see the pattern. He turned over restlessly. It was easy to see how they had come to be in London; it would have been more remarkable if they had not so come together; but now, what now? He could not sum up Julie amid the shifting scenes of the last few days. She had been so loving, and yet, in a way, their love had reached no climax. It had, indeed, reached what he would once have thought a complete and ultimate climax, but plainly Julie did not think so. And nor did he—now. The things of the spirit were, after all, so much greater than the things of the flesh. The Julie of Friday night had been his, but of this night...? He rolled over again. What had she meant at the play? He told himself her tears were simple emotion, her laughter simple reaction, but he knew it was not true....

And for himself? Well, Julie was Julie. He loved her intensely. She could stir him to anything almost. He loved to be with her, to see her, to hear her, but he did not feel satisfied. He knew that. He told himself that he was an introspective fool; that nothing ever would seem to satisfy him; that the centre of his life *was* and would be Julie; that she was real, tinglingly, intensely real; but he knew that that was not the last word. And then and there he resolved that the last word should be spoken on the morrow, that had, indeed, already come by the clock: she should promise to marry him.

He slept, perhaps, for an hour or two, but he awoke with the dawn. The grey light was stealing in at the windows, and Julie slept beside him in the bed between. He tried to sleep again, but could not, and, on a sudden, had an idea. He got quietly out of bed.

"What is it, Peter?" said Julie sleepily.

He went round and leaned over her. "I can't sleep any more, dearest," he said. "I think I'll dress and go for a bit of a walk. Do you mind? I'll be in to breakfast."

"No," she said. "Go if you want to. You are a restless old thing!"

He dressed silently, and kept the bathroom door closed as he bathed and shaved. She was asleep again as he stole out, one arm flung loosely on the counterpane, her hair untidy on the pillow. He kissed a lock of it, and let himself quietly out of their suite.

It was still very early, and the Circus looked empty and strange. He walked down Piccadilly, and wondered at the clean, soft touch of the dawning day, and recalled another memorable Sunday morning walk. He passed very familiar places, and was conscious of feeling an exile, an inevitable one, but none the less an exile, for all that. And so he came into St. James's Park, still as aimlessly as he had left the hotel.

Before him, clear as a pointing finger in the morning sky, was the campanile of that stranger among the great cathedrals of England. It attracted him for the first time, and he made all but unconsciously towards it. Peter was not even in the spiritual street that leads to the gates of the Catholic Church, and it was no incipient Romanism that moved him. He was completely ignorant of the greater part of that faith, and, still more, had no idea of the gulf that separates it from all other religions. He would have supposed, if he had stopped to think, that, as with other sects, one considered its tenets, made up one's mind as to their truth or falsehood one by one, and if one believed a sufficient majority of them joined the Church. It was only, then, the mood of the moment, and when, he found himself really moving towards that finger-post he excused himself by thinking that as he was, by his own act, exiled, from, more familiar temples, he would visit this that would have about it a suggestion of France.

He wondered if it would be open as he turned into Ashley Gardens. He glanced at his watch; it was only just after seven. Perhaps an early Mass might be beginning. He went to the central doors and found them fast;

then he saw little groups of people and individuals like himself making for the door in the great tower, and these he followed within.

He stood amazed for a few minutes. The vast soaring space, so austere in its bare brick, gripped his imagination. The white and red and gold of the painted Christ that hung so high and monstrous before the entrance to the marbles of the sanctuary almost troubled him. It dominated everything so completely that he felt he could not escape it. He sought one of the many chairs and knelt down.

A little bell tinkled, Peter glanced sideways towards the sound, and saw that a Mass was in progress in a side-chapel of gleaming mosaics, and that a soldier in uniform served. Hardly had he taken the details in, when another bell claimed his attention. It came from across the wide nave, and he perceived that another chapel had its Mass, and a considerable congregation. And then, his attention aroused, he began to spy about and to take in the thing.

The whole vast cathedral was, as it were, alive. Seven or eight Masses were in progress. One would scarcely finish before another priest, preceded by soldier in uniform or server in cassock and cotta, would appear from beyond the great pulpit and make his way to yet another altar. The small handbells rang out again and again and again, and still priest after priest was there to take his place. Peter began cautiously to move about. He became amazed at the size of the congregation. They had been lost in that great place, but every chapel had its people, and there were, in reality, hundreds scattered about in the nave alone.

He knelt for awhile and watched the giving of Communion in the guarded chapel to the north of the high altar. Its gold and emblazoned gates were not for him, but he could at least kneel and watch those who passed in and out. They were of all sorts and classes, of all ranks and ages; men, women, children, old and young, rich and poor, soldier and civilian, streamed in and out again. Peter sighed and left them. He found an altar at which Mass was about to begin, and he knelt at the back on a mosaic pavement in which fishes and strange beasts were set in a marble stream, and watched. And it was not one Mass that he watched, but two or three, and it was there that a vision grew on his inner understanding, as he knelt and could not pray.

It is hard and deceptive to write of those subconscious imaginings that convict the souls of most men some time or another. In that condition things are largely what we fashion them to be, and one may be thought to be asserting their ultimate truth in speaking of their influence. But there is no escaping from the fact that Peter Graham of a lost allegiance began that Sunday morning to be aware of another claimant. And this is what dawned upon him, and how.

A French memory gave him a starting-point. Here, at these Low Masses, it was more abundantly plain than ever that these priests did not conceive themselves to be serving a congregation, but an altar. One after the other they moved through a ritual, and spoke low sentences that hardly reached him, with their eyes holden by that which they did. At first he was only conscious of this, but then he perceived the essential change that came over each in his turn. The posturing and speaking was but introductory to the moment when they raised the Host and knelt before it. It was as if they were but functionaries ushering in a King, and then effacing themselves before Him.

Here, then, the Old Testament of Peter's past became to him a schoolmaster. He heard himself repeating again the comfortable words of the Prayer-Book service: "Come unto Me...." "God so loved...." "If any man sin...." Louise's hot declaration forced itself upon him: "It is He Who is there." And it was then that the eyes of his mind were enlightened and he saw a vision—not, indeed, of the truth of the Roman Mass (if it be true), and not of the place of the Sacrament in the Divine scheme of things, but the conception of a love so great that it shook him as if it were a storm, and bowed him before it as if he were a reed.

The silent, waiting Jesus.... All these centuries, in every land.... How He had been mocked, forgotten, spurned, derided, denied, cast out; and still He waited. Prostitutes of the streets, pardoned in a word, advanced towards Him, and He knew that so shortly again, within the secret place of their hearts, He would be crucified; but still He waited. Careless men, doubtless passion-mastered, came up to Him, and He knew the sort that came; but still He waited. He, Peter, who had not known He was here at all, and who had gone wandering off in search of any mistress, spent many days, turned in by chance, and found Him here. What did He wait for? Nothing; there was nothing that anyone could give, nothing but a load of shame, the offering of a body spent by passionate days, the kiss of traitor-lips; but still He waited. He did more than wait. He offered Himself to it all. He had bound Himself by an oath to be kissed if Judas planned to kiss Him, and He came through the trees to that bridal with the dawn of every day. He had foreseen the chalice, foreseen that it would be filled at every moon and every sun by the bitter gall of ingratitude and wantonness and hate, but He had pledged Himself—"Even so, Father"—and He was here to drink it. Small wonder, then, that the paving on which Peter Graham knelt seemed to swim before his eyes until it was in truth a moving ocean of love that streamed from the altar and enclosed of every kind, and even him.

The movement of chairs and the gathering of a bigger congregation than usual near a chapel that Peter perceived to be for the dead aroused him. He got up to go. He walked quickly up Victoria Street, and marvelled over the scene he had left. In sight of Big Ben he glanced up—twenty to nine! He had been, then, an hour and a half in the cathedral. He recalled having read that a Mass took half an hour, and he began to reckon how many persons had heard Mass even while he had been there. Not less than five hundred at every half-hour, and most probably more. Fifteen hundred to two thousand souls, of every sort and kind, then, had been drawn in to that all but silent ceremony, to that showing of Jesus crucified. A multitude—and what compassion!

Thus he walked home, thinking of many things, but the vision he had seen was uppermost and would not be displaced. It was still in his eyes as he entered their bedroom and found Julie looking at a magazine as she lay in bed, smoking a cigarette.

"Lor', Peter, are you back? I suppose I ought to be up, but I was so sleepy. What's the time? Why, what's the matter? Where have you been?"

Peter did not go over to her at once as she had expected. It was not that he felt he could not, or anything like that, but simply that he was only thinking of her in a secondary way. He walked to the dressing-table and lifted the flowers she had worn the night before and put there in a little glass.

"Where have you been, old Solomon?" demanded Julie again.

"Seeing wonders, Julie," said Peter, looking dreamily at the blossoms.

"No? Really? What? Do tell me. If it was anything I might have seen, you were a beast not to come back for me, d'you hear?"

Peter turned and stared at her, but she knew as he looked that he hardly saw her. Her tone changed, and she made a little movement with her hand, "Tell me, Peter," she said again.

"I've seen," said Peter slowly, "a bigger thing than I thought the world could hold, I've seen something so wonderful, Julie, that it hurt—oh, more than I can say. I've seen Love, Julie."

She could not help it. It was a foolish thing to say just then, she knew, but it came out. "Oh, Peter," she said, "did you have to leave me to see that?"

"Leave you?" he questioned, and for a moment so lost in his thought was he that he did not understand what she meant. Then it dawned on him, and he smiled. He did not see as he stood there, the clumsy Peter, how the two were related. So he smiled, and he came over to her, and took her hand, and sat on the bed, his eyes still full of light. "Oh, you've nothing to do with it," he said. "It's far bigger than you or I, Julie. Our love is like a candle held up to the sun beside it. Our love wants something, doesn't it? It burns, it— it intoxicates, Julie. But this love waits, *waits*, do you understand? It asks nothing; it gives, it suffices all. Year after year it just waits, Julie, waits for anyone, waits for everyone. And you can spurn it, spit on it, crucify it, and it is still there when you—need, Julie." And Peter leaned forward, and buried his face in her little hand.

Julie heard him through, and it was well that before the end he did not see her eyes. Then she moved her other hand which held the half-burnt cigarette and dropped the smoking end (so that it made a little hiss) into her teacup on the glass-topped table, and brought her hand back, and caressed his hair as he lay bent forward there. "Dear old Peter," she said tenderly, "how he thinks things! And when you saw this—this love, Peter, how did you feel?"

He did not answer for a minute, and when he did he did not raise his head. "Oh, I don't know, Julie," he said. "It went through and through me. It was like a big sea, and it flooded me away. It filled me. I seemed to drink it in at every pore. I felt satisfied just to be there."

"And then you came back to Julie, eh, Peter?" she questioned.

"Why, of course," he said, sitting up with a smile. "Why not?" He gave a little laugh. "Why, Julie," he said, "I never thought of that before. I suppose I ought to have been—oh, I don't know, but our days together didn't seem to make any difference. That Love was too big. It seemed to me to be too big to be—well, jealous, I suppose."

She nodded. "That would be just it, Peter. That's how it would seem to you. You see, I know. It's strange, my dear, but I don't feel either—jealous."

He frowned. "What do you mean?" he said. "Don't you understand? It was God's Love that I saw."

She hesitated a second, and then her face relaxed into a smile. "You're as blind as a bat, my dear, but I suppose all men are, and so you can't help it. Now go and ring for breakfast and smoke a cigarette in the sitting-room while I dress." And Peter, because he hated to be called a bat and did not feel in the least like one, went.

He rang the bell, and the maid answered it. She did not wait for him to give his order, but advanced towards him, her eyes sparkling. "Oh, sir," she said, "is madame up? I don't know how to thank her, and you too. I've wanted a frame for Jack's picture, but I couldn't get a real good one, I couldn't. When I sees this parcel I couldn't think *what* it was. I forgot even as how I'd give the lady my name. Oh, she's the real good one, she is. You'll forgive me, sir, but I know a real lady when I see one. They haven't got no airs, and they know what a girl feels like, right away. I put Jack in it, sir, on me table, and if there's anything I can do for you or your lady, now or ever, I'll do it, sir."

Peter smiled at the little outburst, but his heart warmed within him. How just like Julie it was! "Well," he said, "it's the lady you've really to thank. Knock, if you like; I expect she'll let you in. And then order breakfast, will you? Bacon and eggs and some fish. Thanks." And he turned away.

She made for the door, but stopped, "I near forgot, sir," she said. "A gentleman left this for you last night, and they give it to me at the office— this morning. There was no answer, he said. He went by this morning's train." She handed Peter an unstamped envelope bearing the hotel's name, and left the room as he opened it. He did not recognise the handwriting, but he tore it open and glanced at once at the signature, and got a very considerable surprise, not to say a shock. It was signed "Jack Donovan."

"MY DEAR GRAHAM, [the letter ran],

"Forgive me for writing, but I must tell you that I've seen you twice with Julie (and each time neither of you saw anyone else but yourselves!). It seems mean to see you and not say so, but for the Lord's sake don't think it'll go further, or that I reproach you. I've been there myself, old bird, and in any case I don't worry about other people's shows. But I want to tell you a bit of news—Tommy Raynard and I have fixed it up. I know you'll congratulate me. She's topping, and just the girl for me—no end wiser than I, and as jolly as anyone, really. I don't know how you and Julie are coming out of it, and I won't guess, for it's a dreadful war; but maybe you'll be able to sympathise with me at having to leave *my* girl in France! However, I'm off back to-morrow, a day before you. If you hadn't run off to Paris, you'd have known. My leave order was from Havre.

"Well, cheerio. See you before long. And just one word, my boy, from a fellow who has seen a bit more than you (if you'll forgive me): remember, *Julie'll know best.*

"Yours, ever,
"JACK DONOVAN."

Peter frowned over his letter, and then smiled, and then frowned again. He was still at it when he heard Julie's footstep outside, and he thrust the envelope quickly into his pocket, thinking rapidly. He did not in the least understand what the other meant, especially by the last sentence, and he wanted to consider it before showing Julie. Also, he wondered if it was meant to be shown to Julie at all. He thought not; probably Donovan was absolutely as good as his word, and would not even mention anything to Tommy. But he thought no more, for Julie was on him.

"Peter, it's started to rain! I knew it would. Why does it always rain on Sundays in London? Probably the heavens themselves weep at the sight of so gloomy a city. However, I don't care a damn! I've made up my mind what we're going to do. We shall sit in front of the fire all the morning, and you shall read to me. Will you?"

"Anything you like, my darling," he said; "and we couldn't spend a better morning. But bacon and eggs first, eh? No, fish first, I mean. But pour out a cup of tea at once, for Heaven's sake. *I* haven't had a drop this morning."

"Poor old thing! No wonder you're a bit off colour. No early tea after that champagne last night! But, oh, Peter, wasn't *Carminetta* a dream?"

Breakfast over, Peter sat in a chair and bent over her. "What do you want me to read, Julie darling?" he demanded.

She considered. "*Not* a magazine, *not La Vie Parisienne*, though we might perhaps look at the pictures part of the time. I know! Stop! I'll get it," She ran out and returned with a little leather-covered book. "Read it right through, Peter," she said. "I've read it heaps of times, but I want to hear it again to-day. Do you mind?"

"Omar Khayyám!" exclaimed Peter. "Good idea! He's a blasphemous old pagan, but the verse is glorious and it fits in at times. Do you want me to start at once?"

"Give me a cigarette! no, put the box there. Stir up the fire. Come and sit on the floor with your back to me. That's right. Now fire away."

She leaned back and he began. He read for the rhythm; she listened for the meaning. He read to the end; she hardly heard more than a stanza:

"Oh, threats of Hell and Hopes of Paradise!
One thing at least is certain—*this* Life flies;
One thing is certain, and the rest is lies—
The flower that once has blown for ever dies."

They lunched in the hotel, and at the table Peter put the first necessary questions that they both dreaded. "I'm going to tell them to make out my bill, Julie," he said. "I've to be at Victoria at seven-thirty a.m. to-morrow, you know. You've still got some leave, haven't you, dear; what are you going to do? How long will you stay on here?"

"Not after you've gone, Peter," she said. "Let them make it out for me till after breakfast to-morrow."

"But what are we going to do?" he demanded.

"Oh, don't ask. It spoils to-day to think of to-morrow. Go to my friends, perhaps—yes, I think that. It's only for a few days now."

"Oh, Julie, I wish I could stay."

"So do I, but you can't, so don't worry. What about this afternoon?"

"If it's stopped raining, let's go for a walk, shall we?"

They settled on that, and it was Julie who took him again to St. James's Park. As they walked: "Where did you go to church this morning, Peter?" she asked.

He pointed to the campanile. "Over there," he said.

"Then let's go together to-night," she said.

"Do you mean it, Julie?"

"Of course I do. I'm curious. Besides, it's Sunday, and I want to go to church."

"But you'll miss dinner," objected Peter. "It begins at six-thirty."

"Well, let's get some food out—Victoria Station, for instance. Won't that do? We can have some supper sent up afterwards in the hotel."

Peter agreed, but they did not go to the station. In a little cafe outside Julie saw a South African private eating eggs and bacon, and nothing would do but that they must do the same. So they went in. They ate off thick plates, and Julie dropped the china pepper-pot on her eggs and generally behaved as if she were at a school-treat. But it was a novelty, and it kept their thoughts off the fact that it was the last night. And finally they went to church.

The service did not impress Peter, and every time he looked at Julie's face he wanted to laugh; but the atmosphere of the place did, though he could not catch the impression of the morning. For the sermon, a stoutish, foreign-looking ecclesiastic mounted the pulpit, and they both prepared to be bored. However, he gave out his text, and Peter sat bolt upright at once. It would have delighted the ears of his Wesleyan corporal of the Forestry; and more than that it was the text he had quoted in the ears of the dying Jenks. He prepared keenly to listen. As for Julie, she was regarding the altar with a far-away look in her eyes, and she scarcely moved the whole time.

Outside, as soon as they were out of the crowd, Peter began at once.

"Julie," he said, "whatever did you think of that sermon?"

"What did you?" she said. "Tell me first."

"I don't believe you listened at all, but I can't help talking of it. It was amazing. He began by speaking about Adam and Eve and original sin and the Garden of Eden as if he'd been there. There might never have been a Higher Critic in existence. Then he said what sin did, and that sin was only truly sin if it did do that. *That* was to hide the face of God, to put Him and a human being absolutely out of communication, so to speak. And then he came to Christ, to the Cross. Did you hear him, Julie? Christ comes in between—He got in between God and man. All the anger that darted out of God against sin hit Him; all the blows that man struck back against God hit Him. Do you see that, Julie? That was wonderfully put, but the end was more wonderful. Both, ultimately, cannot kill the Heart of Jesus. There's no sin there to merit or to feel the anger, and we can hurt, but we can't destroy His love."

Peter stopped, "That's what I saw a little this morning," he said after a minute.

"Well?" said Julie.

"Oh, it's all so plain! If there was a way to that Heart, one would be safe. I mean, a way that is not an emotional idea, not a subjective experience, but something practical. Some way that a Tommy could travel, as easily as anyone, and get to a real thing. And he said there was a way, and just sketched it, the Sacraments—more than ours, of course, their seven, all of them more or less, I suppose. He meant that the Sacraments were not signs of salvation, but salvation itself. Julie, I never saw the idea before. It's colossal. It's a thing to which one might dedicate one's life. It's a thing to live and die gladly for. It fills one. Don't you think so, Julie?" He spoke exultantly.

"Peter, to be honest," said Julie, "I think you're talking fanatical rubbish."

"Do you really, Julie? You can't, *surely* you can't."

"But I do, Peter," she said sadly; "it makes no appeal to me. I can only see one great thing in life, and it's not that. 'The rest is lies,' But, oh! surely that great thing might not be false too. But why do you see one thing, and I another, my dear?"

"I don't know," said Peter, "unless—well, perhaps it's a kind of gift, Julie, 'If thou knewest the gift of God...' Not that I know, only I can just see a great wonderful vision, and it fills my sight."

"I, too," she said; "but it's not your vision."

"What is it, then?" said he, carried away by his own ideas and hardly thinking of her.

Her voice brought him back. "Oh, Peter, don't you know even yet?"

He took her arm very tenderly at that. "My darling," he said, "the two aren't incompatible. Julie, don't be sad. I love you; you know I love you. I wish we'd never gone to the place if you think I don't, but I haven't changed towards you a bit, Julie. I love you far, far more than anyone else. I won't give you up, even to God!"

It was dark where they were. Julie lifted her face to him just there. He thought he had never heard her speak as she spoke now, there, in a London street, under the night sky. "Peter, my darling," she said, "my brave boy. How I love you, Peter! I know *you* won't give me up, Peter, and I adore you for it. Peter, hell will be heaven with the memory of that!" There, then, he sealed her with his kiss.

* * * * *

Julie stirred in his arms, but the movement did not wake him any more than the knock of the door had done. "All right," she called. "Thank you," and, leaning over, she switched on the light. It was 5.30, and necessary. In its radiance she bent over him, and none of her friends had ever seen her look as she did then. She kissed him, and he opened his eyes.

"Half-past five, Peter," she said, as gaily as she could. "You've got to get a move on, my dear. Two hours to dress and pack and breakfast—no, I suppose you can do that on the train. But you've got to get there. Oh, Lord, how it brings the war home, doesn't it? Jump up!"

Peter sighed. "Blast the war!" he said lazily. "I shan't move. Kiss me again, you darling, and let your hair fall over my face."

She did so, and its glossy curtain hid them. Beneath the veil she whispered; "Come, darling, for my sake. The longer you stay here now, the harder it will be."

He threw his arms round her, and then jumped out of bed yawning.

"That's it," she said. "Now go and shave and bath while I pack for you. Hurry up; then we'll get more time."

While he splashed about she sought for his things, and packed for him as she never packed for herself. As she gathered them she thought of the night before, when, overwhelmed in a tempest of love, it had all been left for the morning. She filled the suit-case, but she could not fasten it.

"Come and help, Peter," she called.

He came out. She was kneeling on it in her loose kimono, her hair all about her, her nightdress open at the throat. He drank her beauty in, and then mastered himself for a minute and shut the case. "That all?" she queried.

"Yes," he said. "You get back into bed, my darling, or you'll catch cold. I'll be ready in a second, and then we can have a few minutes together."

At the glass he marshalled his arguments, and then he came over to her. He dropped by the bedside and wound his arms about her. "Julie," he whispered, "my darling, say you'll marry me—please, *please!*"

She made no reply. He kissed her, unresisting, again and again.

"Julie," he said, "you know how I love you. You do know it. You know I'm not begging you to marry me because I've got something out of you, perhaps when you were carried away, and now I feel I must make reparation. My darling, it isn't that. I love you so much that I can't live without you. I'll give up everything for you. I want to start a new life with you. I can't go back to the old, anyhow; I don't want to: it's a sham to me now, and I hate shams—you know I do. But you're not a sham; our love isn't a sham. I'd die for you, Julie, my own Julie; I'd die for the least little bit of this hair of yours, I think! But I want to live for you. I want to put you right in the centre of everything, and live for you, Julie. Say 'Yes,' my love, my own. You must say 'Yes,' Why don't you, Julie?"

And still she made no reply.

A kind of despair seized him. "Oh, Julie," he cried, "what can I say or what can I do? You're cruel, Julie; you're killing me! You *must* say 'Yes' before I go. We'll meet in Havre, I know; but that will be so different. I must have my answer now. Oh, my darling, please, please, speak! You love me, Julie, don't you?"

"Peter," said Julie slowly, "I love you so much that I hardly dare speak, lest my love should carry me away. But listen, my dear, listen. Peter, I've watched you these days; I've watched you in France. I've watched you from the moment when I called you over to me because I was interested and felt my fate, I suppose. I've watched you struggling along, Peter, and I understand why you've struggled. You're built for great things, my dear— how great I can't see and I can't even understand. No, Peter, I can't even understand—that's part of the tragedy of it. Peter, I love you so that my love for you *is* my centre, it's my all in all, it's my hope of salvation, Peter. Do you hear, my darling?—my love, it's my one hope! If I can't keep that pure and clean, Peter, I ruin both of us. I love you so, Peter, that I won't marry you!"

He gave a little cry, but swiftly she put a hand over his mouth. She smiled at him as she did so, a daring little smile. "Be quiet, you Solomon, you," she said; "I haven't finished. There! Now listen again, Peter: you can't help it, but you can't love me as I love you. I see it. I—I hate it, I think; but I know it, and there's an end. You, my dear, you *would put me* in the centre, but you can't. I can't put *you* out of *my* centre, Peter. You *would* give up God for me, Peter, but you can't, or if you did, you'd lose us both. But I, Peter—oh, my darling, I have no god but you. And that's why I'll worship you, Peter, and sacrifice to you, Peter, sacrifice to your only ultimate happiness, Peter, and sacrifice my all."

He tried to speak, but he could not. The past days lay before him in a clear light at last. Her love shone on them, and shone too plainly for mistake. He tried to deny, but he couldn't; contradict, but his heart cried the truth, and his eyes could not hide it. But he could and did vent his passion. "Damn God! Curse Him!" he cried. "I hate Him! Why should He master me? I want you, Julie; I will have you; I will worship *you*, Julie!"

She let him speak; and, being Julie, his words only brought a more tender light into her face. "Peter," she said, "one minute. Do you remember where you first kissed me, my darling?—the first real kiss, I mean," and her eyes sparkled with fun even then. "You know—ah, I see you do! You will never forget that, will you? Perhaps you thought I didn't notice, but I did. Neither you nor I chose it; it was Fate; perhaps it was your God, Peter. But, anyway, look at me now as you looked then. What do you see?"

He stared at her, and he saw—how clearly he saw! Her sweet back-bent head, her shining eyes, the lamp-light falling on her hair out of the night. He even heard the sea as it beat on the stones of the quay—or thought he did—and felt the whip of the wind. And behind her, dominating, arms outspread, the harbour crucifix. And she saw that he saw, and she whispered: "*Do* you hate Him, Peter?" And he sank his head into her hands and sobbed great dry sobs.

"Ah, don't, don't," he heard her say—"don't Peter! It's not so bad as that. Your life is going to be full, my beloved, with a great and burning love; and you were right this morning, Peter, more right than you knew. When that is there you will have place even for me—yes, even for me, the love of what you will call your sin. And I, my dear, dear boy, I have something even now which no devil, Peter, and no god can take away."

He looked up. "Then there's a chance, Julie. You won't say 'Yes,' but don't say 'No.' Let us see. I shall take no vows, Julie. I haven't an idea what I shall do, and maybe it won't be quite as you think, and there will be a little room for you one day. Oh, say you'll wait a while, Julie, just to see!"

It was the supreme moment. She saw no crucifix to sustain her, but she did see the bastard Spanish dancing-girl. And she did not hesitate. "No, Peter," she said, "I would not take that, and you never could give it. I did not mean such place as that. It never can be, Peter; you are not made for me."

And thus did Julie, who knew no God, but Julie of the brave, clean, steadfast heart, give Peter to Him.

* * * * *

The maid came in answer to her ring. "Will you light a fire, please?" said Julie. "I suppose Captain Graham has gone?"

"Yes, mam, he's gone, and he felt it terrible, I could see. But don't you fear, mam, he'll be kept, I know he will. You're that good, he'll come back to you, never fear. But it's 'ard on those they leave, ain't it, mam?—their wives an' all."

"Yes," said Julie, and she never spoke more bravely. "But it's got to be, hasn't it? Would you pull the blind up? Ah, thanks; why, it's sunny! I'm so glad. It will be good for the crossing."

"It will be that, 'm. We gets the sun first up here. Shall I bring up the tea, madame?"

"I'll ring," said Julie, "when I want it. It won't be for a few minutes yet."

The girl went out, and the door shut behind her. Julie lay on still for a little, and then she got up. She walked to the window and looked out, and she threw her arms wide with a gesture, and shut her eyes, and let the sun fall on her. Then she walked to her little trunk, and rummaged in it. From somewhere far down she drew out a leather case, and with it in her hand she went over and sat by the fire. She held it without moving for a minute, and then she slowly opened it. One by one she drew out a few worthless things—a withered bunch of primroses, a couple of little scribbled notes, a paper cap from a cracker, a menu card, a handkerchief of her own that she had lent to him, and that he (just like Peter) had given back. She held them all in her hand a minute, and then she bent forward and dropped them in the open fire.

And the sun rose a little higher, and fell on the tumbled brown hair that Peter had kissed and that now hid her eyes.

Milton Keynes UK
Ingram Content Group UK Ltd.
UKHW041200040324
438885UK00007B/527